ELITE DANGEROUS
PREMONITION

by
Drew Wagar

ELITE DANGEROUS
PREMONITION

by
Drew Wagar

An Elite: Dangerous Novel
Discover the Elite: Dangerous Video Game
http:// www.elitedangerous.com

400 Billion Star Systems
Infinite Freedom
Blaze Your Own Trail

Elite Dangerous: Premonition is based on the definitive
massive multiplayer epic space game, Elite: Dangerous, by
Frontier Developments and sequel to Elite: Reclamation.
www.drewwagar.com

ISBN: 978-0-9931-3967-3 (sc)
ISBN: 978-0-9931-3968-0 (e)

Frontier Developments plc rev. date: 8/18/2017

Contents

Thanks To:

A project as complex as this one ultimately became is not the effort of a single person. I don't think anything like this has been tried before. It was convoluted, difficult and required a high degree of co-ordination between writers, players, designers, editors and management. I have endeavoured to thank as many as I can, though it's impossible to thank everyone.

My wife Anita, sons Mark and Joshua, and Abbey – For allowing me the time both to write this and manage all the in-game events required to make the story work. They got me back with their constant 'Friendship drive charging!'

David Braben – Thanks for allowing somebody outside of Frontier to contribute to the story. At the end of the day I'm just another fan, so to be allowed to discuss the background lore, make my own suggestions and be trusted with writing something new was a pleasure and a privilege.

David Walsh – Thanks for all the commercial support in getting the project off the ground and assistance throughout.

Michael Brookes – For everything that didn't fit into any of the other categories, lore checks, answering questions at all hours of the day on any topic and generally making sure things happened. I know you did a lot more on my behalf than you would care to admit and I don't know what half of those things were, so thanks for all of them anyway!

Jo Scott – For all the legal stuff. I don't understand a word of it, so I'm glad someone else does.

Ian Dingwall – Ian coordinates all the GalNet entries that form the backdrop to Elite: Dangerous. He took my contributions and wove them into the overall storyline, making some valuable suggestions along the way and tweaking everything for consistency.

Steve Kirby – My main interface to the design team at Frontier. Steve co-ordinated all the in-game assets built to support Premonition and was crucial to providing in-game ways for players to influence the evolution of the story line. To see stuff from my stories made 'real' within the game was a thrill for me. I hope you enjoyed what he and the design team achieved.

Thanks also to the artists, developers, audio, QA, support and server teams at Frontier. Having seen what they do at close range I can only offer my humble thanks for all the dedication and sheer hard work. Elite: Dangerous is a thing of beauty.

Janesta Boudreau – For all the organising around production and promotion. Boundless energy, late nights and brilliant co-ordination. Such a pleasure.

Tamara Tirjak – Who translated all those bizarre clues into other languages and retained their meaning, a frightfully complex task.

To my editor, Mae – She took a rough old manuscript, shot through with hundreds of problems after trying to put together this complex and overwhelming project, and turned it into something amazing.

To my copyeditor, Noah Chinn – Every single typo you didn't have to put up with was sorted by him, along with numerous tweaks and enhancements.

Dan, Gabi and Anne-Marie at Fantastic Books Publishing – For all those other bits and pieces that need doing between typing words on a computer and turning them into real pages.

Amelia Tyler and Jay Britton – for bringing some of my characters to life inside the game with their voice acting talents. Incredible.

Ed Lewis and Zac Antonaci – As the community managers these guys ceaselessly promote the game and the players' groups within it. They support the conventions and player led events. They have to front good news and bad, carrying it off with aplomb. Thanks for your support throughout and involvement in getting this project off the ground.

To Fozza – For the writer's interview, along with MahdDogg, FireyToad, DjTruthSayer, Selezen and the guys on the Brocast (Commanders Shabooka, Josh Hawkins, Turjan Starstone and GreyTest) for having me on their respective shows and streams.

To Obsidian Ant – For his amazing collection of videos and somehow being in the right place at the right time to cover them – funny that! Obsidian's videos were very useful for me to keep abreast of events around the galaxy. Keep up the good work!

To Commander Erimus – Who worked so hard on organising resources, teams and events, co-ordinating things behind the scenes.

To my team of conspirators – Those players who worked with me to generate events, spread news, role-play characters and situations so as to further the story. Zenith, Isaiah, Cornelius, Firey Toad, Kerrash, MahdDogg, DjTruthSayer, Selezen Lake, John Hoggard, GreyTest, Dave

Howard Schiff and Malic Tolsen. The Children of Raxxla, Loren's Legion and all the other factions for their role-playing.

To all those who took part on April 29th – It will be a day long remembered!

And to the fans – Thanks to those of you who've been with me since the beginning, during the 1984 onwards 'lenslok years', since the fan-fiction days, through the long night of waiting for a new game. For those who backed my first book, for those who clamoured for another one. For those who loved *Reclamation*, for those who expressed their confidence in my ability to write the story of Elite: Dangerous. For those of you who have sunk untold hours into the game, trying to figure out what was going on, for the 'threadnaughts' and the 'tinfoil', some of your ideas were much better than the ones I came up with!

The Elite: Dangerous Community is a wonderful thing, long may it continue.

Author's Note

It's very difficult to know where to start with all this.

I was enormously privileged to be able to write my first Elite: Dangerous book *Reclamation* back in 2013. I was a fan from the very earliest days of Elite, back in 1984, when it first appeared. I was the right age to be swept up in the franchise and to follow it throughout the many years since. I doodled wireframe Cobra Mark IIIs on my school textbooks, much to the annoyance of my schoolmasters. I was smuggling narcotics out of Riedquat at the tender age of 13; fortunately, my parents didn't ask too many questions!

The mad rush of the original Kickstarter and the writers' packs is now, itself, part of the lore of the game, a piece of history. I'm forever indebted to those who backed me in 2012 and allowed me to begin on this adventure, all anew.

Reclamation has been warmly received. Even now, new readers are finding it and getting engrossed in what I wrote. For a writer, there's nothing better than knowing your story has entertained and delighted someone. I tried very hard to nail the 'atmosphere' of Elite: Dangerous and combine that with my own style of story-telling and high adventure, mixed with characters that would prove memorable. I hoped fans would see it as a quality piece of work, pitched at the right level and doing justice to the remarkable game Frontier Developments has created.

But I didn't expect what happened next.

I didn't expect forum threads hundreds of pages long dissecting every last nuance of what I'd written, looking for clues to the mysteries I'd alluded to in the story.

I didn't expect hundreds of emails thanking me for what I'd written, or dozens of invites to appear on streams and online shows.

I didn't expect patches, banners, trophies, maps, mugs (Mug!) and the occasional biscuit.

I didn't expect a part of the galaxy to be named after me.

I didn't expect to be commissioned to write this book by the very people who created the game.

But most of all I didn't expect players to adopt my characters, bring their own imaginations into the game and role-play their own adventures based upon the seeds I'd planted in *Reclamation*. The dozens of player factions that have taken a cue from my first book were not planned by me in any way shape or form, but it was amazing to see them take form, grow and establish their own lore. Some of them, like the Children of Raxxla and Loren's Legion, have adopted characters direct from the pages of *Reclamation*. There have been poems, artwork, petitions and even an in-game memorial service for fallen fictional characters. I don't think anyone could have paid me a higher accolade.

This is a wholly new phenomenon. I can't think of another example of where players have had the opportunity to bring their own stories into a game, based upon a book, which was, in turn, based upon that game, and then find parts of those stories folded back into another book. The word 'meta' is rather over-used nowadays, but this truly is worthy of the original meaning, being 'above and beyond' both game and book, where players have enjoyed and partaken in the storyline. It has often felt more like teasing something into shape than actually writing a novel.

In many ways, this book has been written by those players. There are twists and turns as you might expect. Many of those have been caused, sometimes unwittingly, by players responding to events in game, or simply generating their own events because they can. I've even been able, anonymously, to take part in some of those events and get a feel for how they worked. Many of those events deserve a book in their own right and there are some amazing escapades that take place; daring rescues, impossible exploration trips, mad sporting events … happening almost every week.

A single book cannot hope to cover the activities of a galaxy full of players. As I write this there are something like 2.1 million copies of Elite: Dangerous out there, with thousands of users playing the game at any given moment across four hundred billion star systems. I have a mere few thousand words to do justice to all of that.

This then is a snapshot of some events, a thread running through the unfathomable scale of space, looping in as much as I felt could be covered. I have had to be very hard, brutal even, in selecting what I can include and what I can't. It's been tough to balance the needs of storytelling against the desire to bring in as much as I can in terms of the vast array of player contributions. Inevitably many will be disappointed that a facet of the game, or some notable event isn't represented. This is not a reflection of the efforts of players, or the worthiness of what they have done. It's simply down to having to be ruthless on time and scope.

I wholeheartedly appreciate the trust that the Elite: Dangerous community has placed in me, even if that has been very scary at times. Many have said that this book couldn't be in safer hands. Thank you for that. I'm so grateful for the support and encouragement I've received whilst putting this book together.

This has been a far tougher assignment than my first Elite: Dangerous novel. The scale and scope have been close to overwhelming at times. I have had to take breaks away from the writing to regain a sense of perspective. It has been a labour of love, but a labour nonetheless. I can truthfully say I have done my very best to do justice to Elite: Dangerous and its staggering player community. It is all of you who have made this game what it is.

I hope you enjoy a retelling of your story.
Right on, Commanders.

Drew,
May 2017.

Excerpt from recovered journal, circa 3302, author unknown.

They used to say witch-space was haunted; haunted by the ghosts of ships that first went out there and never came back.

Yet it's not haunted. It's stalked.

Stalked by the superpowers; Federal, Imperial and Alliance, each vying for superiority amidst the harsh and radiation-soaked vacuum of space, led by powerful figureheads playing a game with entire star systems as their pieces. Thousands die in minor wars of propaganda, their loyalty remembered for fleeting moments. Adherents zealously spout the righteousness of their leaders and castigate rivals.

Stalked by the factions; those who squabble and fight under a thousand different banners in an endless cycle of conflict to secure a patch of transitory territory, each struggling to assert its will across stations, outposts and systems.

Stalked by pirates; those who prey on and interdict ships in the hope of securing a lucrative cargo from a hapless trader. Most kill by necessity, fighting to keep their ships running and put food on the table. Some kill because they enjoy the pain, slaughter and mayhem they cause.

Stalked by bounty hunters; those who look to make money from the crimes and misfortunes of others, their ships bristling with advanced weaponry. Hardnosed and callous, only credits count in their measurement of all that is worthy.

Stalked by traders; the masses who scour the space-lanes for the next best profit run, ferrying goods and cargo from one place to another on an endless quest to better themselves, afford a bigger or more luxurious vessel and retire to a planet somewhere quiet and safe.

But it isn't safe out there.

It's dangerous.

If you live and work in space you make your choice and choose your role. No one tells you what to do. There is no guarantee of success whichever route you take. The only certainty is uncertainty. Watching your scanners for the trace of another ship which you must assume is hostile, because the chances are … it is.

Most, regardless of their politics or allegiance, play out their existence within the boundaries of the core worlds, a bubble of human civilisation a few hundred light years in radius, roughly centred on the star system humans call 'Sol'. It is here that humanity writes its history, fights its wars, and stages its coups, thinking itself of great importance.

Only a few look beyond the artificial boundary that rings the edge of civilisation. Those scant hundred light years are but the tiniest mote when weighed against the splendour and scale of the galaxy. Equipped with new vessels, those who can't resist the siren song of the unknown venture forth into the darkness. Tentatively at first, but then with increasing vigour, they chart courses across the emptiness, even reaching as far as the galactic core and the far-flung loneliness of the remote galactic arms.

Those who go gain a new perspective on the antics of the core worlds. Out there, in the silence that reigns amongst the nebulae and the neutron star fields, humanity's influence seems insignificant. Explorers push on outwards in the hope they will discover … what exactly?

There are rumours, of course, stories that filter back from borderland trading outposts. Ships that return from long ventures in the void with crews gone insane, or ships that are found abandoned in the darkness. The tales tell of lost planets, lost civilisations, strange beacons, crashed vessels and drifting cargoes. There is life out here, too. Explorers catalogue primitive life-forms on a thousand worlds, but, so far, contact with a recognisable intelligence eludes them.

It's said by some that humanity did encounter another race out here. If so, it was decades ago and that first encounter did not go well. Perhaps the barriers between harmonious co-existence were too great, the differences in habitat and culture insurmountable. Alleged accounts suggest that human and alien retreated to lick their wounds.

Perhaps they will return. Perhaps they're already here.

Yet, for those who can see, the signs are there. Curious growths have been seen on planets not far from the boundaries of the core. Nicknamed the 'Barnacles', these strange entities defy classification or explanation – biological for sure, but an order of construct very different from anything humanity has created. Other explorers have encountered strange probes and artefacts drifting amongst the stars, emitting signals which contain coded information pointing to … something. Still more have tracked clues that lead out into the darkness, across barren rifts of space, but seem to lead to dangerous dead ends in the depths of nowhere, far from any assistance.

But, perhaps, there are those who know more. Who is to say what secrets lie hidden in vaults, encrypted documents and sealed memories? While some strive to shine a light on the truth, others may work equally hard to keep that knowledge concealed. They might take the view that humanity isn't ready for those revelations, working in secret for hundreds of years, protecting humanity from itself. It could be they consider themselves above the hoi-polloi, above the factions and even beyond the remit of the Empire, the Federation and Alliance, concerning themselves with the enduring, not the ephemeral.

If such people do exist, they would know all too well that truth is a dangerous thing.

They might well fear a premonition of things to come …

Prologue
AD 3270

Syreadie sector, Formidine Rift, Uninhabited

The stars had thinned out, the galaxy hung as a remote backdrop, a faint edge-on glow, shrouded in dust and gas. Even the glow of the core was muted at this distance, thousands of light years from civilisation, untold parsecs from home.

For aeons little had changed out here, the stellar density low and composed mostly of pale and cool red dwarfs, consuming their hydrogen in such a miserly fashion that they would orbit the galactic centre many times before any change in their appearance could be detected. Many would live on long after all the brighter stars in the galaxy were consigned to violent deaths as twisted neutron stars, blazing white dwarves or the bottomless pits of black holes.

Out here, all was still. Nothing changed.

A bright point of light appeared in the darkness, blue and actinic, crackling out of the nothingness with a flicker of electrical discharge.

A ship. A huge ship, silhouetted against the glow of distant stars.

Wherever it was from it had come a long way. The duralium plating of its hull was tarnished and radiation scarred, the bright paintwork that had once adorned it cracked and faded in the harsh vacuum of space. Navigation lights blinked purposefully in the darkness, outlining the contours of a vast vessel. The ship's engines flared briefly, bringing the ship to a relative halt, stabilising a slow rotation. All was motionless save for the stately spin of enormous wheeled midsections providing a pseudo-gravity to those within.

Inside the bridge, the lighting was muted, a soft red glow aimed at preserving night vision for the crew. The Stardreamer interfaces retracted from their reclined couches, no longer needed now that the interminable hyperspace transit had concluded. The crew stretched, leaning forwards, turning attention to their consoles and instruments. The ship was checked and secured before the scanners were deployed. Most of the crew completed their tasks within a minute. The science officer was conspicuously busy, feverously working her displays and adjusting controls.

Aerials, dishes and other scanning implements deployed from various orifices across the hull of the ship, some spinning around and discharging electromagnetic pulses into the void, while others measured gravity wave fluctuations and ambient radiation levels, all aimed at quickly and definitively mapping the stellar system the ship had found itself in.

Let it be this time…

The captain, with the rest of the bridge crew, waited for the science station officer to report.

She looked up after examining her instruments, a deep sigh escaping her as she did so.

'We have a G class star, sir,' she said. 'Nine planets. The world we're in orbit around is confirmed as … terraformable.'

A cheer broke out amongst the crew and the Captain indulged them. They'd been hunting for weeks out in this forsaken black corner of the galaxy.

Thank Randomius for that. The last of this cargo to drop off, then we can go home. Still six months hard hyperspace travel, but at least we'll be heading in the right direction.

'Excellent news.'

'It maybe tidally locked at this range,' the science officer reported. 'But it looks stable enough. We're picking up methane and low concentrations of carbon dioxide in the atmosphere. Looks like we have a biosphere.'

Good enough.

'Tell the passenger we've found the last one. And break out the terraforming equipment.'

'Aye, sir.'

The passenger. The captain cast his mind back to the beginning of the trip; a passenger with a secret cargo. Not all that unusual, many passengers required a certain discretion in their dealings. In this case it had been several thousand tonnes of 'specialist equipment.' In his experience that usually meant contraband weapons or drugs, but it seemed he'd been wrong.

A cargo that size you'd need dozens of ships, there's nothing that big, nothing you could possibly afford to hire or buy …

Then the destination was discussed.

He'd fallen about laughing.

Ten thousand light years!

The passenger hadn't laughed and had waited patiently for him to stop. The captain had explained the problem. A year-long round trip, no refuelling stops, no repair stations. No one had ever gone out into the void so far. It couldn't be done. You'd be lucky to make a quarter of that distance before suffering a major malfunction that would leave you marooned in deep space far from help. Nobody would be coming to rescue you that far out. No one.

Then the question.

Could it be done?

Nothing is impossible, of course, but it was farcical. You'd need redundant components, self-repair ability, legions of spares, a crew that could cope with the isolation, a ship of a size and specification that only a major government could even think of funding. The cost alone …

How much?

He named a figure, three, maybe four times as much as he thought it would take.

More than the total gross planetary product of some entire systems!

It was then he knew he was in trouble. The passenger had extended a hand.

'We have the ship. A deal, Commander?'

He'd been shown a holofac. An enormous vessel, the size and scale of an Imperial Interdictor but designed for deep space exploration, the long haul … the *Zurara*.

The preparation had taken months, conducted in secret, a condition of the deal. Their destination was unknown, their purpose unknown and any questions to that effect were positively discouraged.

And no captain is happy not knowing what he's carrying in the hold.

He'd had to put up with that condition too. Armed sentries were stationed around the cargo bay. Not even he had been allowed inside. Only one phrase had permeated the crew by the time the ship was ready to depart, whispered in corridors and private quarters or in the mess halls under their breath.

Formidine Rift.

Formidine meant 'terror' in some ancient old Earth language, according to his science officer. Nice. A course was plotted outwards from the core worlds to the edge of the Perseus galactic arm; an astonishing distance that had never been contemplated before. Not even automated probes had gone out that far. Hell, not even telescopes could see what was out there due to the interstellar dust and gas. It was uncharted.

But we weren't the only ones going out there, so it seems.

A few very discreet inquiries had informed him that several other ships had been requisitioned at the same time. All big ships, mostly Anacondas. All stripped and fettled for long distance, long duration travel. A massive fleet of ships, unmarked, unaffiliated, unnoticed, all heading out into the void in different directions.

Wonder how many of them will make it back? I wonder if we will make it back …

'Sir?'

The science officer's voice interrupted his reverie.

'Yeah?'

'The passenger has confirmed the system is good to go. They're deploying the last … package.'

'Good news.'

'I think so, sir.'

'Helm!' the captain called, raising his voice a little. 'Plot us a course.' He looked around the bridge crew, they were all looking back at him with relief and excitement in their eyes. 'Plot us a course back home!'

'I've been updating that one for weeks, sir,' the helm officer said. 'Laid in and plotted. Nine thousand eight hundred and twenty-three light years to go …'

The distant rumble of the cargo bay doors opening echoed through the ship's bulkheads.

'Standard protocol, sir?' the science officer asked.

The captain nodded. 'The usual drill.'

The science officer tapped commands into her console. Scanners and consoles aboard the bridge went dark. With a crackle, the comms system also went dead.

Don't scan the cargo, don't scan the cargo. We're just the delivery team. We aren't to know what they're deploying, whoever they are …

They waited in the darkness, the faint hum of the life support systems the only sound. After a few minutes, they heard the cargo bay doors closing again. The faint thump resulted in the smallest of jolts.

'I'm guessing that's it,' the captain said. 'Power up the systems.'

The science officer tapped at her console again.

'Aye sir, powering up …'

Systems beeped and flashed, consoles illuminating briefly before fading out again. The procedure was tried again, with the same result.

The Captain frowned, stomping over to the console in his mag-boots to stand alongside the science officer.

'What's the problem?'

'Systems won't engage, sir,' the science officer reported. 'Main power is offline. The reactor has gone cold.'

'Cold? Re-initialise it!'

'I'm trying, sir!'

Down in the cargo bay, a passenger sealed themselves into one of the auxiliary cargo bays, fusing the doors to ensure they could never be opened again. Throughout the massive vessel, other conspirators were undertaking their own special tasks in tandem.

The passenger smiled. The crew wouldn't succeed. They might discover that the reactor's hydrogen fuel had been inexplicably vented into space before their time ran out, but it mattered little. Without motive power, nothing could be done about that. Perhaps they would puzzle over it in the limited time available to them. The instinct to survive remained strong in them. They might try to break into the cargo hold. Even if they succeeded it would avail them nothing. There were no answers to be found there.

The mission had been concluded successfully. The passenger's life's purpose was fulfilled. Nothing else was left to be done. The mission was too important to risk any of them returning to the core worlds. Sacrifices had to be made; some sacrifices had to be involuntary.

The passenger felt no remorse for the fate inflicted upon the crew, nor any particular consideration for personal mortality. Years of conditioning, drug therapy and psychological manipulation had seen to that. Only the purpose remained. The purpose was all.

The passenger took out a small capsule, turning it over for a brief moment, before swallowing it without further preamble.

Hexedit. A drug for occasions such as these. Painless. First you forget, then you forget how to breathe ... then you forget how to live ...

Without the reactor the ship would radiate heat into space at a rapid pace. First, condensation would appear on the windows, freezing into bright crystals of ice across the exposed surfaces. Then, as the temperature continued to drop, the crew would experience shivering, slow movements and lack of coordination.

Heart rates, respiration and blood pressure would fall. Speech and thinking would drift into dreams, which would be frozen forever, unchanging, drifting forever in the darkness between worlds. Before long they would submit, one by one, to the frigid chill of the void.

What was planned to be hidden – would remain so.

Coulter city, Tionisla system, The Old Worlds

The ship was old; that much was clear. Its design dated back hundreds of years, but such was the versatility of the craft, they were still being manufactured even now. This one was ancient, though, a relic of a time long past. Old-tech shield generators pushed power fore and aft, a single flux-stained gun emplacement graced the forward view. Since this ship had been in its prime governments had risen and fallen, systems had changed hands, people had lived …

And died …

Her hands shook on the flight controls, resulting in a slight yaw to starboard. She corrected it instinctively in the old-fashioned way, rolling and pitching the ship back into line.

The harsh and business-like tones of SysCon echoed through the bridge.

'Cowell and MgRath Romeo Echo Bravo. *Cor Meum Et Animam*, you are cleared for approach to Coulter City.'

'Ack SysCon.'

Her voice sounded tired even to her own ears. She needed rest.

I'm not as young as I used to be …

She bit her lip for a moment and then chuckled to herself. Well over a hundred years! She couldn't tell whether she'd spent more on ship outfitting or skin regeneration. She had pushed back the ageing process, defied time itself as best she could. But even with the technology of the 33rd century, there were limits. Would she see the 34th? That was the plan.

Not young by any stretch of the imagination!

Age spots dotted her hand and her grip wasn't as steady as once it was. The green glow from the scanner console lit her face in an unflattering way. She could see it reflecting in the cockpit windows.

An old lady …

Grey hair, with just a hint of brown, simply brushed into two neat folds on either side of her head. There was little else of note; she wore no earrings or adornments.

And this last trip was just too long a time in the void …

She looked down at the scanner, seeing the hyperspace routes she had laboriously plotted; a track across the stars to the edge of the galactic arm. Thousands of jumps traced all the way back here to the Old Worlds.

Riedquat. Hope I never have to visit that godforsaken system again.

The comm systems buzzed for attention.

'You are cleared for landing on pad four-two.'

'Confirmed.'

Focussing her concentration she adjusted the trim of her ship and watched as it slowly cruised into the enormous Coriolis space station. There was a familiar rumble as the ship passed through the energy barrier that allowed the interior space to be pressurised.

Wasn't like that back in the day …

The old ship descended towards its allotted pad and settled gently in the weak artificial gravity. A faint clunk signalled the ship was secure.

'Docking successful. Engines disengaged.'

She leant back in her pilot's chair, surveying the scene. The sight of the central corridor of the station wrapping around her to meet itself half a kilometre above her head always felt reassuring. The strange flatness of a planetary surface felt a little 'wrong' somehow. She was a creature of space, born there, her family had made their living in the void for three generations.

True, but there are five generations now…

She had never had children, she'd never found the time. Her older brother had, though. He'd met some pretty woman and they'd settled planet-side on Tianve. They'd had kids, and those kids had grown up and had their own children. She had four nephews and nieces, and more than a dozen great-nephews and great-nieces. Not that she'd seen most of them.

I'm just the mad space-travelling aunt they warn them about, I expect. Always 'out there' somewhere …

She had tried, but she wasn't the family type, and when she'd lost …

Long time ago now.

It still hurt though. He'd kept her grounded, kept her wanderlust under some kind of control. Sure, they'd had adventures across the charts and across the core worlds, but there had always been a reason; they'd made things better, or made some kind of difference.

We had forty years; many don't get as much …

Afterwards, she'd spent a long time depressed, bereft of any meaning to her life. She merely watched the holofac news vids, the appalling, flaccid and cheaply made entertainment shows. She saw the end of Galcop, the rise of the Alliance, new technologies arrive, mature and become obsolete.

And then the rumours started …

She'd written notes about the time before. Those strange dreams of her youth where things were similar, but they just weren't the same. The dreams had been so vivid it was as if they were more tangible than reality itself.

Sometimes she reread those notes, just to keep the dream alive. It felt important somehow, as if they were a real memory … a memory that had, for some unknown reason, been pushed aside in favour of something new.

This universe she'd lived in … it felt … wrong, as if it were missing a crucial ingredient; a flavour that should have been present. She could never quite figure out what it was. There was an ethereal feel to her life, which had grown with the advancing years. It gnawed at her. There was a secret here. Something had changed … and she hadn't.

The rumours … of the aliens …

She'd awoken from her torpor. A purpose again! She would find out what had happened, chase the rumours.

She'd chased them all right, trying to ascertain their veracity, but every clue led to a dead end. Every sure fire certainty dashed. What her dreams had told her was commonplace turned out to be elusive. Decades of her life spent chasing … was there really anything to chase?

They used to drag us out of witch-space. Attack with droned ships. Eight-sided shapes, organic and fluid, yet malevolent…

The official stories didn't tally with what she thought she knew. Outside of legend and myth no one remembered them. There were no artefacts, no alien-items. Nothing but stories of a half-concealed conflict that no one really believed anymore. They'd laughed at her.

She rubbed her shoulder. It ached whenever she thought about them.

She'd followed a rumour she had heard. Strange dark-hulled Anacondas commandeered and sent out into the empty reaches of the galaxy. A huge vessel escorted into the darkness for an unknown mission. None had ever returned. She'd uncovered documents describing their preparation, how they'd been stripped down for maximum jump range, fitted with new-fangled automated field maintenance units, crews selected for having minimal family attachments.

But their purpose had eluded her.

So she went looking for them, making many trips out into the darkness. She had spent months, even years, out in the void with nothing to show but a catalogue of new worlds that no one had ever visited, but none of them had shown anything more devastating than a few benign microbes.

But now I know. They never came back. The history books are blank because they were blanked. Now I can't even trust myself with this knowledge. I can't manage another trip. This will have to rest for someone else to uncover, if there is anything to uncover. Maybe I'm just crazy. A crazy old lady chasing ghosts …

She shook her head and cast her mind back.

This last trip.

She'd found it, abandoned and derelict out in the darkness. The evidence she'd been hunting for. That knowledge was too dangerous to transmit, too dangerous to store, too dangerous to even remember.

I've got to do what I told myself to do, without even knowing why …

She had to cross-reference what she found in the archives. Most were inaccessible, at least legally, and it had taken a while to work around those restrictions. Credits always worked eventually, it was just a matter of finding the right individual. What she had found were only footnotes, vague references and anecdotes. She had found little that substantiated her findings, just some strange and unconfirmed rumours of the Alliance being involved … and remnants of information regarding a mysterious ship.

Polaris?

The system was still permit locked, and it wasn't the only one it was impossible to reach.

Something is being concealed. Proof might be thin on the ground, but I found some evidence. I found where they went. One day someone is going to figure this out. I've left the clues. When the time is right they will be found once more. I must prepare them for that, pass the torch…

She tapped the holofac. Her fingers fumbled on the controls, activating the ship's status panel rather than the comms unit.

Combat Rank: Elite
Explorer Rank: Elite
Trading Rank: Elite

She sighed and jabbed the correct controls.

Not Elite enough though. Can't even hit the right damn switches anymore!

A three-dimensional holofac projection appeared before her with the image of an annoyingly young and fresh-faced man.

I used to look that young …

'Communications. How can I help you?'

'Tionisla Historical Society.' Her own voice sounded gruff and unpleasant.

'Just connecting you.'

She waited as an irritating jingle played out. It was the same one she'd heard last time she'd been here.

'Priest's perfect protopolyps! Tuttle's tasty therapsabladders! Last real food before witch-space!'

Don't they ever change those ads?

The holofac cleared and the jingle faded.

'Dan Mayweather speaking. How can I help you?'

She leant forward. 'I have something for you. A document. It's important it is filed correctly. Here's my ID. That should make things clear.'

A series of text and markers scrolled up the holofac display. The man at the other end examined it and then blinked in surprise.

'Oh …' The young man swallowed, his eyes flicking back and forth as he read the text on his screen. 'Yes, ma'am.'

'That's Commander to you.'

The man swallowed again but didn't say anything.

'Here's the document.'

She flicked her fingers towards the projector and the words 'Last Will and Testament' appeared alongside a document graphic.

The young man looked pale even through the holofac projection.

'The graveyard? But I'm not sure that's even allowed … are you sure?'

She smiled. 'It's all been arranged, trust me.'

'But if they allow you to do that, it means …'

She contented herself with a smug smile and waited. There had to be some compensation for being old after all.

'I'll get that stored straight away, ma'am … I mean … Commander.'

'You do that.'

She saw the acknowledgement trace come back.

Just a few more things to do.

She looked around at the cockpit. It looked as old and tired as she did. The ship was a veteran of more trips through the void than she could count, with more light years under its engines than anything else she knew, even the long distance exploration vessels.

Been around the galaxy more than once if you add it all up!

A tarnished name plate fixed below the main scanner caught her eye, the text illegible. She reached down and rubbed at it, the grime of many years pushed aside after a few vigorous attempts.

Cobra Mark III: Eclipse Class. Apocalypse Engineering Special Edition, 3142.

That made her chuckle again.

Special Edition? Once perhaps, but not anymore! Time has passed us both by, my old friend.

She shut down the remaining flight systems and eased herself out of the pilot's seat, her knees protesting with the effort. Even the seat was saggy and worn.

She made her way through to the midsection, switching the onboard systems into their respective maintenance modes.

One scarred panel made her pause. The switches were long since dead. She flicked them up and down just for the nostalgia, memories surfacing in her mind.

'Should have taken that out decades ago, hasn't worked since ... damn it. Too long ...'

She caught sight of the old manufacturers' names on the other panels with a twinge of sadness. Many of these companies didn't exist now, gone bust or acquired by bigger corporations. The ship was a relic of another century, maybe even the last of its kind.

Ingram, Lance and Ferman, Kruger, Irrikan, Zieman, Cowell and MgRath ...

She rested her head against one of the bulkheads for a moment to steady herself.

You've been a good ship. Now you have just one more job to do, but you can rest a while before that last duty.

She triggered the external hatchway. With a clunk and a hiss of equalising pressure, it lowered itself slowly to the ground. A set of steps folded out.

She walked down, stepping onto the floor of the pad, looking back up.

The hull above her was tarnished and scored, the victim of too much fuel scooping in the blazing coronas of stars beyond count. There was even the squat dome of a bomb housing she'd always meant to remove. She had never got around to it, not that it mattered. It hadn't been a viable weapon for decades.

She walked over to the maintenance bay, where a lone supervisor was working at some kind of console. He looked up as she approached.

'I hope you're not expecting me to be able to repair that thing,' he said. 'I'd have to dig out my grandsire's old repair manuals and I can tell you now that we don't have any parts in stock.'

She glared at him.

'What was your grandsire's name, boy?'

'Carruthers. Malcolm Carruthers.'

'I remember him. I can see the family likeness.'

'You knew my grandsire?'

'I knew him,' she replied.

And he was a flux-stained ass too.

'How old are you?' the young man demanded, turning to look at her more closely.

'It's rude to ask a woman her age. Didn't they teach you that?'

'Sorry, ma'am.'

'It's Commander, dammit!' she snapped. 'Time was when Elite combateers used to command a little respect around these parts.'

'Elite? You are Elite?'

The incredulity in his voice made her fists clench.

'I've killed more pilots than you've had stim packets, kid. I know they've messed with the rating system, but I'm Elite whichever way you look at it. Now, are you going to stop yapping and ask me what I need?'

'I've already told you, we can't fix that old…'

'I'm not asking you to fix it. I just want it cleaned up. Paint job. I want her to look her best. The old school one with the white wireframe relief on the black background.'

The young man spared a glance towards the battered ship behind her.

'Is it even worth it? You'll never sell it, except to a museum maybe.'

Years ago she'd have punched his lights out, but it wasn't an option for her now, however much she wanted to. She walked up to him, craning her neck to look into his eyes, fixing him with a stare that made him recoil under the gaze of brown eyes that were cold, hard and brutal.

'You get it bright and shiny,' she whispered, 'and I'll ask Commissioner Hughes to let you keep your job. How does that sound?'

The young man gulped.

'You know … the commissioner?'

She grinned. 'Oh yes, I know him. And he owes me a favour or two.'

She left him with that pleasant thought, and limped away, cursing the stiffness in her legs.

* * *

She sat in one of the less salubrious bars on the station, hidden in a dark corner. The bar was just below the rotational axis, the artificial gravity was lower here, she found she couldn't tolerate much above half a gee anymore. She took a sip from her drink, annoyed at how her hand shook when she did so. A plastic 'glass'. Anlian Gin was still her favourite, even though it was hard to come by nowadays. You couldn't serve it in actual glass, it tended to dissolve it.

Once I liked to be left alone, now I'd prefer not to be …

She scolded herself. Choices had been made and her life had taken the course it had. She had few regrets other than not having more time with … She took a generous gulp of her drink.

Across from her a news holofac was blaring out quick snippets of information. She ignored them for the most part, but the sharp trumpeting sounds of an Imperial announcement jolted her out of her reverie and she looked up.

'… And the Empire congratulates Senator Algreb and Lady Loren on the birth of their first daughter Corine. Dignitaries are already en route to the Haoria system to celebrate…'

Haoria? Never heard of it. Damn overstuffed Imperials. Not that the Federation is any better. Wish we were back in the good ol' Galcop days …

The years prior to the collapse of that old political institution had been shambolic and uncertain. No one quite knew which side they were supposed to be on. Then the Federation and the Empire took over, and the hyperdrive routes were established. Whole new organisations had appeared, the Alliance being the most notable. Factions rose up everywhere, almost overnight it seemed, quickly settling into battling against each other for territory.

Politics. I hate politics. Everything has changed. But the Empire… that might work… the Lorens was it?

She scrutinised the holofac display, watching until the article finished and moved onto the next piece of news.

We tried the Federation… that didn't work out so well. They'll have to deal with her one day …

She chuckled. She'd even taken a trip to Earth once. She'd found the planet where humanity had originated rather underwhelming, pretty much everything had been manicured to hide the tortured past of the planet, there was little evidence of what had gone before. It was too touristy for her liking.

Achenar, seat of the Empire, was more enchanting, but the overbearing Imperial attitude, baroque architecture and oppressive culture got to her after only a few short days. She had never felt welcome in Imperial space anyway.

And the Alliance? The new kids on the block were just that; young, idealistic, full of energy … and making exactly the same mistakes as their forebears.

I'm a trader by heart, lone-wolf, just me and the void. That's all I ever really was any good at. Searching for the truth. Me and a ship against the galaxy …

The news channel flipped over to a tech story.

'… Dramatic new progress has been made with a revolutionary new hyperdrive mechanism. Known as 'frame shifting', it is believed that if early prototype tests are successful, the new units have the potential to cut transit times from days and weeks to just seconds, heralding a new dawn for interstellar commerce and exploration. It will be years yet before the technology leaves the research labs, but it promises a revolution in space travel unseen since …'

Good luck getting that to work. I still remember the Antares! Seconds though … that would be something to see.

Somebody sat down opposite her, she looked at her guest with a faint smile.

'You took your time.'

The figure was cloaked, face concealed behind a bland close-fitting face mask. Only the eyes were distinguishable; dark and cold.

'You couldn't elude us forever.' The voice was muffled, probably modified by the mask to conceal the identity of the owner. A man, though.

She chuckled. 'I'm surprised an old lady like me managed to give you the slip for so long.'

'You must not reveal the information you have acquired.'

'What information?'

The figured sighed. 'Do we really need to play out this charade once more?'

'Indulge me,' she replied.

'You know why.'

'Because it might reveal the truth? People might find out what you've been concealing all this time?'

'The time is not right…'

She laughed. 'The time is never right, is it? Was it the right time when Galcop collapsed? Nope. How about when the Alliance came to power? No, not then either.'

'Secrets last longer than lifetimes, longer even than yours. We operate on a timescale far longer than mere decades. The Wheel turns…'

'Glad to hear it,' she replied. 'But people have a right to know…'

The man shook his head. 'People are better left in ignorance, getting on with their petty concerns without knowledge of a greater narrative that would freeze their hearts and cause panic across civilised space.'

'And who appointed us arbiters of humanity's destiny, anyway?'

'We did.'

'Convenient, that. Don't you see the slight flaw in that reasoning?'

'Are you going to comply?'

She leant forward, fixing her gaze upon the man.

'You know me well enough to know I don't give an overcooked trumble about complying. I am going to do what I think best.'

'You know we will have to take steps to … deal with you.'

She smiled. 'And you think I haven't already taken that into consideration? Do you take me for a fool?'

He didn't respond for a moment.

'Even I don't know what I know,' she said with a smile. 'I made sure of that as I went along. Trust no one, not even me! I dealt with your agents all along and I know your tricks – I taught most of them! It don't matter if you kill me or torture me, I've made sure the clues will come out someday and there is nothing you can do about it.'

'We will not torture you,' the man said, after some consideration. 'You have served us well for many decades, only now…'

'Now you realise that I despise what we stood for,' she snapped. 'What you still stand for. Why not kill me? No one is left who would care, or even notice.'

The man paused and regarded her for a moment.

'We never waste anything with… potential.' He leant back and folded his arms. 'I suggest you finish your drink.'

'Going to zap my mind again, are you?'

He nodded.

'Yes, we are.'

* * *

She had enjoyed being a librarian. It had been a long but uneventful career. She had worked hard in the Ferenchian research institute for her entire working life and now she had finally retired. Oh, it wasn't much, but it was enough to live on, to see out her final years in comfort, perhaps take up a hobby or two and rest after a life well lived.

Her co-workers had given her the obligatory send-off. She had been rather overwhelmed, truth be told. They had suggested she go home early and advised her to rest. She was only too happy to go along. Two of the younger librarians had escorted her in an aircar. She watched out of the window, looking at the spacecraft that flitted overhead conducting their business from the nearby spaceport. Space had never interested her. *Keep your feet firmly planted on the good soil*, that's what her father had said. Those memories were vague now, she found it difficult to recall her past. Age, of course.

Everything seemed remarkably quiet when she returned home. Neat and tidy; somehow newer and more pristine than she thought it ought to be. Somebody must have cleaned and prepped everything. Her colleagues were so kind and thoughtful, if a bit intense.

Retirement was going to suit her.

As the months passed, it proved true. She gained a little more energy, relaxing from having to do the chores of work. She would receive visits from her colleagues and the doctors. They always had some new pill for her, a booster injection or some such. It broke the monotony of the days which otherwise would have blended together into an undifferentiated blur.

One such day she sat down when they had all left to find she had received a message. The holofac receiver showed a small indicator, slowly spinning in the air.

She hadn't received a message before. It was odd. She had no family left. Her parents had died long ago and she had no brothers or sisters. Most of her friends had long since passed away and those that remained would come to see her in person. She had hardly ever used the comms system.

'How strange,' she muttered.

She gestured towards it and a little envelope icon appeared in the air before her, spun and then turned into a short string of characters.

I advise you to sit down and pour yourself an Anlian Gin.

She blinked in surprise.

'Anlian Gin?'

It was a tipple she was fond of; hard to get hold of and very expensive. How she'd got a fondness for it she couldn't remember anymore, it was long ago.

But no one knows my little foible … surely!

Guiltily, she looked towards one of the storage lockers in her apartment. She walked slowly across and took out a plastic decanter.

With shaking hands, she poured some of the liquor into a plastic shot and then signalled for her chair to come across to her. She eased into it and lowered herself into a comfortable position, looking at the text again.

She gestured.

The text vanished, replaced with a holofac image.

She frowned.

It was her.

Her own face looked back at her and then smiled.

'Hello me, this is you. The real you.'

Her image looked rather smug and self-assured.

'Whoever you think you are at this point, I'm afraid I have bad news. Everything that you think you know is false, manufactured in the diseased mind of one of their agents. Do not reveal this message to anyone. Do not trust anyone, even those you consider your closest friends or family. I have no idea what your life may be like at the moment, so I can't really advise you. What I can tell you is who you really are …'

A cruel joke, obviously. Some sort of prank call. She paused the recording and was almost about to delete it …

But nobody knew about the Anlian Gin, nobody!

After a moment she signalled for it to resume.

'You were born in the year 3122 in orbit of the Tianve system. You are a space pilot, an Elite combateer of some notoriety. You can gauge the truth of this assertion by contacting the Tionisla Historical Society and asking for the last will and testament of …'

Her image spoke a name.

A name that she was sure she'd never heard, but somehow it resonated in her mind.

Another word came, flickering through her mind, meaningless and obscure.

Ragazza!

'… In the Tionisla system you will find your … our ship. The documents will educate you and tell you what you need to do. There's a hundred credits for expenses. You'll find another message waiting.'

The image took on a softer expression.

'I am sorry for what this message must mean to you. I do not know what life you think you have led, how happy or sad you are with your present situation. All I know is that whatever you think is real … is not. There is a story here which has been suppressed, a story that should be told and has been quite deliberately hidden by shadowy powers operating beyond the law. You, me … us …. We're part of it and they've tried to stop us. Be in no doubt that it is something very important. And be careful!'

Her image flipped her a jaunty salute.

'Good luck, fly safe and … Right on, Commander.'

The image faded, with a quick flash showing the location of the Tionisla system itself. It was many light years away.

She was trembling, so she drank the remainder of the gin in one hit.

For minutes she stared at the now silent holofac without moving.

Something jogged in her memory. A dark-haired man, a young woman with brown hair; space, love, adventure, lasers firing … missiles! A green dark-hued ship almost silhouetted against a backdrop of stars. Snatches of some kind of remarkable saga amongst the stars.

Can't be true …

Tionisla was such a long way away. A trip into space, at her age?

Her heart jumped in her chest, surprising her. A fierce joy surged through her as visions flashed through her mind: distant stars, a sunrise fading into blackness, the flash of spacecraft hulls against the dark. A calling … no, a yearning!

She got unsteadily to her feet. Another phrase came to her mind, not quite realised.

Elite combateers, we always … always …

There was a mischievous grin on her face.

'Well then … let's go make a difference!'

Chapter One
AD 3302

Capitol, Achenar 6d, Achenar system, Empire.

The Beluga liner was a thing of beauty. Its enormous bulk had been well disguised by its designers, dainty and elegant despite its huge girth and length. Bright blue starlight flickered from its highly polished hull, sparkling across the expansive windows tapered along the flanks of the vessel.

Before it lay a world of green and blue, wreathed in cyan clouds, reflecting the light of the distant star. In the distance beyond lay a ringed gas giant. This world, whilst bigger than ancient Earth, was merely a moon in this system.

Many would have recognised it, if not from the spectra of the blue-white star, then from the myriad lights visible across the terminator and into the dark side of the world, or by the busy streams of traffic dotted along flight corridors to and from the surface. It was obviously highly advanced and heavily populated.

Achenar 6d.

Capitol.

The beating heart of the Empire.

Founded a thousand years before, the Duval Empire was, perhaps, the greatest single political entity the universe of humanity had ever known. Its origins lay shrouded in controversy, with murder, greed and conquest having played their part. It had long ago split from its great rival, the Federation, and fought many wars against it throughout recorded history. At times it had to fight for its survival, at others it had been the oppressor in wars of attrition and conquest. It had long been ruled by a genetically secured line of male heirs stretching back into antiquity.

Today the Empire spanned thousands of systems, its territory enveloping hundreds of cubic light years. Across this senators ruled and patrons served, all paying homage, at least in public, to the Emperor herself, Arissa Lavigny-Duval. Her elevation had been a recent affair and she had retained the old title, not content with calling herself Empress, her own rise to power a matter of contention and controversy that remained unresolved in the minds of many.

Everything was strictly regimented. Every individual knew their place on the rungs, from the lowliest slave through to the highest denizens of the Senate. Rituals, processions, rites and the many parades and soirees of polite society reinforced rules both spoken and unspoken. Even the clothing, hairstyles, make-up and accessories wove a subtle message for those who knew how to read them.

Two such patrons stood within a lounge on the great vessel, behind the wide viewing windows of the liner, gazing out at the bright crescent of the planet as it swiftly grew before them. The captain, aware of the passengers aboard, had brought the ship towards the planet on a circuitous route, ensuring a captivating view of their destination at all times.

The patrons could not have contrasted more. One was painfully thin, his gaunt figure portraying an air of worry and concern that was matched by the deeply etched lines upon his face. An older man, bent with the pressures of political life. He wore a huge pair of ocular enhancers that were perched precariously upon the end of his nose, looking for all the world like a pair of ancient spectacles from times gone by.

The other was perhaps three times his size, an obese extravagance of a man. A swarthy face graced by a neatly trimmed goatee was the most immediately obvious feature, with chubby digits dripping in rings and jewellery, accompanied by an air of joviality. Only the eyes gave away the fierce determination and ambition that resided within. Despite the vastness of unappealing flesh, there was a sharp intellect at work.

Both men were dressed in traditional Imperial fashion, rather reserved by modern tastes and somewhat at odds with the current vogue in the core systems of the Empire. Both were draped in copious quantities of fine linen, subtly secured against the rigours of zero-gee and space travel.

'I have anticipated my visit to Achenar for quite some time,' the thinner man said. His voice was cracked, impatient and terse. 'But not in this manner, not in disgrace, begging for favours from whatever powers that might take an interest in our plight.'

The larger man laughed.

'My dear Patron Zyair,' he began, his voice rich and melodious. 'Do not fret so. This is Capitol, a world brimming with opportunities for exploit …' He corrected himself. 'For such as us to do great works in the service of our mighty Empire.'

'May I remind you, Patron Gerrun, it has taken us more than a full year to extract ourselves from that debacle in the Prism system? That I have had to bow and scrape the knee to that insufferable snob of an Ambassador for all that time?'

Gerrun pursed his lips. 'Ambassador Cuthrick is an acquired taste, I'll admit. Though he can hardly be held responsible for the duties he was asked to perform by…'

'That woman,' Zyair almost spat. 'Did I not advise against that sordid plan? That she was unsuitable for the role she was pushed into? Conspicuously unsuitable! Dalk paid the price for his lack of judgement. And what did she do? Abrogate her responsibilities and dash off into the darkness… I was proved right, was I not?'

Outside, the crescent of the planet continued to widen. The ship was dropping down towards the terminator, aiming for local dawn on this particular point on the planet. As they watched, the patrons saw the Achenar star sink towards the glowing atmosphere of the planet.

'You were indeed, my friend,' Gerrun acknowledged. 'But events will catch up with Lady Kahina Loren, have no doubt.'

'And how so?' Zyair demanded. 'It is because of her we have no place in Prism, no Senate to serve, no citizens to administer. With one fell swoop, she cut us off at the knees. Impotent! Cast out into a political wasteland. Tarnished goods. If it had not been for the assets we had accrued in that time we might have been forced into slavery.'

'Calm, calm,' Gerrun tutted.

'Calm?' Zyair turned on Gerrun. 'When our political future lies in ruins? I do not share your optimism that a visit to Capitol will solve all our problems. None here will wish to be associated with an errant senator. Our reputations are forever sullied, associated as they are with that wretched Loren girl.'

Gerrun smiled at him and raised an eyebrow.

Zyair looked at him with a frown. 'I know that look. You have a plan already in flight. Pray tell me what is you are scheming?'

Gerrun rocked back gently in his mag-boots, the lack of gravity agreed with his constitution and certainly made his bulk rather more manageable, though one did have to keep a wary eye on inertia in zero-gee. Already the faint grip of gravity from the planet below was making itself felt, before long it would increase in strength as the ship descended. It felt rather akin to being in a lift that was constantly about to arrive at the desired floor. A faint pressure in the legs.

'It is our, shall we say, intimate knowledge of Lady Kahina Loren,' Gerrun said with a chuckle, 'that has currency here on Capitol.'

Zyair blinked. 'How so?'

'We have knowledge of her thinking, insights into her character and behaviour,' Gerrun said. 'First-hand experience of dealing with her antics. Such things are now of interest in high places. With the right introductions, exchanges and promises of service, we can use that to our advantage. The sins of the past can be washed away, and with a little fortune, we can look forward to a more exalted position. Perhaps we might even hold sway over her downfall …'

'Her downfall,' Zyair licked his lips. 'That would be a sweet morsel I would savour for a long, long time.'

The ship rumbled about them, superheated plasma flashing outside the windows in arcs of disrupted atoms. The liner was entering the atmosphere. Within, faint tremors were all that could be felt. Below, the lights of cities on the dark side glowed brightly, an impossibly complex yet elegant network of concentric lights, interconnecting in straight lines, arcs and swirls.

'You have arranged this?' Zyair said after a moment's thought.

Gerrun pursed his lips.

'It's fairer to say that I was contacted, and thus made the most of the opportunity,' he replied.

'Contacted? By whom?'

'I would rather not speak their name here, my friend,' Gerrun said. 'Call me old-fashioned if you will, but there is no need to take unnecessary risks. Let's just say that our Lady Kahina has ruffled more than a few feathers in the past and our contact would prefer discretion in these matters.'

Zyair nodded and looked out through the windows as the ship continued its descent. The superheated plasma faded away and high clouds were flickering past the windows, cyan on their tops, matched with a startling pink on their undersides in the bright light of dawn. The star had sunk to the horizon. Already the tallest building could be seen, rising far above the towering cloud decks. Their destination was not far ahead.

'But I think you'll recognise her,' Gerrun said with a wink. 'She is quite distinctive.'

Zyair frowned as he looked out at the approaching planet. Then his eyes widened in appreciation.

'Ah …' Zyair said.

Edge of the Frontier, two hundred light years from Sol

Myriad stars pricked the darkness of space. Not far away from here was the border, the boundary, the limit of known space; the edge over which only those who couldn't resist the siren song of adventure dared to go; those to which 'dangerous' was just a substitute for exhilaration.

They call it the Frontier.

Out here, against the slowly fading embers of red dwarfs, the sharp light of blue-white supergiants and the deadly peril of uncharted neutron stars, was the void. For uncounted kilometres there was nothing, with perhaps just the occasional asteroid to break the monotony.

This was a dull system, a waypoint of little note in the grand scheme of things. Its central star had no planets, celestial mechanics long ago having determined that the region was poor in elements beyond the essential hydrogen. A lone K class star blazed away as it had for uncounted millennia. It would continue to do so long after the events occurring around it had run their course and been long forgotten.

Yet today, the unchanging vista was interrupted.

Something was moving in the upper atmosphere of the star, a faint spark of light. In moments the spark had grown to a plume of radiant energy, a curving discharge of energised particles, glowing fiercely as their components were shattered by the passage of the intruder.

Whatever it was, it moved at an impossible speed, already it had looped a quarter of the star in a recklessly close trajectory, actually within the corona, just skirting the edges of the enormous flares writhing across the star's surface.

Having traversed half of the surface the object broke off its close inspection and the plume arched away into space, cooling and fading from sight. For a moment the system was unsullied once more, before, with a burst of coruscating energy, a ship materialised out of nothingness.

It was elegant, bright white against the ebony backdrop of the void, extended vents glowing with radiated heat as they cooled. It had a wide low shape with graceful nacelles left and right, from which plumes of engine flux exhaust were being expelled. The ship's form was instantly recognisable to anyone of human origin. Classic curves blended with organic shapes, a Gutamaya design.

An Imperial Clipper.

The hull plates were illuminated by subtly arranged lighting, ensuring the vessel's name could be seen.

Seven Veils.

The vents cooled to a dull crimson and then retracted gracefully against the hull. The engines throttled down, thrusters in the nose of the vessel firing to bring the vessel to a relative halt some forty light seconds from the star.

The cockpit was at the bow of the ship, a wide transparent canopy affording the occupants a superb view into space. Two pilots' chairs could be seen, set forward within a wide and expansive bridge, tell-tale instrumentation lights blinking around them purposefully.

Only one of the chairs, on the starboard side, was occupied. A dark-haired and dark-skinned figure sat secured, garbed in a generic flight suit and surrounded by the glowing holofac displays that signalled the ship's status. The figure gestured with a brief hand motion and the images faded out with a shimmer.

Hassan Farrukh Sharma listened as the ship's drives faded into silence, leaving nothing but the background hum of the ventilation system aboard the *Seven Veils*. The ship still impressed him, even after several months of flying it. It was fast, efficient and a technological tour de force. All the systems aboard had been upgraded to the most expensive and powerful componentry available, its owner had seen to that. She had high standards, and accepted nothing less than the best.

Somehow though, he missed the tatty old Eagle he had once flown. In every measurable way it had been an inferior ship, but there was something about this new Imperial ship that he didn't like. Flying it, he felt as if he were permanently underdressed for an important occasion. He should be wearing a uniform or even a tuxedo, ready to attend some elegant soiree or convention. It was too flash, too flamboyant.

Still, pilot to a senator's daughter. You could have done a lot worse…

It was fair to say she had turned his life around. Two years before he'd been a naïve young impecunious hotshot out to prove himself to the void. Today he was effectively the captain of a multi-million credit Imperial warship, bristling with the best that the shipyards could provide.

But it wasn't the ship, the credits, or even the lifestyle that had truly beguiled him.

It was her.

Salomé.

Officially the Imperial Senator Lady Kahina Tijani Loren, yet Commander Salomé since the cataclysm in the Prism system. She was the daughter of the late Senator Algreb Loren who had once held court over those worlds. Fierce and haughty in the manner of the Imperials, she was nonetheless charismatic and intriguing. She knew it too, using her talents to woo and influence high-ranking officialdom and inspire an almost zealous loyalty amongst the disaffected spacers, traders and explorers she had encountered on her voyages.

It was a far cry from how they had originally met. He'd stolen her, or at least the pod in which she was contained at the time, from the notorious pirate lord, Octavia Quinton. She had been smuggled out from her homeworld dead, or so it had seemed. In truth, it was a complex political game being played by the Empire, the Federation and a group of 'Reclamists' who were all vying over the future of the Prism system.

It was he that had given her the name Salomé.

She stepped out stark naked, threw her guts up over the floor and screamed at me. Not very senatorial…

He chuckled and then sighed. He liked her better that way. The naïve and vulnerable Salomé, rather than the proud Imperial stateswoman, Lady Kahina Tijani Loren.

And yet, her true motivation eluded him. She was a mixture of both now, driven by a singular purpose. A purpose she kept to herself. She slipped between her personae with fluid ease. Who was to say who the real person was?

He'd taken Salomé to the edge of beyond and further still. They had charted the depths of the galaxy, beyond the spiral arms, crossed the core and its fearsome supermassive black-hole, still onwards until the galaxy became a faint smudge in the viewport.

Hassan shivered at the thought. Out there, thousands of light years beyond the fringes of civilisation, the loneliness was immense. The first trip had been following a vague trajectory plot which had taken them to the EAFOTS sector, past a beautiful if ghostly pair of nebula known as the Heart and Soul. They had been following a clue, a strange data log that Salomé had dug up from a secure Imperial data bank. It had been left there over thirty years before.

The stars did thin out, the galaxy was just hanging there and the dangers of space almost ended us, but we never found whatever it was we were supposed to be looking for.

Unfazed by the lack of success, Salomé recruited others to her cause. She was convinced there was something out there, more than just convinced – driven. Precisely what it was remained a mystery. Hassan was bemused at how willing so many were to follow her out into the black. Misfits and social outcasts in some cases, but well-to-do traders and explorers amongst them, some with enormous resources at their disposal.

Salomé had proved herself adept at corralling them. She seemed utterly convinced there was a secret that had to be unlocked. Clues that needed chasing, rumours to be investigated. More exploration trips followed, culminating in a voyage across the heart of the galaxy to the far fringes of the opposite rim, only to rendezvous with more of those who followed her, tens of thousands of light years from civilisation. Sharing information, comparing data, looking for more clues.

And her warnings. Trouble in the core worlds ... something she knows that she won't tell ... not even to me.

And still she was searching, following some crazy old lady's rambling instructions. The toil of hyperspace travel never seemed to weary her. She was a true explorer, always looking to the next jump, the next system and beyond.

They'd amassed a vast quantity of exploration data in their travels and were now heading back towards the core worlds and civilisation once more.

That old lady may just have been insane, how would we ever know? Perhaps this is some wild goose chase and she's out there somewhere, cackling away in a retirement home...

Satisfied the ship was secure, Hassan activated his mag-boots and allowed them to snap to the decking before he gestured for his harness to release him. With an Imperial flourish, it neatly retracted and furled itself efficiently away. He stood up and stretched.

A sigh escaped him.

The door at the rear of the bridge snapped open. Hassan felt his heart quicken with anticipation as he turned.

She walked in, elegant silver mag-boots clicking sharply on the flooring, graceful despite the zero-gee, her measured gait the product of years of expensive upbringing. As was her usual habit, she was dressed in a flowing dark gown cleverly secured by some expert designer with an appreciation of the difficulties women of substance faced aboard ship. Raven dark hair framed a striking, yet somehow severe, face. She was not a beauty in the manner of the celebrity holovids of the core worlds, but there was a wildness to her expressions and a strength to her stance and bearing that Hassan had seen deployed many times to great effect. Gray eyes completed her slightly haunting visage. It was a face that had engendered the loyalty of thousands; men and woman who would, and had, lain down their lives for her.

Me included ...

'Am I to assume we have reached the end of our route?' she asked.

Her voice told another story. It had the distinctive Imperial lilt, combined with a measure of arrogance, determination and grit. Hassan had watched as she'd faced down pirate lords, criminals and bounty hunters. She had a brutal edge. He'd seen her cut down opponents with a deft thrust from the antique Holva blade she wore when travelling and he'd experienced first-hand her unarmed combat prowess.

Never cross Salomé …

Hassan nodded.

'We're here, two hundred light years out from the edge of the core worlds. We're fuelled, ready for …'

'Whatever awaits.'

She had a habit of finishing people's sentences. She liked to dominate, to push and coerce. It was her way.

'What are we waiting for this time?'

Some hint of impatience must have crept into his voice. She looked at him.

'Bored, Hassan?'

'We've travelled the length and breadth of the galaxy chasing this mystery …'

'And we will keep searching until we find out what lies behind it. There is a secret here, long hidden …'

She turned to look at the console, activating the communications holofac. There was nothing new on display. A faint frown crossed her features. Hassan had seen the look before. She was expecting something.

More secrets …

'And for how long?'

She looked around again.

'This is no whim,' she said. 'Need I remind you how difficult it was to extract the information from the databanks? How much I had to risk to confirm whether it was really true?'

'I was there, remember?'

Her eyes narrowed.

'Are you losing faith in what we're doing? There is a truth here that some do not want us to find …'

Hassan shook his head. 'There is so much else we … you and I … could be doing. It's been a year …'

'You and I?' she asked, now looking straight at him. Hassan felt his heart lurch. 'You're my pilot. What do you mean? Do I not pay you generously enough for your service?'

He was spared having to provide an answer by a soft melodious tone from the communications panel. Salomé turned, calling up the transmission with a wave of her hand.

'Our rendezvous,' she said, a faint smile playing on her lips.

Hassan moved over to stand beside her. Her perfume rose up around him; subtle and entrancing, full of promise tantalisingly out of reach. He summoned up the galactic chart and a course plotted itself across the star systems. He could see it was heading into the core worlds. It ended in a region he'd heard of but never visited.

'Tionisla,' Salomé said, running a hand through her hair. 'I thought it might be.'

'You've been there?' Hassan asked. Tionisla was an independent planet, a long way from Empire space. Hassan recalled the name from a history lesson, but the details eluded him for the moment.

'I may have,' Salomé responded. She turned and tapped him gently. 'Our course, if you please, we need to be there as soon as we can.'

Her hand rested on his shoulder for a long moment. He indulged a brief daydream where he took her hand in his, pulling her into his arms, finally bending her to his will and …

'Hassan?'

He blinked.

'I'm on it.'

You stupid fool. After all this time … Never in a million years would she even think … but if she did … just maybe …

He stomped down on the desire, the feelings and the lust. It retreated within, smouldering gently. The course needed plotting. He buckled himself back into the pilot's chair and fired up the controls.

The newsfeed flickered to life on his right, a scrolling list of items as the ship synchronised itself with the nearest outlets. He hadn't checked the feeds for some time; there was a lot to catch up on. One particular item caught his eye and he pulled it across for inspection.

'…And in a dramatic turn of events, it has been revealed that Jaques, the cyborg bartender who famously modified his entire space station and prepped it for an audacious hyperspace jump across the galaxy has been located! Jaques, who had been given up for lost when the station failed to materialise at its destination at Beagle Point on the opposite side of the galaxy, has been confirmed to be intact and well but in an obscure location most of the way towards the galactic core, some twenty two thousand light years from the core worlds. Intrepid explorers have already begun the trek out to him with spare parts and supplies. It appears the station was badly damaged by the ambitious transit and is unlikely to move again …'

Hassan rubbed his chin.

Better not show that to her, she'll want to go!

Thus distracted, he pushed the thoughts away and he began the task of plotting the route and prepping the ship for yet another series of hyperspace jumps. Within minutes he was ready, adjusting the ship's course to match. He looked out at the distant stars.

'Here we go again.'

***

Salomé retired to her cabin, securing the door behind her with a sigh.

Tionisla? Circling back there once again? What is it about that system?

With the ship in the depths of space there was no need to lie down, but she approached her sleeping bunk regardless and climbed upon it. She gently secured herself as she felt the ship begin to move.

She closed her eyes, trying to keep her mind blank, to concentrate …

But the images came. Ships smouldering as they were struck by beams of fierce energy, a twisted wreck spinning past, the screams of the innocent haunting her as they did every time she closed her eyes.

You have your war, signorina …

She clenched her eyes shut against the memories, trying to erase the images from her mind, but to no avail. She could never forget what she had done, what she had sanctioned. The words she had uttered mocked her in her own proud Imperial tones.

Armies fight battles! That is what they are for!

They had fought her battle, fought over her home, the emerald moon of Chione. Thousands had died, that blood was on her hands, she had instigated that conflict. She had tried to make amends in whatever way she could, using her rank as a means to extend remorse. Relatives had been compensated, entreaties to the other powers made. Her efforts had been accepted by some, ignored by others and seen as cynical by those she thought might have helped her. Some, thinking she sought the throne of the Empire, had spun the media against her.

I wish I could change it all …

And then this mystery. A threat to the safety of all so she was led to believe, something she could perhaps solve. A way to atone for her sins, to protect the people of the galaxy from some nameless threat. Or so it seemed.

Am I any closer to solving this riddle?

She felt the ship adjust course and then heard the unmistakable sound of the frame shift drive charging.

Tionisla, will I find my answers there?

Chapter Two

Deep space, Chontaiko system, Empire

Bright metallic hulls glinted in the darkness. The intense glare of a white dwarf was the primary illumination, harsh and hostile; the white-hot remnants of a star, its very core dense beyond imagination.

'Flight leader to group, form up for jump. Key frame shifts for sync. Confirm wing beacon lock.'

The lead ship, a Clipper, was at the head of a small convoy, taking a shipment of Imperial slaves to Mu Koji. The convoy itself consisted of a series of Type-7 freighters, their bright white paintwork the only obvious clue to their ownership. Bulky, ugly and slow, they were nonetheless a perfect ship for hauling large quantities of cargo across the void.

The fleet was guarded by a phalanx of Imperial Eagles, nippy little single-person fighters that had proved themselves in many battles. They flew alongside the bigger ships, watching their scanners for traces of anything they needed to respond to. The life of a fighter escort was mostly mind-numbing tedium, punctuated here and there with moments of absolute fear and mayhem.

Just a few more jumps to Mu Koji …

The convoy was a long way out of the core worlds. The Empire had some ambitious expansion plans in the Pleiades sector and Mu Koji was seen as something of a strategic location to further that end. The slaves were required to work on reinforcing the Empire's interest in the system. Ships, bases, installations and weapons. It all had to be built. Given the nature of the many convoys that had been sent out this way, it appeared it had to be built quickly.

Guess the cold war is heating up after all these years ...

The freighters lumbered into position, ready for the next jump in the sequence. The flight leader scanned his controls from within the cockpit of the Clipper. All ships had reported in, they were ready. His hand moved towards the holofac control that would synchronise the jump for all ships.

He frowned.

The far right side of the holofac had shifted from its normal display. He looked at it for a moment, unable to fathom what it was telling him.

Wanted?

Comms crackled from the console.

'Skipper?' One of the freighter pilots was calling him. 'This is a little odd. I think I've got a problem with the flight computers.'

The flight leader flicked on the comms to respond. 'Don't tell me, you just got tagged fugitive.'

'Er … yeah. You have it too? Weird. Apparently, I've just picked up a two hundred thou credit bounty!'

The flight leader flicked up the status indicator. His was even higher. True, he was rated an 'expert' on the combat scale, but …

400,000 Cr!

'You should try shooting me. Hold tight for a moment everyone,' the flight leader instructed. 'I'm going to try a system reboot and see if we can clear this. It's probably duff data from our last stopover.'

He instructed the computer to shut down the onboard systems. The holofac displays flickered and died. The life support systems cut out momentarily as the ship reset itself. For long moments there was nothing but silence as the ship drifted in the darkness. It was strange to hear nothing, the gentle cycling of the air systems and power conduits aboard ship always gave rise to a background hum in normal flight.

Reminds you how empty the void really is.

The computers flashed back on, the holofac displays crashing with static for a moment before steadying and displaying information once more. The flight leader checked the log.

Damn.

'No change,' he reported. 'I suggest we get to Mu Koji as fast as we can and get the ships checked over for data transmission problems. Everyone got the same symptoms?'

All the pilots in the convoy reported variations on the theme.

All the computers go duff at the same time? This doesn't feel right … at all. Like someone just painted a target on our backs …

'Standby for jump.'

No sooner had he engaged the jump controls when another series of warning messages appeared on the displays.

Frame shift inhibited by factor of 12. Disruptive mass.

Mass locked?

'Escort! We have company. Break and defend!'

The crashing sizzle of static and a repeating vibrato thump echoed out of the comm system.

Jammed!

He wrenched the Clipper about, transferring power to the engines to make the turn. The Clipper yawed violently to one side as it struggled with the abrupt change of momentum. Laser fire and explosions were crackling around the convoy. The scanner was suddenly alive with movement, all sorts of undistinguishable marks, flickering uncertainly.

Ambush!

Ships flew out of the darkness. Pythons, Anacondas. With a sickening lurch in his stomach, the flight leader saw their weapons discharge. Some serious firepower, more than the convoy could deal with.

He deployed his own weapons. The Clipper was no lightweight, it was the most powerful ship in the convoy by some way, yet it was seriously outmatched here.

Ident checks buzzed across the displays, the flight leader only sparing them a cursory glance.

Federation markings. Warmongering dogs!

One of the Eagles exploded to his starboard side, lighting the cockpit with fierce yellow light for a brief moment. One of the freighters heeled over, its flank burning under the assault of intense heavy multi-cannon fire from a pair of Pythons.

The escort was down, the freighters ripped to shreds moments later. The Clipper was next. One Python was damaged by return fire, but the remaining group of attackers turned and concentrated their assault.

The result was a foregone conclusion.

The Clipper reeled in the onslaught. The flight leader punching out one last desperate message as the ship failed around him.

'Convoy Delta Romeo Victor to Mu Koji base. Attacked by Federation forces en route. Convoy destroyed! Repeat, convoy destroyed! Federal vessels attacked without provocation …'

Shields offline!

The staccato impact of weapons fire echoed throughout the hull. The Clipper spun out of control, one of its nacelles ripping free from the main body of the ship. More fire poured into the beleaguered vessel.

There was a flash. Then there was nothing but spinning debris, slowly dispersing into the darkness.

Emerald, Cemiess system, Empire

Emerald was a terraformed world, and far the better for it. The climate was mild, with atmospheric regulators still operating to influence the weather whenever required. The Cemiess system itself had a chequered history, having been a point of contention between the Federation and the Empire many times in the past.

In part due to this, it had become the only Imperial system where slavery was illegal, though this was circumvented by a thriving black market that somehow always seemed to find a way not to come to the attention of the authorities. Ironically, this meant that trading slaves in the system was far more lucrative than elsewhere, at the risk of traders being caught smuggling and thus being fined or having their ships confiscated.

Today was not a good day for a smuggling run. The main station in the system, Mackenzie Relay, was flanked by far more than the usual number of system authority vessels. Squads of Vipers were patrolling the perimeter of the station's safe zone, scanning all approaching ships and shepherding them into long queues for processing.

Traders grumbled. Anyone without a pre-arranged docking slot, which was pretty much everyone, was being held beyond the station entrance. Two Imperial Cutters were positioned before the station, conspicuously not answering any hails whatsoever. Enquiries as to what was happening went unanswered.

A few ships were allowed in. Surreptitious scans revealed that they were carrying arrays of transmission technology and other high-tech goods. A small flotilla of Couriers brought in an array of notable Imperial dignitaries, backed up by a larger Imperial Clipper.

The ships made their way, after a brief pause for scanning, past the Cutters and through the station's docking entrance. Bright light reflected off their polished white hulls. Landing struts extended with typical Imperial flourish and the ships spread out, drifting slowly towards their respective landing pads and settling themselves down.

The glare of exhaust flux faded away as the ships shut down their engines. A small army of automechs moved in to service them; refuelling, repairing damage and adjusting onboard systems.

The portside airlock of the Clipper irised open as a boarding ramp was extended towards it. Moments later, a team of four individuals in work-a-day overalls marched out and filed across the walkway. They spared the enormous interior of the station a quick glance and then walked on, arriving on the expansive loading floor of the docking area. Once they had vacated the pad, a brief gesture from the leader was all it took to dismiss the ship.

With a hiss of equalising pressure, the Clipper sank out of sight behind them, lowered into a cavity below, there to be unloaded.

The four stepped up to an alcove marked 'DeCon' and stepped through with no hesitation. They were all long-term space travellers. Not for them the indignity of requiring vaccinations and injections to combat the plethora of space-borne maladies.

The lead figure, the technical leader of the group, stepped up to the embarkation officer who was waiting for them.

'You made good time,' the officer said.

'Good ship,' the tech-lead responded, 'and the Admiral was able to straighten a few routes for us.'

The officer nodded. 'I have your inventory listed as holofac transmitters and image enhancers. You part of the vid crew?'

'Just the techies. We're here to set up the AV down in the park.'

'Let me see your IDs,' the officer said, looking at the patches on the crew's overalls. It was a familiar circular emblem.

Holovid Tru 3D Tech Comms Team.

The tech-lead extended his palm and his colleagues did the same. The officer tapped a command into the commtab he held and scrutinised the result.

'You're good. Cleared for access to green zones. You should get a nice view of the speech today.'

The tech-lead shrugged, 'We'll be too busy monitoring the feeds, and besides, we've heard them all before. Blah blah, Federal scum … blah blah, won't stand for it any longer … blah blah, follow me if you're a true Imperial …'

The officer laughed. 'You've got him pegged. Make sure you get his good side. I hear he's quite particular about that.'

The tech-lead grinned. 'We'll get him, don't worry about that.'

***

A quarter of the way around the station interior, another group of individuals were hunched over status displays. Their uniforms were grey, just a shade above black, severe and immaculately tailored. Enhancements concealed their eyes behind reflective shades, but furnished them with a direct connection to intelligence data systems, allowing almost instantaneous queries on any subject to be made with just a brief flick of their eyes. Hair was neatly trimmed, cut short in the manner of most space travellers.

They were rarely seen, their identities unknown. Each looked very similar, with any distinguishing features having long ago been removed or adjusted by surgery. They operated as a collective with singular purpose. Recruited from the cream of the Imperial educational establishment and then subjected to brutal training that only a few graduated from, they were set apart from even the highest echelons of the Empire. They were a tool of the Emperor herself.

Double I, Double S.

The Imperial Internal Security Service.

Two of their agents were crouched over a holofac representation of the local star system. As they watched, a new indicator appeared on the chart; a ship making its arrival into the system. Within moments, a series of ID markers appeared alongside it, identifying the ship and providing distance, bearing and ETA. The marker turned blue and pulsed on the display.

'He's here,' noted the first. 'Wing beacon has been activated.'

'Fighter escorts are homing in,' the second replied. 'All station traffic is now on lockdown. Nothing is going in or out.'

The first nodded and scrutinised the display for long moments, deep in thought.

'Do you think it's a duff lead?' the second asked.

'Most likely, they usually are. There are dozens of threats against him every week. Federals, disaffected factions, controlled systems that don't like being exploited. He's made a lot of enemies. There is always someone lining up to take a pop at him.'

The second agent didn't answer. Politics was simply a mechanism for change as far as the IISS was concerned. They were partisan to most of it, serving she who stood above the morass of feuding and scheming that defined the upper-middle ranks of the Imperial elite.

'These guys, though,' the first agent said. 'They have a special place on his list. They killed the old Emperor and almost cost him his place in the Senate. They certainly destroyed any chance he had at becoming Emperor himself. Their mistake was making it personal, so he vowed to eradicate them. He did a pretty thorough job; billions were spent on combat bonds to take down their ships and destroy their bases.'

'So, why …?'

'You can't eradicate any of these factions completely. There is always a handful who survive, and they go on to cultivate a new round of insurgency. Or it's just plain revenge. Too many are caught in the crossfire, and rightly or wrongly hold the antagonists on either side responsible for their pain and suffering.'

'Emperor's Dawn.'

The first agent nodded.

'Regardless of whether this tipoff is accurate, our task today is to keep him from harm, and that's precisely what we will do.'

One of the status screens flickered with a feed from the station exterior.

Space crackled and writhed outside Mackenzie Relay. A sinister looking darkness ripped and clawed at the very fabric of space, bright discharges of energy flickering around it. The rip widened, sooty and opaque.

From it emerged a vessel, sleek and grandiose, yet intimidating at the same time. It nosed forward, majestic and serene, aware, but somehow disdainful of the awe that its arrival engendered in those who watched.

The bulk of the ship became visible; a vast edifice of sparkling whiteness, flowing curves and glistening hull illumination. To the rear was an enormous circular section, slowly rotating amidst the structure of the ship, providing the comfort and familiarity of artificial gravity aboard for those whose rank or privilege allowed.

Mighty engines blazed forth with disrupted energy flux; bringing the ship to a gentle halt before the station.

The Imperial Majestic-class Interdictor *Imperial Freedom* had arrived.

And with it, the Admiral of the Fleet. Senator Denton Patreus.

Mars High, Mars, Sol system

Saffron du Maurier watched as the ship came through the docking bay. It wasn't a pretty vessel, more a squat collection of triangular panels formed into a hunched looking spacecraft. It had an aggressive air about it, and Saffron knew this particular ship had been optimised for combat, with a surfeit of guns and defences both seen and unseen.

She watched from the observation deck as it lowered itself onto a pad with a brief flare of thruster flux. A Federal Assault Ship, so its owner was proud of saying. It meant little to Saffron. She ran a hand through her short curly hair.

The name plate was just visible on the flank.

HSC Umbral Whisper.

Saffron smiled. The pilot was her closest friend. They'd had a lot of fun together in the past, though it had started as a relationship of mutual convenience. Saffron was a reporter for the Federation Times, with a steady job and a long career ahead of her.

The pilot of the ship was a little less … predictable.

Commander Scarlet Ashcroft was the owner. Saffron saw her emerge from the boarding ramp, already barking out some instructions to the dockhands clustered around the base of the ship. They nodded and scurried away from her. Saffron could see Scarlet's signature hair, even from here. The startling red colour wasn't her only distinguishing feature.

Saffron made her way down to the docking level and walked onto the pad, just as Scarlet was leaving it.

Scarlet looked up and saw her, her neon red hair falling slowly down around her in the low-gee. Her blue eyes were in sharp contrast to her hair, that and her oddly pale skin. The two women couldn't have been more dissimilar. Saffron's skin was as dark as Scarlet's was pale, her own eyes a deep brown.

'You're late,' Scarlet snapped.

'You're early,' Saffron countered with a shrug of unconcern.

'Keeps you station-side layabouts on your toes,' Scarlet replied. 'I know how soft you people live up here.'

'Better than going three weeks without a shower,' Saffron retorted. 'Have you bought a second outfit yet? Smelled you coming even before you got docking permission.'

Scarlet grinned, as did Saffron. They embraced.

'Good to see you again,' Scarlet said.

'You too.'

They turned and entered a lift, taking them down to a lower level within the station.

'So, got any gossip for me?' Saffron asked.

Scarlet moved her head to one side. 'Drink first, then talk.'

'Still like those ghastly Leestian Evil Juices?'

Scarlet smiled. 'Makes me look spooky.'

Saffron laughed. 'You don't need any help with that. You ever check out your holo-me? That last tech service agent you fancied almost had a heart attack.'

The station bar on this level was an ordinary affair. It was early morning local time, so they settled in a quiet corner, Saffron with a coffee and Scarlet with her Evil Juice. It was an odd beverage, but it suited her; a bright, almost fluorescent green liquid, contrasting vividly with her hair.

'So, come on then, what have you been up to?'

Scarlet leant forward. 'I signed up with Canonn Research.'

Saffron blinked. 'They let you in?'

'What's that supposed to mean?'

'They're just a bunch of crackpots, doing … fake sciency-stuff, aren't they?'

'They investigate mysteries,' Scarlet said, taking a sip from her drink. She grimaced. 'I wish they could brew this stuff properly off-world. Going to have to take a trip back to the Old Worlds for the real thing.'

'Canonn?' Saffron reminded her.

'Oh yeah. Listen, they've been investigating this weird stuff happening out in the Pleiades. Barnacles they call them …'

'I remember the articles. Organic growths or something, aren't they?'

'Leave the xenobiology to me,' Scarlet said. 'I have qualifications, remember?'

Saffron put on a silly voice. 'I bow to your amazing expertise, oh great one.'

'Shut up,' Scarlet said. 'There's more to this than is public. These things aren't just growths, they produce stuff. Meta-alloys, they've been called. This stuff is weird. It fixes stuff it's brought in contact with …'

'Fixes stuff?'

'Yeah. If you process it, you can insert it into broken equipment and it … I don't know how, but it starts working again. Like it figures out what the problem is and turns itself into replacement parts all by itself.'

'Weird.'

'That's not all,' Scarlett said. 'Canonn is investigating all sorts of stuff. I got access to some of their records. People going missing, bizarre discoveries, ships disappearing, coded messages. They have all sorts of records and a bunch of people checking them out, I reckon.'

Saffron looked at her. 'Please tell me you're not turning into a conspiracy nut.'

Scarlet pulled out a commtab and fired up its holofac transmitter.

'You check this lot out and tell me what you think.'

Saffron took the commtab, peering at the small display. A brief glance showed her that there was a huge amount of information contained within the files.

Antares, SpaceFlight One, Barnacles, Unidentifed artefacts, Formidine Rift, Imperial Ascension, President Halsey …

Saffron looked up. 'You really think there's a story in all this? This is tabloid stuff, not for a mainstream media publication. We ran an article on Canonn just last month, calling them harmless nutters. We can't retract that.'

'Just …'

'And I've looked into this Rift thing before, too. It's just a wild goose chase concocted by some crazy Imperial woman who went psycho last year …'

'Read it,' Scarlet said. 'Do what you do. Research it.'

Saffron sighed. 'All right, but only because it's you.'

Scarlet smiled and downed the rest of her drink.

'You'll see.'

Chapter Three

Arcanonn Headquarters, Thompson Dock, Varati, Independent

Dr. Arcanonn of the Canonn research group allowed himself a moment to relax. There was no leaning back in zero-gee, but he consciously went through his muscles and eased them one by one. The stress had taken a toll on all who worked for the institute. Two years of exploration and investigation, sometimes helped and sometimes hindered by the authorities.

They had acquired a lot of data in that time. He thought back to the initial discoveries in the early part of the previous year; convoys carrying secret and unknown artefacts. Artefacts that were clearly not of human origin, notwithstanding all the ridiculous assertions that they were manufactured and placed in the void to distract explorers. They were organic in general form, but their structure was not strictly biological. Somehow they were active, almost alive, the product of a technology that had little in common with that of humankind. Despite almost constant investigation over the year since they had been located, their purpose was unknown and only the broadest understanding of their behaviour catalogued. They remained an enigma.

Before him, a rotating image floated. A faint blue nebulosity was lit by a series of bright blue stars in a close cluster. Around it was a sphere of markers, glowing softly in red. A scale indicated they formed a shell perhaps a hundred and fifty light years in diameter. Every discovery catalogued and marked.

'Impressive work, Commander Red Wizzard,' Arcanonn said to himself, appreciating the thoroughness of the plot and the detail it showed. He turned it about with a gesture, examining it from all sides.

Red Wizzard ... I wonder what his real name is?

He'd seen this behaviour often. This curious breed of spacer, the itinerant commanders, had some peculiar habits. They were fiercely proud and protective of their vessels, whether they were humble Adders or massive Anacondas. They lived in their ships, happier in the void than planetside, making their way through the darkness, defining their own rationale and purpose to life. Many had strange names that, presumably, had some great significance to them. It did make for some odd conversations at times.

Never mind, back to the task at hand …

The first clues had emerged. Free in space, the artefacts would align themselves in a particular direction. Triangulation studies indicated that regardless of their location they would point towards the Merope system, a previously unremarkable member of the Pleiades star cluster. The artefacts would also emit waves of radiation akin to scanner pulses, and contained embedded data with schematics of the ships that encountered them, seeming to imply that humans weren't the only ones trying to catalogue their encounters in the dark.

There is an intelligence at work here. Some kind of reconnaissance … of us! But by whom?

Arcanonn gestured to a nearby holofac display, and the schematic of the Merope system appeared alongside the previous plot.

Merope 5c.

A barren moon, of little note in the grand scheme of things, it had hitherto warranted no entry at all in the galactic database. Explorers, getting wind of the Merope system being of interest, had swarmed into the area. Arcanonn had counselled care and instructed the members of his research institute to proceed with caution, applying rigorous process and procedure to their own investigations.

And it paid off.

Earlier in the year a pair of pilots, commanders who went by the names of Octo and Snax, whilst overflying the moon, came across something unusual on the surface. Lit by the fierce glow of Merope, it appeared as a large, vaguely conical object, surrounded by a dozen or so spikes protruding from the ground. The central structure had a distinctive symbol on its side, the meaning of which remained unclear even now.

The spikes themselves had green pods or buds growing from them. Despite urgings to the contrary, many unaffiliated pilots took it upon themselves to open fire on them. The 'Barnacles', as they came to be known, proved disturbingly immune to both energy and projectile weapons, but generated a curious material in response to the assault.

Meta-alloys …

It was quickly discovered that this material had an unusual property. It seemed able to enhance or repair technology, somehow taking on the form and function of damaged componentry and then becoming those components.

Almost as if it were alive, and understood the nature of the device it was inserted into …

There were no other signs of 'life' in the traditional sense. Meta-alloys did not move, eat, excrete or otherwise ingest anything, but they certainly had some remarkable chameleonic capabilities.

Despite warnings advising pilots to exercise care and protestations about the lack of understanding about what precisely this stuff was and what it was capable of doing, the meta-alloys quickly became the 'must-have' commodity across the core worlds, bartered in common markets.

A modern day gold rush … and this stuff is now all over the place, unaccounted for. If you were looking for a way to infect us … this would be perfect.

It wasn't long before the superpowers took an interest. Capital ships were seen guarding key locations as they were discovered. The price of the new material on the open market skyrocketed within days, and within weeks became effectively unobtainable. Piracy and smuggling between the worlds of the Pleiades and the core became rife.

Humanity never learns …

A buzzing sound interrupted his musings.

Arcanonn gestured again and the holofac disappeared, to be replaced with the image of a young pilot. Arcanonn recognised him from a briefing several weeks before.

'Commander Luffy,' he said, reading from the ident system. It wasn't possible to transmit messages without ident checks. It was against the law for a start, and even criminal elements had to procure expensive fake identities to make transmissions.

Luffy nodded, bowing his head in respect. 'Apologies for interrupting you, sir, but I think we've found something you'll be interested in.'

Arcanonn looked up. 'Show me.'

Luffy's image was replaced with a grainy view of a cargo hold. It wasn't clear what ship it was, but that wasn't what was drawing the doctor's attention.

An object could clearly be seen, nestled in the cargo bay. It was akin to the strange artefacts he had just been reviewing, but bigger, more complex …

'Where did you find this?'

'Ross 47, sir. Convoy. We … ah … recovered it from them.'

'Initial assessment?'

'Definitely the same composition, but no obvious outputs at this time. It appears to be inert. We have listened on all EM frequencies and subjected it to the usual tests. No response.'

'Excellent work,' Arcanonn said. 'Bring it back for further analysis.'

The holofac faded.

Arcanonn sighed. He would have to play politics once again in an attempt to keep this new discovery secret for as long as possible. He could feel his muscles tensing in response.

It's all about the science.

He chuckled.

Well, that explanation will do for now …

Mackenzie Relay, Cemeiss system, Empire

The AV crew took a lift down a level, into the interior of the docking area. There they were reunited with their ship, now securely held within the bowels of the station, its docking ramps extended and its cargo bay open and unloaded. A series of large canisters had already been removed from the ship by the automechs, and had been arranged in a tidy stack near one of the landing struts.

The crew supervised the movement of the canisters into a freight lift, then stepped in alongside and punched in the codes for their destination. The door hissed shut and the sound of heavy machinery unbolting echoed through the chamber.

'Hold tight,' the tech-lead said, and pressed a final illuminated control.

The elevator dropped, accelerating downwards at a ferocious speed. Before them, through the windows of the lift, the interior hull of the station flashed past, a blur of bulkheads, structure and conduits. All four had braced themselves, knowing what to expect.

After a few moments, the acceleration slackened, leaving them weightless save for the curious effects of the Coriolis force, which seemed to gently tug them away from the windows. They were already moving at hundreds of metres per second. The lift continued 'downwards' and then emerged into the open. The occupants were treated to a spectacular view of their surroundings.

The lift was descending one of the two major support struts from the docking hub to the external habitation ring some two kilometres below.

'Below' was a relative term, of course, but it made sense. From the hub, all directions were 'down'.

The four instinctively leant to one side as the Coriolis force began to take hold more strongly. It felt as if some invisible hand was pushing at them harder and harder. Support struts blurred past at regular intervals as the lift continued its meteoric descent.

Outside the windows, the sheer overwhelming scale of the station was revealed. It was a vast construct, the end product of centuries of engineering prowess and home to millions of inhabitants. From the cylindrical docking hub, itself a marvel of complexity where arriving and departing ships were serviced and managed, the station extended back for several kilometres. Here were power plants, processing facilities, hydroponic bays and all manner of equipment devoted to the upkeep of the station.

Those who worked here also had their accommodation nearby. The vast majority did not enjoy a view out of the station; such an outlook came at a premium. There was very much a strata to society aboard. The richer you were, the better the view and the more gravity you enjoyed.

For those with the means, the ultimate display of station-side wealth was to own a property in the habitation ring itself. It was a wonder of design; a transparent roof gave natural light to beautifully manicured gardens below. There were lakes, small woodlands, rivers and ornamental gardens. Many were private properties, but some were open to the public, so that they might enjoy them and, of course, gain an appreciation of their relative rank in society. It gave Imperial citizens something to aspire to. Filters across the transparencies would adjust the illumination to simulate planetside sunrises and sunsets, with the occasional artificially manufactured mist to add a little poetry to the experience.

The lift began to brake its descent. Already they had descended three-quarters of the way. The tech-lead looked up. The hub was now some distance away, the ships arranged before it tiny sparkling marks in the light of the Cemiess star.

Aside from one. An Imperial Majestic-class Interdictor was slowly approaching the station, its two-kilometre bulk intimidating even from here.

'It's him.'

The view was lost as the lift descended the final distance into the ring, coming to a halt with a jolt. The door snapped open to reveal a plaza edged with green grass. Beyond was a marble palace, designed with an ingenious forced perspective to look bigger than it actually was, fronted by fountains. Before it were arranged hundreds of chairs in neat ordered rows, framing a dais upon which was set a plinth with a stylised eagle emblazoned on it, the Imperial insignia clutched in its talons.

More security guards quizzed them and then escorted them, with their equipment, towards the perimeter.

'Let's get our gear set up,' the tech-lead said, 'Speech is this afternoon. We've got work to do.'

High above, ships continued to jostle for position.

The *Imperial Freedom* was too large a vessel to dock directly with the station. Once it had been secured, an Imperial Cutter came alongside, docking just clear of the bigger ship's rotating habitation ring. Small fighter craft organised themselves into neat formations about it, with other ships nearby remaining in an escort pattern. The constant ping of scanner traces flickered across the displays as they swept the area, looking for anything out of the ordinary.

Eventually, the Cutter disengaged, lifting gracefully away. Docking clearance was requested and granted immediately, a formality for such a distinguished guest.

Fighter craft fell in behind the Cutter as it moved towards the station hub and then entered the bay. No other ships were allowed to move for the duration of the manoeuvre, the interior defences of the station on high alert for any infractions. If necessary, they could dispatch any vessel in moments and deal with the debris later. Station orbit space justice was hard, brutal and efficient. All pilots respected the rules.

The Cutter set down on pad zero-two, the most prestigious location in the dock. Its undercarriage unfurled with the craftsmanship typical of Imperial tastes, flamboyant and elegant, the forward strut serving as a wide stepped walkway from the interior of the ship.

Guards, dressed in immaculate bright white uniforms and decorated with a variety of distinguished honours, descended immediately, quickly trotting into place on either side of the walkway. All held weapons at the ready. Seasoned observers would have noted they were state-of-the-art laser rifles; powerful, accurate and deadly.

Next came a series of aides, standing to attention in ordered rows. At some unseen signal they all stepped smartly to attention, saluting in the Imperial fashion. A group of officers of high rank marched onto the pad, surrounding the station commander himself.

The steps of the Cutter echoed to a single set of footsteps; heavy, deliberate and self-assured.

The man was tall, his bearing military and erect. His uniform was an ensemble of maroon and black, cross-belted with a sash that ran from his left shoulder down to the right side of his belt, buckled at the hip with an Imperial insignia. His scalp was partly shaved in the manner of military pilots, though he retained something of a quiff, rakishly brushed to one side. A neatly trimmed beard framed a face that was accustomed to power. Dark eyes briefly looked to the left and right under heavy brows.

At this slight signal, the officers stepped forward, smartly turned and saluted again. The station commander stepped forward an extra pace.

'Fleet Admiral Patreus, welcome to Cemiess. It is an honour …'

'No need for the preamble, Commander,' Patreus responded, continuing to walk forward. The station commander turned on his heel, almost stumbling to reverse course and keep up with the long strides of the Admiral. The officers fell in behind them.

'Admiral?'

'To business. My time is precious, Commander. Is everything arranged?'

'Everything is prepared, Admiral. All dignitaries are aboard and accommodated …'

'I care little for the lackeys. The communications hub and the coverage across the major newsfeeds is what concerns me.'

'All arranged with triple redundancy, Admiral.'

'Sufficient. Security?'

'We have IISS agents deployed, station security has all traffic embargoed for the duration and everything has been searched and searched again.'

Patreus nodded. 'See to it that it continues that way. I hold you personally responsible for the duration of my stay.'

The commander gulped. He understood his role well, but having it articulated somehow made it far worse.

Carey Terminal, Chi Orionis system, Federation

Lasers flashed about the cockpit, lighting the interior with sharp, swiftly moving shadows. The shields flickered as they repulsed hostile fire. Four other ships, small agile fighters, darted and jockeyed for position amongst the spinning asteroids. The staccato thrum of multi-cannon fire crackled through space.

A pilot watched the battle from his own compact cockpit. Before him, an Imperial Fighter lost its shields and began to stream sparks from a damaged hull. It tried to flee, twisting and turning, but it was shoved up against the long flank of one of the asteroids, with the pilot's own ship in a superior position.

Just as I planned…

He nosed his ship down, triggering a boost. Despite being flung back into his seat, his grip on the controls remained secure and his aim sure.

The comms system chattered around him, the tournament commentary half unheard.

'… Nice move there by Commander Falchion, looks like Commander Chenth is in trouble, lost his shields …'

His hand closed on the trigger, unleashing the multi-cannons once more. They spat blistering fire from either side of the cramped cockpit.

The Imperial fighter dodged as the tracer lines cut across its bow, then clipped the asteroid and spun up out of control.

Easy kill. That's why they call it close quarters combat!

A quick yaw was all it took and the arc of multi-cannon fire intersected with the beleaguered vessel.

A brief flash thumped out against the asteroid. A moment later, twisted blackened debris spun past the canopy of his ship.

'… And Commander Falchion takes the lead! First blood!'

Raan Corsen, callsign Falchion, grinned and adjusted the power configuration of his ship.

Full pips to shields, let's see where everyone else is …

He brought the nose of the F63 Condor around. It was a tough little ship, fast and manoeuvrable, but lacking in shields. With his preferred loadout of low-powered kinetic weapons, he could afford to divert most of the ship's power into the engines, giving him an edge over the weightier and slower ships he was often up against.

Three ships still out there.

He looked at the scanner, not seeing any telltale markers on the scanner. Not really a surprise, these pilots were the best. This was the final. Billions of folks across the core worlds and the borderlands, perhaps even out to the frontier, were watching the ultimate round of the Melee Masters Arena Championship.

Before he had a chance to assess anything else, the commentator interrupted him.

'… And Commander Nakamura equalises for the lead! Burnt out Commander Yansig with those twin beams. That's a fierce ship he's got there. Favourite for the win here, of course. Fresh from winning gold at the AZ Cancri Crucible …'

'Yuri,' Raan muttered under his breath.

He'd come up against Yuri Nakamura before. He was a brutal pilot. They said once you were in his crosshairs you never got out again. That wasn't quite true, but he had a kill count and a kill-to-death ratio that was the envy of most other Arena veterans. From what Raan had managed to pull together on his background, Yuri had been some kind of high-level military pilot in the Federation. He had the skills for sure.

And last time, he handed me my ass …

Yuri flew a tricked out Eagle. It was bigger and heavier than the Condor, but what it lost in speed and turning it made up for in sheer firepower and thick shields. Twin beam lasers quickly made a mess of lesser ships. One mistake in front of him and you were dead.

As Yansig just found.

Stealth was your friend in the Arena, and Raan's ship was perfect. Low emissions, and a loadout aimed at staying cool. Behind him, just out of sight of the cockpit, were twin heatsink launchers; their job – to dump excess heat on demand, effectively making his ship invisible to scanners long enough to get out of visual range.

Only Yuri knows that trick well enough. And he only needs a single bead on me to take me down …

Raan had learnt his tricks well, having trained with some of the best in the business. The Atlas Corporation, over in Attilius Orbital, was probably the best Arena flight school in the core worlds. He had a plan to go back to them if he won, rumour had it they offered some serious money for military missions, but only if you could demonstrate the skills.

But if I can win here, they'll take me for sure!

His ship was still hugging the flank of the asteroid, hiding in its shadow. As he watched, another ship crept into view, cautiously making its way between the tumbling rocks.

It was a Sidewinder. An odd choice of vessel to have made it this far, but that just proved the pilot's worth. Raan could just make out the SAS decal of the Sidewinder Appreciation Society. Some folks just loved the old ship, some were even mad enough to go exploring in the things.

But made a mistake here …

The Sidewinder was running cool; there was nothing on Raan's scanner. He'd got lucky. With a gentle nudge to the thrusters the Condor came about, the Sidewinder drifting into his crosshairs.

Raan closed his thumb on the trigger.

Shields flared in the darkness. A heat signature appeared on the scanner. Raan locked onto it, registering the name of his current opponent.

'… Unlucky for Commander Terriel there. Looks like she got stealthed from behind! Never a nice way to get caught …'

A spray of metallic particles spewed from the rear of the Sidewinder and its engines flared brightly as it tried to boost away. Chaff, aimed at trying to confuse the gimballed tracking mounts that inferior pilots used to make up for their lack of aiming ability.

Raan smiled, throttling up to match.

'Won't work on me, girl.'

The Condor's weapons were fixed, locked in place. They were harder to aim but more powerful and, crucially, immune to being decoyed. There was no way a Sidewinder was going to outrun a Condor, either. Tracer fire blistered over the Sidewinder's shields. Raan watched them flicker, fold and collapse.

Now kinetic fire shattered into the Sidewinder's hull. Raan could well imagine the sparks and cracking sounds the other pilot would be experiencing, he'd been on the receiving end of it often enough. Not the time to panic.

The multi-cannons clicked empty.

Reloading …

Precious moments ticked away. The Sidewinder was damaged, but not dead. If it could get away in the confusing maelstrom of tumbling debris it could hide, lick its wounds and come back. Clearly, that was Commander Terriel's intention. Raan could not afford that to happen.

'… And another kill for Commander Yuri. That's two to him as he takes the lead from Commander Falchion …'

Damn. He's finished up and he knows where we both are!

Ahead, the Sidewinder was jinking left and right, jawing and turning erratically, trying to throw him off. It was doing a good job. What the ship lacked in speed it made up on its ability to turn, and it could pretty much do it in any direction. Raan almost lost sight of it at one point, craning his neck up to see where it had gone.

The multi-cannons completed their loading cycle.

Raan flipped a toggle and hit the boost.

'Flight assist off,' the computer intoned.

The Condor spun about its axis, moving vertically whilst rotating at a dizzying speed. Raan braced himself against the disorientation.

The Sidewinder came into view. Almost face on.

Raan had already triggered the weapons and the Condor strafed past, ripping the Sidewinder to shreds.

A flash and a cloud of smoke and debris.

'… And Commander Falchion equalises! A deft move there with the off-axis tactics he's become known for! Only two competitors left now. It's come down to this. Speed and guile versus firepower and ruggedness. Falchion versus Yuri! These two have only met twice before and both times Yuri has come out on top. Can he make it three for three, or will Falchion deal the killing blow this time …?'

Raan equalised power all around and triggered a heat sink. It would give away his position, but Yuri already had that from the previous fight. Right now he needed stealth. If Yuri found him first he didn't stand a chance. Yuri had been a couple of klicks away when he'd killed the Sidewinder, but it looked like he'd played the same trick.

There was nothing on the scanner.

Not that I'd expect there to be. He's the best there is …

In previous bouts, Yuri had played a waiting game with him, allowing him to make the first move, relying on his ship's ability to soak up damage to give him a chance to bring his big guns into play. Would he try the same thing again? The strategy worked well.

Raan knew he wouldn't be able to take the Eagle out in one attack, he needed two strikes.One for the shields, one for the hull. That meant getting on Yuri's six twice in succession. It wasn't going to be easy. Some precision flying was going to be called for.

His heat signature was as low as it was going to get. He continued visual scanning, but there was no sign of the other ship. He gave the thrusters a little nudge, keeping close to the surface, but careful not to graze it and discharge what little shield power the Condor could summon.

'… Looks like they're both being real careful. Both know what is at stake here. We're seeing the final showdown between the galaxy's best CQC pilots …'

Below him, the asteroid was slowly rotating, bringing the rest of the asteroid field into sight. The view stretched out for millions of kilometres, but the Arena boundaries were set to just a short range. Stray beyond it and you'd forfeit the match, out of bounds. You couldn't run. You had to kill and win.

There! A heat signature!

Yuri must have activated his drives and made his move. Something was glowing on the scanner behind one of the rocks ahead. Raan jockeyed himself into position, trying to get a good angle. The heat signature was still obscured, but it would come into view in a moment.

'… Interesting move …' said the announcer.

By who?

Raan was poised, his finger on the trigger.

The scanner pinged. Instinctively, he opened fire, only to see a missile streak across his view.

Damn! Decoyed!

Then came the glare. Laser beams streaked perilously close to the flanks of his ship. He dumped all power into the engines and triggered the boost.

'Flight assist off.'

The Condor spun and yawed, an elusive target for the heavy weapons of the Eagle. A single blast of laser fire found its mark, the shields draining away with terrifying rapidity, fading from bright cyan to dim crimson on the heads-up display. He triggered his remaining heat sink and dived away, leaving the Eagle trailing behind.

'Geez, he's good.'

'… A great move there by Commander Yuri. Used a missile as a signature decoy and then snuck around the back of a 'roid! Only a smart bit of evasive flying saved Commander Falchion that time. His shields are almost gone. Does he have what it takes …?'

Got to get on top of this!

He still had a trace on the Eagle. It looked like Yuri was also out of heat sinks and his blast from the beam laser had cooked his ship a little. The heat signature was still bright on his scanner and he was invisible.

Won't last forever. Got to make use of it …

He wrestled the Condor into position between two of the larger aster-oids as the Eagle moved past.

'My turn.'

He adjusted the tracking of his weapons. This was a new tactic. The multi-cannons spat again, but they were aimed precisely this time.

Sub-system targeting.

The Eagle boosted the moment the fire hit, but he was ready for that. The Condor snuck into place behind it, unleashing a constant barrage from its kinetic weapons. Shields flared under the assault, but the Condor hung on tenaciously.

'… And Commander Falchion makes his move! Is it too little too late …?'

The Eagle's shields flickered and died. Then the multi-cannon fire found its mark.

Raan saw the damage report on the scanner. He'd taken out Yuri's shield generator.

Yes!

'… And Commander Yuri has damage! Commander Falchion has neu-tralised his shield generator and he's running light armour on his Eagle! That makes him vulnerable too …'

Raan ducked his ship behind an asteroid as Yuri's Eagle twisted away, still streaming sparks from the damage he'd inflicted. He'd hit it hard, harder than he'd expected.

He pushed maximum power to his shields, hoping to rejuvenate them in time for the next confrontation. That would put the fight on an even footing. All he had to do then was …

Incoming call …

'Shit! Not now!'

Incoming call …

He didn't have a choice. He was supposed to be at work. In fact, he was at work, using his employer's high bandwidth connections to the core infrastructure to give him the best possible chance of winning the Arena bout. He couldn't afford a decent link at home, not on his salary.

He toggled the feed from the Arena off in his VR specs and blinked as his eyes readjusted to his surroundings. He was sitting at a plain cubicle, a basic holofac interface before him covered in documents and administra-tive monitors. He tapped the receiver in his ear.

'Raan Corsen, I'm busy at the moment …'

'This is deputy administration Benz, Corsen. I'm expecting those admin stats today and I need an hour to incorporate them into my reports. When are you …'

'I'll have them for you, sir. I just need …'

'Can I just confirm that you'll have the metrics, ordered by category?'

'Yes, definitely.'

Something else was playing in Raan's other ear.

'… This is strange, Commander Falchion is just flying straight and true, he's a sitting duck. What does he think he's playing at? Look, he's come to a dead halt right out in the open …!'

No, no, no!

'I'll need the sequences, too.'

'You'll have them, now I really need to …'

'Just one more thing.' Benz paused for a long moment. 'If you could format them up and break them down by annual expenditure, that would be really useful for me. You see, the monthly notifications …'

'… Commander Yuri has spotted him, he's coming in … he's hesitating too … he doesn't know what to make of it either …'

'Got it. It'll be done in the hour. Bye!'

Raan tapped the receiver again and cancelled the call, gesturing for the high-bandwidth connection to re-establish itself in his VR specs. He blinked as the cockpit of the Condor seemed to materialise around him. He grabbed at the imaginary controls. It took a moment for the link to settle down.

'… He's coming in … Is something wrong with Commander Falchion's ship …?'

Come on, come on, come on!

The Condor jolted around him as the link finally hooked up. Beam lasers flickered around the cockpit as he mashed the throttle forward, hit the boost and flipped a toggle.

'Flight assist off.'

'… No, he's still there … He's coming around … Look at that machine go …!'

The Condor flipped over. Raan kept the ship moving vertically, out turning the Eagle and bringing his weapons to bear. At close range, the Eagle was a big fat target for the tiny Condor. The twin multi-cannons lit up, shredding the hull of the larger ship.

Raan saw one of the wing pods peel away and the Eagle began to tumble out of control. He let the guns spin out to the limits of their magazines. They sputtered to a stop, ready to reload.

The Eagle spun a further half turn and then exploded.

Faint cheers and screams sounded behind the commentator's voice in his right ear.

'… What a move! Suckered Yuri right into point blank range by playing dead and then took him out! Such moxie! That was a big risk, but what a payoff! We have a new champion of the Melee Masters' Arena, and it's Commander Falchion!'

Raan let out a breath and cancelled the connection once more. Sweat dripped down his nose and he wiped his brow. As his cubicle faded back into view, he gestured for the galactic news feedbacks to display on the desktop holofac. He could already see it updating.

Commander Falchion wins the Melee Master's Arena Champion in a tense final bout, luring his opponent to his doom in an innovative move which is sure to go down as one of the greats. Commander Falchion's true identity remains unknown, but he is known to be connecting from the Chi Orionis system.

'Yes!'

Raan looked up. He hadn't meant to say anything. He needn't have worried. His work colleagues were seated around him, unperturbed and unaware. The VR specs were a neat piece of kit and well worth the expense, a complete sensory bypass. His heart was still pounding from the match.

The admin screens were still before him.

'Back to work then.'

Chapter Four

Mackenzie Relay, Cemiess system, Empire

Banners fluttered in the artificial breeze. Music could be heard, classic Imperial marches for the most part, played by dress musicians who proceeded in military ranks around the seating area. Dignitaries, celebrities and other worthies from across the Empire were treated to refreshments, exotic wines and hors d'oeuvres by legions of slaves. Entertainers kept them all amused with slight-of-hand tricks, acrobatics and other acts of skill. The chatter of thousands echoed above the perfectly manicured lawns of the habitation ring.

As with all Imperial soirees, it was important to watch and to be seen. Fashion moved quickly and it was an opportunity to find one's place within the pecking order, observe the influencers and follow their leads. Measures of personal wealth, rank and position were assessed, weighed and calculated via snatches of fawning conversation, the cut of a dress, the tilt of a hat or the opulence of jewellery on display. Behind the smiles and the polite comments of appreciation lay a battle no less vicious and hostile than those that took place in the vacuum of space. Imperial high society was a caustic cauldron of subtly shifting loyalty, allegiance and power.

Newsfeeds from the Imperial Citizen and Imperial Herald, two rival news organisations with their own fierce animosities, competed for the best coverage of the event. It was not often that a senior member of the Imperial hierarchy gave a public speech. They had already been briefed on the contents, of course, so that they might issue reports in a timely fashion, reports that had already been approved by the Admiral's communications and PR staff.

Across the Empire, billions more watched. Some watched out of interest but most watched out of duty via the holofac entertainment channels. Programming had been interrupted, at huge cost, to cover the speech. The Admiral had deep pockets.

Trumpets announced his arrival. The assembled masses turned, conversation dropping to a muted background buzz, as a succession of military personnel marched onto the dais. Holofac cameras swung around to capture the moment. Even the illumination subtly adjusted itself, allowing spotlights to pick out the dais more effectively. Sunset came early at the Admiral's bidding.

A voice boomed across the throng, supported by holofac text feeds, which would relay the spoken words in text form for convenience.

'Senators, Patrons, worthy dignitaries, friends and citizens of the Empire, Cemiess is graced and honoured today. The liberator of Durius and Quivira, dispatcher of the Emperor's Dawn, Commander of the Imperial Navy, Servant to the Emperor herself. Be upstanding for Fleet Admiral Denton Patreus.'

Tumultuous applause greeted this announcement, less for the words than for fear of not being seen to be enthusiastic. The crowds were just as much a part of the show as everything else.

Spotlights focussed in on the plinth that stood atop the dais. Camera crews moved in as close as they could, wrestling with security teams.

Patreus could now be seen, his uniform stark and bold. He raised a hand to the crowd, gaining another burst of adulation, turning to the left and to the right to ensure he covered all who had assembled beneath him, not forgetting a glance of appreciation to the cameras and a clear mouthing of the word, 'Thank you' for their benefit.

The applause slowly dropped away.

Patreus looked around, taking a moment to observe the crowd. He was too shrewd a politician to allow a trace of the disdain he felt for them all to show. His expression remained one of calm authority, a hero of the Empire, here to serve. Yet he despised the ranked masses of Imperial society with their constant fawning and socialite games. Military power was all that mattered, to turn and influence entire star systems. These events were nothing but tools, necessary tedium to influence the outcome of a bigger agenda.

He straightened and began.

'Senators, Patrons …'

There was a hiss and crackle, followed by a burst of feedback from somewhere below. Patreus could see the reporters and press teams looking around in abject shock, trying to find the source of the problem.

Measured as always, Patreus took it in his stride, gesturing to the audio-visual teams and throwing a smile to the crowd.

The crackle stopped.

'If I might be allowed to continue?' Patreus asked, looking down from the plinth. As one, the press team below gulped and nodded, many bowing in a ridiculous attempt to look servile.

He looked back up at the crowd.

'I do believe we're ready … Senators …'

A fierce rising hum burst out from nearby. Patreus turned to see where it was coming from, fury now etched on his face. He caught sight of one of the camera crews, standing around a camera mounted on a tripod just beyond the press ring. He frowned. They seemed unconcerned at the noise. The camera was pointing directly at him. He could see down the lens, where a faint red glow was swiftly growing in strength.

A cry broke out, amplified across the assembly.

'THE SUN HAS NOT SET FOR THE EMPEROR'S DAWN!'

Pandemonium broke out. Patreus found himself roughly hauled aside as someone wrestled him to the ground.

What followed was a burst of noise and light, shocking in its intensity. Patreus saw a stream of energy incinerate the plinth where he'd been standing a moment before, leaving nothing but flaming wreckage. He hit the ground hard, crashing into the dais, his breath knocked from him. Screams rent the air, the sounds of people panicking and running in disarray. Smoke clouded his vision, burning in his nostrils and causing him to cough violently.

'This way, Admiral!'

Patreus looked into the eyes of a man dressed in the uniform of IISS and felt himself dragged up and away from the dais. His ears were ringing, his head spinning with disorientation. He heard the sound of gunfire, more screams. Sirens sounded, counterpointed by the harsh barking of orders.

A hatchway, cunningly concealed in the lawn behind, opened up and revealed a set of stairs leading down and away. Now, surrounded by a group of the IISS staff, Patreus was wrestled out of sight, the hatch closing behind them. The noise and hubbub were cut off.

'Are you injured, Admiral?' one asked. The rest were busy on secured commlinks. Patreus heard snatches of conversation

'The Admiral is secured…'

'Countermeasure three successful…'

'Targets isolated, but…'

'I'm fine!' Patreus said, pulling himself upright and dusting himself down. 'But we eradicated those scum … Did you get them?'

'A moment, Admiral.' The lead IISS agent held up a hand, reviewing information that scrolled in his line of sight.

'Four individuals. Suicide. No … wait. One is alive … we have their ship … masquerading as AV crew. Checking back on permits and authorisations now …'

Patreus' gloved hands clenched and his lip curled in anger.

'I personally decimated them,' he rumbled. 'We crushed them under our boots. No way did they do this without assistance. Find out who organised this. Interrogate that survivor! I want them dealt with, permanently!'

New California, Epsilon Eridani system, Federation

Epsilon Eridani was, unarguably, the most luxurious and exotic of holiday destinations for the well-heeled clientele of the galaxy. At just over ten light years from Sol, most of its visitors were of a Federal inclination, but such was its reputation that it attracted people from all over the core worlds.

The main planet, New California, had been terraformed in the late 30th century and hosted the galaxy's most famous theme park – in fact, the entire planet was essentially a playground. It was impossibly picturesque, with carefully manicured gardens, fountains, copses, woodlands, glorious scenery and climate control that actively managed the rainfall and atmospheric preferences of visitors in order to provide the best possible experience. VIP visitors could even buy the weather they preferred, as long as they booked far enough in advance, though it did make for an odd experience for long term residents.

Nestled amongst all this were some of the most expensive and comfortable hotels in the core worlds. Entrance to the theme park was extortionately costly, a once-in-a-lifetime vacation for most. Clients could choose from all sorts of experiences, many augmented by character actors for authenticity, ranging from the sublime, via the exotic and erotic, to the ridiculous and extreme. So compelling was the experience on offer that highly trained psychiatric counsellors were on hand to allow clients to prepare prior to their visit, adapt during it, and adjust afterwards on their return to normality.

Rumour had it that it was a favourite haunt for private detectives, making easy credits on behalf of jealous partners who suspected their significant others of indulging in a little too much of the twilight entertainment on offer.

The Interstellar Trade Franchise was not an organisation of much note in the grand scheme of things, but it did know how to hold a successful conference. How much of its membership was due to the fact that it held its annual meetings on Epsilon Eridani wasn't clear, but no one had ever complained.

Two individuals, men dressed in smart but casual attire, were leaning out across a hotel balcony, taking in the balmy evening air whilst enjoying a drink. Sunlight still drenched them as the warm star slowly dropped towards the horizon. A bright point of light was already visible in the sky, a star from a nearby system.

The first man gestured towards it.

'Sirius is bright this evening.'

'Sirius is always bright,' the other acknowledged, with a chuckle.

'Acquisitions going as planned, I presume.'

The second man nodded. 'I think we can say it's safely in hand. The board are being adequately compensated for their … flexibility in looking favourably on our proposal.'

'This new hyperdrive tech …'

'We are aware of its importance,' the second man said, lowering his voice. 'However, we cannot be seen to be precipitate. We can't afford to have unwelcome counteroffers made. If news of this were to emerge to the general populace …'

The first man shuddered. 'Every grubby spacer between here and Fehu would be after it.'

'Precisely. Under our guidance, the board is moving in the correct direction. How sad that the chairman's health is so fragile.'

'It is?' The first man seemed surprised for a moment. 'Ah … I see. I assume his strategic vision doesn't align with the company's long-term financial best interests?'

The second chuckled again. 'You are correct.'

'Can I assume that his company may have some difficult times ahead?'

'We live in a time of great economic turmoil.'

'Excellent news.'

The men clinked their drinks together.

***

Many kilometres above, five more individuals had just taken their places for dinner. The Epsilon Eridani Crystal Sky restaurant didn't take reservations in the usual fashion. People were invited to attend according to predetermined criteria based on wealth, influence and agenda. The cost of the meal was as stratospheric as the altitude the restaurant occupied above the planet, but the careful selection of invitees ensured that any potential embarrassment over such humdrum considerations, such as mere cost, was never a factor.

The restaurant itself was suspended twenty kilometres above the surface. Low enough that the patchwork of the planet below could be appreciated with a pleasant tinge of blue atmosphere during the day, but high enough that the vista at night afforded a view of space far superior to those available on the orbital space stations. Here, clientele could appreciate the majesty of space without all the tedious lack of gravity or the motion sickness that never sat too well with the galaxy's premiere chêfs de cuisiné.

Vast panoramic windows looked out above and below the deck where guests dined, with both the floor and ceiling given the option of becoming transparent on demand. Chairs, tables, even cutlery and utensils were crafted out of crystal, leaving occupants with the distinct impression that they were magically suspended in a dream world far above the hoi polloi, and just a step down from the vastness of space.

Only immediately below, in the superstructure that supported the observation deck, were more traditional materials employed. Here could be found the kitchens and preparation rooms for the staff that served the galaxy's most influential people. Arrival was by specially chartered, and appropriately luxurious, air cars from a plush reception lounge at ground level.

Tonight's group of five required absolute privacy; lighting was subdued and uneven, allowing all of them to recline in shadowed locations. By arrangement, there was no one else present in the restaurant this evening, and their staff and attendants had been thoroughly vetted for suitability, trustworthiness and willingness to voluntarily undergo courses of hexedit; a memory altering drug often used to adjust the recall of events as needs dictated.

Some of their faces would have been recognisable to many in the galaxy, with others being completely unknown. Here though, all were equals. There were no names; they referred to each other merely by their responsibilities.

Talk was inconsequential for the most part, but as the main course drew to a conclusion the conversation started in earnest.

'News from the tech sector looks encouraging,' said one, draining his wine glass. His responsibility was for 'Infrastructure'. In other circles, he would have been the chairman, but this organisation had no such arrangement.

'Indeed,' said the woman two places to his left, or 'Finance' as she was referred to here. 'Both Gutamaya and Core Dynamics have issued profit warnings. Sirius stands poised to assist any companies suddenly found to be in dire straits. We have dispensed with various aspects of governance, compliance checking and the various regulations that were blocking progress.'

'How did you achieve that?' Infrastructure asked.

Finance grinned. 'A push for innovation. Paperwork can be such a chore, after all. We will reinstate it when the next crisis looms and cite lack of oversight as the driver.'

'Ah … we're at that point in the cycle,' Infrastructure said, with a nod. He leant back as a smartly dressed troupe of waiters and waitresses began clearing plates and refilling glasses. None of them interacted with the group, carrying out their tasks efficiently and with complete indifference. Within moments they had swept away again, cutlery and crockery removed.

'It's about a five-year run now,' Finance replied. 'Used to be ten or more not that long ago.'

'We can't afford for the stakeholders to be at a disadvantage for too long,' said a thin man between them, 'Exo.' His responsibilities included exploration and the affairs of worlds beyond the borders of the core worlds. 'Unease prompts unpredictability.'

'I can put your mind at rest there, my friend,' Infrastructure said, taking another gulp of his wine. 'There will be good news for them before too long if Fleet Admiral Patreus gets his way.'

'Time to void the London Treaty?' Finance asked, raising her eyebrows. 'So soon? Are we moving that up the agenda?'

'We'll need time to construct the necessary ships, my dear,' Infrastructure replied. 'Whilst efforts to fuel the tensions between the Federation and the Empire have been perhaps the easiest part of this whole affair to organise, there is a significant lead time due to restrictions elsewhere. Nonetheless, there is so much latent hatred between the factions that one merely has to suggest the possibility of infringement and the various military leaders immediately sense an imminent war.'

Finance nodded. 'Various Federal and Imperial convoys have been attacked, as per our previous minutes.'

'Appalling warmongering,' Infrastructure said, with a chuckle. 'But at every stage it appears that the convoys in question were ferrying illegal cargoes. Most disreputable.'

'Remarkable what a little misinformation can do,' Finance said with a nod. 'Both sides have valid claims; both believe they have been subject to unprovoked attacks. The diplomats are trying hard, naturally, but I don't expect to see our objectives in this matter being thwarted now. They've been spoiling for a fight for years.'

'They've been trivial to manipulate. Child's play, in fact. I foresee no trouble in meeting our schedule in that area, as long as the treaty is abolished shortly.'

'That's good to hear,' Finance replied. 'It would appear that Mu Koji is going to be the flash point we've been working towards.'

The waiters and waitresses returned with the dessert course. A collection of exotic and beautifully sculpted dishes, some enhanced by miniature force fields to retain their appearance. The group of five eagerly welcomed them and conversation faltered for a few minutes whilst the sweets were consumed.

'And so, to the next item.' Infrastructure said, dabbing his mouth with a napkin as the dishes were once more cleared away. 'Poor Patreus deserves a little success after all his recent troubles, surely. What do you think, Personnel?'

Personnel was a small and rather fierce looking woman to his right.

'He's not the most charismatic of fellows, but he's perfectly positioned to be the one who rips up the London Treaty after recent events. We can arrange for appropriate Federal outrage at his sabre rattling. As you say, they are very easy to coerce.'

'Excellent.'

'After all,' Personnel said, 'His standing has improved dramatically since someone tried to kill him. He seems to have attracted the sympathy vote.'

'And full marks for orchestrating that little adventure,' Infrastructure replied, with a roguish wink. 'I thought it went down rather well.'

'We were happy with the end result,' Personnel replied. 'Though I'm looking forward to the day we can remove him once and for all.'

'Patience, my dear,' Infrastructure replied. 'He has his uses. Society?'

Society was the final member of the group, sitting opposite

Infrastructure. A jovial fellow to look at, but a steely glint was always visible to those who knew him.

'We're running a number of campaigns to keep the populace entertained and diverted. The various Arena championships have proved quite diverting and also surprisingly lucrative. There's very little to concern ourselves with overall, though the itinerant independent spacers, as usual, are the key concern.'

'Irritating parasites,' Exo chimed in.

'How so?' Finance demanded. 'We make considerable currency off the back of their trading and bounty hunting exploits, not to mention taxes, tolls and ship and equipment exchanges. In fact, finding enough diversions for them to spend their credits on has proved something of a challenge.'

'Damned explorers,' Exo replied. 'Everywhere you turn there they are, poking their noses where they have no business doing so.'

Society nodded. 'Yes, rather a law unto themselves. Quite what possesses them to head out into the void on a whim and a prayer is rather beyond me, but they do represent a significant danger.'

Infrastructure nodded. 'The risk of being exposed prematurely.'

'Indeed,' Society replied. 'We've given them all sorts of financial enticements to stay away from any areas of interest, naturally. Community goals promising rich rewards seem to retain their allure for the most part. For the determined, we provide other enticements, luring them into areas where they can be … embroiled in some unfortunate accident in the depths of space.'

'Exterminated,' Exo said. 'Like the infestation they are.'

'Quite.' Society grinned. 'Exploration is rather dangerous, after all. It helps maintain the allure of it all.'

There was a general chuckle from around the room.

'We never anticipated how many there would be, unfortunately,' Society continued. 'The advantage of all this new technology we've graciously allowed them to benefit from. One group has crossed the width of the galaxy, you know, rather grandiosely calling itself the "Distant Worlds Expedition."'

'I recall the Galactic Network doing a feature on them,' Infrastructure said with a nod.

'It should never have been allowed,' Exo grumbled. 'We should have destroyed them to prevent further such sorties.'

'Destroying them too often leads to mystery and myth and rumour,' Society said. 'If an area of space becomes known to be dangerous they swarm like flies towards it. Do not underestimate the driving force of curiosity. These explorers thrive on it. One sniff of an enigma and they set off on a quest to locate it, with barely any justification at all.'

'We should be harder,' Exo said.

'Worse still are these so-called scientists headed up by our old friend, Dr. Arcanonn,' Society said. 'They've proved remarkably adept and working through the lines of obfuscation we've thrown in their way, and there are others besides. Naturally, they're chasing myth and rumour for the most part, based on very scant evidence indeed, but many of them are proving tenacious in their investigations. We won't be able to keep a lid on it much longer.'

'You think the trumble will soon be out of the hold, so to speak,' Infrastructure said.

'Surprised they haven't found it yet, to be frank,' Society said. 'There have been enough leaks.'

'And what do we do when they find it?' Exo demanded.

'We use it to our advantage, of course,' Society replied. 'We already have the relevant articles primed and ready to go; all manner of disinformation will be promulgated. The Federation and the Empire can be relied upon to attempt to blockade the site. A little fear we can use to our advantage.'

'On an exploration note, the necessary detailed data still eludes us,' Infrastructure pointed out.

'It's only a matter of time before the Dynasty expedition is discovered too,' Exo said. 'They'll find it eventually. We can't stop them looking. With that, the plan is exposed … if it makes it into the popular press …'

Drinks were now served – red, rosé, white, green, alcoholic and not so. Some were brewed from grapes, others from more exotic foundations.

'Which brings us neatly to our second individual of note,' Finance said, savouring a sip from a glass of vintage Teorgian chardonnay. 'The denizens of the Empire do seem to be the flavour of the month.'

'Ah yes,' Infrastructure sat forward and steepled his fingers in front of him. 'Our errant Senator.'

'She's been exploring for quite some time now, and her motivations are elusive,' Society said. 'She has the data we need, but she has proven adept at evading our grasp. I fear she has outside assistance of some kind.'

'And who could do such a thing?' Finance demanded.

Personnel rubbed her chin. 'Who else? It's her. It has to be the lady.'

There was silence for a moment.

'That complicates matters,' Infrastructure said. 'Are we aware of the lady's whereabouts?'

'Not at present,' Finance said. 'She knows our reach and how to avoid it.'

'Naturally,' Infrastructure said, 'She was one of us. In the meantime …'

'We believe she is using the Senator as a proxy, or perhaps a protégé.' Finance added. 'Training a new generation of troublemakers.'

'We've been working at some length to portray the Senator as rather less than desirable,' Society said. 'When she does show herself …'

'Excellent work by the Imperial Citizen,' Exo added. 'But it's not sufficient. She must be disgraced and taken out of circulation.'

'You seem unconcerned,' Infrastructure noted, looking across at Personnel.

'I have already taken steps to deal with the problem. We have discovered that she is returning to the core worlds. We have sown a few seeds of discontent already. She has made a few enemies along the way, who we can take advantage of. There are certain statements in the past we can make use of, not least a strong dislike of Admiral Patreus. She has even drawn the ire and jealousy of a certain People's Princess.'

There were murmurs of appreciation from around the table.

'Ah … Very clever,' Infrastructure said.

'Could she be drawn into the Cemiess system, perhaps?' Finance asked.

'By a curious coincidence, yes,' Personnel replied. 'Leave it to me. The Princess has been told that the Senator is returning and has been advised on what to do about it.'

'Then I think I can see how we can procure the exploration data we need,' Infrastructure replied with a satisfied air.

'Would you care to elucidate?' Exo demanded. 'Explorers are all trouble and she's the worst of them. Cultivating a following amongst the universe's disgruntled and itinerate communities. With her rank as Senator, the legal situation is most complex …'

'We have taken that into account,' Finance replied. 'She has been absent for some time, giving us various legal precedents. Her system is currently being exploited by …'

'Our heroic Admiral of the Fleet,' Infrastructure finished, with a broad grin.

'I see,' Exo said, a faint smile of appreciation playing on his features. 'It would be gratifying to be rid of her at last too.'

'It will be a distinct pleasure,' Society added. 'She has caused no end of problems, but I think we can contrive something appropriate for her before she exits our story.'

'We will leave it in your capable hands then,' Infrastructure said. 'We meet again in two weeks, I believe?'

The talk returned to the inconsequential once more. Business concluded, the members of the group disbanded, still under a cloak of anonymity.

Chapter Five

Capitol, Achenar 6d, Achenar system, Empire

The Achenar Hall of Justice was a vast columned space, its pink quartz, dusky marble and slick surfaces a contrast to the more baroque architecture of Imperial tradition. The domed roof, a hundred metres high, flaunted glorious scenes; the defeat of the Federation, the settlement of planets, the terraforming of new worlds. The line of the Duval family interweaved across it, tracing back centuries.

The area was off limits to public citizens, but the nobility of the Empire, or those with certain ranks or sanctioned business to conduct were permitted entry. Across the expansive floor were placed statues wrought in white marble, honouring those deemed to have succeeded in furthering the aims of the Empire through their endeavours.

The building had a counterpart two miles to the north, the ancient Hall of Martyrs. That was built in a similar style, but of black obsidian, paying homage to those that had died in the Empire's service. It was rumoured that some brave martyrs had their fate thrust upon them less than willingly, and had been entombed within the columns whilst still alive.

By contrast, the Hall of Justice was a rather less sombre affair, a frequent meeting place for those with delicate transactions to negotiate and a venue for meetings deemed unsuitable for prying eyes. Direct surveillance, already uncouth by the public standards of the Empire, was both banned and actively prevented.

Visitors reached it by the wide expanse of steps leading up from the piazza, checked by security guards before being allowed to proceed. Today, the hall was bustling with activity. Several notable senators were in attendance, but security was particularly tight around one anteroom off to the left of the main entrance.

Two patrons, one remarkably frail and thin, the other large and overweight, could be seen talking with the guards outside. After a brief exchange, they were permitted entry.

Patrons Zyair and Gerrun were ushered within. The thick panelled doors closed behind them.

A woman stood before them, young and beautiful in an anodyne way.

Both men bowed low, in deference to her far higher rank within the echelons of Imperial society. For her to even acknowledge them was a remarkable courtesy, but she inclined her head in greeting.

'Patrons, I trust your journey from the Prism system was not too arduous?'

The voice was clear, sharp, but affected; a voice that had been trained and tutored, retaining little of its original timbre.

Zyair and Gerrun rose slowly back to their full heights.

'Princess Aisling, this is an honour unlooked for...' Gerrun began.

'I imagine it is,' Aisling replied. She was dressed in a surprisingly simple one piece dress that did little to disguise her figure. Her hair was instantly recognisable, a bright blue reminiscent of the unfiltered light from the Achenar star. Her features perfectly made up, as sharp and as expressionless as a porcelain doll.

'To grant us an audience ...' Zyair gushed. 'We are at your service, Princess.'

Aisling wasted no time.

'I understand your position, patrons,' she said. 'You seek to serve a new senator, to restore your privilege and honour after the disastrous outcome of events in Prism.'

'Disastrous is perhaps not the right word ...' Zyair ventured.

'Oh,' Aisling looked surprised. 'Then you need no assistance, you will restore your virtue within society after your own fashion, will you?'

Gerrun coughed, shooting Zyair a warning look. 'Your Highness is right, of course, we agree with your assessment. Disastrous, absolutely, and our part in it unfortunate and inexcusable.'

Aisling nodded. 'I would like to help you, truly I would, but my hands are tied. Imperial honour is such a tortuous beast to navigate. I'm sure you understand. I cannot be seen to interfere with senatorial positions or matters of patronage. I have so many problems I need to overcome ...'

Zyair sighed, but Gerrun moved quickly forward.

'I completely understand, Your Highness. We didn't come here hoping that you would intercede on our behalf, perish the thought!' Gerrun ignored the consternation growing on Zyair's face. 'You are elevated far above such tawdry concerns as the welfare of lowly Patrons such as we.' He paused and then lowered his voice. 'But if lowly patrons could find a way to relieve you of the problems that vex you ...'

Aisling smiled and tilted her head up a little. 'You served a senatorial family in the Prism system, did you not? The Lorens, I believe, yes?'

'Yes, indeed, Your Highness. We served the late Senator Algreb Loren for many years before his untimely demise at the hands of sordid revolutionaries.'

'Untimely indeed. And that upstart daughter, what was her name?' Aisling was looking idly out of the room's large windows, her voice carefree, but her posture was tense.

Gerrun looked at Zyair once more, a faint smile playing on his lips.

'You mean Lady Kahina, Your Highness? Algreb's third daughter, if memory serves.'

Aisling's smile faded and was replaced with something like a sneer.

'Kahina, yes. That was her name.'

Gerrun coughed again. 'We served her for some time,' he said. 'Is there something we might be able to tell you about her? How can she, mere Lady that she is, be of concern to such as you?'

Aisling licked her lips and paused before responding. 'She came here to Achenar last year, caused quite a stir with what she said and did. Some even thought she might make a play to be Empress herself.'

'She always had delusions of grandeur,' Zyair ventured. 'Heed her not …'

'Indeed she did,' Gerrun continued. 'Shameful conduct. Headstrong and naïve all at once.'

'Yet she attracted a following and continues to do so,' Aisling said. 'I have seen the reports. Her exploits attract many from beyond the Frontier. Even here in the core of the Empire, she has her admirers. People who should know better than to be swayed by her lies and deceits. People who should follow … others, more worthy of attention.'

Aisling's face was set in a pout.

'Her conduct should not concern you,' Gerrun replied smoothly. 'She is far away from here …'

'Reports say she is coming back,' Aisling said, interrupting him. 'She is likely to return here to Achenar, seeking publicity for herself once more. I wish to avoid any contrary opinions being expressed. She must be … discouraged from peddling her nonsense. Put in her place.'

'I quite agree,' Gerrun said, nodding gamely. 'Her presence will only lead to discord.'

'There can be only one People's Princess, of course,' Zyair added, taking his cue.

'Quite,' Aisling said. 'I have nothing against her, of course. It must have been difficult to deal with the death of her family and the actions of those around her, though I'm sure you both tried very hard to advise her as best you could.'

Gerrun and Zyair mumbled enthusiastically in agreement.

'But the situation here is fragile. Her presence would make things so much more … difficult. If only there was a way to discourage her from coming here, or, if needs dictate, to reveal things about her …' Aisling's tone took on a harder edge. 'So that she never bothered us again.'

Zyair had an idea. 'Perhaps the loyal Imperial press might run some articles about her, to set the record straight about her … shortcomings?'

'An excellent idea,' Aisling said, with a nod.

Gerrun cleared his throat. 'We are aware of those she trusts, those she is closest too,' he said. 'We may be able to bring some … influence to bear.'

Aisling smiled sweetly. 'That would be most welcome.'

'We will see to it immediately.'

Aisling nodded and moved to dismiss them before turning back, as if in afterthought.

'Oh,' she said innocently. 'I have something for you.'

'Princess?' Gerrun asked.

Aisling took a small and elegant sealed container from one of the desks along the wall. It appeared to be made of wood, but as she brushed her hand across it, the telltale marks of a holofac image appeared in the air before her. A quick gesture with her fingers and the container opened, folding back to reveal its contents.

She picked it up and brought it over to them. Both patrons peered into it.

Inside, nestled on a plush purple velvet cushion, was a large brooch, or perhaps a medallion. It bore the mark of the Pilots' Federation, a stylised pair of griffon's wings. Around that was a strange reptilian creature with a sharply spiked tail and jaws agape.

'What is this?' Zyair asked.

'It was found here on Achenar,' Aisling said. 'The last time your errant senator visited.' Aisling reached into the box, her fingers flickering in some kind of sharp light. Gerrun and Zyair recognised the hue of a biological sanitiser, ensuring that no impurity would be retained by anything contained within; no bacteria, no humidity … no fingerprints.

Aisling held the medallion up for their inspection, turning it around in her elegant fingers. On the reverse side was a word.

Gerrun and Zyair mouthed it silently.

Salomé …

'It was hers,' Aisling confirmed. 'A calling card. If it were to be found somewhere incriminating …'

'Very unfortunate,' Gerrun said. 'But quite an unarguable piece of evidence.'

Aisling smiled and dropped the medallion into the container, the brief flash of light ensuring any contamination had been eradicated.

'Can I trust you with its safekeeping?' she asked.

'We can assure you ...' Zyair began.

'… that it will be returned to its rightful owner at the appropriate time,' Gerrun finished.

Aisling nodded, a faint smile playing on her lips.

'You know,' she said, languidly turning away. 'I've just had an idea. I am aware of a senator in need of loyal patronage, such as you both might be able to provide. As luck would have it, I will be seeing him within the next month. Perhaps I will be able to put in a good word for you.'

'I hope so, Your Highness,' Gerrun said.

Aisling's voice was hard again, a smile forced upon her face.

'I hope so too.'

She held out her arm, her hand limply proffered. Both patrons prostrated themselves at her feet and kissed her hand.

'You are dismissed.'

Wicca's World, Alioth 5, Alioth system, Alliance

It wasn't what Tsu had expected.

A faint buzz. Her chosen alert sound. A series of letters formed in her view.

Interview in ten minutes. Urgent assignment. Don't be late. 9:59

Just a text trans? What was that supposed to mean? Ten minutes!

Her Tianvian nettle tea would have to wait. She'd barely get back to the office in time if she left now. They'd told her to expect an assignment later today, but in the afternoon. There was supposed to be a chance to review the mission before being interviewed for the task in hand.

How can I be ready, there's not even a brief!

She scanned the text again. There was nothing more, just the countdown.

9:39, 9:38, 9:37 …

She had no choice.

She gestured for the bill and paid it with a quick authentication nod. She stood up, smoothing down her elegant one-piece white dress and stepped away from her table. High heeled glossy shoes matched the dress and heightened her bearing. She looked across the courtyard, its textured surface a stylised version of the Alliance emblem, seeking out and summoning a taxi. By the time it had landed beside her, she'd already indicated her destination.

Alliance Interpol HQ.

The taxi joined the traffic stream, thrusting rapidly upwards and threading its way high above the pedestrianised ground level streets and walkways. Tsu summoned up her bio as it would have been presented to whoever the client was. They might ask her anything, it was worth refreshing it in her mind.

Client Name :	*Singh, Tsu Annabelle*
Client ID :	*720551*
Rank :	*Inspector, Alliance Interpol*
Age :	*24*
Endorsements :	*Top of class graduation, Alioth Prime training facility*
	Special commendation, Alioth Shipyards
	First class honours, Advanced Encryption and Interception

There was more, but she knew most people didn't scan down to the detail. Whoever they were, they probably needed her encryption expertise. More than likely she'd be joining some forensic review of a criminal investigation, some kind of accountancy foul up, maybe embezzlement or some such. She'd probably have to gain access to a bunch of protected files to prove something one way or the other. Crypto skills were quite thin on the ground; it had been a smart move to study it. Her salary reflected the scarcity of her skillset.

Seems urgent though.

That was odd. She'd been on a number of assignments so far, and whilst each client liked to get moving as quickly as was practical, they typically took their time over the recruitment of seconded staff.

Hope that doesn't mean it's a rush job. I hate those.

She straightened her fingers, checking her fingernails. They were white too, customised that morning to match her dress and shoes. Long, thin, shaped and polished immaculately. She didn't go in for some of the full spectrum bio body-mods common amongst the well-heeled in society, but a few choice tweaks, well chosen, made all the difference.

Neat and tidy. The way I look, the way I work.

The taxi slowed and dropped to street level. The Interpol building was nestled amongst the other major structures of the city centre, an imposing edifice towering high into the sky, and currently lost in the clouds perhaps four hundred metres above. As she looked up, a ship passed overhead, rumbling through the sky.

She had always taken an interest in spaceflight, and had her pilots' qualification with excellent sim scores. One assignment had taken her off world, a quick piece of investigation into some illegal trade dealings between the Mizar and Alcor systems, but she hadn't ventured out of Alliance space yet.

She paid and left the taxi, walking confidently across to the entrance. Tsu looked aside as the retina scanners identified her and the doors snapped open. A text message flashed in her view.

Level 80. Meeting room 6A. 3:40

That made her blink. Level 80 was the reception suite and 6A the biggest room. Those meeting rooms were only used for the extremely high-value clients. They were luxuriously appointed with guest rooms and six star hotel-style accoutrements and accommodation. She'd been there on a tour once, impressed at the opulence and glamour of the state rooms and banqueting halls. It was a far cry from the sterile cubicles and dull panelled meeting rooms she was used to.

She moved to the elevator and touched the graphic for the necessary floor. Others filed in beside her, noticing the floor she had selected. She could feel them looking at her, wondering what she might be doing on the 80th floor. She ignored them, maintaining a disinterested air, but inwardly thinking exactly the same thing.

Must be an important organisation if we're trying to impress them. But ... no brief! Going in cold ...

Her fellow travellers vacated the elevator as it continued its ascent, leaving her alone for the last section. The doors opened into a panelled reception area.

To her surprise, there was a troupe of guards at the doors. They looked up as she stepped towards them, one speaking rapidly into a cuff transceiver. Another made a surreptitious scan and then, apparently satisfied, beckoned her across.

Standing beside them was her boss. Tsu could see his face was suffused with anger.

'What are you playing at, Singh?'

Tsu frowned. 'What do you mean?'

'Organising meetings with clients without consulting me?' He stepped close and leant over her. It was his favourite tactic. Tsu refused to be intimidated and didn't lean back as others did. They came uncomfortably close, face to face. 'Don't go over my head. I deal with the accounts, you just do the work. I'm level 2, remember? You earn that position.'

Yes, I know, I'm a level 3 …

'I haven't organised the meeting.'

'What?'

'I got the summons not five minutes ago. I assumed you'd organised it.'

That left him nonplussed. Tsu enjoyed his discomfiture. She knew her boss saw her as a threat. He knew she was brighter and smarter than he was and he wanted to ensure he enjoyed as much success from her work as he could before she eventually got promoted past him. Right now, he had the managerial position and she didn't. So, she was biding her time.

But if he didn't organise it … who did?

'I'd better not be late,' she added, with acid primness. 'Clients first, yes?'

'They must have forgotten to cc me in on the meeting,' he said. 'Let's sort this out.'

He walked across towards the guards, Tsu following behind him, dutifully.

The guards straightened as they approached.

'We're here for the meeting,' her boss said.

'Only her,' the guard said, with a brief gesture towards Tsu.

'But I'm her supervisor!'

'I don't care who you are,' the guard replied, holding up his hand and generating a holofac that flickered between the two men. Tsu could make out a representation of her sitting at the sidewalk café. 'Just her.'

Tsu stared at the holofac in surprise.

Someone has been scanning me all day. That's illegal!

'What?' her boss spluttered.

'We have orders that only Miss Tsu Annabelle Singh is permitted,' the guard finished. 'That's her, not you.'

'But this is ridiculous, who is going to manage the administration, forecasting, planning and resourcing …'

Meeting room 6A. 1:50

The text flashed in Tsu's line of sight again.

'I'll just have to manage the best I can,' Tsu said primly. Moving around her boss, she approached the guards, who stepped aside to let her through. She turned to see them close ranks again, their beefy frames interposed between her and her boss.

Her boss looked even more furious.

'I expect a full report on the outcome, Singh! On my desk before the end of the day …'

She smiled sweetly at him and then looked at the nearest guard. She rolled her eyes. The guard grinned.

She walked on through the doors and swallowed as they snapped closed behind her. There was an open corridor just beyond, framed by huge arched windows wrought in the typical no-nonsense Alliance style. Form followed function, she appreciated the design. She was far above the clouds now and the Alioth star was blazing bright white through the plexiglass. The meeting room was on her right, the largest on this side of the building. The panelled doors were closed.

She paused at the threshold and took a deep breath, ready to face whoever might be inside. The doors slid smoothly aside for her.

Then she stepped in.

The room was empty. She spun around to check, but she was alone.

The room was almost bare, the panelled walls undecorated, the floor laid with an expensive but dull tan coloured carpet. The Alliance emblem, emblazoned proudly on a holofac plinth in the middle of the room, was the only obvious adornment, apart from two plush reclining leather chairs.

Tsu walked forward. Nothing seemed unusual. From the long-ago tour, she remembered the room set up as a conference venue. Was that the norm and had it hastily been changed for this interview? There was nothing on the plinth, no summary, no brief. Nothing.

And only two chairs?

She moved over to the window and looked out. Cloud blanketed the view, lit by the fierce white of the Alioth star. The faint but enormous arc of the Alioth 5 gas giant could be seen in the background. Transports came and went in ordered rows, punctuated here and there by larger spacefaring vessels. She recognised a squad of the new Viper Mark IV, their freshly gleaming duralium hulls flickering in the glare. They were escorting a much bigger ship, a lumbering freighter.

Lakon Type-9.

The buzz sounded in her ears again. The timer had reached its countdown.

Meeting room 6A. 0:00

On cue, the door behind her opened with a faint swish. She turned to see a man walk in; he gestured for the door to close and then locked it behind him with a wriggle of chubby fingers.

He was tall and well built, probably twice her weight and rather portly. He was dressed in a smart but casual maroon and beige jacket with matching trousers. A quiff of greying hair stood up from his head and as he turned Tsu saw a jowly, but friendly looking face.

An instantly familiar face.

Her mouth dropped open in surprise.

The man grinned and gave her a jaunty Alliance salute, fist closed against his chest and then extended outwards palm open. She reciprocated automatically.

'I see I won't need to introduce myself.'

Tsu ran her tongue over her lips and around her mouth.

Say something, you idiot!

'It's a pleasure, Prime Minister.'

Am I supposed to curtsey, or bow … or …

'Edmund is fine.'

He held out his hand. She stepped forward to take it. It was all she could do to place one foot in front of the other.

Edmund Mahon! The Alliance Prime Minister? Here in person, to see me on my own. What does this mean? Professional, Tsu, you're a professional. Stay focussed. He's chosen me because I must have been recommended to him. I'm worth this …

The handshake was firm but friendly. She hoped her palms weren't chill with sweat.

'It's good to meet you, Tsu. For introductions, consider that I'm well acquainted with your profile. I have something I need you to do for me.'

Tsu swallowed, unable to respond.

'Shall we?'

He gestured to the two chairs. She nodded, recovering herself.

'Of course.'

She sat down as he lowered himself into the opposite chair and leant back. She sat perched on the edge of hers, trying to decide whether to cross her legs or not. She contented herself with placing her knees to one side and ankles to the other.

'You come highly recommended by the establishment here,' Edmund began. 'I apologise for the slightly unorthodox approach, but, as you know, I'm not the greatest fan of bureaucracy.'

'You've met my boss?'

'Fortunately not. But he sounds precisely the sort of person I don't need to waste time with.'

Tsu couldn't stop a smile forming on her lips. The Prime Minister was famous for cutting to the chase and getting things done. He was, perhaps, the most effective Alliance Prime Minister there had ever been. His soft and friendly exterior was said to hide a tough determination, firm will and a cunning mind. Tsu had no doubts on that score.

'I prefer the straightforward myself,' Tsu said.

'One of the reasons I have selected you,' Edmund continued. 'Alongside the skills you clearly have.'

'How can I help?'

'Are you aware of the Engineers?'

Tsu blinked. The Engineers were a curious set of characters. Individuals stationed far out in remote locations around the core worlds. She'd read a few of the bios that had been assembled on them. The official stance had been to tolerate their presence but to keep tabs on their activities.

'I've heard of them, though "engineers" seems to be the wrong word for them …'

'Tinkerers, illegal modifiers, criminals?' Edmund asked.

'If you say so,' Tsu replied.

Edmund frowned. 'I like that you're tactful, but I'd prefer to hear your opinion.'

Be direct! He has no time for those who don't know their own minds …

'Criminals then,' Tsu answered, thinking quickly. 'They operate outside of any jurisdiction, making modifications to ships that have no external quality assurance, no oversight and no regulation. These modifications are potentially hazardous, but grant the owner abilities which could easily make them a threat to official government or military forces.'

'Not bad.'

'Most have shady pasts of some kind or another,' Tsu added. 'A few are seriously hardened criminals. All of them have assets measured in the multi-trillions, giving them the means to run and operate well-defended bases that are the equal or superior of many military installations. They provide unusual and bespoke upgrades to shipping.'

Edmund seemed to relax in his chair, regarding her for a long moment. Tsu held his gaze. Then the grin was back.

'I've chosen well,' he said. 'I would agree with your analysis. We've heard of ships doubling their jump radii, having weapons that can penetrate shields in a fraction of the time anticipated.'

'Does this have something to do with the assignment?'

'Straight to the point, I see,' Edmund said. 'Yes, it does. Does the name Turner mean anything to you?'

Tsu was surprised. Virtually everyone with a decent level of security clearance knew the name 'Turner.'

'As in, "The Turners"?' she asked.

'Yes,' Edmund said, his eyes narrowing. 'Tell me what you know.'

'The interesting stuff starts with Mic Turner, I guess. Co-founder of Argent Inc. He worked with Meredith Argent way back in the 3250s. Argent was a major company specialising in state-of-the-art exploration ships, if I remember correctly.'

'Correct.'

'The story goes Mic was searching for a supposed alien race called the Thargoids, but disappeared without trace. There's a monument to him on Argent's Claim, I think. It's one of those stories that has grown in the telling, like the Thargoids. It's all rumours and hearsay …'

She saw him raise his eyebrows.

'It's not hearsay?' she asked, feeling her stomach contract in a mixture of alarm and excitement.

Edmund licked his lips.

'Mic Turner,' Edmund said, 'had an interesting life. Have you ever heard of INRA?'

The Intergalactic Naval Reserve Arm?

Tsu tried to recall her history. They had been a clandestine group, operating beyond Federal, Imperial or Alliance jurisdiction, perhaps even above them. Ancient history now, though.

'I've heard them mentioned in the records, there's doubt as to whether they were real or not, however.'

'Oh, they were real all right,' Edmund said.

'And the Thargoids?' Tsu asked, not sure she wanted to hear the answer.

Just tales, stories told to kids to freak them out. Armour plated insectoid killers lurking on the edges of space … nonsense, surely?

'Evidence suggests that they're real too, though no one has seen any sign of them for over a hundred and seventy years.'

Tsu swallowed.

'Much of the whole story is true,' Edmund explained. 'Intelligence reports suggest that INRA developed a bioweapon and used it against the Thargoids way back in the past – perhaps we wiped them out. Mic Turner went looking for the Thargoids a hundred years later. He may have found them, we'll never know. It's more likely that Mic found out something about what INRA did back then and got killed for it. INRA was disbanded shortly afterwards.'

Tsu's head was spinning.

'But what has this got to do with the Engineers?'

Edmund leant forward. 'One of the Engineers is a chap by the name of Bill Turner.'

Related? Or just a coincidence …?

'He operates locally,' Edmund continued, 'Alioth 4a. Specialises in drive thrusters and speed upgrades. Oh, we've checked him out dozens of times; spot audits, unannounced inspections, he always comes up legit. Always pays his taxes, records all straight and even.'

'That I didn't know. And you think he's suspiciously clean?'

'Squeaky.'

'He's a relation to the other Turners?'

'He has claimed to be an illegitimate son in the past. Whether that's true or not we don't know. We've got no precedent to bring him in for questioning, and if we did, we'd likely blow our only line of investigation.'

'Which is?'

'Where you come in.'

Tsu waited. Edmund steepled his fingers in front of him.

'We've detected that Bill is receiving encrypted transmissions from an external source. We've tracked it back to the Federation. The Chi Orionis system, to be precise.'

Tsu hadn't heard of it, but she assumed it was a fair distance away.

'We've been trying to decrypt it, with no success thus far.'

Tsu shook her head, 'And you won't. If it's being broadcast across holofac on FTL it will be using a massive rotating cypher, probably prearranged in some fashion. You'll never crack it in a million years without knowing the key.'

Edmund smiled. 'Not my field, but I'm sure you're right.'

'You want me to take a look at this and see what I can do?' Tsu was disappointed, it was a mundane task without much possibility of success.

'No.'

Edmund sat back and regarded her for a long moment.

'Explain,' Tsu prompted.

'I want you to find out who is sending it, and why.'

That wasn't what she had expected.

That means travelling to Chi Orionis. A real assignment. Off world. Spaceship travel!

A thought occurred to her.

'When you say "you," you do mean a team …'

'No, just you. I want this low key. Very low key. Bill is up to something and if he is related to old Mic Turner, it could be very serious indeed. If he gets spooked by a big investigation, we'll lose track of whatever this is.'

Tsu felt her heart pound and her stomach lurch.

Solo!

Edmund continued. 'I want you to travel to Chi Orionis and see if you can locate the source of the comms from the other end, decipher it and solve this mystery. Once you find out, I want you to report back to me directly, no intermediaries. This is a private assignment.'

In person?

That was most irregular. Alliance Interpol investigations were usually covered by multiple layers of governance and administration. There would be briefings, planning sessions, team roles, retrospective analysis, debriefs …

Edmund must have seen something of this on her face as he continued.

'I know this is a little different from your usual work. I've arranged the necessary exclusions. The fewer people who know, the better. This could be very significant. There may be a lot more to this than meets the eye.'

'Do you have anything on Chi Orionis itself?'

'Federal democracy, pretty small in the grand scheme of things,' Edmund replied, 'Total population is around the thirty million mark. A couple of starports. The best lead we have is that there is a small startup company there that has set up in the last couple of years. The comms from Bill Turner started about six months after they were up and running. Could be a connection. I've prepared a dossier for you.'

'What's the company called?'

'MetaDrive.'

Tsu's thoughts raced for a moment.

MetaDrive? As in Meta-alloys? They come from those strange 'Barnacles' found out in the Pleiades sector ... a chap who claims he's related to old Mic Turner of the Thargoid rumours from way back when ... talking in crypto to a location in the Federation! About what?

Edmund must have been watching her expression as she digested the information.

'A lot to take in, I know,' he said. 'But if there is a connection between Bill and Mic, and if that leads to the Thargoids in any way, shape or form, we need to know.'

Tsu looked up, barely able to contain her excitement.

'When do I leave?'

'Immediately.'

'I'll need a ship, some specialist comms equipment ...'

'I've had a ship prepped for you with everything I think you'll need,' Edmund said, pulling out a small commtab from his inner pocket. A holo-fac representation of a wedge-shaped ship appeared above it as he pressed his thumb down.

Viper Mark IV ...

'It's not one of ours. We keep a few of these about painted in Federal colours for exactly this sort of mission. Not the most glamorous of ships ...'

Tsu shook her head. 'No, it's what I would have chosen. Unremarkable, common, blends in anywhere, no political overtones, reasonable turn of speed. Perfect for a bit of surveillance and can hold its own in a fight.'

Edmund nodded. 'Glad you agree.'

'I'll go direct to the spaceport.'

Edmund nodded, apparently satisfied.

'Your usual pay will be doubled for the duration,' he said. 'And there'll be a bonus upon your return. Bear in mind that you're beyond Alliance influence. If something goes wrong ...'

Tsu nodded. All Alliance agents knew the drill. They all carried the drug.

Hexedit.

A simple tablet or patch. In small doses, it was useful to 'manage' undesirable memories. In greater concentrations, it dissolved the connections between neurons in the brain. First you forgot what you knew, then you forgot how to walk and talk, then you forgot how to breathe – in that order. The perfect solution for leaving no questions answered.

There was no known antidote.

Edmund stood up.

'Good luck, Miss Singh.'

Tsu took his hand and was rewarded with a firm shake.

The meeting was over.

Chapter Six

Orbital graveyard, Tionisla system, Alliance

The *Seven Veils* dropped out of hyperspace with a faint surge of deceleration. The Tionisla star swam into view. Salomé didn't flinch as the vast ball of plasma swelled before them. The exit from hyperspace never failed to draw a gasp from those not used to star-flight, but it was routine and unremarkable to her now.

'These are the co-ordinates,' she said to Hassan, watching as he punched them into the flight computers. A targeting reticule appeared in their forward vision.

'Lagrange point,' Hassan noted. She watched as he steered the ship. Millions of kilometres of empty space flashed past unnoticed as the star fell behind them, its orange glare casting shadows around the cockpit.

Salomé watched the eerie flicker of light as the frame shift drive dispelled its energies and the *Seven Veils* dropped into normal space. The sound of the thrusters echoed up through the cabin as the ship's sublight engines engaged and regained attitude control of the ship.

Ahead, countless prickles of light marked the darkness, almost star-like, but twinkling in the glow of the corona.

Stars don't twinkle in space. This is it …

She watched as a vast collection of faint traces appeared on the *Seven Veils*' scanners. She frowned, squinting out of the cockpit windows, seeing Hassan leaning forward alongside her, trying to get a better look.

This was where she had been told to go.

'What is this place?' he asked.

'It's called the graveyard,' Salomé answered, her voice low.

Luko brought me here once before …

She watched Hassan pull on the throttles and the *Seven Veils* eased into the tumbling menagerie ahead. She cast her mind back and the image of the swarthy Italian trader appeared in her mind. Luko had rescued her when she'd crashed on an almost deserted planet. Somehow, he'd been there too, marooned with a broken down ship that he'd repaired from the wreckage of hers. He'd not taken sides in the conflict in the Prism system, but had rescued her when Octavia had tried to kidnap her and steal her body.

Octavia …

She shuddered. She didn't want to think about that experience.

Salomé could just make out the tumbling remains of monuments, ancient ships tethered to enormous markers; great lumps of metal, with the words and symbols still visible after untold centuries in the vacuum. It was a bizarre and otherworldly sight. The markers were rarely less than a hundred metres across. There were corroded chrome-alloy crosses, titanium stars and duralium henges. All the strange symbolic shapes of all the worlds, minds and faiths that had come to die in this ancient mausoleum.

'You know about this place?' Hassan's voice was hushed.

'Not much, but I have been here once before,' Salomé said softly. 'It was a final resting place for the rich and famous. Long time ago … It's existed for at least two hundred years, but it fell into disuse.'

'What happened?'

'Politics of yesteryear. The Old Worlds, brought low by the Federation and the Empire. Once they were a mighty power, now no one remembers outside of the history texts. Did they teach you about Galcop in educlasses?'

Hassan shook his head, still captivated by the view from the windows of the *Seven Veils*.

'Not much call for old politics on an agri-world. Quite the reverse, actually. We tried to forget about history.'

Salomé smiled. 'I was taught at length by tutors. Most of it was deathly dull, but a few bits I found interesting.'

Many of the abandoned ships were ancient, their lines simple and angular. Most were of a type neither of them had ever seen before.

'The Galactic Cooperative,' Salomé said, wistfully. 'Long gone now. They used to be the main power in this part of space. An interesting organisation, they were a little like the Alliance is now, but they only held jurisdiction over space and the stations, never the planets below.'

Hassan nudged the ship into the edges of the graveyard.

'Should we even be here?' he asked, his voice low as he gazed at the huge and sombre gravemarkers slowly drifting past the ship. 'Isn't this trespassing …? Wow, look at that!'

Salomé looked across to where Hassan was pointing.

A great crystalline structure, a puff-ball of diamond-bright needles, easily a hundred metres across. Within it, she could just see a body, dressed in a red military-style uniform, hovering in stasis at the centre of the great construct, illuminated by focussed light from the Tionisla star. She watched it with a strange sense of awe as it passed them on the port side.

'We don't touch, we don't interfere,' Salomé said. 'Those are the rules. We are just paying our respects to ...'

'To who?' Hassan asked.

Salomé didn't answer. She squinted, looking forward.

Hassan wove the ship around, ensuring that he gave each monument sufficient clearance. The graveyard was huge, and the shadows of the great tombs made this strange sanctuary of the dead into a place of innumerable hideouts. Some of the ancient vessels and artefacts were enormous.

Salomé gestured with her hand. 'There! Over there.'

A dilapidated ship could be seen in the distance, surrounded by the wreckage of other vessels. As she watched, a light winked on and off briefly. She blinked. A red light, flashing on and off, directed at them. The ship was painted black, with curious white strips at the boundary of its hull panels, making it look like a framework rather than a finished ship.

Hassan was peering at it.

'That looks like ...'

Salomé smiled. 'Yes. The same kind of vessel as Luko's ship. It is one of his beloved Cobras, I think.'

Hassan flipped on the *Seven Veils'* external hull lights in acknowledgement and manoeuvred the ship closer.

'Definitely a Cobra,' he said, squinting at the big ship. 'Old one, too.'

'We need to dock with it,' Salomé said.

Hassan rotated the *Seven Veils* so the two ships were belly to belly. A few moments later, there was a metallic clunk as the respective airlock mechanisms joined and sealed. Green lights flickered on the dashboard.

Docking complete. Engines disengaged.

'All ok,' Hassan whispered. 'Power and atmosphere confirmed on the other side. Good to go.'

There was a crackle from the narrowband comms. After a brief moment of static, a heavily disguised voice spoke.

'Kahina Loren? You come alone and unarmed.'

The comms went dead.

'Are you sure about this?' Hassan asked. 'If you run into trouble ...'

'Too late for that,' Salomé answered. 'That is, if we're going to find out what this mystery is all about. Keep watch. If you don't hear from me within the hour, leave.'

'But …'

'No, Hassan,' she said, trying to take the sting out of her voice. 'Do not worry about me. Get to safety.'

She could tell she hadn't convinced him by the look on his face. There was more there, concern for sure, worry too … and other feelings of …

I don't have time for this now.

She took a commtab with her, turned on her heel and left the cockpit, making her way down through the luxurious decks of the *Seven Veils*. Salomé stepped into the airlock mechanism, waiting for it to run its cycle, conscious of her heart beating fast in her chest.

Two faint clunks and then the sound of equalising pressure echoed through the bulkheads around her.

The opposite hatch swung back, revealing the form of a woman, cast in silhouette by the glare. She was nonchalantly poised against the interior, despite the zero-gee. The bulkheads beyond were dimly lit, but seemed in remarkably good repair considering the dilapidated exterior of the vessel.

The two women stared at each other for a moment. Salomé recognised her. She had met her once before, whilst recruiting support for her exploration quests out in the void. The woman seemed completely unchanged, even her clothing was identical. Salomé registered a small wiry frame, fit and supple. Her age was difficult to determine, but she wasn't young. Her eyes were dark, her skin olive. She wore her hair in an unusual array of coloured spikes and was dressed in a tight fitting full-length tunic. There was something odd about the way she moved; it was almost mechanical, almost too precise to be human.

'You …'

'Still struggling for words, I see.' the spiky-haired woman said. 'Cat still got your tongue, even after all this time?'

Salomé sighed.

Cat? One of these days I'm going to find out what a cat is …

'You do … er …' The spiky-haired woman frowned. 'You do have a speech function? Or are you one of those early "semaphore and gormless grin" androids?'

'I am not an android,' Salomé retorted, taken aback by the woman's forthrightness.

'Oh God,' she replied. 'Where's the off switch? That Imperial accent. I think I prefer you silent …'

Salomé opened her mouth to reply, but the woman cut her off.

'Quickly now, follow me. Time is pressing.'

The spiky-haired woman turned on her heel and strutted away. Each footfall was sharp and measured, precise and even, clicking sharply on the floor in time with the steps of her mag-boots. It made Salomé feel clumsy in comparison. She hurried to keep up.

'Will you explain what this is all about? I've chased your clues from …'

The woman stopped and huffed impatiently. She looked back.

'Feeling put out, are we?' The woman winked. 'Come on, Lady Kahina. Or Salomé.' She followed the wink with a mischievous grin.

'Who are you?' Salomé demanded. 'I don't even know your name.'

The spiky-haired woman laughed.

'That's because you don't need to know my name …'

She climbed out of sight, disappearing into an alcove above.

The airlock cycled behind her and locked into place, Salomé had no choice but to follow. She knew the layout of the Cobra well, and this one was little different inside from the one Luko owned. The woman led her up through the decks into the cargo bay, its interior functional and drab compared to the ostentatious design of Imperial vessels. Salomé could immediately see the ship was ancient. Few of the control panels were powered. The ship seemed to be a derelict.

'Welcome aboard the *Cor Meum Et Animam*.'

That voice!

Salomé turned to see a woman, a very frail looking old lady, standing behind her. Salomé recognised her immediately. She had seen her only once before, more than two years ago.

The old lady from the hospital! But even older … so much older!

'You've done well, Senator Loren. Well enough, at any rate.'

The old lady's voice was raspy and dry. The spiky-haired woman stood just behind her, protectively.

'I've done what you directed,' Salomé replied, gesturing with the commtab she held. 'All the data is here. The results of several missions by many talented explorers …'

'Yes, we've followed your antics with interest, as have others,' the old lady interrupted, her voice no less authoritative despite the waver in its tone. 'Quite an air of mystique you've drawn up about yourself. Very Imperial.'

Salomé bristled, but let the jibe pass. 'You told me misdirection was key, flamboyancy comes easily to us in the Empire.'

The old lady moved forward, struggling a little with her mag-boots.

The spiky-haired woman stepped forward as if to help, but the old lady batted her away.

'The time for that is past now,' the old lady said. 'Let me have the data.'

Salomé passed her the commtab. 'I found the three markers, but most of it is encrypted. Do you know how to unlock it?'

'I may do.'

Salomé sighed.

Is there to be no end to these games?

The old lady had paused. She was turning the commtab over in her hands. Salomé could see she was trembling, her hands shaking.

Age, fear, or something else?

'This …' the old lady began. She stopped, breathing in and out. 'This … is what they've tried to hide. It's all here. The Imperial databanks, the re-mote systems, the Pleiades …'

'What does it mean?' Salomé asked. 'You owe me an explanation. I've travelled thousands of light years for this … to the rift, to …'

'Owe you, do I?' the old lady replied, waving a hand and turning aside. 'You took this quest of your own free will, as did all the others.'

'I completed your quest,' Salomé returned. 'I organised people, we followed your clues, did your dirty work for you. I must have an answer. The least you can do is …'

The old lady faced her, a steely glint in her hard brown eyes. Salomé recoiled, despite herself.

'You just wanted a way to soothe your soul, Imperial girl. That was the deal.' The old lady laughed at the expression on Salomé's face. 'We choose wisely, you know. We tested you to see if you had the smarts, and you came through. We offered you a way to do something for the good of others after your mistakes at Prism, and you have. Your contribution here outweighs your sins. The galaxy is safer as a result of what you've done. Go in peace.'

'It's not enough,' Salomé said. 'I have spent two long years following the clues you left. I demand an explanation!'

The old lady looked at her for a long moment, before a grin broke out on her face.

'It figures,' she said. Salomé heard the spiky-haired woman chuckle from behind her. She turned to look.

The spiky-haired woman stepped forward. 'You weren't satisfied with my explanation, if you recall,' she said, directing her words to the old lady. 'You were just as belligerent.'

'Maybe, maybe,' the old lady replied.

'Enough!' Salomé said. 'Enough with the games!'

The pair of women exchanged a look with each other.

The spiky-haired woman turned to Salomé. 'We can't tell you everything, because much of it has been hidden.' She paused. 'Hidden by us deliberately, not even we know it.'

Salomé shook her head. 'I don't understand.'

'Which is a good thing,' the spiky-haired woman said. 'The less you know the less you can reveal. Suffice to say this secret has been the death of many, and it will continue to kill people.'

'What secret?' Salomé asked. 'What is this all about?'

'That's …'

An alert echoed through the cargo bay. All three women turned in surprise.

Audio from Salomé's earpiece crackled in her ear. Hassan's voice, high and alarmed.

'Inbound ships! Look like Federal Dropships, at least four. Heading this way, scanning range in under a minute …'

'Who …?' Salomé began.

'Federation,' the spiky-haired woman said, looking at some monitors on the cargo bay bulkhead. 'Closing fast, how did they …?'

'They've found us, it doesn't matter how,' the old lady snapped. 'Come here!'

She gestured to Salomé.

'Come, now!'

Salomé moved to her. The moment she was in range the old lady grabbed her wrist and turned her hand over, palm upwards. Next moment, she slapped her other hand down hard on Salomé's. There was a moment of sharp pain as something burrowed into her flesh. Salomé ripped her hand back, fighting the instinct to break the old lady's wrist in response.

'What did you …?'

The old lady grinned and then picked up the commtab, quickly jabbing at its surface. There was a faint beep and an audio query.

Delete all contents. Confirm?

'Wait!' Salomé said as the old lady's finger came down on the commtab. 'The data!'

'Don't worry. It's safe,' the old lady said. 'You've got it.'

Salomé looked at her palm, where she could see a small red lump. It was sore.

'Bio-trace,' the old lady said. 'Clever stuff, stores data in unused DNA strands. Won't show up on a security scan.'

'How do I unlock it?'

'You?' The old lady laughed. 'You can't.'

'But …'

'Remember Cuculidae!'

'I … what?'

'Cuculidae!'

'What does that mean?'

'Ask your Italian friend.'

'Luko? But how would he …?'

'And I suggest you run,' the old lady said. 'If they catch you with me, they'll almost certainly kill you.'

'What about you?' Salomé demanded.

'Oh, we've done our part,' the spiky-haired woman said, stepping alongside the old lady. 'Don't worry.'

'One minute to scan range!' Hassan's voice interrupted her again.

'But what do I do?' Salomé demanded. 'Where …?'

'Don't get caught,' the spiky-haired woman said with a smile. 'Get your people to search the Conflux and Hawking's Gap, too. There's more to be found, the key …'

'More searching in the void?'

'Look for the key,' the old lady said. 'You'll find it. Now, run!'

Salomé stumbled backwards and fled. She scrambled down the companionway to the airlock and threw herself through.

'Hassan, decouple. I'm aboard. Get us out of here!'

Serebrov Terminal, HR 6421 system, Independent

Serebrov Terminal in the HR 6421 system orbited an unremarkable rocky moon, and the terminal itself was merely a standard Coriolis affair. But that location had a saving grace. The moon's own orbit was remarkable, just a few thousand kilometres beyond the edge of a dramatic system of rings circling endlessly about a strikingly blue gas giant.

Normally the view relaxed Commander Erimus Kamzel, but today it was unable to work its magic. His jaw was clenched, the usually clean-shaven face sporting two days' worth of stubble.

She hasn't contacted us. She promised she would. Something must have gone wrong …

Erimus led a faction known as the Children of Raxxla. They had a chequered history, born due to a heady mix of dissatisfaction with the politics of the core worlds and a desire to uncover the mysteries of the cosmos they had reason to suspect had been concealed by those in authority. They were an eclectic mix of explorers, entrepreneurs and disaffected combat-hardened veterans.

Beside him stood a woman, with short-cropped dark hair and a vaguely Asian look about her. Alessia Verdi acted as the spokesperson for the group, heading up their communications division. Her expression was taut too, with lines of worry etched on her face.

'I'm going to go and take a look,' Alessia said. 'It's been too long, we should have heard by now.'

Erimus nodded. 'Fly safe, take no unnecessary risks. I fear positions have shifted and someone is making a move …'

Alessia nodded. 'I will scan her route and then return as soon as I can.'

Their leader was the ex-Senator of the Prism system – Lady Kahina Tijani Loren, known to the Children of Raxxla as Salomé. It was she who had issued their proclamation.

I can recall her words, still ringing in my ears …

Erimus watched Alessia go. He knew she was perhaps Salomé's closest confidant outside of her immediate circle of friends. She was the daughter of Luko Prestigio Giovanni, a trader, so he claimed, who had once rescued Salomé when she'd crashed on a distant desolate world.

Although Alessia is the first to admit she doesn't know what her father's background is!

Erimus toggled a holofac recording. He knew the words off by heart after all this time, but they still gave him comfort as Salomé's image took form in the space before him, her tones strident and sharp.

'Citizens of the Empire, Peoples of the Federation, the Alliance and those from the independent worlds. I call out to you at a time of great galactic turmoil. Our great organisations have a bloody history, but we had achieved a relative peace; an understanding between the Empire, the Federation and the Alliance.

'But now our leaders have fallen to fighting and squabbling over territory, waging petty wars, wasting lives and resources, setting sibling against sibling, parent against child … and for what? A few lines on a chart; gains and successes that are wiped out within days. Thousands have already died in the name of these Powers.

'Surely humanity is better than this? Can we not build a stronger future, one that we can all be proud of? Can we not choose peace?

'Our peoples all suffer under their leadership. I know there are many of you who desire peace and would take a stand against this infighting. Who no longer wish to be pawns in their game.

'You know me. I was once a senator of the Empire. I released my homeworld from the blight of those that would subdue it, now I would see all people free from manipulation and exploitation.

'I call for those who would resist the powers; the lone-wolf fighters, those who have lost their homeworlds, the disaffected, those just trying to make a living in the void and feel forced to take a side, those who see the false promises and futility of supporting these people and to all who have suffered at their deeds. Those who wished our history might unfold … another way.

'Know there are those who care about your peril, that would show concern for your losses and who share your fears for the future.

'Now is the time. Show the void there is an alternative to the constant Pyrrhic *victories* we endure week after week as systems are taken and lost at the whim of those who care nothing for the plight of those affected.

'Fight for freedom, fight for peace and fight for a stable and prosperous future for your children, and your children's children.

'Join us. Become a child of Raxxla.'

And they had come …

Hundreds upon hundreds of commanders had joined the cause. Some joined because they believed, others because they wanted to make a gesture to the authorities, others just for the exploration quests that the Children had made the heart of their missions.

The Children of Raxxla had taken part in the expedition to Beagle Point, that far-flung system across the galaxy, diametrically opposite to Sol, seeking clues about the myths and legends that filtered back from the darkness. Salomé herself was investigating something; she had undertaken her own quests and asked for assistance on numerous occasions. The Children had always come to her aid.

But now …

Erimus rubbed his chin.

Overdue … and she's never late.

That meant something had gone wrong. And if it concerned Salomé, it was going to be something very wrong indeed.

Orbital graveyard, Tionisla system, Alliance

The scanner was hard to read with so many contacts. Even the derelicts were still giving off low-level infrared. The four Federal dropships stayed in close formation as they searched through the graveyard.

'There.'

A stronger heat source showed on the scanner, flickering uncertainly. They would be in range in moments and able to get a detailed scan.

The commander of the lead ship squinted forwards, trying to make out their quarry, but the shifting bulks of hundreds of ships defeated his eyesight.

For a moment the heat signature pulsed brighter, but then it steadied and became a solid reading on the display.

'Scan!'

He watched as the information scrolled up on the auxiliary holofac display.

Cobra Mark III
Registered : Cor Meum Et Animam
Life support module subsystem activated

'Got you at last.'

It took only moments for the four ships to surround the dilapidated Cobra. Docking for the lead vessel followed, closely guarded by the three remaining vessels.

There was no response to hails, but that had been expected.

Security protocols quickly overrode the locking mechanisms on the airlocks and the commander and two of his guards forced their way in, weapons clutched in their hands.

They moved through the interior cautiously and methodically, sweeping each compartment, covering each other, before moving onto the next. The cargo bay was their destination; they didn't hesitate, but burst in with weapons drawn.

Nothing moved within. There was little save the faint hiss of the air processing systems.

The commander looked around him, studying the floor, ceilings and bulkheads with a practised eye. Nothing seemed amiss.

'Escape pods.'

They moved across the cargo bay floor, mag-boots clanking rhythmically.

Both pods were activated, but unlaunched. Their vision plates were fogged, obscuring whatever was inside. The commander signalled to the nearest guard and they both punched in the code release, before stepping back, weapons at the ready.

The doors hissed, clunked forward and retracted to the side. Mist swirled out, thick and impenetrable. The commander waved his hand, trying to disperse it.

There was nothing.

Decoyed!

He turned as he heard the click of a weapon being primed. One his guards yelled and jolted back as a laser beam flash-burned across him.

The commander flung himself to one side, bringing up his own weapon and training it on target. He saw a woman step through the mist, a weapon clasped in her right hand. He got a brief impression of wild hair, arranged in a bizarre series of spikes.

He fired. It was a charged round. Designed to incapacitate, but not to kill. His aim was good. It hit her square in the chest, fizzing and sparking.

She stepped forward, somehow unaffected by the electrical blast.

That should have dropped a 100-kilo marine …

His men fired similar weapons, and a crackling cacophony of sparking electrical shorts enveloped the woman's body.

She staggered back, shook her head and kept coming, firing her own weapon and taking out another of his men.

'Lethal force!' he yelled, jabbing at his own sidearm and resetting the ammunition selector. This time it would kill …

He fired, hitting the woman again. She was thrown backwards this time, her mag-boots' grip on the flooring broken. She landed heavily against a bulkhead.

And then got back to her feet.

The commander stared in dismay. The left side of her face was oozing blood now, and her right arm was twisted at an awkward angle. Her chest was blackened and burnt from the blast, clothing torn, ripped and smouldering. In places her skin was gone completely, revealing …

Metal.

Cybernetics!

She was bringing the gun back up again.

'Kill her!'

More blasts, the shocks smashing her back into the bulkhead repeatedly. The gun she carried was shot from her hand and she dropped forward, her body falling its length to the floor and then bouncing up to rock gently in the zero-gee, secured by a single mag-boot.

Smoke, acrid and harsh, filled the room, making it difficult to see. The commander and his men cautiously moved forward.

Her body lay twisted backwards, still now, a mixture of blood and mechanism. Through ripped flesh they could see an internal skeleton of metal, her bones and organs supplemented by machinery and components. As they drew close they saw her eyes open.

'You're too late,' she managed to say, blood coating her lips. 'You're always too late.'

A cough and a shudder. Her eyes lost focus, staring upwards to the ceiling of the cargo bay.

'Randomius ... lady of fate ... take me now ...'

Her breath sighed out of her, accompanied by a faint electronic whine that spiralled up for a moment and then cut out. Her body drifted amidst them.

'Search the ship from stem to stern. Pull every data bank and node. She's got to be here somewhere ...'

Orerve system, Alliance

'Did they track us?' Salomé demanded.

Hassan shook his head. 'No, they didn't get a scan before we jumped. We'll have left a high wake, though, if they're equipped to read it ...'

'Little doubt about that.'

The *Seven Veils* had made the jump to hyperspace and was already a couple of systems away, but the big ship's jump range was limited, even with the upgrades to her systems.

'Where are we heading?'

'We need to get to Luko.'

'Luko?' Hassan asked, bewildered. 'Why?'

Salomé looked furious. 'Because he knows something about this ...'

'But how can he?' Hassan asked. 'He's never been involved with …'

'They know him. So he knows,' Salomé answered. 'And he never told me.'

'I don't understand.'

'Just plot a damn course!' Salomé snapped. 'If those ships identified us, they'll be trying to track us. Whoever that was, we've got to lose them.'

'They'll blockade the immediate systems if they're smart …'

'Divert towards Achenar. Those were Federal ships. We can hide more easily in Imperial space.'

Hassan replotted the hyperspace jumps and watched as the computer came up with a suggested route.

The targeting reticle snapped to a new system, away from the plane of the galaxy visible in the forward windows. Hassan banked the *Seven Veils* around and triggered the jump.

Frame shift drive charging …

Orbital graveyard, Tionisla system, Alliance

The old lady sat in the cockpit of the ship, just as she had sat there so many times before. The ship had taken her to the edge of beyond, thousands of light years around the galaxy. It had done everything she could possibly have asked of it. Now its last duty was upon it.

And mine …

Thumps echoed from behind her. Her co-conspirator would have tried to stop them. Futile, of course, but every moment was precious. Her sacrifice had bought enough time …

She looked at the text on the console before her, a last message for the universe to decipher. Only those with a knowledge of the past would be able to make sense of it, only those who had the intelligence, education and discretion to prove themselves worthy of the challenge.

Ancient myth, clues in the darkness. It will lead them to the answers at the right time …

The words were strange, echoes of legends from the distant past. A summary, or a culmination, of all the clues she had left to point the way.

The River to the underworld, Gaia's daughter all unfurled. Fourth minor bear in vain, by viper's sting was slain …

The strange poem continued for many stanzas, she didn't have time to review it all. It was ready though, encoded in the transmission and it would be found in time. She toggled the holofac receiver and a man's face appeared.

She nodded at the holofac image before her.

'I have sent her to you,' the old lady said. 'She has to connect the final pieces. She is the last one. They have found us, so you can tell her everything.'

The man nodded. She looked at his grizzled hair with fondness. A neatly cropped salt-and-pepper moustache and beard framed a swarthy face counterpointed by a bright pair of eyes. His voice had a strange accent. She knew it to be Italian.

'Is there …'

'There is nothing to be done. See to her now, she is all that counts. I have sent her to you. She must complete what remains.'

'She will not be happy.'

The old lady grinned. 'We never are. She is going to head to Achenar, I expect. She will need your help.'

The man nodded. 'I will be ready.'

'And Luko …'

'Yes?'

'Thank you,' she said, blinking rapidly and wiped the back of her hand across her eyes. The skin came away moist. 'And goodbye.'

'My Lady, it has been molto honour …'

More thumps from the rear hatch. It cracked open a centimetre. She gestured to the holofac transmitter.

'Time to go.'

'Addio …'

She cancelled the holofac transmission and sighed. She reached out a trembling hand and flicked a switch. A faint green light on the console was the only obvious result.

The rear hatch failed and was jolted open. She spun her pilot's seat around and faced the commander.

She bit down on her lower lip.

'I don't remember you, of course,' she said, with a wry smile. 'Your bosses have done their handiwork too well after all these years. But I'm sure you remember me. You're too late, as usual. I have a new protégé.' She grinned. 'Good luck with the chase.'

The commander clearly had his orders. She watched as he raised his weapon.

After all this time they are actually going to …

Gloved fingers closing on a trigger. She gasped.

… kill me!

The pain was less than she expected. It was neat and tidy. She approved of the marksmanship. Her strength ebbed.

Good fortune, Salomé … make a difference …

Blackness, deeper than any void she'd ever traversed, swirled around her vision. Voices from her past called to her. A lover she had lost, friends, people she had known …

Elite combateers … they always finish what they start …

Only the faintest words from the world of reality reached her. She dimly heard the commander barking orders.

'Scan the graveyard, look for any ships that are jumping out. High wakes, anything. Move!'

A familiar face. An arm held out in greeting. Her last breath was a gasp of recognition.

Oh … Jim!

Void. Endless void.

***

The Dropships had taken only minutes to locate the telltale evidence of Salomé's ship leaving the Tionisla system. Wake scanning technology allowed them to identify the destination of any given hyperspace jump. These were tough multipurpose combat vessels, ideally suited to tracking and pursuing other spacecraft. Modified with superior jump range in mind, they could catch other ships with ease, often jumping ahead of them and forming blockades to catch the unwary.

They were favoured by system authority jurisdictions and navies across the core worlds for this very reason.

'Last jump was the Agartha system,' the commander said. 'Spread out across this trajectory and scan for fuel scooping ships that look like they're in a hurry.'

The Dropships veered off in different directions before disappearing into the darkness with abrupt flashes of energy.

***

The Cobra lay abandoned in the graveyard, gently drifting alongside all the other relics, its drives cold and dead, no navigation lights blinked from its darkened and sombre painted hull. Even in the silence of space, the graveyard had a deathly stillness that transcended the vacuum. Its on-board systems, having detected there were no longer any persons aboard, cut power to the life support systems and liquidised the atmosphere within back into storage tanks.

After a couple of hours, a faint light pulsed in the dim and age-tarnished cockpit of the ship. A console illuminated briefly, power supplies summoning some last reserves of energy from almost exhausted reserves.

A small hatch popped open on the exterior of the vessel. From it rose a small antenna dish. It spun around for a moment and then aligned itself more carefully with a series of short jerks, compensating for the slow roll of the craft. Keen observers would have noticed it was pointing just above the galactic plane, right between a pair of fuzzy patches of light. Distant nebulae near the constellation of Cassiopeia.

Inside the cockpit, a stream of noise signalled a transmission of some sort. A sequence of letters flashed across the single holofac display.

... O T S E A F O T S E A F ...

The symbols repeated several times before the holofac flickered and died. The few remaining lights faded out. The antenna retracted into place as the ship continued to drift in the darkness.

Hera system, Independent

Another star swam into view as the *Seven Veils* dropped out of hyperspace. The fuel tanks were low now. Hassan adjusted course and rolled the ship around so the star was above, glowing fiercely above the canopy a mere few million miles away. The ship vibrated as it pushed against the increasing gravity well.

Ahead, huge loops of plasma arced before them, casting a shimmering orange light across the hull of the ship. Cooling fins extended, radiating heat away into space, fighting a losing battle against the fearsome energy output of the star.

Fuel scooping ...

Hassan's grip on the flight controls was knuckle-white. He hated this. Fuel scooping in haste.

Too easy to make a mistake, get too close and the safeties will cut in, but we'll be stuck there waiting for the cool-down sequence ... completely vulnerable!

Slowly, the fuel tank indicators crept up, but not as quickly as the temperature gauges. Red lights glowed in warning as the ship struggled to keep itself cool.

Warning. Temperature critical.

There was a distinct smell of overheating electronics, an unpleasant hot metal aroma wafting through the cabin. The star was rolling away above them. The strange sound of the fuel scoops funnelling in the solar plasma and liquefying it echoed from below decks.

Still need more ...

With agonising slowness, the fuel tank continued to fill. Hassan almost felt he could smell the burning as the ship's temperature soared past safe limits.

Come on ...

Hassan pulled the ship away from the star, relieved to see the temperature begin to drop. The fins retracted and the ship surged away into the darkness.

Fuel scooping complete.

A flicker appeared on the scanner. Another ship arriving from hyperspace. Most likely a trader, simply doing something similar to them, refuelling for another jump ...

Scan detected ...

'Shit! They've found us.'

'Jump now!'

'We don't have the whole route plotted ...'

'Just do it. What system is in range?'

Hassan flicked the holofac system roster on his left-hand side and scrolled down the list.

'It's someplace called Cemiess ...'

'Cemiess it is, go! We've got to escape this trap. I need to speak to Luko!'

Frame shift drive charging ...

Hassan pushed the throttles to their stops, willing the ship to accelerate. It responded sluggishly, still hampered by the overwhelming mass of the nearby star.

We're being herded; somebody wants us to go this way ...

The *Seven Veils* flickered and disappeared.

***

The GalNet feed burbled to itself as it had done for years, the holofac transmitter doing its job oblivious to the fact that no one was paying it the slightest attention. The patrons of the bar were far too interested in, or inebriated by, the contents of the tankards, glasses and other beverage containers around them.

'An unusual event occurred recently, which hasn't been seen for over a hundred years. A new ship was introduced into the Tionisla Orbital Graveyard.

'Originally a final resting place for the fantastically rich and famous in the 3100s, the graveyard fell into disuse after the general economic slump that beset the Old Worlds at the time.

'Something of a backwater today, Tionisla was once a major trading hub and communication complex in times past. With the graveyard itself having fallen into disrepair, with many of its relics vandalised and looted, it came as something of a surprise when the request was received by the Tionislan government.

'Despite the odd circumstances behind the request, the Tionislan government has surprised observers by moving swiftly to ensure that the application was processed forthwith. Tionislan administrative red tape is typically appalling, even for hard-nosed bureaucrats. In this case, the individual appears to have been some kind of celeb, perhaps warranting a fast track of some kind.

'Just before the vessel was moved to its final resting place, an onboard beacon briefly activated, transmitting a series of curious characters in a repeating sequence. This continued for a few minutes until a power failure silenced it. The significance of this transmission, if any, is unclear.'

"'I shouldn't worry about it," said Grace Mayweather, "We see this sort of thing all the time. A last bit of mischief – tricks, codes – even traps for the unwary sometimes. Pay it no heed. They're just messing with your head from beyond the grave! People go mad trying to work these things out, they never mean anything."'

Chapter Seven

Pleiades sector, Uninhabited

'I suppose you're wondering what it's all about. The clues. The messages. Well, I'll tell you. We found something, me and my associates. Something the whole galaxy will want to see. You want to know what it is, right? Well, I'd love to tell you ... but with information this valuable, I'd be a fool to give it away for free ...'

'Yeah, buddy, but you need to give us something.'

Commander Noctrach had been puzzling over the words for quite some time, sifting them for any hidden meaning, but coming up blank. He cursed and flicked the holofac off.

What kind of stupid message is that, anyway? We're being played here.

Noctrach had joined the Canonn research group only a few short weeks before, intrigued by the mystery of the Barnacles and with the blessing of his own faction, the Maxwell Corporation. Codes and secret scripts weren't his thing. Searching and reconnoitring though? That he could do.

His ship, the FRV *Physeter*, was originally a fairly ordinary Federal Dropship. Retired from the Navy, he'd modified it for deep space exploration and reconnaissance. It had proved a worthy workhorse.

The wideband comms flickered for attention. It was his Canonn colleagues calling in. Noctrach recognised the oriental features of Commander Balalaika. For some reason, he insisted on having the suffix 'x3' listed alongside his name. Noctrach had no idea what it meant. A moment later, Commander Ihazevich's image popped in alongside.

'Hi, Commanders.'

Balalaika wasted no time with introductions, it was not his style.

'I think I have decoded the audio. Thought we'd give it a whirl before reporting it to that pompous ass, Arcanonn.'

'Really?' Noctrach was surprised. The best brains in Canonn had been puzzling over that one for weeks, each potential explanation more outlandish than the next. They even had a word for the fruitless attempts to decode the enigmatic message ... 'tinfoiling.'

'Another clue came through. Community work over in Cail. Pleiades sector, somewhere along the AB vector.'

Noctrach's heart sank.

'That's still dozens of systems. It'll take years.'

Balalaika grinned. 'Lucky you have my humble genius at your disposal, then. I cross-referenced the chart from the audio with any systems on the AB vector.'

'And I found a match,' Ihazevich said, his laconic voice indicating little other than the bare facts.

'What! Where?'

'Pleiades Sector AB-W B2-4 9 A.' Ihazevich said, looking at a readout. 'It's a barren moon. According to the stats, it has not been explored yet.'

'Can't check it myself, too far out,' Balalaika said. 'Can you?'

Noctrach fired up the galactic chart and examined it quickly.

'A few jumps, but doable.'

'It is the same for me,' Ihazevich replied.

'One more thing,' Balalaika said. 'We have what looks like a latitude marker. Minus 26. That's all I have.'

'Should be enough, if it's accurate.'

'Good hunting, commanders.'

Balalaika's image faded out. Noctrach turned to Ihazevich.

'Shall we?'

'You will have to move very swiftly to arrive there before me.'

'I'll take that challenge …'

***

It was hidden in the dark, deep in the shadows cast in stark contrast to the unending grey vista that stretched out beyond. How long it had lain there could not be easily determined. Days, months, years … perhaps aeons. Little changed on this airless rocky world in many lives of humans. There was no air, water or other corrosive agents, no plate tectonics or volcanism, and only the occasional meteorite impact to break the monotony.

Today though, lights flickered in the sky far above. They slowly grew in brightness and size until the forms of angular vessels came into sight, their thrusters and hull lights casting erratic illumination around the base of a rocky outcrop.

With a brief flurry of dust, the ships settled, motion ceasing for long minutes. Then, silent in the vacuum, hatches opened, depositing small six-wheeled vehicles onto the surface. These scurried forwards, quickly at first, before slowing to a crawl.

Their own lights illuminated the shape, throwing an artificial glow across it.

Vast petals, bent and broken, with a faintly iridescent sheen, were cast haphazardly about the rocky surface. In the centre lay a twisted ovoid shape, curved and clearly the heart of whatever vehicle or creature had come to grief in this lonely location.

It was cast into sharp relief by the bright lights, its vast bulk dwarfing them into insignificance. The last resting place of something that had nothing to do with the humans that looked upon its wreck with awe and fear.

Unknown. Alien?

***

The holofac news transmission continued to burble to itself unattended.

'… Fleet forces continue to build in the Mu Koji system, with Imperial and Federation forces battling over Military Intelligence, whilst over in Pleiades Sector AB-W B2-4, an Imperial Interdictor is reported heading towards the wreckage of the now infamous unknown ship …'

Commander Watts waved at the holofac idly, cancelling the transmission. He'd been listening to it over and over. As with most news broadcasts, there was no additional information to be gleaned after the first few minutes. He caught sight of himself reflected in the canopy. The goatee and long wavy hair looked a little unkempt. Exploration did that to you.

Empire's trying to lock down the sector. Unbelievable. They think they have an automatic right to …

Gravity warnings began to flash. His Diamondback Explorer was closing on the moon.

No name yet, just Pleiades Sector AB-W B2-4 9 A. Gotta get there quick, capture some footage and scans before the opportunity is lost.

The ship shuddered around him as the fail-safes dropped him out of supercruise, the moon now an icy landscape before him. It was a long way out, the starlight was faint with little heat.

Faint creaks and groans came from the superstructure around him as the ship settled into the moon's gravity well. Vertical thrusters ignited and began adjusting the ship's course as it glided down towards its destination.

Watts reviewed the geo-location plots.

Three valleys, just like the newsfeed. This is the right place.

He squinted. There was something there. More than one object, several … some were above the surface …

The contact display lit up with a red-tinged warning and a rough authoritarian voice echoed through the cockpit.

'No unauthorised ships allowed in this area! You have ten seconds to comply!'

Watts spun the scanners rapidly through the targets that were flickering on the forward edge of his scanner. The biggest confirmed his fears.

An Interdictor. They're already here!

Watts' onboard computer flashed up a warning.

Ship scan detected. 'Shit!'

The rough voice came again.

'We've got a contact in the restricted zone. Engage with impunity, weapons free! Target is a Diamondback Explorer, Commander Callsign, DriftedIsland.'

He pulled back on the controls. The Diamondback roared as power was transferred to the engines, but the ship was sluggish in the growing gravity and yawed to one side. The massive bulk of the Imperial Interdictor slid into view. Watts adjusted heading and barely managed to arrest the descent of his vehicle, slipping over the smooth white hull of the enormous Imperial ship. He got an uncomfortably close view of a massive dual-barrelled cannon amidships. Fortunately, it didn't fire.

Once clear, he could see the stars again, the Diamondback was gathering speed.

'Frame shift …'

He toggled the controls, jabbing at the necessary buttons. Plasma erupted behind him and the shields flickered.

The computer flashed up more messages.

Frame shift inhibited by factor of 12. Disruptive mass!

'Don't need this! Faster, dammit!'

More plasma fire. The shriek of shields stressed to breaking point. The Diamondback lurched and jolted. The scanner was a blur of angry red flickering marks.

Boost! Too many ships …

Then came the countdown. Watts centred the controls, as the timer hit zero.

'Engage.'

Stars flickered and seemed to surge towards him. He was out of their range and not a moment too soon.

A glance at the readouts showed it had been a close thing. The shields were virtually gone. The lightweight alloys of the hull wouldn't have been much protection against Imperial fighters. The exploration loadout of the ship wasn't up to running a gauntlet.

I got lucky. Lesson learned. Better not push it …

A few light years in towards the core worlds, another exploration vessel was having trouble with the authorities.

Flickering blue light scattered off the name plate of the ship as it slowed in the strange aura of supercruise and submitted to the vessels that had caught it.

Snake Eyes.

It was a Python-class ship, sturdy and well made, if rather slow and bulky, the design had been around for hundreds of years. This one had a slightly chequered past, its current owner having stumbled across it in the depths of space, abandoned by its former crew after an unfortunate canopy breach.

Hey, it was a free ship!

He still felt a little guilty about it, but it wasn't illegal …

'Scan detected!'

I hope …

Two Vipers. Federation markings, slotting in behind him. The scanner showed they had hardpoints deployed. Ready for a fight.

'Commander Skolios, you are entering a combat zone, be advised that we are not able to provide system authority response in this sector. Capital ships are incoming and this is likely to be a war before long. Avoid the exclusion area.'

'Copy that,' Skolios returned. 'Just here to capture the story …'

There was a disparaging laugh over the comms. 'Unarmed? Rather you than me, buddy.'

The Vipers peeled away, apparently satisfied. They had little to worry about on his account; the *Snake Eyes* had triggers all right, but no guns, just cameras. It was kitted out for speed and survivability.

Skolios grinned to himself.

GalNet Space Photojournalist of the Year, here we come!

He'd watched the growing tensions carefully, working out fleet movements and making good educated guesses as to the waypoints the two power blocks would use. He was sure it was going to happen here and happen soon …

The *Snake Eyes* rolled. Quickly, he corrected the turn and looked up. Barely two kilometres away space was writhing and twisting. A black shadow crackled, lit from within by bolts of lightning.

Federal Battlecruiser. Yes!

He rolled the ship around to get a better view as the massive bulk emerged from hyperspace. He could make out the enormous identification plates.

FNS Gellan.

The cameras aboard his ship whirred, taking in the scene before him and converting it to holofac footage he'd be able to transmit back to civilisation the moment he cleared the zone.

Contacts flickered on the scanners, a new formation of ships. He turned the cameras onto them, seeing a brace of Imperial fighters swooping in, peppering the Federal battlecruiser with small arms fire. It responded in kind, light multi-cannon and plasma weapons forming a defensive arc around the ship. The Imperial fighters veered off and a troupe of Federal Condors swooped in behind, trading fire.

Just the warm up act …

Space crackled again, light blazed around the form of another ship, sleek and elongated, festooned with weapons that spun around and opened fire even before the entire ship had emerged from transit.

Majestic-class Interdictor! It's happening …

The Imperial ship was further away, having materialised on the starboard bow of the Federal battlecruiser. Weapons streaked across space. Bulkheads ruptured, spewing crew and equipment into the void.

Wow! There's not been a battle like this since that skirmish in the Prism system … almost war then, got to be the real deal this time.

Huge turrets spun and locked. Beam and projectile weapons clashed in the void, space was littered with debris. All the while, smaller ships looped and spun around the larger vessels, fighting their own battles amidst the carnage.

Something flew out of the darkness. Wreckage, most likely. It cannoned off the *Snake Eyes'* shields and sent the ship into a dizzying spin.

Beam weapons tracked, turreting around to line up with his vessel.

'Shields offline,' the computer announced.

'Time to get out of here!'

Skolios wrestled the controls back and forth to counter the spin and push the engines to full burn. The Python roared up away from the battle.

Just wait 'til this gets out on GalNet!

Deep space, Atlantis system, Empire

'I have them, sir. Fuel scooping Imperial Clipper, registry *Seven Veils*. They're jumping now. Scanning wake … Heading for Cemiess.'

The commander grinned. 'All ships, jump to adjacent systems, best possible speed.'

'We not going in after them?' one of his colleagues queried.

'Not our part. We're only here to ensure they don't escape.'

His pilot handled the manoeuvre, allowing him to settle back in the secondary seat and contemplate the moment.

'So, the threads are entwined, as we suspected.'

He triggered a secure commlink, watching as a series of encrypted data links organised themselves, redundantly transmitting via several different relay points.

The response was immediate, audio only. He'd never seen any faces; that was not how it worked.

'Commander?'

'We are tracking a vessel that made a rendezvous with the lady.'

'Which ship?'

'An Imperial Clipper. The *Seven Veils.*'

There was a distinct pause from the other end.

'Most gratifying, Commander.'

'We've chased them into Cemiess as required.'

'Excellent. Hold station, Commander. We will do the rest.'

***

The *Seven Veils* burst out of hyperspace, still trailing plumes of plasma from its brush with the previous star.

'We're almost out of fuel,' Hassan said. 'It will take five minutes to refuel via the scoops …'

'Too long,' Salomé said. 'Head for one of the moons. We can hide there easily enough.'

The ship turned and headed out into the darkness, accelerating away from the star.

Hassan watched the scanners, a few other ships were showing, but a quick surreptitious assessment showed they were not on parallel courses. Most were heading out-system, towards the main station, Mackenzie Relay.

'Who the hell are these people?'

Salomé sighed. 'Hired hands, most likely. Paid to do the will of whomsoever wants the truth of all this hidden.'

Blips appeared on the scanner. Hassan scrutinised them.

'Heading this way.'

'See if you can outrun them.'

Hassan cancelled the target lock he'd been using and pushed the engines up to full power, watching the speed rapidly increase. Already the ship was flitting through space at many times the speed of light.

Salomé accessed the comm system, rapidly typing out a message.

Erimus, advise the Children of Raxxla to expand their expedition to the Formidine Rift. Whatever lies there, we must be close to discovering it. It is vital that we find out what it is. I'm sorry I can't meet with you in person …

She gestured for the first line of the text to be sent, but the comm system buzzed angrily in return.

Unable to transmit. Message failed.

'We're being jammed,' she said. 'Erimus will be expecting a message to relay, but if we can't notify him, then they'll never know …'

The scanner marks astern were closing rapidly, clearly trying to catch them.

'They're overhauling us,' Hassan said. 'Thirty light seconds … they're going to ...'

With an abrupt twist, the ship spun off course. Disrupted frame shift energy coruscated outside the canopy, a dizzying whirl of blue and cyan. Stars whirled about them, the ship pitching and yawing as if possessed.

Interdicted!

Salomé could see that Hassan was trying to wrestle the ship back on course. Onboard flight computers provided him with a vector, but it jumped and spun away regardless of what he tried. The Clipper was simply too heavy and ungainly to match the agility of whatever it was that was trying to wrench them back into normal space.

Not going to work. Submit and we'll run!

'Don't fight it!' she yelled.

Hassan pulled the throttles back and heard the drone of the engines as they spiralled down their efforts to evade the pursuers.

With a flash and a horrendous groan, the *Seven Veils* materialised back in the universe of traditional physics, spinning and yawing out of control, its thrusters trying in vain to bring its erratic motion under control.

Hull integrity compromised!

The spin subsided. Hassan was shaking his head to clear it. Salomé could feel the nausea rising in her stomach. It was enough to make even the hardiest pilot feel sick.

Four ships streaked out of the darkness.

Hassan pushed the throttles to their stops and diverted all power to engines. The *Seven Veils* surged forward.

Frame shift drive charging …

'Let's see if we can lose them this way …' he said.

Laser fire crashed against the shields. The healthy cyan glow of the shield indicators quickly faded to a dim red. The *Seven Veils* wasn't set up as a fighter, but as a long duration exploration vessel. Fighting wasn't an option …

Shields failed!

Salomé heard the unpleasant crackling as laser fire burnt across the hull, swiftly followed by the heavier thumps of multi-cannon rounds.

Thruster malfunction!

Power-plant malfunction!

Frame shift drive offline!

'They're taking out the modules!' Hassan yelled.

The ships streaked around them. Salomé could see they were Imperial vessels, bright white against the darkness of space. But they bore no markings, no faction or system identifiers.

She feverously brought up the comms system, setting it to wideband transmission, diverting all the ship's remaining power.

Facece system, Empire

Several systems away, a rugged gunmetal grey ship hung in the darkness of space. The Diamondback Explorer was not the most aesthetically pleasing ship to behold, but it was designed for a role and it performed it well. The pilot aboard was carrying a cargo of medical relief supplies by direct request from the Emperor herself, but the ship was off course, making a wide swing out to the edges of Imperial space.

Lyrae looked at her schedule. She could still make the deliveries, but this diversion wasn't going to look good if she got tracked. Questions would be asked, questions she'd rather not answer. She was supposed to be on station in the Facece system, not out here, halfway to the Pleiades cluster.

But those stories ... if it's true and we really have found evidence ...

Curiosity had got the better of her. She had to know, so she'd worked her schedule to allow herself to make a major detour.

Static crackled on the wideband.

Some kind of long range transmission?

Whatever it was, it was weak. She boosted the gain, trying to make it out. A heavy rhythmic thumping overlaid the signal. Someone was trying to jam it. Static laced the faint sounds of a woman's voice, high with distress.

'... dine Rift expedition is ...'

Lyrae adjusted the comm system, struggling to make out the words.

'The situation is out of control, they do not want us to find ... oh, no ... I have incoming ships ... hostile ... they ... Hassan! Evasive! Before ...'

She triangulated the origin of the signal, quickly working out its origin. It was dozens of light years distant, back in her deployment loop. The Cemiess system.

'Commander, receiving you. Advise on your precise position.'

Static crackled back, buzzing in her ears.

'Heavy fire ... mayday! Imperial markings! Traitors ... shields are down, we're taking damage ... it's ... I thought I sensed his arrogance! How dare ...'

She managed to get a comm-trace locked despite the interference. The sender's profile popped on the nearby holofac display. She recognised it; her name had been splashed across the GalNet newsfeeds in recent weeks, and not in a nice way.

'Commander Salomé ...'

She was something of an enigma, some claimed she was the missing Senator of the Prism system, Lady Kahina Loren, others that she was a troublemaker lurking on the edges of the core worlds, fanning the flames of discontent amongst the disaffected. Some claimed both.

Lyrae adjusted her own transmitters, sending out a call to her colleagues, running similar errands to hers in nearby systems. Only one responded. Her faction, the Chapterhouse of Inquisition, was spread thinly across the core worlds.

'Quantum Delpha, acknowledging …'

'Commander, we have an Imperial civilian under attack in the Cemiess system. Transmission is being jammed, unlikely system authority ships will receive it.'

'Plotting course now …'

Lyrae activated her own frame shift drive and plotted a course.

'Commander Salomé, Lyrae here! We're fifteen minutes out and en route. Standby!'

The transmission crackled again. The woman's tones were calmer now, measured, but still laced with fear.

'Commander Lyrae. We're … boarded. I only … moments. Please get … the Children of Raxxla … Commander Erimus … tell them I have uncovered … The Rift … Hawking's Gap … Conflux are somehow … strange happenings in the Pleiades … they must find out before …'

There was a rapid burst of noise, shouts and scuffles, then the comms went silent, other than the faint background hiss of distant stars. As she watched, the now vacant holofac was filled with a news article from the Imperial Citizen. Lyrae listened in bewilderment and increasing anger as the article played out.

'You 'stards!' Lyrae cried out, punching the console in frustration. 'You lying 'stards! How dare you twist the truth like this …'

The smug voice of the broadcaster finished in assured tones.

'… Beautiful, charming and charismatic she may well be, but the truth is Lady Kahina is a bloodthirsty, scheming, manipulative and selfish individual who will stop at nothing to achieve whatever she is aiming to do. Do not trust a word she utters.'

The holofac display faded out.

Mackenzie Relay, Cemiess system, Empire

'Demand? What demand?' the station administrator yelled. 'Get those ships out of there! They're blocking the designated flight path.'

'They refuse to move, sir,' the operator replied. 'They claim they're blockading the system.'

'Blockading the …'

The administrator stared at the holofac monitors. Sure enough, a flotilla of ships had positioned themselves outside the station perimeter and were blocking incoming vessels. They were firing warning shots across the bows of approaching traders, who quickly turned and retreated out of range. The offending ships were clearly well armed, and whilst no threat to the station, he wasn't convinced his system authority vessels were immediately capable of mounting a resistance.

'Who are they and what the hell do they want?'

'Their idents show them to belong to a faction called the Children of Raxxla, sir,' the operative said, shaking his head in bewilderment. 'They claim we're holding somebody and demand her release.'

'Who?'

'Somebody called Salomé.'

'Who the hell is Salomé?' the administrator demanded. No one had an answer for him. 'Tell them we have no one in our jurisdiction by that name and that if they don't end their blockade immediately I'll get the Imperial military in here to boil their backsides!'

Chapter Eight

Location unknown

Lights, harsh and bright, blistered into his eyes. Hassan flailed back but was brought up short. He was held in restraints, somehow secured to a chair, his wrists tied to its arms. It was rock solid, bolted to the floor. He heard the heavy clunk of mag-boots moving around somewhere nearby.

Everything was blurry. He blinked rapidly, trying to clear his vision.

'He's awake. Advise the patrons.'

Patrons?

He heard a door slide open and the mag-boots clicked away. He could just make out figures ahead of him. One seemed huge, the other thin and tall.

'All yours,' said a voice. The door slid back with a hiss of pressure. 'Let us know if you need our assistance.'

He could see better now. Two men in Imperial garb, swathed in robes secured by jewel-encrusted brooches and clasps. The larger of the two lowered himself into a chair across from him, whereas the thin one remained standing.

Gravity. We must be on a planet or a moon somewhere ...

Hassan frowned. He'd seen these two before. His memory came back.

Boarded! They stormed the ship, stun weapons! Imperials ... but why?

'Hassan Farrukh Sharma,' the large man intoned, his voice deep and gravelly. 'We have the pleasure of making your acquaintance once again. I trust our Imperial guards haven't left you too incapacitated. Stuns are rather like being inebriated, so I understand, though obviously without the prior pleasant effects.'

The man was smiling genially.

Hassan shook his head to clear it.

These two, they were patrons on Prism, I remember them from Salomé's ceremony ...

The large man caught his look of recognition.

'Ah ... light dawns. You see, Zyair? Our fame has spread a little.'

Zyair and ...

'Gerrun,' Hassan managed to say.

'Indeed,' Gerrun said. 'My traditional acknowledgement would have been to say that I am at your service, but alas, I'm afraid we're not at your service at all at present. Though, if you cooperate, you may find yourself at ours.'

Hassan was struggling to follow Gerrun's mode of speech.

'Cooperate?'

'Do as we say,' Zyair said, enunciating each word as if talking to an idiot.

'You were Salomé's pilot, I understand,' Gerrun continued patiently.

Hassan bucked against his restraints.

'What have you done with her?' he demanded.

'She has been arrested,' Gerrun said.

'And charged,' Zyair added.

'With what?' Hassan asked. 'She's done nothing wrong.'

'On the contrary,' Gerrun said, his face split by a wide grin. 'The attempted assassination of Fleet Admiral Patreus, whilst I can certainly sympathise with and appreciate the motivation, is very much considered to be a crime.'

'Patreus?' Hassan spluttered. 'She didn't …'

'The evidence rather suggests otherwise,' Gerrun finished, smoothly. 'She's been aligning herself with many rather ne'er-do-well factions for quite some time now.'

'No,' Hassan said. 'She's being framed, you can't let this happen. You know Salomé, she wouldn't do anything like this …'

'She does have a rather bloodthirsty reputation, alas,' Gerrun said. 'Running people through with swords does spring to mind, alongside an unfortunate habit of starting space battles. A most unpleasant experience for all concerned.'

'The youth of today,' Zyair tutted and rolled his eyes.

'As an accomplice to that attempt,' Gerrun said, in an offhand manner while examining the tips of his fingers. 'Imperial justice is likely to treat you rather …' He turned to look Hassan right in the eye. 'Well … zealously. They do take rather a dim view of this sort of thing. Execution is quite commonplace.'

Hassan felt a wave of panic wash over him.

'Of course,' Zyair added, 'We want to help. Protest her and your innocence and such like …'

'But she is innocent!' Hassan yelled. 'She's hasn't attacked Patreus …'

Hassan saw Gerrun glance at Zyair with something akin to a smile of satisfaction.

'Perish the thought!' Gerrun said. 'We will be doing our utmost to ensure Lady Salomé is cleared of these accusations. We're merely asking for your help in this.'

'Such an Imperial beauty, is she not?' Zyair said. 'Charismatic, charming …'

Hassan swallowed. He couldn't stop the image of Salomé that swam into his mind, dressed in fine white silk, the dress hugging her figure …

Zyair coughed for attention.

'However,' Gerrun continued. 'Imperial justice is a tricky beast at the best of times. If she is found guilty, your position will be rather … awkward. It might be advantageous for you to vouchsafe certain information about her …'

'I won't betray her!' Hassan said. 'I …'

'Well, my fine fellow,' Gerrun said, getting to his feet. 'Fine sentiments indeed. Doubtless your feelings for her will be some comfort to you in the brief but painful moments that lie ahead. I'm glad we had this little chat.'

'Likewise,' said Zyair, who had also stood up and was making preparations to leave.

'But … why?' Hassan demanded, a frown creasing his forehead.

'Salves the conscience to know we tried,' Gerrun said, patting Hassan's shoulder.

'We wouldn't want anyone to accuse us of not trying,' Zyair said. 'Though we rather thought you'd be more accommodating, based on your previous experiences at the hands of that … now what was her name?'

'Olivia?' Gerrun mused. 'No … Ah, I have it. Octavia, that was it.'

'You're right, of course,' Zyair agreed.

Octavia Quinton!

She had tortured him. Visions of a knife, embedded in his palm, his shoulder … she was a sadistic drug baron who inflicted pain for her own titillation …

The door snapped open at some unseen signal. Hassan could make out guards outside, dressed in Imperial uniforms. He could see the one in the lead was holding some kind of metal instrument. Hassan's eyes widened as he made out a cudgel.

'Fleet Admiral Patreus is rather vexed,' Gerrun said and winked.

Hassan squirmed in his chair, but it was to no avail. Gerrun and Zyair stood aside to let the guard in. A shadow fell on Hassan, the guard was so tall he was blotting out the light in the cell. The cudgel was raised in one hand and tapped into the palm of the other.

'No …' Hassan managed, bucking against the chair in a frantic attempt to break free. He heard footsteps and then the sound of the cell door sliding closed.

The guard advanced, the cudgel raised, glinting in the light.

***

Salomé was marched unceremoniously through the corridors of the ship. She was cuffed at the wrists, her sword confiscated. She was escorted by two guards in Imperial attire. Judging by the interior, the ship was a Cutter, a svelte ship ideal for ferrying around important dignitaries and their entire support staff. Through portholes in the hull she briefly caught sight of a desolate grey surface, a moon or other body. They could be anywhere.

She was pushed onwards to the midsection, which, in classic Imperial style, was decked out luxuriously in the manner of the plush hotels of the home systems. A door ahead slid back with an efficient whirr.

She didn't move, but was shoved through regardless.

'Ah …' said a voice. 'Senator Kahina Tijani Loren, or just Salomé, perhaps. A pleasure once again.'

Salomé's eyes widened.

'You …'

Her gaze took in the obese frame of Patron Gerrun, reclining on a chaise longue, helping himself to fruit from a bowl. Across from him sat another man she recognised, Patron Zyair. They were the pair that had schemed with her erstwhile mentor, Dalk Torgen. A scheme that had ended up with her family being assassinated and herself put through months of torment to reclaim her homeworld.

'How dare you!'

She had made short work of their careers in the Prism system upon returning to power. With Ambassador Cuthrick's help, she had banished them from her home, not caring what happened to them. The last she had heard was some obscure report of them falling upon hard times on Achenar, but she had not paid heed.

Perhaps I should have done.

'Dare?' Zyair said. 'We dare much.'

'When Cuthrick gets to hear about this …'

'Powers rather greater than pompous old Ambassador Cuthrick Delaney are in play,' Gerrun said, his smile still firmly in place. 'You did little to cultivate allies in the heart of the Empire, and since you did not take the opportunity to avail yourself of our sage counsel in the Prism system …'

'You schemed against me,' Salomé retorted. 'Perhaps I should have run you through too.'

She saw Zyair step back, though Gerrun seemed unfazed.

'Empty threats, my dear,' Gerrun said with a chuckle.

'Then this one will not be,' Salomé said. 'I have allies beyond the Empire. Snatching me out of space will not have gone unnoticed. Release me and I'll be lenient. I know what you want.'

'Do you indeed?' Gerrun answered.

Salomé scoffed. 'Position and power in your case, money, wealth, prestige and a life free from complication in his.' Salomé gestured towards Zyair. 'I know you well enough.'

Zyair nodded. 'A fair appraisal.'

'Indeed,' Gerrun said. 'Though missing one element.'

'And what is that?' Salomé demanded.

Zyair licked his lips, but it was Gerrun who spoke.

'Revenge,' he said.

Salomé looked from one to the other.

'I do appreciate it's somewhat unrefined,' Gerrun said, 'But it will be most satisfying to have you brought low for the benefit of our amusement. And others in positions of even greater influence than yours share our agenda.'

'You just try it …' Salomé growled.

'Oh, we already have it planned,' Gerrun said. 'It's no accident that we have interdicted you here in the Cemiess system. Such an opportunity was too good to pass up. Loose ends being tidied, that sort of thing.'

'And shocking behaviour on your part,' Zyair said, his face cracking into an unpleasant grin.

A frown grew on Salomé's face. 'My part?'

'Trying to assassinate Fleet Admiral Denton Patreus,' Gerrun said. 'Gauche, even for you, but entirely in character.'

'Patreus?' Salomé gasped in astonishment.

'He will be delighted the individual that bankrolled his would-be assassins has been found.' Zyair said.

'You can't prove this; it's a charade, complete nonsense!'

She lurched forward, but the pair of guards held her tight.

Gerrun smiled. 'Of course it's a charade. And a well-orchestrated one at that. But you've been careless, Senator.' Gerrun dripped scorn on the title. 'Did you really think your antics would be ignored? Those little speeches railing against our Imperial benefactors? Leaving your calling card where it might be found …?'

Salomé's eyes narrowed. 'What?'

'Those deluded fools from the Emperor's Dawn faction,' Zyair said. 'Flocking to your banner.'

'Who in the void are the Emperor's Dawn?' Salomé asked, confused.

'I'm surprised you don't remember,' Gerrun said. 'They have admitted swearing undying loyalty to one Commander Salomé, erstwhile Senator Kahina Loren of the Prism system, sworn to carry out her wishes. That is, they did swear, before they were unfortunately killed whilst trying to escape.' Gerrun looked over towards Zyair. 'Your little detail as I remember? A very nice touch I thought.'

Zyair smirked. 'A little flair is sometimes required.'

Salomé's mind raced through their scheming, trying to figure out what they were trying to accomplish.

'What do you want of me?'

'Of you?' Gerrun said. 'We want nothing at all, my dear. We simply want the satisfaction of seeing you fall from grace. A fall far worse that the one you inflicted upon our good selves.' His voice hardened. 'We want you to experience the uncertainty, the fear …'

'The humiliation and the turmoil …' Zyair added.

'The shame and embarrassment …' Gerrun continued.

'The loss of face and respect …'

'And end up wretched and alone, your rank and reputation soiled beyond redemption,' Gerrun finished. 'We, on the other hand, will be elevated back to our right and proper positions.'

'I still have those who will intercede on my behalf,' Salomé said, struggling against the guards. 'You won't get away with this.'

'On the contrary,' Zyair said. 'We have cultivated powerful friends in your absence, waiting for the opportunity. It is they who want you, or rather, don't want you. Our needs are more emotive. Revenge will satisfy us completely.'

'You could say our stars have aligned,' Gerrun said. 'There are many who would like to see you … dealt with.'

'They will not get what they want,' Salomé returned, 'I have taken steps to ensure that.'

'Your dalliance as the patron saint of explorers?' Gerrun answered. 'The Children of Raxxla? They are busy making fools of themselves here in Cemiess as we speak, pawns in the game and unaware they are being played. Those we serve have means, subtle and otherwise, to extract what they wish from you.'

'Then let Hassan go, at least,' Salomé said. 'He was merely my pilot. He is innocent of this intrigue and has done nothing to harm you!'

'Commendable concern for your co-conspirator,' Gerrun said. 'But misplaced, I fear.'

'You cannot protect him,' Zyair said, a cruel smile fixed in place. 'Think on how you are responsible for his demise.'

'No, don't do this …' Salomé said. 'Leave him alone!'

'Take her away,' Gerrun said, with a wave of his hand. Salomé was dragged off, struggling futilely.

Gerrun waited until the doors had snapped closed before turning to Zyair. 'I thought that went rather well, all things considered.'

'The sooner she is dealt with, the better,' Zyair replied.

Gerrun chuckled. 'There are many paths we can choose for her at this stage. Right now the obvious one is playing out, but there are others that need consideration.Those require some insurance to guarantee we can take advantage of them should the need arise.'

'Insurance?' Zyair asked.

'Leave it with me, my dear fellow,' Gerrun replied. 'Her co-pilot should suit our needs perfectly. He's proved himself to be a flexible chap in the past and he clearly carries a torch for our dear ex-senator, if I read him right. I think we can take advantage … I mean … appeal to his better nature. Some drugs may help, too.'

'Do what needs to be done.'

Gerrun chuckled. 'I will deal with it immediately.'

***

Consciousness returned. Hassan could barely see; the world about him vague and blurred. Pain though, that was clear and present.

The guard, the cudgel …

Hassan tried not to remember, but the guard had been thorough and practised. He'd asked no questions, simply pummelled Hassan into oblivion. He could smell sweat and taste blood on his swollen lips. He could hear his breathing come in ragged gasps.

Voices swirled about him, loud and confusing, echoing in his mind. He shuddered.

Words didn't make sense, he must have passed out.

He hung, slumped forward, supported only by his wrists, still secured to the arms of the chair. He raised his head, just able to make out the guard. The cudgel cradled in his hands, stained with dark smears.

'I trust you remember well enough now,' a voice said. Hassan struggled for a moment to sort the words into an order he could comprehend.

Patron …

'A rather primitive technique, I will admit, but effective nonetheless.'

Gerrun …

Hassan managed to look up at him with one eye, the other was swollen shut.

'Are you prepared to be more reasonable this time?' Gerrun asked. 'Alas, I will not be able to repeat this offer a third time, it seems unlikely you will … survive the experience. Zyair does not have the stomach for such things, but I have to admit I rather relish them.'

'I …'

'Before you make your decision,' Gerrun said. 'I must advise you that we have taken advantage of the situation to fully evaluate your predilections.'

Hassan gaped at him, uncomprehending.

'We know what you desire,' Gerrun explained. 'Rather unethical, of course, probing your memories and psyche without permission, but such are the times we live in. I am prepared to offer you a deal.'

Hassan blinked, but didn't otherwise respond.

'If you're not interested, we can proceed with the inevitable. You are completely expendable, my young friend. Your demise will be rather drawn out, naturally. Such is the nature of things.'

Gerrun signalled to the guard, who moved forward, the cudgel raised once more.

Hassan juddered against his restraints and shook his head.

'No …' he rasped. 'Tell me …'

'Very well,' Gerrun said, settling into a chair opposite him. 'Lady Kahina has betrayed the Empire and will stand trial for the attempted assassination of Fleet Admiral Patreus. Whilst not wishing to presume the outcome of our Imperial justice system, it would seem likely that bad news awaits her.'

Hassan shook his head.

'No ... not true ...'

'I'm afraid it's a foregone conclusion, my young fellow. There is nothing you can do about it. You can either profit from the situation, or ... well, I don't think I need to explain the details, do I?'

Hassan shivered.

'Clearly not,' Gerrun continued. He tapped the table and a holofac image appeared. It was Salomé, standing in a flowing gown, slowly rotating between them.

'Quite a beauty, is she not?' Gerrun said. 'I can understand your infatuation.'

Hassan swallowed at the sight of her.

'You might call it love, or lust, or obsession,' Gerrun said. 'But she is a senator, a high-ranking Imperial lady, far out of the reach of your grubby little hands. Unrequited love! Poets have waxed lyrical across the centuries of such tragedies. Lovers separated by society, or class or allegiance.'

'I won't ...'

'Betray her?' Gerrun said. 'That tired refrain? I know, my friend. I know. But we don't want you to betray her, we want you to ... cherish her, occupy her ... ensure she no longer causes such consternation in the echelons of Imperial society.'

Hassan frowned, 'But ...'

'But how?' Gerrun said, his smile widening. 'She is a formidable spirit, is she not? A wild sprite, impossible to tame? Oh, but there are ways ...'

Gerrun tapped a control on the holofac and Salomé's dress faded away, revealing her naked body, slowly revolving between them. Her lithe form, slim and athletic from her constant practice and prowess with her sword blade. The curve of her ... enticing, beguiling ... Hassan could not stop staring at her image. Desire, hot and blinding, grew in him. The room faded away about him, there was only ... Salomé.

'We can arrange for her personality to be moulded,' Gerrun said, his words throbbing through Hassan's consciousness, warm and convincing, almost reassuring. 'Refined, perhaps. Given inclinations more in keeping with your desires. In short, we can give her to you, a lover, an adoring companion. She can be yours, Hassan, in every way you would wish. We can see this done.'

Hassan was trembling now, his gaze still locked on Salomé's form.

'There would be money too, of course,' Gerrun continued. 'Enough that you would never again need to concern yourself with anything that you did not wish to do. Everything you ever wanted.'

'Or …'

Gerrun shrugged and the guard moved one step closer. Salomé's holofac image flickered and faded, drawing a sigh of dismay from Hassan. The room and its occupants came back into his vision.

'I think you know where the alternative lies.'

Hassan slumped, nodding.

'In exchange …?'

Gerrun smiled, leaning forward slightly.

'Then listen closely, my young friend.'

Carey Terminal, Chi Orionis system, Federation

Raan logged onto his terminal. Holofac displays flickered around him and then faded to grey with the words 'Access Denied' flashing across them.

'What the…?'

A prerecorded message appeared in his line of sight.

'Raan Corsen, you have been found to have violated your terms of employment regarding inappropriate use of company resources whilst at work. Report for assessment, meeting room 46 Delta, in five minutes.'

'Shit!'

A timer started counting down in his vision.

4:59.

A cold slice of fear burrowed into his stomach. The tech-heads here were cleverer than he'd given them credit for. Piggybacking the holofac link to the Arena games should have gone unnoticed, but somehow they'd managed to track him.

But I need this job …

He couldn't afford to pay for the high bandwidth holofac link you needed to take part in the games from his apartment, not on his operative's salary. It was way too expensive. Excuses came to mind. He wasn't causing any harm, was he? MetaDrive had bandwidth to spare; he'd done it out of hours too, not like it was going to cause any interruptions to business. He worked hard, didn't he? Better than those freeloaders all about him.

4:30.

He got up from his desk, stumbling as he did so, and almost tripping over his chair. A few of his co-workers looked around and smirked.

They know … someone must have reported me!

He gritted his teeth and made his way along the corridor, staring fixedly straight ahead. The meeting room was several floors above and he used one of the travel pods that lined the outside of the building to get there.

The pod deposited him near the top of the building, just below the executive suites. He walked out, navigation markers flickering in his vision, directing him to the meeting room.

A quick retina scan greeted him. The door opened as he approached and closed again behind him.

It was a typical meeting room. No windows, nothing but the usual table and chairs. No one there, either.

He walked around the room before settling into one of the chairs opposite the entrance, trying to force himself to relax.

I've got good appraisals, probably just get a warning. Won't need to worry about it in the future, the winnings will cover the cost of a decent link of my own next time …

The door opened and a man came in, walking quickly. He dropped a commtab on the table and gave a gesture. The door sealed itself behind him.

Raan gasped. A tall dark-skinned man with a shock of bright blue hair and a conspicuous scar across his face was staring at him. His expression was dour, irritated and annoyed.

Femi! Why is he here?

Femi Dakarai was the chairman of MetaDrive. Raan had seen his image on the monthly newsletters and updates, even seen him once giving a speech, but had never expected to meet him face to face.

Femi looked down at Raan, his dark face creased with a frown.

'Stealing my bandwidth, eh? Thought we wouldn't notice?'

Raan's carefully prepared speech had evaporated.

'I … er …'

'I built this company up from scratch. Didn't put it together so folks like you could sap it out from underneath me.'

Femi flicked his fingers over the commtab.

'Least you won, though.'

Raan's mouth fell open, but he still didn't speak.

Say something! Your job is on the line!

'So,' Femi continued. 'Process says you get fired, I dock your salary and you'll likely never get a job in this system again. Any reason I shouldn't follow through on that?'

'It was out of hours,' Raan managed. 'I was working late on a submission too …'

'My time, my kit, my resources,' Femi interrupted.

'I worked the extra time…'

'I already paid the overtime, fluxstain!' Femi countered, slamming a fist down on the desk.

Raan jolted back, but anger flared in him.

'Yeah? And why is someone like you involved, anyway? Just get admin to fire me, why don't you?'

'You little shit …'

For a moment Raan thought Femi was going to hit him, but his face broke into an abrupt grin. 'You're right. Smart kid, after all. I need something doing and I want you to help me.'

'What?' Raan answered, confused. 'Me … help you? But …'

'Or I can fire you,' Femi added, the grin vanishing in an instant.

'What do …' Raan croaked, his mouth dry. He coughed, trying to get his voice working again, 'you want doing?'

'You hid your tracks pretty well,' Femi said. 'It wasn't the IS guys who picked you up, it was me. I watch the Arena games from time to time. You're pretty good.'

'Er … thanks.'

'Good, but dumb,' Femi snapped back at him. 'With your talent you could have worked a sponsorship deal. Imagine if you'd had a MetaDrive logo on the side of your ship when you took down that Yuri guy.'

'I …'

'That was the reason I paid to find out who the hell you were,' Femi said, his voice betraying his anger. 'Imagine my surprise and embarrassment when I found out the perpetrator works in my own fucking company! Next time you bring it to me, clear?'

'Yes, sir!'

'Since you seem good at dodging the IS team, I want you to look into something for me.'

'I'll do it.'

'This isn't in the rulebook, kid. Get caught and we didn't have this conversation. I'll let admin deal with you straight.'

Raan's eyes were wide now.

What is this all about?

'Er …'

'I want you to scan the exec files,' Femi said. 'Do it out of hours, remote comms, whatever you think best.'

'What, here at MetaDrive? I mean, don't the execs work for you?'

Femi nodded but didn't say anything.

'What am I looking for?'

'Something called Project Dynasty,' Femi replied.

'Dynasty? What does that mean?'

Femi gave him a look.

Dumb question!

'Report back to me if and when you find something. Keep it quiet. News leaks, you're fired. Get caught, you're fired. Can't be bothered, you're fired. I'll make it worth your while if you're successful. You got it?'

Raan nodded.

'This could be your big break, kid. Don't screw it up.'

Femi got up, picked up his commtab and left without further acknowledgement. The door slid back into place.

Raan realised he'd been holding his breath.

'Woah …'

He blew out his cheeks, not sure whether to be relieved or anxious.

Chapter Nine

Serebrov Terminal, HR 6421 system, Independent

The holofac transmission was low bandwidth and on an emergency channel. Erimus struggled to make out the words in the distorted audio.

Alessia!

'Imperial ships are … the place.' Her voice was high pitched with worry, fading in and out. 'No sign of Sal …'

She's being jammed …

'Ambushed … managed to … them this time, heading back to Serebrov, it's the …'

A blast of static crackled across the link, blanketing her words. Erimus winced, trying to make it out.

'It's going down … rendezvous in the Cemiess … interdicting ships. I am safe, will be with you within the hour …'

Erimus sighed in relief. 'That's good, just get back here in one piece. I had an update from Commander Lyrae regarding Salomé's disappearance. One last directive, more sectors to search. The mission is already underway, but our resources are stretched thin.'

'Roger that.' Alessia's voice came through clearly for a moment. 'They are interdicting and attacking anyone and everyone trying to keep a lid on this, lots of innocents being caught in the crossfire …'

And they're going to blame this on us …

Carey Terminal, Chi Orionis system, Federation

Raan didn't immediately begin working late at the MetaDrive offices. He figured it would look a little suspicious if he suddenly started putting in long hours. Instead, he volunteered for extra duties from his supervisor who was all too willing to load him up with additional work. Before long, he had a backlog of reports and analyses that would require dozens of hours of overtime.

Might as well get paid for this! Entrepreneurial and all that …

His coworkers listened, without much sympathy, to his laments of woe about his workload and simply left him to it. It seemed they hadn't figured out his moonlighting on the Arena circuit, but were just glad someone else was taking flak from management rather than them. Raan watched as everyone else headed out to catch the latest holofac immersion vid-series exported from the Federal entertainment networks.

Speaking of which …

He fired up the holofac comms and scanned his lists of contacts. He grinned when he saw one particular individual was online and toggled the connect control.

'Hey loser!'

A severe and inscrutable face looked back at him.

'Oh, it's you.'

'Still sore about that last result?' Raan asked.

'I'll get you next time, not falling for that ruse again. You got lucky.'

Raan smiled. Yuri Nakamura was both a rival and a friend. They'd never met in person, but shared a respectful remote acquaintance over holofac comms. Unlike Raan, Yuri had the credits to play the Arena without all the subterfuge Raan employed. That meant he got the accolades under his own name, not just a pseudonym.

'Trying out for the Leesti lightweights now? I hear they're looking for volunteers.'

'Cute.'

Yuri was looking at something out of sight of the holofac imager.

'You busy, dude?' Raan asked.

'Not really … just, you know …'

'What's up, buddy?'

Yuri sighed. 'I don't know, kinda lost my way with these Arena bouts. It's the same old faces every time, same risks, same rewards. I want to do something … I don't know … significant. Thinking of shipping out on a real ship, maybe doing some work for a system authority that needs a good pilot.'

'You know any good pilots?'

Yuri chuckled. 'You're really on form today, aren't you?'

Raan grew serious. 'It's dangerous out there, no restart option if you make the wrong call …'

'I know, probably a bit crazy. How about you?'

'Just work, you know. Got to get those credits.'

'Yeah, got to be hard being the poor guy. Thanks for the call. Fly safe.'

The holofac flickered out. Raan frowned for a moment before shrugging and getting back to work.

It was no use doing a direct search. That was unlikely to turn anything up and would probably trigger any surveillance tech in place to monitor such activity. No, he had to somehow trick the systems and make it look like genuine research activity.

He hit upon the idea of doing what he liked to think of as a 'side-load', slipping in additional queries into his document search routines for legitimate data and only analysing them at a later date. If anybody tried to figure out what he was up to, they'd have to wade through petabytes of data and, even then, it would be almost impossible to prove it was a deliberate hunt for something specific.

A few days passed before he hit on something. He made copies and extracted the data in a different format, burying it across multiple data storage silos in order to prevent anyone from being able to prove he had a complete copy of the document.

As it turned out, the message was stark and brutal. It was a comms piece, buried in a secured data-pipe. Something he had employed to attempt to hide his own use of company resources.

Project Dynasty.

Auditors will be presented with sufficient evidence to launch their inquiries week commencing 11/09/3302. Board members agree that they will unanimously approve the takeover on 15/09/3302 and the acquisition will take place shortly afterwards. Whilst public protestations will be made there will be no de facto objection. The board will require that the issue is dealt with in the same timescale. All technical data relating to the project will be made available once the formalities have concluded. We look forward to an ongoing relationship with Sirius Corp.

Raan reread the passage several times, not sure what it meant. There had been rumours circling for a while that MetaDrive had some financial problems. Auditors and consultants had been swarming all over the place recently, digging up information and generally causing a nuisance, but that was normal behaviour for auditors.

But Sirius Corp?

Most of the founding employees of MetaDrive were ex-employees of Sirius, having left the monstrously big corporation in order to work in a less regulated and less constrictive environment.

Selling out? Selling out what, though?

There was only one thing to do. Raan tapped in the codes Femi had given him and left a message.

'Got something I think you'll want to see.'

***

Raan found himself in the same room as before, awaiting Femi's arrival. Five minutes had already gone beyond the scheduled time and there was no sign of the chairman. The holofac in the room buzzed for attention. Raan acknowledged it.

Text flickered in the air before him for a moment. Raan recognised the establishment of some kind of encrypted link. Then Femi's face appeared. Raan couldn't tell where he was, there was no background detail visible.

'You got something for me?' Femi asked, wasting no time on preliminaries.

'I found some comms,' Raan replied. 'Project Dynasty …'

Femi's eyes narrowed. 'What does it say?'

'The board, they're planning on selling out to Sirius when they make a hostile takeover bid for MetaDrive in the next week …'

Femi swore and leant back. 'So, that's the game. Paid off by Sirius, every last one of them. The bastards have been leaking documents to the auditors for weeks, trashing the share price and talking us down. Well, they aren't going to get it.'

'Get what?'

'Something important,' Femi replied. 'Something I need you to deliver.'

'Deliver?'

'You can fly, can't you?'

'Er …'

'And you're still an employee with a dodgy record that I haven't yet cleared …'

'But you said …!'

'Do this and I'll clean it up for good, and reward you into the bargain. It's vital that those 'goids over at Sirius Corp don't get their hands on this. I'm too obvious; you on the other hand …'

'How much?'

Femi grinned. 'I like your style, kid. I'll give you a hundred thou and you can keep the ship.'

'Ship? What ship?'

Femi gestured and the image of a bright white shiny vessel appeared. Raan's eyes widened in appreciation.

'I know you like fast fighters,' Femi said. 'This is my Buckyball racer, tuned for speed and agility, but still packing some heat. I need you to get to a man by the name of Bill Turner. You'll find him on Alioth 4a.'

'Alioth? But that's in Alliance space …'

'Yeah,' Femi answered. 'Get there and get back quickly. Bill will know what to do. Don't get caught and don't get scanned. I doubt Sirius will be very lenient. Oh … and you'll need this.'

A code appeared in Raan's line of sight rather than via the holofac, a sequence of numbers.

'For the hatch and the flight controls. I already have the Alioth permit. I suggest you leave now, it's only a matter of …'

The holofac crackled with interference and went blank. Raan stared at it uncomprehendingly for a moment before staggering up.

Someone was monitoring that … and if …

He bolted from the room.

Deep space, Talitha system, Alliance

The Viper Mark IV sported a matte grey titanium paint job, with a pair of parallel stripes of crimson. It was a tough ship, perhaps the preeminent fighter ship of its class. The Mark III version had long been the mainstay of many a system authority fleet, but it had served for decades and was in danger of being outclassed by newer designs issuing from Gutamaya and Core Dynamics.

The Mark IV shared the same purpose as its predecessor, though; speed, agility, toughness. Vipers had a reputation for tenacity in battle and this newer version had an even sharper bite than before.

The one Tsu was flying was called the *StarStormer*.

She checked the telemetry aboard her new ship. She had just left Alliance space, hyperspacing in consecutive leaps according to a pre-determined route.

Don't forget the drugs …

The zero-gee. Her first flight had been gut-wrenchingly unpleasant. Nothing prepared you for the shock of feeling like you were falling down a bottomless pit the moment you left the clutches of gravity. She'd taken the meds to counter it, but it had been a couple of days before she fully recovered.

But she could see the appeal. Flying a ship through the darkness of space worked on the soul, there was a call out here, endless freedom. She'd never before understood why some would incarcerate themselves in a metal coffin and head off into the void on a long-range exploration trip. Now she had an inkling as to their mentality.

Before her lay the worlds of the Federation.

They had a very different ethos from what she was familiar with. She had yet to experience their culture first hand, but the prevailing view was of corporation-controlled decadence. The Federation was driven by its constant economic stress that required more resources, more investment, constant growth and indifference to the needs of individuals. It was a very old political structure, presidential in form, with an elected representative at the very top. The present incumbent, President Zachary Hudson, had little real power and was more of a figurehead.

So she'd been told, anyway. He was all over the newsfeeds.

Not that I know much about politics …

She had made the transit in a leisurely fashion, stopping at trading ports along the way, partly to ensure she was never low on fuel and partly to see a little of the life of a spacefarer. It was not quite as she had suspected. In some of the stations she received a friendly, if distant, greeting. In others, outright hostility. It seemed that in some places 'spacers', the group of people she now found herself categorised within, were not trusted, often not welcome and frequently viewed with deep suspicion by the general static populace. In most though, indifference was the most common response.

Time to concentrate. She had a mission. There was no time to be distracted by idle flights of fancy.

She'd worked out a pattern to the old transmission that Alliance intel had intercepted. It typically occurred on weekdays, outside of normal working hours. Tapping into it had been tricky, but the *StarStormer* was equipped with various eavesdropping tech she had been at pains to ensure had not to come to the attention of any patrols. It had been the only difficult part of the mission thus far, avoiding the system authority security scans. Those would have definitely shown that there was something a little odd about her ship.

She couldn't break the encryption; the computers aboard the ship were not nearly powerful enough even to try. That wasn't the point, though. It was the source she was interested in.

Her final jump took her into the Chi Orionis system. The star flared before her, but she quickly banked the ship onto a new vector, heading out into the darkness. Once she felt she was far enough for surveillance to begin, she dropped the ship out of supercruise, throttled back the engines and switched off power to as many modules as she could spare. Only the comms system and life support remained active. Unless she was very unlucky, no one would be able to find her. Her ship lay silent and cold; practically invisible.

Then she waited.

If the transmission came on cue she'd be able to triangulate it. Right now she didn't know if it was planet-side or in orbit, or perhaps even out in the void of the system somewhere. She needed to narrow it down.

The canopy crackled with freezing condensation as the ship radiated heat into space. This was the dull part of the job, waiting for the next clue.

The *StarStormer* hung motionless in the darkness, starlight flickering from its hull.

Beyond the canopy, the ghostly light of the Milky Way cut diagonally across the view. Tsu watched it for a while, marvelling at the complex beauty of the combined light of four hundred billion stars, interstellar dust and nebulae portrayed before her. Even the short trip from Alioth to Chi Orionis had seemed a long way, but the galaxy map had revealed how trivial her little jaunt was when measured against the size of the galaxy itself. She'd heard that explorers had ventured to the other side, some remote destination they had nicknamed 'Beagle Point' after the first explorer who had discovered it.

Bored, she flipped on the holofac systems and brought up the local news. A broadcast was playing out. A young woman was trying to inject enthusiasm into what was a dreary piece on some company financial problem.

'*... appear that the financial affairs are far more complex than a mere lack of investment.*

Auditors, reviewing their accounts, have found a series of payments to undisclosed suppliers without the evidence of necessary checks and balances being in place.'

The feed cut away to a fat, balding man. Tsu could see the description underneath his image. Gary Marshall, Senior Auditor of BigSix.

'*It's a big mess. We're placing the company in receivership. It needs a buyer and quickly.*'

Then the image cut back to the young woman again, still earnestly talking into the camera.

'*The Chairman of MetaDrive Inc., Femi Dakarai, was not available for comment.*'

Tsu sat bolt upright.

MetaDrive?

Quickly she replayed the segment, listening for the details before allowing it to continue on.

'*Shares in MetaDrive Inc. plummeted on the news, but Sirius Corp unexpectedly volunteered to prop up the smaller company.*'

Another cut, this time to a wizened looking chap with a thin gaunt face and watery blue eyes. Apparently, he was the marketing manager of Sirius Corp's hyperdrive research division. He had an untrustworthy look upon his face, if Tsu was any judge of character.

'*We've been interested in collaboration for a while, and were in talks as to how we might license MetaDrive's exciting new technology. We have no wish to see them go under due to financial problems.*'

Information was scrolling up the side of the holofac with details on the company in question.

That looks distinctly dodgy!

She pulled up information on Femi Dakarai, and only got a limited profile from the dossier Edmund had given her. Not much was known about him other than he was rich. He had an interest in Buckyball racing, Arena competitions and had a race-prepped Imperial Eagle stored in the hangar at Carey Terminal.

Tsu thought to herself for a moment. It was as good as any a place to start, and it would beat hanging around out here in the void. She could just as easily keep up the surveillance, and it might give her a chance to pick up extra information.

She cancelled the holofac and fired up the ship's modules. With a rising hum, the ship readied itself. A quick flip of the navigation markers and she had a course plotted. She pushed the throttles.

Frame shift drive charging …

'Let's go see what we can find.'

Deep space, Location unknown

'See the galaxy, they said. It will be fun, they said!'

Commander Jaschish pushed back in the cockpit of his Asp, looked out at the distant stars and swore.

Bored!

Two days before, he'd signed on with the Fuel Rats, a curious organisation, with no particular affiliation to any faction or superpower. There were no leaders, no assigned jobs. They offered little in the way of remuneration either, but acted as a sort of loose commune. It was a good place to hide away from prying eyes. No questions asked, no answers required. The Fuel Rats' stern mantra echoed in his mind.

If we do our best, then collectively we'll be awesome …

They helped out stranded pilots and they took pride in being good at it. That was it. Nothing more, nothing less.

We've got fuel, you don't. Any questions?

There was only one rule Jaschish had come across. Something the other Rats took with almost religious observance.

The Q word. Say it as often as you like, but never accidentally …

'Stupid rule,' he muttered to himself. 'Worse kind of superstition. Even if you did say it was quiet that would hardly mean …'

'Dispatcher to Commander Jaschish. We have a rescue required in the ER 8 system, can you assist?'

No way …

Jaschish leant forward and triggered the galaxy map from the console. A quick review indicated that the ER 8 system was but a few short jumps away. He triggered the comms.

'Dispatch, this is Jaschish, can confirm. Details please.'

Static crackled for a moment before the dispatcher's voice came through. 'Target is the Imperial Clipper *Eclipse*, pilot is a Commander Alesia. Confirm.'

'Confirmed.' Jaschish said.

Odd.

Very odd, in fact. Most of the Fuel Rat runs were to assist inexperienced commanders, running across space ill-prepared and ill-educated about the rigours of space travel. Many ran without a fuel scoop and failed to take into account the distances involved. But lack of money and inexperience went hand and hand, those pilots typically flew inexpensive vessels, simple and easy to maintain.

An Imperial Clipper was none of those things. Nor would its owner be short of cash. Why would they have run out of fuel within the boundaries of the core worlds?

Jaschish was nervous. He'd heard stories from the Rats regarding unscrupulous pirates who had lured in some of their members in order to ambush them. This didn't feel right. His Asp Explorer was a lightweight ship, not armed to the teeth. It would be no match if the Clipper turned hostile.

I signed up, though, got to take the rough with the smooth …

He charted the necessary course and triggered the hyperdrive systems.

Ratted up and ready …

A few short jumps brought him to the ER 8 system. As requested by protocol, the Imperial Clipper was emitting a wing beacon, allowing him to home in on it easily. The ER 8 system played host to a dull brown dwarf; they used to call them 'dark systems.' A fuel scoop was no use here.

He adjusted course and matched the supercruise velocity to bring him alongside, dropping from frame shift with his hand on the triggers, ready to defend himself if it turned out to be necessary.

The proximity lock was spot on, he reappeared in normal space only a couple of kilometres from the other vessel.

As expected, the Imperial Clipper hung in the darkness, its hull reflecting the gleam of distant stars. He toggled the narrowband comms.

'Commander Alesia, drop shields and power down all modules other than life support. Fuel transfer will begin when status is confirmed.'

Now let's see what happens.

It was standard procedure for the Fuel Rats. If the other ship wasn't willing to ensure the safety of the rescue ship, they could do without the rescue.

Jaschish watched the scanners carefully. The shields on the other ship faded out with a flicker and a scan confirmed the ship was powering down.

So far, so good.

A closer inspection showed that the ship was badly damaged. He could see streaks of tarnished hull, the blackened stains of missile impacts. A dull red glow came from one of the engine nacelles. The ship was in a bad way.

Been in a fight, by the look of it.

Jaschish made a quick scan of the area, but no other ships were in the vicinity. Either the Clipper had eluded them, or it had destroyed them.

The comms crackled and a woman's voice sounded across the narrowband comms. Jaschish recognised the affected tones of someone from the Federation.

'Thank you for coming to my rescue.'

Federation woman in an Imperial ship. How does all this make sense?

'You're safe now, Commander,' Jaschish said. 'Will deploy fuel limpets in a moment. How come you ended up here without fuel?'

There was a long pause from the other end of the comms.

'I was ambushed,' came the answer. 'Only just escaped with my life. Case of mistaken identity, I think. I was just travelling through the Cemiess system and Imperial ships just attacked ...'

'Pirates?'

'Might have been.' The woman's voice was vague and defensive. 'They ID'd me and opened fire without warning. Tried the comms. They claimed I was someone called Alessia Verdi and I was in league with some Imperial senator or something. I tried to tell them they had the wrong person, but they weren't taking any explanations, just fired their guns... Alesia! One S, I kept saying! Alesia! But they didn't care.'

Jaschish looked at the status indicators. The Clipper was hauling no cargo and her profile wasn't listed as wanted. No reason for a pirate or a bounty hunter to bother her. He toggled the trigger for the fuel limpets. The small remote-controlled craft zipped across the space between the two ships, connecting with the beleaguered Clipper and depositing the precious fuel into its tanks.

'Looks like they hit you pretty hard,' Jaschish said. 'Fuel should be coming in now.'

'It is,' the woman's voice replied. 'Thank you once again. How can I repay you?'

'No need,' Jaschish said, thinking of the Fuel Rats' mantra. 'Just let folks know about us.'

'I will,' she said. 'Your assistance will not go unnoticed. You may have just saved my life.'

It didn't take long to refuel the ship. Jaschish backed his ship away as the Clipper powered up its systems.

'Fly safe now,' he said, as the Clipper cruised past.

The comms crackled once again.

'Safe is no longer an option for me, I'm afraid,' the woman said. 'I would not mention my name in Imperial space if I were you. You may find it brings you bad luck. I've had it with all this crap, I'm going exploring, next stop Colonia!'

Frame shift charge detected...

The Clipper accelerated, boosting away with a crackle of engine flux. Moments later it flashed into the distance, leaving nothing but a faint trail, slowly dispersing into the void.

Jaschish ran his tongue over his teeth.

'What the hell was all that about?'

Chapter Ten

Capitol, Achenar 6d, Achenar, Empire

The great palace of the Duvals rose above the skyline of Capitol, seat of the Emperor on Achenar 6d. The palace was silhouetted in the evening glare from the blue-white light of the Achenar star as it lit clouds heavy with rain a glowing purple. Just visible alongside was the Hall of Martyrs, obsidian black, the vaults of those who had fallen in the service of the Empire, entombed forever.

Perhaps half a kilometre from the palace stood an administrative building known as 'The Complex,' a name that was deliberately ambiguous. It too was a vast building, towering into the sky, its upper levels penetrating the clouds. The moisture was redirected around it by intricate force fields, ensuring no unseemly marks or stains tainted its exterior. Rain was directed away, downwards to street level, where it would sully only the poorer citizens of the city, far from the concerns of the bourgeoisie above.

Penthouse suites atop the building afforded their occupants breathtaking views of Capitol. Wide windows, decorated with baroque duralium lattice work, rose several dozen metres in height.

From one such window, a woman, dressed in a simple white gown, could be seen staring out through the rain, one hand pressed up against the glass. A cowl was drawn across her head. A lock of dark hair fell in front of her face; she brushed it back behind her ear absentmindedly.

She had been brought here against her will. She did not have to test the doors to know they were locked. The rooms were designed to be entirely secure. She knew her movements and any words she uttered would be monitored.

A prison by any other name.

It was luxurious enough. Her rank deserved it and honour demanded it. Political prisoners were often kept here, sometimes for life, in order to 'manage' them. Innocent until proven guilty, of course.

Not that there is much doubt of the outcome of this. They have sprung their trap and I am caught.

Salomé paced the floor of the suite. She had been permitted no external communications, no way to contact anyone.

No way to contact Erimus or Cuthrick …

She was on trial for the attempted murder of Fleet Admiral Denton Patreus.

Ridiculous, but clearly they have manufactured evidence to justify this claim.

She stopped pacing for a moment.

But who are 'they?'

It seemed unlikely that Patreus would have the wherewithal to organise something of this nature. For all his faults he was a straight talker and a straight shooter. Salomé had no significant dealings with the Emperor herself, so that seemed unlikely – she would have bigger issues to consider than the antics of a minor senator. That Gerrun and Zyair had turned on her could be explained by their own motivation for revenge. It seemed they were working for someone, but who?

Salomé resumed pacing.

Aisling Duval? Zemina Torval? What did they stand to gain? Someone was framing her for this, but who could it be? And why?

It all came back to that transmission she had uncovered at the old lady's behest. Salomé cast her mind back two years. She could see herself in her mind's eye, crouched over the holofac transmitter.

Whatever it is, it's something that Galcop, the Imps and the Feds don't want us to see …

The old lady had played her and she still didn't understand the rules of the game. She'd followed the clues into the Federation, researched the historical archives of Galcop and found tantalising clues that directed her outwards across the galaxy. She'd searched long and hard, but found little other than rumour and hearsay.

By her efforts and the others she had gathered to the cause along the way, thousands of worlds had been scanned and classified. Derelict ships found and investigated, curious anomalies explored. She'd gathered all that exploration data with the express instruction to bring it back to the lady.

The old lady must have known she was going to be ambushed.

This was part of her plan? To frame me? But why? To what benefit? And what does Luko know about all this? What is hidden in that exploration data I unearthed?

The bio-trace must contain the answer, but how to get at it? She rubbed at her palm. The slight soreness was long gone now.

The only saving grace is that no one knows it's there, or how to extract that data now. Not even me.

They had taken her ship. She had no doubt it would have been stripped down to bare metal and every single bit of data aboard analysed to the nth degree. They would find nothing. She had it all. She looked at her palm.

Right there.

A tone buzzed through the suite. Someone approached.

There was no reason to refuse entry, she signalled with a gesture for the door to open. There was no point in attempting an escape, she knew guards would be stationed outside. Such an attempt would give whoever it was behind all this even greater latitude to make her life miserable.

The door slid back.

As she expected, two guards stood in the frame, dressed in typical Imperial uniforms, weapons readied. But they stepped back almost straightaway.

Salomé blinked in surprise as a woman walked between them.

Her …

She was quite diminutive, small and neat, with a mischievous grin and a slightly salacious manner about her. Her hips swayed with exaggerated femininity. She was slim, dressed in a tight-fitting white garment that she appeared to have been sewn into. Her complexion was flawless, make-up exquisitely applied, her face framed by earrings with Imperial insignia marked in gold. Yet she stood proud and aloof before Salomé.

It was her hair that was her signature piece. A blue that matched the hue of the system's star itself. Achenar blue, Royal blue, Imperial blue …

The People's Princess.

Aisling Duval.

What does she want with me?

Salomé watched as Aisling moved towards her and then stopped, turning on a heel and dismissing the guards. The door closed behind her.

'I assume I am safe in your presence?' Aisling asked, turning to regard Salomé once more. 'You won't skewer me with a cunningly concealed sword like your other adversaries?'

Salomé didn't respond. Aisling knew full well that she had been disarmed.

'No,' Aisling mused, 'You're a little more subtle than that nowadays, aren't you?'

'Are you here for a reason?' Salomé asked.

'Are you busy then?' Aisling said. 'Plotting some new murder attempt?'

'You know very well I had nothing to do with …'

Aisling walked past her and made her way over to the windows to look out, before turning once again.

Here to tease me, or actually offer me something?

'You really thought you could swan in here from your provincial little system and get away with murder?' she asked, her voice laced with acid sweetness. 'You even had designs on being Emperor. Have you any idea how ridiculous you look?'

'I'm not the one wearing a stupid wig,' Salomé replied. 'And I had no designs on anything. I wanted nothing from the Empire save reassurances that my homeworld would be left undisturbed.'

'Yet you left it to fly off into the void, chasing dreams. Denton did you a favour, you know, without him your precious little homeworld would have been overrun in weeks, regardless of your wishes. I think you would refer to them as … Federal Scum … you have such a way with words.'

'Fleet Admiral Denton Patreus loves the military, loves conquest and loves expansion,' Salomé replied. 'He took Prism because it was advantageous to him. That's all. He did not care for my people or my world.'

'You admit you hate him then?' Aisling asked.

'I admit nothing,' Salomé said. 'The facts will speak for themselves.'

That seemed to amuse the princess and she walked a little further around the suite.

'You're not altogether wrong,' Aisling answered. 'He has the virtue of being predictable.'

'What do you want?' Salomé asked, tiring of the sparring.

'What makes you think I want something?'

Salomé sighed and tilted her head in annoyance. 'What other purpose can you have?' Her voice took on an impatient edge. 'Why else would the darling princess of the Empire visit a disgraced senator from the wretched provinces?'

'You know you're finished,' said Aisling, her voice colder now. 'Everyone knows you're guilty. You'll be stripped of your rank and title, and no fancy speech can save you.'

'I know how the games are played,' Salomé answered. 'I will not take part in them. Nor make things easy for others.'

'I would have thought you would have learned a little discretion by now,' Aisling replied. 'Your mistakes have cost you dear in the past.'

Salomé frowned. Aisling smiled at the confused look on her face.

'Oh yes, I know a great deal about it all, Lady Kahina Tijani Loren. A great deal.'

Salomé's eyes widened.

'Zyair … and that egregious Gerrun! So, they're working for you then.'

Aisling nodded. 'Thoroughly distasteful as they are, they have their uses. Gerrun is a rather able politician. You should have cultivated friends rather than growing enemies. Their patronage is mine now. They have related some quite entertaining stories about you. Have you not read what the Imperial Citizen has written?'

'That squalid rag matters little to me.'

'I thought Zyair's contributions rather well composed, myself,' Aisling replied.

'You are welcome to them,' Salomé snapped. 'They care only for their own ambition. I would warn you of their conduct. They will turn on you …'

'Oh, I am in no doubt about that,' Aisling said. 'But they need me more than I need them. Needy folk are easy to use and cajole.'

'And using people is what you're good at, isn't it?' Salomé replied, her voice cold.

'A talent we both share,' Aisling retorted. 'Don't deny it. You know how this game works.'

'Say what you must and leave me,' Salomé snapped.

'I could defend you,' Aisling said, giving Salomé a coquettish look, 'They have given me such knowledge that could, perhaps, sway the debate one way … or another.'

Salomé took a deep breath.

So … her agenda then. She fears a loss of standing. She's no longer in the ascendency and has no way to pull herself higher …

'And what do you ask in return?'

'You have a certain …' Aisling pursed her lips for a moment. 'Allure. A following amongst the disaffected, those unhappy with the politics of the Empire, even the core worlds themselves. You can reach out to the Federation, perhaps even the Alliance and the independents in a way that others cannot. In short, you have influence. That is an attribute I could make use of.'

Salomé saw Aisling's plans in a moment of clarity. With Salomé's support, many factions might turn to Aisling. She was already growing in popularity with her stance against slavery and modernisation of rules within the Empire. Patreus had the military, Emperor Arissa the control. Aisling needed more leverage. Salomé might provide it.

It might work … perhaps I could play along. Does she really have some influence, or is this just her using the situation to her advantage?

'Of course …' Aisling said, running a finger down Salomé's arm and whispering in her ear. 'The Empire needs only one darling princess of the people.' Her voice turned hard, her gaze sharp and fierce. 'And that is me.'

'You want me to pledge my allegiance to you,' Salomé said, deadpan. 'What do I get? Prismatic shields for my ship? Or do you have other some other wonderful enticement?'

Aisling smiled. 'Between us we will turn all heads. I will give you a position of power in my organisation. I will guarantee patronage of Prism. Another strong, beautiful Imperial woman at my right hand. Youth, vigour and beauty. All will love us and follow us. Together we could take everything.'

It might actually work … we could do this.

'And in exchange, you would influence this trial in my favour?'

The coquettish smile and voice were back. 'Denton can be turned easily enough. There are ways.'

'And I would be your lackey from this time forth.'

'I would see you were rewarded.' Aisling sounded hurt. 'Prism returned to you, just leave the admiration of the Empire for me.'

Sell out to Aisling? She has a lot of popular support, her anti-slavery stance would be a problem … but not insurmountable. Away from the trial I might be able to … but it's all bribery and corruption. What the Empire is always accused of! Is this what we have become? It truly is rotten to the core! She would cast me aside the moment I am no longer useful and dispose of me another way. I must stand against these figureheads to expose what lies behind all this. I will face this trial!

'No,' Salomé said, slowly shaking her head. 'I will not be a puppet to a spoilt brat.'

She saw it coming, and grabbed Aisling's outstretched hand before it could slap her face. Salomé twisted Aisling's arm around, applying the edge of her hand to a vulnerable pressure point in the princess' wrist. Aisling screeched in pain before Salomé released the grip.

'You are a barbarian!' Aisling hissed. 'How dare you touch me? You will pay for this, Lady Kahina Loren. I will let Denton rip you to shreds!'

'Do what you will. I defy you. The truth will come out.'

'The truth?' Aisling laughed. 'The truth is what we will make it.'

'Anyone with half a brain will see this is a setup. There are those out there that believe in me and will not let this lie.'

Aisling smiled cruelly. 'No. They will stand aside if they value their continued existence. The truth is you did try to murder Denton and so it will be found. All will be convinced you hate him and tried to kill him!'

'Oh, I despise the man,' Salomé said, with a cold laugh. 'But if I had wanted him dead, he'd be dead. There is nothing I do better than revenge.'

Aisling pushed past her and gestured for the exit. As the door opened she turned with a final flourish.

'You will regret this,' she said. 'Punishment will be … severe. Doubtless Gerrun and Zyair will have some suggestions on how to temper you. Your life is over. No one can save you now. I was your last chance.'

'Then I'm grateful I won't have to speak to you again,' Salomé said. 'Good day, Princess Duval.'

The door closed, leaving Salomé alone in her incarceration once more.

Carey Terminal, Chi Orionis system, Federation

Raan had quickly moved back down the MetaDrive building towards his workstation. Arriving on his floor he noticed his colleagues were clustering around the room's main holofac projector, where a news article was being broadcast live. He could just make out the words.

'*… Sad news from the Chi Orionis system this morning with the news that Femi Dakarai, Chairman of the relatively new company MetaDrive Inc. passed away this morning after a short illness. Dakarai had been taken ill last week with suspected 'burnout' from working so hard on the financial backing that the new company required. Board members reported that he was working very long hours and had been showing signs of stress for many months. The arrival of auditors appears to have been the final straw …*'

'Shit!'

Raan could see two suited figures standing off to one side, near his workstation. It looked like they had been going through his stuff. As he looked they turned around and caught sight of him. One gestured briefly to the other and they began to walk towards him. Raan turned and fled.

He got to the lift which would take him down to ground level and jabbed his palm against the call panel. The panel lit up red and the words 'Access Denied' appeared above it.

They've already killed my ID …

The doors of the lift immediately to the right opened unannounced. Raan leapt inside and slapped his hand on the close button. The doors slammed shut behind him and the lift began to descend. He let out his breath only to look up and find a group of people looking at him.

He swallowed as he recognised the board of MetaDrive, all five of them, except Femi.

'Afternoon,' he said, clenching his fists to stop from trembling.

Someone just murdered Femi … maybe it was one of them!

They acknowledged him with a brief nod and resumed their discussion, taking no further interest in him. The lift opened on the ground floor and he moved out, looking in every direction as he walked out across MetaDrive's reception area. There were security guards at the doors, but they didn't seem to be looking for anyone.

Just get through the doors, walk casual!

The holofac above the reception desk flickered and changed from the news report about Femi. It was tinged with red, with an urgent message from MetaDrive security.

'A junior employee of MetaDrive Inc., Raan Corsen, has been suspended from the company and is wanted in connection with 'Audit Irregularities'. Please advise if you come into contact with him. A reward is offered for his safe return.'

The message was accompanied by an unmistakable picture of him.

Raan kept moving, keeping his head down, not making eye contact. He reached the external doors and only then looked up. The nearest security guard was looking at him with a faint frown. Raan gave him a jaunty thumbs-up as the external doors of the building opened. The guard smiled, nodded and then paused.

'Hey, you!'

Raan looked over his shoulder and saw the board members pointing at him.

'Stop him!'

But he was outside, running.

He could hear feet behind him, but he kept going. He ran, at breakneck speed, across the traffic line that ran outside the building, heedless of the vehicles abruptly adjusting their courses to avoid him. The sounds of thrusters firing echoed around him and a blast of hot air nearly knocked him off his feet.

The MetaDrive building was opposite a park. A lake curved majestically away in front of him, fringed with leafy trees and vegetation. He ran into it, narrowly avoiding holidaymakers and romantic couples who were strolling in the opposite direction. The trees gave him a little cover.

'Stop that man!'

Got to get to the hub! Let's hope they don't know about the ship …

He darted left into thicker vegetation, ignoring the scratches that the thorns inflicted on him. A crashing and cursing from behind told him he'd bought himself a bit of time. He chanced a look back, seeing the security guard from the entrance struggling through the undergrowth about fifty metres back.

The main station strut leading up to the hub was a few hundred metres away. He squeezed through the shrubs until the hub access station came into view. He could see there was a massive queue lined up for transports upwards. His heart dropped within him and he scanned around for a moment looking for an alternative.

Service elevator!

Hardly anyone used them because they had no seating and the acceleration was fierce, all the better for him, though. He started running again.

By the time he reached it, his breath came in gasps, his body ached in places he didn't know he had muscles. The support strut stretched high above him now, half a kilometre of metal construction vaulting above until it intersected with the distant hub of the space station.

The service elevator was unoccupied and he banged at the hatchway, fell inside and closed it behind him, punching in the codes to take him up. As he did so, he looked out of the windows, seeing the security guard arrive at the base. The elevator rumbled and started to rise.

He saw the guard's face suffuse with anger.

To his surprise, the guard leapt towards him, vaulting over the protective rails and bodily launching himself at the elevator. A dull thump indicated the guard had made the jump. Raan saw him claw his way alongside the windows and peer in, mouthing something at Raan.

The elevator began its rise, the ground dropping away with terrifying rapidity. Raan felt himself pushed downwards as if his weight had doubled, aghast to see the guard was still clinging onto the outside. Raan could see his clothing flapping in the wind generated by the ascent.

The fierce acceleration tailed off after a few brief moments. Raan stared as the guard clenched his fist and gestured at him, it was clearly a threat. Raan watched the guard climb and disappear from view.

A moment later, the lift decelerated sharply, almost throwing Raan to the roof.

Some kind of override?

The elevator stopped and then slowly began to descend. Clunks from above signalled that the guard was moving again. Raan could see feet dangling past the windows.

Frantically, he looked around the interior, spying a control panel on the opposite bulkhead. He activated it.

'Elevator status.'

'Maintenance mode activated, returning to base.'

'Cancel maintenance mode.'

'Maintenance mode cannot be cancelled.'

A heavy thump from behind him made him turn around. The guard was back at the doors.

'What caused the maintenance mode?'

'This unit detected anomalous external sensor inputs. Maintenance mode activated, returning to base.'

Sensors ...

Another thump at the doors. The guard was trying to open them!

Raan looked into the control circuitry. It was pretty straightforward stuff. A service elevator didn't need much in the way of sophistication. He could see the cross connects from the detectors feeding into the main bank. It was far simpler than the stuff he worked on at MetaDrive.

Maybe I can ...

He jabbed at the exposed controls, cursing as his hands shook trying to tease the fiddly connectors into an ordered pattern. Outside, the ground was rising up. The elevator was almost back at ground level. He had only moments.

He jabbed at the control panel, routing the gee sensors across and connecting them to the external sensors.

'Anomalous external sensor inputs are now clear. Cancelling maintenance mode. Normal service resuming. State required destination.'

'Up to the hub!' Raan yelled.

'Acknowledged.'

Barely a metre above the terminal the elevator halted. Raan had a moment to turn around and see the guard's terrified expression as the lift rocketed upwards. Stupidly, the guard hung on as the lift rose. Raan could hear a dull scream and stared in horror as the guard's grip slowly loosened.

Then, he was gone.

I killed him …

Raan swallowed, mumbling to himself.

'Not my fault … not my fault!'

***

Tsu had settled her ship on a pad within the docking area. The *StarStormer* looked completely innocuous amongst all the other ships. She arranged for it to be refuelled and watched as the automechs did their work. The gravity was low and uncertain here in the hub, disconcerting after the zero-gee she had acclimatised to. The view overhead was rather overwhelming. Ships were coming and going within the busy station interior. Every location within the docking cylinder was 'down', she found it difficult to wrap her mind around it. Perhaps she'd get used to it eventually.

Satisfied the ship was ready, she swung herself out of the pilot's chair and made her way down through the ship, emerging onto the landing pad itself.

Here the noise of the vessels coming and going was even more notice-able, echoing around her. Speed limits were rigorously enforced, traffic offences were severely punished. You didn't flout the rules inside a space station. The system security services would take you outside and blow your ship to pieces. Justice was harsh and immediate.

There was no sign of an Imperial Eagle, but Tsu hadn't expected to see it. It was probably tucked away in a hangar in the decks below somewhere. A few discreet enquiries might reveal where it was.

She walked across to where a transport was picking up people who had disembarked from a nearby Beluga liner. As she queued up behind them, she caught sight of the holofac newsfeed.

'… *Sad news from the Chi Orionis system this morning with the news that Femi Dakarai, Chairman of the relatively new company MetaDrive Inc. passed away this morning after a short illness …*'

She frowned and stopped to watch. Almost immediately, the feed changed to a shot of a young man and the newscaster rattled off more information.

'*… A junior employee of MetaDrive Inc., Raan Corsen, has been suspended from the company and is wanted in connection with 'Audit Irregularities'. He is believed to be on the run from MetaDrive security teams and any sightings should be reported …*'

Movement to her left caught her eye and she turned.

An Imperial Eagle with a garish crimson paint job was being moved into position on the adjacent launch pad.

***

Raan sprinted into the hangar, rushing up to the hatchway just as Femi had described it. It was locked. Quickly he jabbed in the code Femi had given him, cursing as he got it wrong the first time and the lock responded with an angry buzz. The second time it worked. The door hissed back and allowed him in. He sealed and locked the door behind him.

Safe for a moment, he took a second to look around. He was in one of the bays below the docking zone of the station, where the ships were repaired and maintained. As promised, below him was a ship. Raan stopped for a moment to appreciate it.

The *Whiplash*.

It was a classic fighter profile, updated, smoothed over and upgraded with Imperial flare and style. That and the bright red paint job.

Imperial Eagle!

Raan tapped his mag-boots off and jumped over the rail without hesitation. He drifted down slowly, bracing himself as he hit the bay floor a few seconds later. An impossible leap in a one-gee zone, here near the axis it was an easy feat.

Mag-boots clicked on the flooring as he made his way into the ship, settling himself into the pilot's chair.

It was eerily familiar. He'd performed these actions a thousand times in the immersive experience of the Arena sim suites, but this time it was real.

Get killed out here and there's no coming back for another try next month …

The ship's engines engaged with a faint rumble. Status indicators and holofac projections lit up with messages of readiness. The ship was alive around him. He looked right, seeing the config and weapons loadout of the ship.

A-Class throughout, beam laser and two rapid-fire multi-cannons. Femi spared no expense on this baby …

He toggled the request to launch.

The bay beneath the ship rumbled and the ship lurched, rotating around its centre. Then the entire bay lifted up and the ship was moved into the central corridor of the station.

The comms flickered to attention.

'Gutamaya Romeo Alpha Alpha, you are cleared for takeoff. Ensure you obey traffic restrictions whilst in the vicinity of Carey Terminal.'

There was a clunk from somewhere below and the *Whiplash* jolted slightly to one side.

'Here goes nothing.'

He toggled the vertical thrusters and the *Whiplash* rose from its moorings, the holofac image of the landing pad marker drifting downwards and out of sight. Raan tapped the forward thrusters and the ship began to move towards the narrow docking slit at the other end of the cavernous space.

The comms buzzed again.

'Gutamaya Romeo Alpha Alpha. Departure clearance has been aborted, please return to pad two-four immediately. Acknowledge.'

Damn!

Traffic control within and around stations was fierce. You could get blown to bits just for parking in the wrong place. If they were already onto him …

'Gutamaya Romeo Alpha Alpha. Departure clearance has been aborted, return to pad two-four immediately. Acknowledge.'

Ahead of him, two other docking bay pads were rotating. He could see two ships being lifted into launch positions. Cobras. Mark IIIs, by the look of them. It was bad news. Cobras might not be the last word in offence, but they were quick. Quick enough to intercept the Eagle.

'Time to get out of here.'

Raan signalled for the undercarriage to retract, mashed the throttles forward to their stops, aimed the nose of the ship at the docking slit, and triggered the boost. He hung on for dear life as he was thrown back in his seat, desperately trying to keep the little ship on course.

One mistake and I'll be a stain on the station bulkhead …

There was no time to think. The docking slit rushed towards him, growing menacingly. He corrected, almost catching the left nacelle on the corner of the egress. The force field hummed around the ship as it punched its way through. Raan had a moment to notice the docking guides, or 'toast-rack' as most pilots nicknamed it, before the light faded.

Space, infinite space.

He couldn't help the gasp that shuddered through his lungs.

Somehow, the sims had never prepared him for this moment. He was actually out here, in the void, in the vacuum. There was nothing, literally nothing, between him and the distant stars. The view was all the more overwhelming for actually being real.

Woah …

A message flashed up on the holofac display.

Illegal departure, 500 Credit Fine.

Lasers from the Cobras flashed around him, but the little ship was fleet, quickly moving beyond the range of the station. He boosted the engines again, giving them as much power as he could from the main reactor.

Full pips to engines! How often have I done that … but this time it's real … so real!

Blips appeared on the scanner. Two marks, both astern. A quick spin of the scanner showed them to be the two Cobras. They were in pursuit already. He had to elude them.

He selected a system at random and activated the hyperspace controls.

Mass locked!

He cursed and boosted the engines a third time, watching as the capacitor drained away. The powerplant could recharge only so fast …

Got to buy some time …

More laser fire. The shields flashed and flickered. He spun the ship about and changed course, switching off the flight assist computers. The Eagle yawed and pitched and then struck off in a new direction. Raan could see the Cobras struggling to match the turn.

A third blip. This time it was a Viper launching from the station. It kept its distance, so Raan ignored it, concentrating on the pursuing Cobras instead.

The comms crackled.

'Raan Corsen, you are bound by law to stand down. This is Commander Marcos Kross of the Earth Defence Fleet. We only want to talk to you.'

Earth Defence Fleet? Who are they? Stand down? Talk? Yeah right …

He triggered the hyperspace controls.

Frame shift drive charging …

He knew they would get a notification of his intentions, but there was nothing he could do about it. If he could get a jump ahead he might be able to make a second jump before they figured out the destination of the first.

The progress bar that showed the charging of the drive crept up with agonising slowness. Hyperdrives pushed against gravitational fields, they didn't like other masses being present. You needed clear space, the presence of another ship made it harder ... slower ...

'Come on!'

The engines recharged sufficiently for a further boost. Raan turned the ship about and raced away from the station again.

Space crackled and shifted about him.

Hyperspace ...

He didn't want to think about it. Hyperspace was just plain weird. Chucking a ship through multi-dimensional compressed space in order to ...

The *Whiplash* flickered, accelerated and was gone.

***

Tsu had dashed back aboard the *StarStormer*, followed the Eagle out and then watched the short altercation between it and the Cobras. The pilot of the Eagle knew what he was doing when it came to flying the ship. It was ducking and rolling every which way, making it almost impossible for the Cobras to land a shot on it. Clearly they were out to disable it.

Frame shift charge detected ...

He was making his run.

Raan Corsen ... So what are you up to?

Tsu activated her wake scanner. It would tell her where he was going.

The Eagle turned and then, with a bright flash, disappeared, leaving a parallel streak of exhaust slowly dispersing in space. She toggled her wake scanner onto the location and waited while it decoded the hyperspace destination.

It didn't take long.

'Got you.'

Frame shift drive charging ...

The two Cobra pilots were clearly doing the same thing. All three ships were oriented in the same direction. All spooling their jump drives, striving to be the first to hit critical charge.

Tsu watched as the flickering energies of hyperspace wrapped themselves around her ship.

'This is going to get interesting ...'

Chapter Eleven

Hutton Orbital, Alpha Centauri system, Independent

Infrastructure looked out across the darkness of space. From his vantage point, the Milky Way was a glorious arc stretching out overhead, the combined light of four hundred billion distant stars. The view was augmented, of course, but no less spectacular for it. Out there lay countless dangers and unknowns.

His eyes were drawn to a small patch of stars some way above the plane of the galaxy. They were bright and compact, a star cluster formed of hot blue stars, bathing in the remnants of a faint nebula. Even from the skies of Earth they were a well-known and familiar sight.

The Pleiades.

He couldn't help but shiver.

After all this time, after all the work that has been done, it is this generation that has to face the peril. Have our preparations been sufficient? Only time will tell.

He was sitting in the observation lounge of a remote outpost in the Alpha Centauri system. Hutton Orbital was a curious location. At over a fifth of a light year from the system's jump-in point, it was visited only by freighters on long-haul resupply missions, those who took missions without checking the distance in advance, or those who desired to purchase a curio known as a 'Hutton Mug.' Nothing more than an old-Earth style beverage container, it was inexplicably sought after by some within the galaxy, fetching a price far beyond its intrinsic worth.

Today, the station was quiet. A maintenance interval had been 'planned,' ensuring that the outpost was closed to inbound and outbound traffic for a short duration. Ships hung in the darkness, shut down and awaiting their turn to dock.

The doors to the deck opened and four more individuals entered. He turned and waved in greeting and they took their seats around him.

'Not our most luxurious destination,' Finance grumbled. She was not a fan of spaceflight of even short durations. The extended flight to Hutton Orbital had tested her patience.

'The obvious spots are precisely that,' Infrastructure replied. 'Being off the beaten track does have its advantages.'

'No one comes here who doesn't have a very good reason, or is a little unhinged,' Society replied, settling his enormous frame into one of the recliners. It gently moulded itself about him, gripping him firmly. There was no gravity on the outpost, but somehow it still felt appropriate to 'sit' in a chair, regardless.

'It is the least pleasant location on our roster of venues,' Exo said. He was gaunt and thin by comparison, constantly referring to the commtab he carried around with him and frequently ignoring those around him while he researched a topic.

'Oh, I think it has a certain rustic charm,' Finance said. 'And it's cheap. That's never a bad thing.'

'To business,' Infrastructure said. Pleasantries were always exchanged in this fashion. He had known his colleagues for decades and little they did or said surprised him any longer. They were effective, there was no jostling for position or power, each knew their role and was happy with the responsibilities and accountabilities associated with it.

'First item of business is the matter of our dear friends at Sirius,' Infrastructure said. 'I trust their financial acumen is as sharp as ever.'

'We expect the acquisition of MetaDrive to complete this week,' Finance replied. 'The board were fully compliant with our overall directives. Chairman Femi has sadly passed away.'

'Then we can expect the distribution of the new hyperspace technology forthwith,' Infrastructure said with a smile.

Finance paused.

'There is a problem?' Infrastructure prompted, his eyebrows raised. Society leant forward.

'Femi clearly had some suspicions. He entrusted the technology to a staff member prior to his … unfortunate demise,' Finance said. 'An individual known as Raan Corsen. All other copies were deleted from MetaDrive's data silos with some kind of recursive algorithm. The board wasn't careful enough ...'

'Has this Corsen fellow been apprehended?' Infrastructure asked.

'No,' Finance replied.

There was no hostility at the news. The team had long ago moved beyond blame and accusation as tools to further an agenda. Results were the only thing that mattered. Emotional outbursts of frustration would only slow down resolutions.

'He is being pursued by agents of the Earth Defence Fleet and Sirius' own staff,' Finance said.

'What do you know about this person?' Infrastructure asked.

Society gestured and a holofac representation of a young dark-skinned man appeared in the air above him.

'Raan Corsen was a low-level tech admin in their operations depart-ment,' Society said. 'It turns out that he's also known as Commander Falchion, winner of the recent Melee Masters Arena championship.'

'An interesting connection,' Exo said.

'We believe it's a coincidence,' Society replied, 'but he was able to elude security forces at the company and the station. Naturally, he's a good pilot, if inexperienced in the realities of flying a real ship.'

'And where is he bound?'

'Uncertain at present,' Finance said. 'We have uncovered an encrypted communication between him and Femi. The contents are unreadable, but it is clear they were in touch prior to his departure.'

'So we assume that Femi gave this young chap the only remaining technical data on the new hyperdrive technology,' Infrastructure said. His face was stern. 'We find ourselves in a precarious position.'

The other four remained silent for a moment. The disapproval was far more intimidating than any outburst of anger could have been.

'He will be recovered,' Finance said, her voice catching.

'Yes,' Infrastructure said. 'Otherwise the acquisition of MetaDrive will have been in vain. I believe our priorities are clear.'

'Indeed,' Finance said.

'On to other matters,' Infrastructure looked across to Society and Exo. 'The exploration data ...'

Both men looked uncomfortable too. A frown creased Infrastructure's forehead. It was unusual for events to run beyond the control of the team, for it to happen on two fronts simultaneously was unprecedented.

'... has not been recovered,' Society said. 'Not yet, at any rate.'

'You have the senator, though. I saw the articles about her arrest.'

Society nodded. 'She is safely incarcerated. We also caught up with the Lady ...'

Infrastructure tensed, leaning forward. 'And?'

Society licked his lips to moisten them. 'She is dead.'

Infrastructure sighed and leant back in his recliner, his face registering sadness.

'A fitting end, I hope.'

'A clean one at any rate,' Society said. 'She clearly knew we were coming for her and had planned for it.'

'I would expect nothing less. She knew us too well.'

'She left a message, too,' Society flicked his fingers forward and the image of an old lady appeared. She was thin and gaunt, her silvery hair brushed into two neat folds on either side of her head. Her skin was marked with age spots, with one cheek bearing a scar from some kind of knife wound. Only her eyes seemed youthful, but dark and hard, full of purpose and intent.

She spoke, her voice crotchety but sharp.

'You're too late, as usual. I have a new protégé. Good luck with the chase.'

The image faded.

Infrastructure allowed himself a faint smile. The old lady had always been a step beyond, seemingly privy to knowledge that eluded the team around him. She had been one of their most valuable assets until ...

'The Prism senator is the protégé?' Exo asked.

'It would seem so,' Society said. 'Though it seems she herself is unaware of this, or only has a partial understanding of what the Lady intended.'

Infrastructure shook his head. 'If so, that is by design, not chance. We know the Lady planned in meticulous detail.'

'We recovered the Senator's ship,' Society said. 'The databanks were wiped, there was no exploration data aboard, no commtabs, no backups, no transmissions. The Senator has been scanned for memory alterations with no success. Her pilot, too. The exploration data eludes us.'

'Plan B?' Exo inquired.

'Will need to be accelerated,' Infrastructure said. 'But it is unlikely we can replicate the results in so short a time. We must have that exploration data. The escape routes ...'

'Can I suggest an alternative approach?' Personnel said, entering the conversation for the first time.

Infrastructure turned to regard her. 'Enlighten us.'

Personnel smiled, enjoying her moment.

'Perhaps we could play the girl, rather than the ball.'

Infrastructure frowned for a moment.

'You think the Lady has given the Senator a mission of some kind?'

'Undoubtedly,' Personnel said. 'Why not engineer a way for her to complete it? We have her in custody already. Allow her the means to bring the exploration data to us.'

'It is risky,' Exo said. 'We do not know the Lady's full intentions. If the Senator gets away from our control …'

'The Senator doesn't know, either,' Personnel said. 'We can use that. We also have other ways of managing and reporting on her activities. Our insurance is in place, I assure you.'

Infrastructure nodded. 'Proceed then, but with extreme caution. We have already seen independent pilots trying to influence events around that woman, our plans are fragile enough as it is at this point.'

'Meanwhile, the Federation and the Empire continue their games,' Exo said.

'The aspect of the plan that is unfolding without complication,' Finance said with a nod.

'We must be vigilant, though,' Exo said. 'Itinerant independent Commanders continue to cause problems. An Imperial flagship was forced to withdraw yesterday after a sustained assault from an affiliated league of independent vessels. We cannot underestimate their influence.'

'I am not concerned about the ships,' Infrastructure said. 'The London Treaty will shortly be annulled. That will deal with that particular issue.'

'We are ready with Fleet Admiral Patreus' speech,' Personnel said.

'He's going to have quite a week,' Society said, with a chuckle.

'Agreed,' Infrastructure said. 'You all have your assignments. Apply yourself to them with diligence. This is a critical moment in our operations and things may yet go awry.'

The others looked sombre.

Infrastructure grinned. 'Cheer up, though. I have made a singular achievement this week.'

The others looked blankly at one another.

'Which is?' Finance asked the obvious question.

Infrastructure raised an object in one hand and patted it with the other. It was a simple drinking container with a handle on its side. Across its exterior were a jumble of letters and a stylised representation of the outpost.

'I've been after one of these mugs for years.'

Location unknown, Aries dark region, Uninhabited

Commander Basch Fon Ronsenbur wasn't an average member of the Canonn Research group. It was fair to say he was something of a … well … loose cannon wasn't quite the right phrase, but he had a healthy disregard for rules that kept him on the edge of some of their more official ventures. He preferred the lure of the void, a little uncertainty on the objective and great flexibility in how to interpret his orders.

Loose cannon, somebody probably thinks that's funny …

Thus he tended to be in receipt of some of their more speculative ventures, those that required tact and discretion, and a blind eye turned to the legalities of the situation. He'd been tracing a route given to him by Dr. Arcanonn himself, a delicate tracery of star patterns which probably led nowhere, but were a lead that had to be followed up.

Explore everything, leave nothing unexplored.

Basch had little to show in terms of successes at Canonn. That rankled with him. He'd been with them from the very start, years ago, when they formed, trying to seek out the truth behind the plethora of legends that filtered back from the depths of space.

The chart that Dr. Arcanonn had given him was vague. Calling it a chart was giving it a description it really didn't merit. It was more of a projection, a stylised representation of what a cluster of stars and nebulae might look like from a particular vantage point.

Quite where the good doctor got his information from was unknown, certainly he never revealed that. Perhaps it was to protect his own sources, perhaps it was for other reasons. The upper echelons of Canonn Research were as mysterious as some of the legends they went looking for.

A bottle of maple brandy sat in a receptacle in the dashboard; a little nod to his Canadian ancestry. But the bottle was mocking him.

Can't be opened until I find something.

It had been sitting there for over a year. It didn't look like he was going to be opening it anytime soon.

He squinted out at the stars above the canopy of his trusty Cobra Mark III, comparing it to the star chart in the computer. The Cobra was an old ship now, but a worthy one, fitted out in exploration trim; long range without much in the way of luxuries.

Looks lined up to me... but there's only this moon …

It was a desolate and dreary looking place, billions of square kilometres of grey, grey and more grey, broken up here and there with a crater, a rill, or perhaps a canyon. Nothing he hadn't seen a thousand times before.

The Cobra strained as it maintained its height over the frozen landscape. Gravity was unusually high for such a small moon. Perhaps it had a dense metallic core.

He proceeded in this fashion for hours, tracking back and forth across the barren wasteland with little thought. Where many would have been mind-numbingly bored by such activity, if that was the right word for it, Basch took a certain relaxation from it. He enjoyed the solitude, far from the crowded worlds of the core, far from the politics and the administration of trading. Out here was peace and quiet. Any drama you made was your own.

Which was when the scanners began acting up.

Static clouded the forward reticule and interference covered the heads-up display. Fearing an instrument malfunction, Basch took the scanners offline and rebooted them, slowing the ship while he waited, peering ahead into the gloom.

Ahead, the landscape rolled and undulated as before, however, on the horizon, was a ridge, almost perfectly straight.

Doesn't look natural. Nature hates straight lines … even on an airless world …

The scanners came back on, but the interference was still there.

He switched on the Cobra's hull lights and was rewarded with a faint reflection from the dark surface below. Cautiously, he moved the ship ahead.

Dark shapes …

A strange vista unfolded before him, much of it hard to make out despite the ship's powerful lighting. Sombre and mysterious shadows flickered this way and that as the ship moved across the landscape. Overhead, another moon hung in the sky, casting a further faint glow over the area.

His first impression was of immense age. The place was covered in the same material as the landscape, dust was everywhere, with the bulk of whatever it was hidden beneath it. Shapes were softened by what might have been aeons of dust accumulation.

The next was size. It was enormous, easily as big as a major outpost on airless worlds humanity had settled, and rather similar in overall shape and feel. He pulled the ship upwards to get a better overall perspective and got his first view of the complete area for the first time.

A base, it has to be … but not human …

There was a central dome, offset to one side, with a series of what look liked ringed fortifications around it. What purpose they might serve was anyone's guess. Further afield, an outer wall ringed the main site, enclosing a flattened area that gave the impression of landing space. Certainly it was an ideal place to set down.

Basch did precisely that a few minutes later.

Nothing moved, the dust settled almost instantly in the vacuum. Basch shut down the flight systems and unstrapped the flight harness.

A quick reccie in the SRV, then I'll report back …

The lower hull folded out and down, depositing the surface reconnaissance vehicle onto the ground. It was an ugly, squat affair, reminiscent of a bulbous multi-limbed insect with six wheels at the termination of its legs. It did what it was designed to do, cope with any terrain under any conditions. It even had a limited ability to 'fly.'

Basch had no such need today. He took the SRV on a slow trundle around the immediate area. Here and there were markings etched on the ground, somehow free of dust. In other places there were strange orb-like objects, apparently abandoned on the surface.

Going to have to call in the experts for this one.

Something in particular had piqued his interest, though. There was a faint signal on the SRV's scanner, something that looked like a power source according to the energy profile.

Can't be running, not now, not after all this time …

He moved the SRV slowly across …

And had to grab the emergency brake to stop himself from panicking.

The ground trembled, a faint rattle being the only sound that penetrated up into the SRV. Ahead, a cloud of dust fairly exploded into the air, showering the SRV cockpit with fine debris. Basch retained enough presence of mind to back the SRV away a little …

An object reared out of the ground.

Thrusting vertically into the sky, it climbed in stages, up and up, a mechanism of some kind, getting narrower as it extended. Quickly it was far taller than his little vehicle, taller than the ship even.

Then it stopped. The dust settled and all was still again.

Basch heard hurried breathing, and realised it was him. He could feel his heart racing in his chest.

Then, a glow shone out from the very top of the monument, pulsing in waves. Pulsing with intent and purpose.

Basch watched it for a few moments, feeling the sweat cool and chill on his brow.

Going to need that brandy now!

Chapter Twelve

Location unknown

The next thing Hassan recalled was a bright light. He squinted, the glare driving thumping wedges of pain through his eyeballs straight into his brain. There was a hiss of equalising pressure and the thump of some mechanism sliding around him.

Escape pod ...

He blinked, trying to figure out where he was.

Salomé ... Patrons Gerrun and Zyair ... they ejected me ...

'Slowly, my friend,' said a familiar voice. 'They knock you about pretty good, I think. Here, drink first. Brandy? Scotch? Vodka?'

Hassan looked up into a familiar salt and pepper bearded and moustachioed face. It was twisted in a wry grin.

'What ... happened ... ship?'

'Brandy then.'

A gel pack with a plastic tube was shoved into his mouth and he sucked hard on it, washing the foul chemical taste from his mouth. Travelling in an escape pod certainly kept you alive, but it wasn't a glamorous form of travel.

'Luko. They took her,' Hassan managed to say after a moment.

'And who are they, hmmm?'

'Imperials,' Hassan replied. 'Those patrons that used to work on Prism, they abducted her!'

Luko helped Hassan up out of the pod. It was resting in the cargo bay of an old looking ship. Hassan could only assume it was Luko's antique Cobra Mark III, the *Bella Principessa*.

'... how did you find me?'

'Distress call,' Luko answered. Apparently that was explanation enough. 'Salomé, she hurt?' Luko was peering at him intently.

'I don't think so, they took it out on me, they wouldn't dare to ...'

'They dare much,' Luko said with a shrug. 'Word is they take her straight to Achenar.' He spat. 'They accuse her ...'

'Trying to kill Patreus,' Hassan said.

'They say she tried to kill him,' Luko said. 'Is nonsense, yes?'

Hassan nodded. 'We were herded into the Cemiess system, it was a ruse ... we've got to go get her!'

Luko shook his head. 'In a Cobra? Just the two of us? My friend, you are molto brave, but we can not do such a thing. Is impossible.'

'But the Imperials ...'

Luko sighed. 'It is politics, of course. Now, come. Must get to safety.'

'Wait,' Hassan said. 'There is something else, she said that she needed to speak to you. There was something she needed to ask.'

Luko smiled. 'Is ok, I know this.'

Hassan looked at him with a frown. 'Ok ... what aren't you telling me?'

Luko waggled a finger at him. 'Best not to ask the questions yet, yes? Strange times. Come, we must go. Not safe to stay here in the heart of the Empire, I think.'

Luko led him up from the Cobra's immaculate cargo bay, through the central living quarters and up onto the twin-seated flight deck. For once he welcomed the zero-gee, he didn't think his bruised and battered body would be up to coping planet-side for a while.

The Cobra's bridge wasn't nearly as big and expansive as the Clipper he'd been used to, but it was all that was required. The Cobra was a ship design from another century; they'd simply done a remarkable job in the past. Even now the original specs were still being used, admittedly with greatly updated internal components.

Hassan strapped himself into the co-pilot's chair. It felt good to be back here. Luko's ship was a museum piece, but it felt solid and comfortable; reassuring even. Space hung outside, an exquisite backdrop peppered with the light of distant stars. Hassan sighed with familiarity, looking around him and running his hands over the old-fashioned brass controls. Before him was a bewildering array of physical gauges and displays, a stark contrast to the ubiquitous holofac instrumentation of modern vessels.

'Good to see some things don't change,' he murmured.

'Signor?' Luko asked, looking over from the pilot's chair as he buckled himself into place.

'Oh nothing,' he answered. 'I missed this ship more than I knew.'

Luko grinned. 'A classic Cobra is not just a ship, is ... hmmm ... a way of life.'

'Thanks for rescuing me,' Hassan muttered. 'Just wish we had Salomé too ...'

The lone holofac display in the cockpit was burbling some newsfeed about a new championship where pilots from across the core worlds could compete in mock battles against each other. Hassan watched as ships angled through a twisty course of maze-like passages at breakneck speed.

'This looks like fun,' Luko said, gesturing at the display. 'I might try one day. Though I think maybe my ship too big ...'

'Salomé thought it was a distraction,' Hassan said. 'To give the masses something to occupy themselves so they don't notice the loss of their rights and liberties.'

'Ah ... politics. Always politics with her.'

'She would say that everything is politics.' Hassan said. 'Too complex for me, I couldn't understand half of it.'

Luko shrugged. 'Huh. This I not care for either. But she ... well.'

He nudged the throttles and the *Bella Principessa* leapt forward with a rumble of powerful engines.

'Rescuing you two seems to be my regular job.' He looked across again. 'We not fighting a war this time, I trust?'

Hassan grimaced in response.

'No war. Believe it or not, I think she's trying to stop one.'

'Just checking. Always the big quest with her, eh? Why not just stay out of trouble, relax, enjoy the universe, plenty to see and do without getting involved ...'

Something about his voice wasn't quite right, Hassan decided. An air of bravado, or something else? It was hard to tell.

'You know Salomé ...' Hassan answered.

Luko sighed. 'Alas, I do.'

Hassan called up the navigation charts and studied the surrounding systems.

'I suggest we go to Prism,' Luko said.

Hassan nodded. 'If it's politics, Ambassador Cuthrick might be able to help us ...'

Luko nodded. 'I have the course already, we go molto vito.'

He saw to the onboard systems and then allowed the automation to take over.

Frame shift drive charging ...

'So, they let you go ...' he said softly, looking over to Hassan. 'Why they not kill you?'

Hassan paused before answering. 'I'm not sure. I think they wanted the exploration data she'd acquired. I didn't have it so I wasn't any use to them.

That fat one is a sadistic 'stard. I think he enjoyed the idea of me eventually suffocating in the pod. Salomé didn't store anything in the ship's computer. Just before we'd paid a visit to this weird junkyard in Tionisla ...'

'The graveyard?' Luko queried, 'Ah ... yes.'

'You know about the graveyard?' Hassan asked.

Luko pursed his lips for a moment as if considering what to say. 'I have heard much of it. A strange place, no? They say it is connected with old stories. They say it was once the headquarters of the Dark Wheel ...'

Hassan frowned. 'The Dark Wheel? Aren't they a faction in Shinrarta Dezhra?'

Luko chuckled.

'Somehow I think they are not related,' Luko said. 'Hmmm ... Life, she saw, hope.'

'I'm sorry?' Hassan said, with a frown.

'That's what Shinrarta Dezhra means,' Luko explained. 'Life, she saw, hope. Languages of old Earth I was told. Zhizn, life. Ra'at, she saw. Nadezhda, Hope. Zhizn Ra'at Nadezhda.'

Hassan tried to pronounce it, causing Luko to wince.

'Have you ever been there?' Luko asked.

'Me?' Hassan replied. 'No, you need to be Elite, either as a trader, combateer or explorer before they let you in ... Wait a minute. You've been there? How?'

Luko shrugged and evaded the question. 'There are ways ... Shinrarta is the world of the Founders, they who sit above the Pilots' Federation. Is said they have much power, but they are not the Dark Wheel, I think.'

'You seem to know a lot about all this ...'

'I know my history, signor,' Luko said, tapping the side of his nose with a finger. 'This Dark Wheel, they appear and they disappear. Whenever a crisis occurs, there they are. For hundreds of years they have been turning the pages of the story. The Tionisla system is steeped in mucho ancient lore.' He shrugged. 'And now they take Salomé into their world, eh?'

'It was her secret,' Hassan answered. 'I only took her there; we had to get out quick, that's when we were ambushed by those Imperial goons ... She wouldn't tell me what she was doing ...'

'Perhaps she was wise,' Luko replied. 'Tries to keep you safe, yes?'

Hassan felt the bruises still aching on his body. 'Yeah ...'

'So,' Luko said. 'The patrons' scheme, the Dark Wheel summons and she is now at the mercy of Imperials. What is it she knows?'

Hassan looked out at the distant black emptiness beyond the ship. 'Only she knows the answer to that question.'

The *Bella Principessa* disappeared into the void between the stars.

Capitol, Achenar 6a, Achenar system, Empire

The main thoroughfare of Capitol between the Hall of Martyrs and the Hall of Justice had been cleared of pedestrians a day in advance. Banners now lined its two-kilometre length, the flags of the highest noble Imperial families mingled with royalty. A thousand others fluttered in the breeze, those of innumerable factions loyal to the Empire. Crowds of citizens and slaves jostled behind transparent barricades.

Above, the weather was clear, but the peaceful sky was rent with the sounds of multitudes of ships converging on the city. In neat formations, squadrons of vessels had congregated, overflying the crowds to gasps of amazement. Vessels were a common enough sight out by the spaceport, but this was something else.

Massive Imperial Cutters cruised majestically in the centre, flanked by Clippers on either side, their polished white hulls sparkling in the blue-white light of the Achenar star. Their engines were barely powered as the ships crawled forward, hull lights flashing in an ostentatious demonstration of power, their weapons deployed for all to see.

About them zipped smaller ships; heavy fighters such as Imperial Couriers and the lighter interceptor, the Eagle. Some performed aerobatic displays for the delight of the crowd, their engine flux flaring brightly in the air, and the boom of their exhausts echoing for kilometres around.

Below them, more military hardware was deployed. Ground assault vehicles of different types, some historic and some modern, drove or hovered down the thoroughfare, accompanied by legions of smartly dressed troops marching in formation. Some also bore arms, others were carrying musical instruments. Martial themes serenaded the enthusiastic crowds.

The Achenar Military Tattoo.

It had not been performed for decades, deemed out of place in times of relative peace. A de facto cold war had been the assumed stalemate between the Federation and the Empire for long decades. But now, the mood had changed. Security of its borders was threatened, the stability of its worlds unsure. The Empire had risen to such challenges before, it would do so again.

The event was being covered by all the Imperial newsfeeds, but it was the external feeds that were of more interest to those behind its organisation. The Empire was sending a message; they desired to be certain it was received.

Employees of the Federal Times, a right-leaning corporation-focussed news service, popular with the higher ranks of Federal society, was one non-Imperial organisation covering the story. The holofac recorders were primed but had yet to go live, the reporters were waiting for all clear

'Look at them,' one reporter said. 'Such pomp and show. They're spoiling for a fight, just asking for it.'

The comms controller next to him chuckled. She was checking the various inputs to make sure they had good coverage of all the events of the day. 'Fight's already begun. Haven't you been keeping tabs on Mu Koji?'

'No, I mean a proper scrap, big ships, duking it out, annexation of systems, some cities nuked. You know, a proper war. Not this poncing around, showing off all the time.'

'Won't happen,' the controller said. 'That's what these shows are for. It's just posturing. We'll do something similar at some point soon, probably on Earth. It's a way of showing military might without any danger to your forces.'

'Must cost an absolute fortune though …'

'Not as much as a war. They can't afford to have a war, anyway.'

'Can't afford …?'

'The treaty stops them, and us as it happens, building up a big enough fleet to do any serious damage.'

'Treaty?'

'Sheeesh, don't you know your history? The London Treaty. Signed by both powers back in, I don't know, the late 3270s or something. Limits the number of capital ships they're allowed to run. They can replace anything that gets spaced, but only up to a certain size.'

'They signed up to that?'

'Made good sense at the time. The Empire couldn't stand for an arms race without restructuring their Senate, which would have caused massive upheaval. We didn't want it in the Federation either, the tax hikes would have been unbelievable, especially with the economy being so fragile back then.'

'So rather than war it's just a case of who can put on the best show?'

'You got it.'

On the holofac monitors, the legions of troops could be seen fanning out in an arc and turning around to face the Hall of Martyrs, its huge obsidian columns stretching beyond the angle of the view.

'Big speech from the Quiff coming,' the reporter said.

'You can bet on it,' the controller replied. 'Hope he's well coiffured for the cameras, he'd better not let us down. You know how our folks love to hate him. Make sure you get a tight angle on him.'

'I wonder if someone will take a pop at him again.'

'Doubt it, security will be double tight. Did you see that portable force field emitter they have? Neat stuff, nobody will be able to get close to him.'

'That's what they thought last time. Would be awesome to catch him getting spaced on holofac, that might make my career.'

The controller chuckled again. 'You're a bit bloodthirsty today. That probably would start a war. They'd likely pin it on us this time around rather than that Imperial brat they've got on the hook for it over in ...'

'Shhhh! Here he comes. Look at that grease ball!' •

On the monitors they could see Fleet Admiral Denton Patreus stride onto the wide steps of the Hall of Martyrs. Rapturous applause greeted his arrival, the cheers of appreciation rumbling down the two kilometres of crowds as they caught sight of him either directly or via holofac imagers spread down the thoroughfare. His image loomed large across them, projected into the air above him, a vast three-dimensional representation positioned directly in front of the Hall of Martyrs. The symbolism was blatant.

Patreus looked around, saluted to the crowd and then stood, ramrod straight in a military stance, waiting for the cheering crowds to calm down.

'In the name of our Emperor, ruler of a thousand worlds, arbiter of justice and supreme overlord of our great and distinguished society – I greet you!'

Patreus was forced to stop, drowned out by the cheering of the crowds. Flags and handheld lights waved and flashed; the stamp of feet and the applause counterpointing the fading rumble of the spacecraft and ground vehicles.

'Senators, Patrons, Citizens and honoured guests of the Empire!'

Cheers and roars of appreciation punctuated every word. Patreus could be seen to acknowledge them, raising his hands.

Slowly, perhaps encouraged from within, the crowd settled down.

'Here it comes,' the controller said. 'Let's see if he has anything interesting to say about all this ...'

The reporter zoomed in the monitors, ensuring that Federal viewers would catch every nuance of the Imperial speech.

Patreus paused for a moment. Silence fell, the crowd waiting for their orator to begin.

'Our glorious Empire has stood, built upon the blood of our fathers, their fathers and their fathers before them, from time immemorial. For more than a thousand years, our society has prospered and flourished. We have been attacked, we have defended ourselves. We have faced overwhelming military might, we have prevailed. We have faced covert surveillance and manipulation, we have uncovered it, exposed it and frustrated it. We have thwarted the cowardly and will leave no stone unturned in the pursuits of justice …'

'He's still sore about Cemiess. That Prism girl is going to hang …' the reporter murmured. 'Whether she's guilty or not, she's going down for it.'

'Next week's story,' the controller snapped. 'Focus on this!'

'The Empire remains strong,' Patreus continued. 'Yet these are dark times. Skirmish after skirmish and rumours of war come back from our borders on a daily basis. Threatened we are. Yes, threatened! Threatened by forces we could counter and others we have yet to test our strength against. We would respond, but our hands are tied. We are hemmed in on every side by the depredations of legality and bureaucracy.'

'Hello …' the controller said, leaning forward.

'Thirty years ago we were manoeuvred into a legal trap. Taking advantage of the political instability of the time and in order to protect their financial interests, we were forced to negotiate a treaty with our Federal …' Patreus poured scorn on the next word. 'Associates. A treaty that they claimed would promote peace and prevent war. They even insulted us with its name, harking back to an ancient Federal city. They named it …' His voice soured with distaste. 'The London Treaty.'

'Yet I ask you,' Patreus continued, his voice rising in fervour. 'Have we found peace as a result of this treaty? Or have we found our borders disputed, our expansions thwarted? Have we made great strides in the growth of our ambitions in this universe? No, we have not! For no longer do we have the means to take or even hold our acquisitions. We have been hamstrung, invalided, disabled. And by whom? By the Federation!'

'Shit … he's really going to do it!' the controller said, her mouth hanging open.

'The Federation have always harried us, delayed us, and put before us every obstacle they can bring to bear. Enough is enough. This so-called treaty was foisted upon us by overzealous Federal lawyers and now they use it to limit our ability to defend ourselves in an increasingly hostile universe. This I cannot and will not accept any longer!'

The crowd was silent, now hanging on every word. A million faces were turned to hear Patreus' next words. A billion more watched remotely. He took a moment to look at the assembled masses.

'Ever the theatrics …' the controller whispered.

Then Patreus spoke, in tones of ringing clarity.

'I am proud … Yes, proud! Proud to announce we will be building a new fleet of capital ships, treaty restrictions be damned. We will defend our borders, we will push back the frontiers. In the Emperor's glorious name!'

Patreus pumped a clenched fist into the air. The crowd erupted into cheering, their shouts echoing through the streets of Capitol. Banners and flags waved. The spacecraft returned on cue, roaring back across the masses of people in tight formations. Fireworks and weapons discharged into the air, creating a frenzy of noise and light.

'You're on!' the controller said. 'In five, four, three …'

The reporter waited for the countdown to complete and then spoke.

'And there you have it. Fleet Admiral Patreus has pledged to break the restrictions of the London Treaty at today's military tattoo here on Achenar. The crowds are ecstatic, and it seems that we edge ever closer to a war footing with the Empire, with confirmation that they intend to build a new fleet of capital ships. Tensions between the Federation and the Empire, already weakened, will be further strained by this news …'

'They're really going to do it,' the controller whispered to herself. 'They're really going to start a war …'

***

Fleet Admiral Denton Patreus stepped directly into a transport and was whisked away towards the Capitol spaceport. With the speech concluded there were other matters to attend to, more subtle and certainly more compelling than the tedious orations he was forced to give as the military face of the Empire.

He smiled to himself.

The image of a one-dimensional warmongering fool is well portrayed and firmly believed. If only they knew …

He watched as the spectacular city line of Capitol rolled beneath the viewport. It was an eclectic mix of ancient, historic and modern, all blended successfully into a cohesive whole. Patreus had been to Earth once and had been horrified at the scattered and haphazard arrangement of the buildings in the famous city of London.

London, I doubt I have many favours left there after today …

It had been necessary, a piece of pomp and fluff for the camera, a facile but necessary part of his role. He was tasked with keeping the Empire, not just keeping the Empire safe. There was a crucial difference. The Empire was not a static thing, it had to expand, take new ground. The pioneering spirit that had formed it continued to this day, always looking outwards for new acquisitions.

And if we don't, our economy will, in time, falter. We will stagnate and our Empire will crumble from within.

Patreus was a student of history. He'd read about ancient Rome, knew of the Byzantine, the Ottomans and the Turks. He'd studied the rise and fall of the British in the 20th century and the spectacular collapse of the United States in the 21st – from which the Federation itself had been born. History repeated itself across the centuries. The Tau Ceti Rebellion … Empires had their time in the sun and then they faded. Downfalls shared many aspects in common, failures to respond to threats, failures to expunge the wastrels, failure to curtail freedoms, failure to consolidate gains …

So be it if he needed to play the part of the strutting arrogant military fool. If the Empire prevailed, it was a cost worth paying.

And so this girl …

Patreus turned his thoughts towards his next assignment. It would be more of a challenge. He'd reviewed her biography a number of times, but he had questions that only a personal meeting would answer. He replayed her encounter with Princess Aisling, chuckling at the barbs tossed between the pair. She had spirit and a deft touch, that was clear enough.

But who is she really working for, that is the question. Is she an asset, or a liability? She has a choice, as do I …

The aircar slowed and descended into the private suites of the spaceport reserved for those of stature. He emerged, giving a brief nod to the ranks of guards lined up to greet him as he entered the complex.

A questioning look brought him the answer he was looking for.

'Fleet Admiral. She has been moved,' an aide said, 'She is in the guest quarters. The transport is prepped and will take her to Prism at your behest.'

Patreus nodded.

'Her effects?'

The aide beckoned him over to a sealed canister and gestured for it to open. The top folded back.

'That's all?'

'That's all, Fleet Admiral.'

Patreus took a closer look. There was only a single item. It was a sword, and a vintage one at that. The pommel was carved from bone, the guard wrought of bright-steel and marked with runes of a script he did not recognise. The scabbard was leather, bound with a latticework of fine metal.

He picked it up, marvelling at its lightness, and then drew it to examine the blade. That too was bright-steel, and inlaid with gold filigree. It was the product of a master craftsman, a blade that spoke of lineage, honour and a family tree that stretched back far into history.

A Holva blade, and an ancient one. Made for the Lorens centuries ago, I would guess. A real prize.

It was a weapon of far greater worth than his own family heirloom, the sword he wore buckled at his waist for ceremonial occasions.

'More than a few people have admired that,' the aide commented.

Patreus did not respond, returned the blade to its scabbard, but kept hold of it.

'Her ship?'

Scanned from stem to stern, sir. Nothing found in the ship's systems other than the hyperspace route plots. They show a series of voyages across the chart, but the data involved has been purged. The ship is heavily customised with state-of-the-art componentry, but nothing particularly unusual. It remains impounded.

Seven Veils. She wraps misdirection about even the name of her vessel.

Patreus acknowledged the report with a brief incline of his head.

'I will see her now.'

The aide looked uncertain. 'The weapon, Fleet Admiral? Is it wise to take it with you? She has quite the reputation with it. It has shed blood more than once in recent years.'

Patreus smiled. 'A woman of spirit, substance and capability. Such things should be witnessed, they are rare enough.'

'If you're sure …'

The aide hurried to a pair of doors and unlocked them. Guards stood at the threshold, weapons drawn and prepared, but no one awaited them. Patreus stepped through, the Loren blade held in his hand, his own still buckled beside him.

Salomé was being held in a guest suite, awaiting transport to Prism for the court hearing. As Patreus entered, she was sitting in a chair by the window, looking out across the landing bays of the spaceport back towards the towering skyline of Capitol.

He watched as she turned to regard him. He saw her eyes widen briefly as she realised who it was and saw her glance towards the weapon in his hand.

Prepared, watchful for any opportunity. Good …

'Forgive the intrusion …' Patreus began.

'No, I do not,' Salomé replied. 'I see they are sending all manner of torments for me. Have you come here to kill me ahead of time in retribution for this ridiculous accusation?'

Patreus smiled. 'I merely wait for the wheels of justice to turn in their grooves.'

'Grooves which you have aligned for your own benefit, no doubt.'

'You really think I annexed the Prism system out of spite?' Patreus asked. 'That I did not consider long and hard how best to manage incursions from the Federation?'

'It was not the Federation we feared. We could have handled the situation without the benefit of your …' her lip curled in distaste, 'influence.'

'My influence is what saved your little world from annihilation.'

'Is that what you tell yourself? Is that the justification you use for all of your acquisitions? That you were just "saving" them?' Salomé rose from her chair and walked towards him. 'You appropriated my world without so much as a by your leave, not even a common courtesy. You exploited it, used it as a staging post on your rise to power, wrestling with all the other members of this sordid little powerplaying clique of yours. To add insult to injury, despite the cost to my home, you didn't even succeed in your vainglorious quest to become Emperor.'

Patreus returned her gaze. He had the advantage in height, but her gait and poise were firm and sure. He could see the tone of her muscles and the firm set of her jaw. But most of all, it was the determination that burned in her grey eyes that struck him.

Not one to underestimate …

'Our play for power?' Patreus smiled. 'A game, nothing more. But a game with a purpose.'

Salomé looked distinctly unimpressed. 'Your games cost the lives of thousands.'

'As did yours.'

That stopped her for a moment.

'I had just cause.' Her voice was lower.

Patreus nodded. 'And those who prevail are those worth saving, the pure that survive the refiner's fire, those that can overcome the crucible of war. Those who die … a cost worth the price?'

He saw her blink in surprise.

Patreus walked past her. 'Do not suppose this is all idle posturing,' he said. 'There is a means and a purpose to all this.'

'Ha! A purpose to still elevate you to Emperor, no doubt,' Salomé replied. 'Yet your ambitions were thwarted, were they not? That must have been a bitter pill to swallow for one such as you.'

Patreus smiled to himself. 'I will not deny that such a rise would have pleased me. But it is the Empire itself that is my concern.'

He heard her snort of derision.

'You care for nothing but yourself.'

Patreus turned to regard her. 'The same has been said about you, Kahina Loren, Salomé, or whatever it is you wish to be called. You say you fight for Prism, yet you abandoned it to chase dreams and myths. You instigated a conflict and caused the death of thousands, and yet the lives of those on your precious little moon are largely unchanged. Your people would choose doddery old Ambassador Cuthrick over you. In fact, they have …'

He saw guilt and shame flicker momentarily across her face and knew he'd found a weakness.

'Perhaps you and I are not so dissimilar after all,' Patreus said, lowering his voice. 'Forced by events, duty and society to project an image of ourselves that is at odds with reality.'

That silenced her!

She turned aside and didn't respond for a long moment.

'I am nothing like you.' Her voice shook with the words. She didn't look at him.

'You think I am a warmongering fool, out to expand the Empire's military conquests regardless of the cost,' Patreus said. 'It's true, that is how I portray myself. It's easy enough to believe.'

She didn't answer, but regarded him with an unfriendly look.

'You, on the other hand, are considered a spoilt brat, an over-privileged daughter of a moribund Imperial house, inciting violence and war, sowing the seeds of discontent across the galaxy, cloaked under a mantle of charisma and charm. But that is not your real purpose, is it?'

She opened her mouth to respond and then thought better of it.

He threw the Holva blade at her. She caught it expertly and stepped back as he drew his own sword and pointed the tip towards her.

'Start down this path and be prepared to meet your end,' she snarled, drawing the ancient blade from the scabbard. 'I know how to handle a sword. I do not boast idly.'

Patreus admired her stance. It was practised and ready. Her swordsmanship was no mere story embellished in the telling. She truly knew what she was about.

'So I have heard. But perhaps I offer you an honourable end. Not for you the ignominy of a sentence and imprisonment, servitude, banishment or … reconditioning.'

He struck out at her, an abrupt lunge and slash. She sidestepped immediately, parrying and turning the blade back upon him. It was even faster than he'd expected. Their moves were a blur, exchanging half a dozen cuts and thrusts before they both retreated, sword tips poised.

'There is more to you, Kahina Loren, more to all of this,' he said, his voice barely above a whisper. 'I know you are not guilty of this ridiculous charge of attempted assassination. That much is plain. Given that, it is clear that someone else moves against you. We could work together to search out the truth.'

'Work with you?'

The response was a stinging slash with her sword. He parried and they came close, straining at each other for advantage.

'You have enough enemies already,' Patreus replied, his face inches from her. 'I am not one of them.'

'It's plain to see your ex-lover is behind all this,' Salomé answered. 'And you call me a spoilt brat!'

'She has not the wit for this scheming,' Patreus said. 'Her strings are being pulled elsewhere.'

'She does not concern me …'

'You don't know what you're looking for, do you?' Patreus asked. 'I can make this trial go away, just tell me what you know. I will help you …'

'That's your price, is it?' Salomé replied. 'You're asking me to trust you too? Your darling princess already tried that pathetic line.'

She pushed him back and returned to a ready stance.

'It was not I that accused you of trying to kill me,' Patreus replied. 'It was obvious that this was a setup from the start. I eradicated the Emperor's Dawn, purged them from the stars. For them to come back? Ridiculous. Somebody assumed I would be easy to manipulate and cast you as the villain. Someone who wants to stop you completing whatever it is you're trying to achieve. The princess is a useful figurehead.'

Salomé shook her head. 'A convenient story. More likely you are in league with that blue-haired trollop.'

'Then perhaps a traditional threat will convince you,' Patreus said, his voice hardening. 'You are politically destitute. This court will find against you and the punishment will be severe. It is within my gift to dispel it, but I need your cooperation.'

'Bribery and corruption. I do not trust you, nor will I ever!'

'You don't need to trust me. Just tell me what you know, the trial will be forgotten.'

Salomé held still for a long moment, before lowering her sword, returning it to its scabbard and then throwing it back to Patreus.

Patreus caught it and then looked at her.

She shook her head.

'I will not work with you.'

'You are making a mistake. Signing your own death warrant … or worse.'

'So be it.'

She knows her mind. She is determined to see this through. I would do the same in her position. Yet … she can trust me … but I cannot tell her why …

Patreus spared her one last look. She was not beautiful in the manner of the debutantes and celebrities of Achenar, but she was a striking woman. In another universe, she would have made quite the consort. But she had forfeited that opportunity.

He turned and walked to the doors, signalling for them to open. They slid back with a faint hiss.

'I will see you on Prism then, Lady Kahina Loren,' he said. 'For the final chapter in your story.'

Salomé gave a curt bow. Patreus let out a deep sigh as the doors closed behind him.

The Empire could do with more women like you. A shame it may soon have one less.

Patreus watched as the pre-arranged holofac transmission was relayed to the various news agencies of the Empire. It was necessary to follow through on this farce now, there was no alternative. He didn't blame Kahina for not trusting him, she had no reason to, but there was only one course of action now.

Through the maelstrom and out the other side. Let's hope we survive intact.

He watched as the major Imperial networks slotted the announcement into their programming. The Imperial Citizen, always keen to highlight anything that denigrated the disgraced senator's character, ran the article immediately.

In an unusual display of legal legerdemain, Senator Kahina Tijani Loren has been stripped of her rank of Senator after being deemed 'In Absentia' after abrogating her responsibilities in respect to the Prism system to Ambassador Cuthrick Delaney in 3301.

"She gave up the responsibilities of Senator, it is not reasonable that she is protected by the title and all it accords," said an aide working on behalf of Fleet Admiral Denton Patreus. "Quite frankly, she can hardly be described as a Lady given the accusations against her, but we will allow the courts to make that determination."

Observers have noted that this now means Kahina Tijani Loren will be tried for her alleged crimes based on the rules of her currently nominated homeworld, which is, of course, the Prism system.

Whilst the system remains under the supervision of Ambassador Cuthrick Delaney, it is also heavily exploited by none other than Fleet Admiral Denton Patreus. Kahina is due to be moved from Achenar and will be shortly en route to the Prism system under guard.

"Naïve individuals, without a proper appreciation of due process, might accuse us of a conflict of interest in respect to this matter," the aide added. "However, we can assure all concerned that the Imperial legal code will be adhered to … to the letter."

Chapter Thirteen

Leeson City, Chione, Prism system, Empire

Ambassador Cuthrick Delaney, Acting Senator of the Prism system, stretched and winced as he felt his back muscles pull. He had been hunched over a desk for far too long, reviewing all manner of necessary but inconsequential work that required his oversight or approval. The worst was delegated to underlings, but such was the nature of it, much required his personal view.

He sat back and sighed.

So, she's returning home.

He had been watching the various missives and legal wrangling that preceded any Imperial trial of note. This one had been nothing particularly unusual in that sense, it was only that it concerned someone he knew and had some affection for.

Two years prior, Senator Kahina Tijani Loren had abdicated her executive powers relating to the Prism system to him. Since then, he'd been looking after the affairs of the little moon, trying to rebuild its economy and infrastructure after it was shattered by the brief war that had beset it in 3300.

A war we both had responsibility for starting.

He comforted himself that there had been no real alternative. The Federals had invaded the system and would have stopped at nothing to secure their access to the world's tantalum. He recalled the tense political wrangling between himself and Tenim Neseva, the Federal representative for the region. Warmongering military types on both sides had used the affair as a proving ground for their new starships, with the loss of life being an 'acceptable cost.'

She had taken it hard, though.

True, her actions immediately beforehand had precipitated the conflict, but back then she had been young and naïve, the situation thrust upon her against her will. She had survived and had the wisdom to realise that the stewardship needed a firm and experienced hand.

And this other business …

She had been the ideal candidate to investigate the rumours. She had taken guidance from many. Finance and equipment had not been a problem, and she had popular support that ranged far beyond the boundaries of the core worlds. If there truly was a threat, she was well placed to discover it.

And did she? This trial is merely a move in the game. But who are the players and who are the pieces?

Cuthrick was experienced enough with galactic politics to look for the ends rather than the coarse tactics of the short term, but if there was a master plan at work behind the machinations, he could not perceive it.

He rubbed his forehead.

More at work here than we can see.

That the Federation and Empire were being stoked for a war was obvious. Too obvious. Neither organisation had any desire to have an actual armed conflict of any magnitude. The recent annulment of the London Treaty had sent ripples across the core worlds, but it had been a moribund treaty for some time – more honoured in the breach than the observance. Patreus had merely made public what had been official private policy for some time.

Patreus …

Cuthrick had met him on a few occasions. His lackeys had been interfering in the running of the Prism system, exploiting it for resources and personnel. Prism had a reasonable tactical position on the edge of the Empire. Cuthrick had accommodated the additional bureaucracy as best he could.

But Patreus himself …

Cuthrick had been tempted to dismiss him early on, his perceptions coloured by the media representations of the man, and the impressions borne by those who worked for him. It was only upon meeting him at a reception that Cuthrick had decided to reappraise his own assessment.

For a start, Patreus listened far more than he spoke. That was always an encouraging sign. Moreover, he was quick to identify the fawning timewasters who did little beyond swelling the numbers at Imperial social gatherings. He quickly established where the power lay and worked to associate himself with it. Cuthrick had little affection for the man, but found he could work with him. Patreus had an intelligence he kept hidden from the public. Out there he was all brash and bravado, the belligerent mouthpiece of the mighty Imperial military. In private he was measured and astute, though no less determined to get his way.

Cuthrick reviewed the material before him. Press reports were typically myopic, taking either a positive or negative spin on proceedings dictated by the whims of their readers. He'd enjoyed the coverage of Salomé and Aisling tossing barbs at each other. That ridiculous blue-haired socialite was, surprisingly, exactly the same in person as her image suggested, the epitome of a facile celebrity, being famous for merely being famous; her family line and her youthful comeliness the only attributes of any note. Little surprise she used them to their maximum effect.

And this trial …

Salomé, for all her irritation with Patreus given his interference with Prism, had no real grudge against him as far as he knew. She hadn't been here – how could she? Patreus, most likely, hadn't even heard of her until the events of Cemiess. Someone was forcing them into confrontation. Imperial law ostensibly required formal justice and procedure, but Cuthrick was well aware that in the case of senators, such trials were a foregone conclusion, used to move the players about and curry favour with those in power.

It seemed implausible that Salomé would have had anything to do with Patreus' assassination attempt, and equally unlikely that Patreus would have believed she did.

Why then? And who benefits from this charade?

Cuthrick sighed. Whomsoever it was had yet to play their hand.

A faint tone sounded from the holofac transmitter. He acknowledged it and reviewed the new information that appeared.

Imperial Clipper inbound, scheduled for landing at Leeson City in ten minutes.

He got up and walked outside. Prism's Hall of Justice sat on the northern edge of the Loren Piazza, once the scene of an execrable massacre by Salomé's father, Algreb. Today it was virtually deserted. The area had been deemed off limits to citizens due to the impending trial. Security was discreet but in place, nonetheless.

An aircar arrived and he boarded it, settling into a plush seat as it whisked him swiftly towards the spaceport on the edge of the city. As it circled down, he could see that the Clipper had just arrived, escorted by a series of Imperial warships that continued to hover protectively around it.

He was surprised to see it was Salomé's ship, the *Seven Veils*. Its hull still bore the marks of weapons fire, scorched and burnt along the nacelles and upper surfaces.

Tactless to bring her as a prisoner in her own ship, or is this part of her humiliation?

He disembarked and was met by a phalanx of guards from Loren's Legion. The self-styled faction had taken up military duties in order to ensure stability throughout the Prism system. Cuthrick had found them to be efficient and unexcitable, attributes he found reassuring and useful. Their leader, one Commander Cornelius Gendymion, was a dour-faced individual with an almost permanent frown, but dedicated and dependable.

He was there, overseeing the arrival. On noticing Cuthrick, he turned and strode across the landing apron towards him.

'All secure, Ambassador,' Cornelius said. 'She can disembark safely.'

Cuthrick inclined his head in acknowledgement.

'Good to hear, Commander,' Cuthrick said. 'You've done your duty. Your reputation is well deserved.'

'I would do more,' Cornelius answered. 'If I only knew what that duty might be.'

Cuthrick nodded.

'For now we must let the wheels of Imperial justice turn on their axles,' Cuthrick said. 'Any interference in due process would not be advisable. We have seen what reckless action results in.'

Cuthrick saw Cornelius purse his lips.

'You mean the Children of Raxxla blockading and assaulting ships in Cemiess? Ill-advised, I'll warrant, but somewhat understandable given the circumstances. I've done my best to discourage them from doing anything similar again.'

'Patience wears thin,' Cuthrick replied. 'But precipitate action oft goes awry.'

He sensed the man's frustration. Cornelius was a man of action, held in check by wisdom and experience, though he had little time for the vagaries of politics.

They walked forward towards the passenger boarding ramp of the Clipper, the Commander's men stepping into place smartly behind them.

Imperial guards, dressed in bright white uniforms, funnelled out, their boots thumping on the stairway and taking up station alongside Cornelius's guards.

'Prisoner may disembark.'

Lighter steps sounded on the stairs. Cuthrick could hear the footfalls, not too fast, not too slow. A perfect gait honed through years of fine Imperial upbringing.

Then she came into view.

She was dressed in her trademark green, a simple yet elegant and understated dress she often wore whilst travelling. She wore a necklace, but no other adornment.

Stripped of her rank of Senator ...

She looked exhausted. Make-up and rejuvenation clinics could not hide the tiredness etched on her features. Her poise and countenance looked weary, despite her Imperial bearing. Her eyes were hollow and haunted.

Cornelius and his guards snapped to attention with a sharp salute. Cuthrick bowed.

Perhaps she is no longer a senator, but I will treat her as one, regardless.

Catching sight of them both, a smile broke out on her face and she walked quickly across to them.

'Cuthrick!

She clasped him close in an embrace, catching him off guard.

'My Lady.'

'For now, at least. They haven't stripped me of that title yet.' She smiled. 'But I imagine there is still time. And you, Commander Cornelius. Your service has been exemplary. I thank you for it.'

Cornelius nodded curtly. 'Always at your service, ma'am.'

The senior guard that had arrived with her coughed, noticeably.

'I see I am permitted little time for reunions,' Salomé said aloud. 'Dear Patreus doubtless has some other pressing business.' She looked at Cuthrick one last time. 'I am not concerned with him.'

Then she was gone, marched across the landing apron towards the terminal, to be secured prior to the trial. Cornelius's guards paced alongside the Imperial escort, merely because they could.

Cuthrick rubbed his chin. Cornelius looked at him.

'What did she mean by that?'

Cuthrick glanced at him.

'It means that she doesn't suspect Patreus to be behind this affair,' Cuthrick said, with a frown.

Which begs the obvious question ...

Cornelius voiced it for him.

'So who the hell is?'

'I am not sure ...'

Mars High, Mars, Sol system

Saffron hurriedly tapped in the codes for her communication panel and was relieved to see her friend's face appear in the view. There was some problem with the telepresence system, so they had to resort to vid comms.

The transmission was poor quality, clearly at some significant range, but Scarlet's red hair was unmistakable.

'Hey girl,' Scarlet said. Saffron could see she was in her ship and out in space somewhere.

'Glad I caught you,' Saffron said. 'Listen. I need to be quick, something weird is going on.'

'Tell me,' Scarlet replied.

'I started digging into your story,' Saffron said. 'At the high level, it all looks just as you'd expect, a mad conspiracy theory for the nutters to debate.'

'And …?'

'I dig a little deeper, requisitioned a few data silos from some folks I know. There's another layer here; clandestine comms, secret orders, missing files. That Imperial woman who just got arrested. Lots of feeds point back to companies like Sirius and Wreaken too. President Halsey, remember how she went missing in that ship disaster? That nerdy professor got a mention too … Palin or something. All sorts of stuff.'

'Looks like you found it …'

'There's more. I archived it into a private commtab, locked it down,' Saffron said. 'Picked it up just now and … it's blank.'

'Wiped?'

'Looks like it. Remotely. I don't know how, you're not supposed to be able to do that … I'm a little freaked out …'

Scarlet's voice was no-nonsense. 'Get out of there now. You remember where we first got drunk together?'

'Yes, but …'

'Ship out on a tramp vessel, don't use public transport. Some commander will be going that way, go as a private passenger. I'll meet you there this time tomorrow. No more comms, all right? Just be there.'

'Scarlet …'

'Be there!'

'I will.'

'Don't stop for anything, just move.' Scarlet's face softened for a rare moment of empathy. 'It will be ok, trust me. I'm coming.'

Saffron swallowed and nodded. 'See you soon.'

'You betcha.'

Chapter Fourteen

Jaques Station, Colonia, Colonia nebula

It had attracted many. Rich investors looking for an unlikely but profitable return, the poor looking for a new life, explorers who planned to use it as a handy way station in the void. It was so far away that most baulked at the trip across the vast distance. It took a certain type of individual to make the 'Journey to Jaques.'

Twenty-two thousand light years doesn't look like much on a map of the galaxy, not even a quarter of its diameter, but it's a different matter when you're traipsing the void between lonely stars that no one has ever visited, and quite possibly, no one ever will again.

Jaques himself was a rather eccentric individual. Part cyborg, his transformation from man to machine began during the time he served as a member of the Quinentis Fourteens, a Federal black ops strike team. His unit was captured by enemy forces during the Battle of Hell's Gate.

The intrepid ex-soldier spent close to the next two hundred years improving his cybernetic implants and saving up to buy the eponymous 'Jaques Station.' Slowly, with the patience only a machine can have, he invested money and upgraded the station with various engineering subsystems until it was fully manoeuvrable, equipped with its own engines and hyperspace capability, along with some very advanced sound systems, providing a dark electric beat to what had become one of the most renowned nightspots in the void for young thrill seekers.

Jaques claimed he was only a barman and that he was on a mission 'to discover new beverages, explore distant stars, and bravely go where no starport had been before.' Whether he had some ulterior motive wasn't clear, but he had done little to arouse suspicion.

His roving space station had been wandering the galaxy for forty years and had wound up in the Gliese 1269 system when the announcement was sent out. No one was all that surprised when Jaques indicated that he intended to attempt a hyperspace jump across the entire width of the galaxy. Most just shrugged and said, 'That's Jaques …'

His destination was the newly charted system known as 'Beagle Point.' An unremarkable star system in every way except one; at the time, it was the furthest reachable system diametrically opposite the core worlds, on the far side of the galaxy.

An unheard-of quantity of fuel was sourced by willing pilots who joined in the madness. The station was fuelled and began its jump on the 20th of May, 3302.

And promptly disappeared.

No one seemed entirely sure how long such a jump should take on this unprecedented scale. Hyperdrive technology was not something that most people were intimately familiar with. Days certainly, weeks perhaps …

Once a week had passed, some search activities began to take place. Lonely explorers camped out at Beagle Point reported no sign of the station. No transmissions had been received. The station had definitely entered hyperspace, there was no sign of it at Gliese 1269. Some speculated it had been flung out of the galaxy, most began to assume it had been destroyed.

But a month later a transmission, faint and broken, was received.

'… witch-space … drive engines … station infrastructure intact but … we are …'

It wasn't much, but it was enough for the intrepid explorers of the galaxy to begin triangulating its position. That eventual honour went to a certain Commander Cly, who stumbled upon the station almost accidentally in a routine patrol of distant stars near the core. Completely off course, the station had been found in the obscurely named Eol Prou RS-T d3-94 system, which was almost immediately given the moniker 'Colonia' for ease of reference.

It transpired that the station was in poor shape, in need of major repairs. Once again, long range explorers and traders rose to the occasion, ferrying materials across the long tracts of empty space.

Thus it became a waypoint in the void. More travellers arrived and the station became something of a conversation piece, and then a society all of its own. Entrepreneurs set up auxiliary outposts and surface bases. Before long, there was an economy and governance …

Colonia, the second bubble. It lies against a bright reflection nebula, backlit by thousands of blue-white stars and the glow of the galaxy's core. The skies there are utterly mesmerising, a hundred times the density of the stars visible from the familiar systems towards the rim and far brighter. It is never truly dark with such illumination, regardless of where you travel.

***

Alesia had fled the core worlds, driven out by the intrigue and hostility of the bubble.

That and all that other weird stuff! One S, I said. I'm no Imperial sympathiser!

Born and raised on Brani 6, she had never felt at home in the core worlds. The machinations of the Empire and the Federation left her with the feeling she was locked in a box of their making. She never understood why they would fight so hard and long over such a small volume of space when there was so much territory just a few thousand light years out, and all that it promised in resources, planets and life.

She sold a family business, a popular small resort chain, and used the funds to train for and acquire her pilot's license. Graduating with a lowly Sidewinder, she worked her way up to her dream ship, an Imperial Clipper. When she heard about Jaques Station, she knew she had to go and see it for herself.

The sabre-rattling of the Empire and the Federation had pushed her out; she was looking for a new start, alongside many others.

And after that business with the Empire accusing me of being in league with some criminal … enough! The core worlds are corrupt and cursed with politics. Colonia is free from all that, a new start, a new set of worlds un-tainted by all that history. We can all start again.

Today she was chasing mysteries.

She'd heard of bizarre and otherworldly ruins being discovered across the galactic chart, apparently the ruins of some long dead civilisation that had already been nicknamed the 'Guardians.' Humanoids perhaps, an advanced culture for sure, and long dead so it seemed. As far as she knew nothing similar had been found out in the Colonia region, but there were tantalising hints that these aliens might have been out this far.

And I plan to be first to prove it …

It was a bit of an indulgence, to be fair. She loved exploration and reports had come back that various locales in the Colonia system were showing a variety of curious readings. Most vessels had skimmed through, heading to Jaques Station for repairs without stopping to do systematic surveys.

Many of the planets in the Colonia system had already been surveyed, but she liked the idea of exploring something new. The world of Colonia 3CA was her target, her Clipper smoothly dropping out of supercruise as it approached.

Orbital flight engaged …

The targeting reticule switched modes. She felt the faint tug of gravity from below, it wasn't much, but it felt very strange after the zero-gee of space travel. Around her, the Clipper creaked and moaned as its structural members took up the increasing load.

It was difficult to tell when the planet below stopped being a sphere and became a landscape. It was brown in colour, pockmarked with craters – and sometimes craters within craters. Huge canyons arched across it, hundreds of kilometres in length.

Glide engaged …

The ship slowed further, the ground rising up to meet it. Alesia adjusted course. The canyons looked far more interesting than the craters and they might go deeper into the planet's crust …

Glide complete …

If the Clipper had a weakness it was a tendency to yaw into sharp turns. Its lateral thrusters were relatively tepid for its significant bulk. Alesia made the turn a little too late, catching the lower hull on the rim of the canyon and dislodging a torrent of material that cascaded slowly down in the low gravity. Shields flickered and failed and the hull gave an unpleasant groan.

'Oops …'

The hull condition marker flashed angrily at her.

96%.

'Going to have to pay for that …'

As she pondered the cost of her inattention, the scanner lit up with a signal. She looked at it for a moment, realising that she didn't recognise the pattern.

'Woah … what's this?'

Something down there …

She adjusted course in such a hurry that the ship's engines began to overheat. She cursed, berating herself for being reckless. It was the fastest way to get yourself killed.

'Breathe! And calm! I'm good … calm. Now. Landing …'

The Clipper lowered itself down and over the overhang of a canyon, dust swirling up past the canopy for brief moments as the ship came to rest. No way to land on the tumbled debris of the canyon floor, there was no space for a ship of the Clipper's size. She'd have to drive down.

Alesia jumped out of the flight chair and quickly strapped herself into the Clipper's SRV. Within another minute she was out on the surface, trundling forwards in the wheeled machine, heading for the enigmatic signal.

'I shouldn't … but I'm going to!'

She jammed the throttle forward and the SRV flew straight off the canyon ledge, trailing dust and rocks in its wake as it fell into the canyon.

Alesia had plenty of time to enjoy the experience. The gravity was low enough that the little vehicle took half a minute to reach the canyon floor below. She hit the thrusters to cushion the impact and then jammed the throttles forward again, skidding and crabbing her way across the landscape.

As she roved on, the canyon widened out before her and she was delighted to find a series of active geysers, spouting gases into the faint traceries of atmosphere that clung to the surface of this world.

But the scanner trace is beyond … what can it be? Surely I couldn't have found something on my first recce …

Cautiously, she pushed on through the geysers, more circumspect now. It would not do to get caught in an explosive outgassing. In this low gravity there was a chance that the little SRV might get launched with sufficient force to achieve escape velocity. That would really ruin her day.

The geysers were soon behind her, though, with one of the walls of the canyon looming close, casting a long shadow over the floor.

Something there, hard to see …

She slowed the SRV and switched the external floodlights on to their maximum setting, bathing the area in a bright glow.

The SRV scanner was pinging sharply, emitting unfamiliar sounds. She was close now, whatever it was, she must almost be on top of it. Better slow down.

What is it? Something new?

And then there they were, strange conical projections rising up out of the surface. They seemed confined to the shadowed areas, avoiding the direct starlight. They were big too, at least the height of the SRV in most cases, some much larger. There were hundreds of them.

She prodded the scanners to get more details. She could see the analytic computers working quickly through the scans. It would be only moments before …

There we go.

Chemical analysis flashed up before her. She scrutinised the readings, feeling herself tense with excitement.

Organic?

More analysis followed, and the final criteria displayed on her HUD matched up.

Alien, something that no one had seen before.

I've done it!

She cut the throttles and brought the SRV to a halt, gathering her thoughts for a moment.

Or not.

It wasn't the ruins of a long-lost civilisation. The little craft sat alone, surrounded by a field of vast alien fungi, as far as the eye could see.

Deep Space, Lir system, Uninhabited

The *Whiplash* flickered back out of hyperspace with a brief flash, unmarked in the darkness. It pitched away from the star ahead, setting course, its top-mounted cooling fins extending to radiate the excess heat of its encounter.

Raan looked over the controls.

So far, so good! If I can get a jump ahead …

His hopes were dashed the next moment. Bright marks appeared in space before him, glowing bright like swiftly moving comets, trailing an almost smoky wake, the tell-tale sign of vessels using the frame shift drive.

He was a little way ahead of them, they had dropped out of hyperspace near the star in close formation, probably organised into a wing. A quick scan revealed them to be the same Cobra-class vessels that had been pursuing him.

Damn!

He was going to have to try something different, the Cobras had the advantage in jump range over the Eagle. They were fast, too. No way to outrun them in normal space, frame shift or hyperspace. Quickly, he toggled the hyperdrive subsystem, oriented the ship towards the next star.

Frame shift drive charging …

The bars flickered bright on the heads-up display, the rising crescendo of the drive as it sucked power from the reactor.

Almost there …

Coruscating blue energy flashed around the viewpoint and the ship shuddered off course, jolting him in the flight chair.

Interdicted!

They weren't going to let him go, that was plain to see. Now his next choice, submit or fight the interdiction?

He had the edge in manoeuvrability, but if he lost the Cobras would have him, there'd be no escape. If he submitted he might be able to jump out before they could get a bead on him, but with two on one that seemed unlikely.

Go with your strengths!

He was the Melee Masters' Champion, wasn't he? Fight that interdiction!

He wrestled the ship back on course, watching the escape vector as it was highlighted on the canopy. The ship was sluggish, rolling, yawing and banking almost at random as the disrupted energies of the drive tried to re-establish stability.

The star field whirled outside, the distorted view of the system mesmerising amidst the scintillating blue of the interdiction tether. More than once he almost lost the battle, but he managed to pull the ship back from the brink with a deft hand on the controls.

Whoever was pursuing him had talent, that was for sure.

Interdiction evaded!

With a final jolt, the blue light faltered and faded away, he was free! His attackers would be spiralling around behind him, thrown back into normal space, hopefully with a healthy measure of hull or system damage for their pains.

Bought a little time, now to make use of it …

He jabbed at the controls and the thrumming sound of the hyperdrive subsystem spooling up filled the cabin.

Frame shift drive charging …

The ship hurled itself into hyperspace, the spinning maelstrom of … what exactly?

Raan found that the strange spinning shadows and glows during hyperspace transit began to hold a peculiar fascination. He caught himself looking for patterns, for shapes … Hadn't he seen that before? What were those glows that seemed to pace his ship during the voyage between the stars? It was haunting, and not in a good way …

Witch-space, they used to call it …

A glow ahead signalled the jump was nearly over. The destination star burst into existence, prompting another evasive turn. But this time there was no sign of pursuit.

Got far enough ahead! Yes!

He lined up for the next jump and triggered the jump drive once again.

The computer buzzed angrily.

Frantically, he looked at the diagnostic panel, where a message was glowing.

Insufficient fuel.

'Shit, no!'

With rising panic he surveyed the instruments, noting with mounting frustration that the fuel gauge wasn't lying. He didn't have enough fuel for the jump to the next system on his itinerary. It was too far away.

And those ships will be here any moment!

He activated the holofac subsystem to his left and scrolled through the list of destinations. There had to be something in range!

Two systems. He didn't recognise either of them.

Quick!

No time for a scan, he had to get out of here!

He triggered the jump drive again and the little ship hurled itself across the stars.

The lurid glow of a K-class star lit the canopy upon arrival. He scanned the system, his heart dropping in his chest, a sweat of cold fear forming over his body.

No stations! But it's ok, it's scoopable. Going to have to …

He switched to the opposite viewer, on the right side of the cockpit, looking down the list of equipment aboard.

AFMU? What's that?

He checked the description. Some kind of repair system.

Neat, but where is … no way … no fuel scoop …

He'd marooned himself.

***

Towards the core, the widespread antenna relays of the Fuel Rats' station were buzzing with activity. The dispatchers were working frenetically, guiding their colleagues out in the void to rescue stranded pilots. As they watched, the queues of calls were stacking up.

Busy day.

More appeared on the list. One wasn't too far away and the displays indicated one of the Rats was close by. The dispatcher saw a way to ease the queue a little.

'Commander Jindrolim, this is dispatch, receiving?'

'Commander Jindrolim here,' came the immediate reply.

'Got a target for you, feeding the location to your system now. Target class is Imperial Eagle, ID Raan Corsen. Subject appears agitated, could be under threat. Advise caution.'

'Roger that dispatch. Jumping now ...'

Leeson City, Chione, Prism system, Empire

The day dawned grey and damp, unusual for the time of year in the southern hemisphere of Chione. The daily eclipse had already taken place, with the artificial illumination of Leeson City switched back off. Drizzle fell from heavy leaden skies and a blustery wind swept through the empty spaces of the piazza.

Guards stood outside the Prism Hall of Justice, standing to attention, rifles held across their chests. They wore the dark green insignia of Loren's Legion.

Above them a shadow moved, the clouds riven by the noise of thruster jets. A faint blue glow appeared, and then an Imperial air car emerged through the thick cloud, descending vertically towards the ground, flanked by two well-armed Imperial Couriers.

Their landing gear unfolded smoothly in Imperial style, and the three ships touched down on the expanse of the piazza. Wind blustered the guards, but they stood stoically, knowing their duty.

Lights flickered beneath the air car, illuminating the boarding ramp below. More guards, this time in the black uniforms of Fleet Admiral Patreus' personal detachment. In the midst were two other figures, one dressed in a dark mauve uniform, the other in a green dress. Commander Cornelius had insisted on escorting Lady Salomé to her trial in person. She was bound at the wrists.

The tableaux marched up to the steps of the Hall of Justice.

'I bring Lady Salomé, as required by the summons of the court,' Cornelius said.

His guards lowered their rifles and stepped aside. Cornelius spared Salomé a look. She was pale, but there was little else to read on her face. There seemed little of the determination she was known for, but there was no sign of fear either.

Detachment, or resignation? Is this part of her plan, or is she controlled by others?

She stepped forward and began to climb the stairs to the hall.

Cornelius watched her go. He was not permitted to enter. He stood with his own guards as she walked upwards, flanked by Patreus' guards.

Salomé was ushered inside the hall and the great obsidian doors swung shut with a dull and forbidding clank.

'Farewell, my Lady.'

Chapter Fifteen

Leeson City, Chione, Prism system, Empire

The interior of the Prism Hall of Justice was centred on a great amphitheatre, with tiers of seats in a semi-circle around a central dais. In the centre stood a chair, where the accused sat and waited for justice to run its course.

Salomé identified herself to the court clerk and then was led to that very chair. She looked around as they removed the restraints from her wrists. There were few in attendance. She recognised a handful of senators in the ranks, accompanied by their respective patrons.

Allies of Princess Aisling it would seem ...

A judge approached from another entrance, flanked by two aides, all making their way to an imposing desk set before her, draped with a rich embroidered tapestry of the emblem of the Prism system, emblazoned across the familiar Imperial symbol.

Salomé looked at the three men, not recognising any of them. They weren't from Leeson City, Chione or even the Prism system as far as she was aware. Another set of lackeys in the pay of Aisling?

Accuser, Prosecution and Judge! And no jury. Her influence is everywhere.

Fleet Admiral Patreus approached from another entrance. He was alone and was ushered to one side of the amphitheatre, taking his place in the defendant's row on her right-hand side.

'This court is now in session.'

The judge in the centre got to his feet and produced an obsidian orb from his robes. He struck it down three times on the desk before him. The noise echoed through the hall. Conversation stopped.

'All rise.'

Everyone got to their feet. All but one. All but Salomé.

'You will rise,' the judge said to her.

'I will not,' Salomé replied. Her voice clear and sharp. Mutterings began around her.

'We will add contempt of court to your list of accusations, Lady Kahina.'

'Do as you will,' Salomé replied. 'I do not recognise the authority of this court.'

'This court has been appointed by the express command of senatorial mandate, Lady Kahina …'

'… By the Fleet Admiral who accuses me of his attempted assassination …' Salomé interrupted.

She looked over at Patreus and was surprised to see a smile on his face, which vanished almost immediately.

The judge continued, unabated, talking over her by means of audio amplification. '…in full accord with the directives of Imperial law. You will rise.'

Salomé didn't move for long moments, but then did rise to her feet. The judge sat back amidst mutterings from those assembled, satisfied that he had maintained decorum.

Salomé spoke after a pause.

'I rise only in respect of Imperial law and in confidence of its honourable discharge,' she said.

'You may not apply conditions to senatorial mandates!'

The judge glared at her, but she didn't back down. She returned his look with calm and composure.

He looked at the holofac display before him.

'You have refused legal counsel.'

'I wasn't offered legal counsel,' Salomé answered.

The judge stopped again, discussing with his colleagues for a moment before turning back to her.

'A legal counsellor was provided, were they not?'

'A lackey of Princess Aisling Duval, you mean?' Salomé said with a laugh, 'who knows less about Imperial legal proceedings than I do? Is that to whom you are referring?'

The judge gritted his teeth.

'You have refused legal counsel.'

Salomé sighed.

'If you say so.'

'You have refused legal counsel. Yes or no!'

Salomé looked at the ceiling, rolled her eyes, pursed her lips and then gave an exaggerated shrug and smiled sweetly at the judge.

'Yes.'

The judge let out a deep breath and then turned his attention back to the holofac before him.

'Lady Kahina Tijani Loren,' he said. 'You stand accused of

masterminding the attempted assassination of Fleet Admiral Denton Patreus in the Cemiess System on the 20th of August 3302. How do you plead?'

Salomé's voice was firm and direct this time.

'Not guilty.'

'Not guilty, your honour …' one of the aides snapped.

Salomé fixed him with a glare.

'There is no honour here,' she said.

'In absence of a defence counsel, we will hear your statement,' the judge said.

Salomé looked around briefly, taking in Patreus, the judge, the aides and the assembled throng of people behind her. She heard them leaning forward, clothing rustling, the odd cough. She waited until she was sure she had their full attention.

'I am Lady Kahina Tijani Loren,' she began, her voice crisp and sharp. 'Third and only remaining daughter of the late Senator Algreb Loren of Chione. I abdicated my senatorial responsibilities to my loyal servant Ambassador Cuthrick Delaney in July of 3301 in order to undertake several exploration journeys to remote parts of the galaxy in the year following.

'I made contact with many different organisations in that time, who all shared exploration as a primary mandate. I was returning from one such expedition, intending to arrive at Achenar in time for Empire Day, when my ship was interdicted and boarded in the Cemiess system.

'From there, I was accused of this nonsense, that I had somehow masterminded an assassination attempt on Fleet Admiral Patreus. I have been in Imperial custody ever since. Quite clearly, I had nothing to do with it and this court should disband immediately in order to prevent further waste of valuable time and resources.'

'It is my decision as to whether this court remains in session, Lady Kahina,' the judge said. 'Do you have anything else to add?'

'I do not.'

'Then we will hear the case for the prosecution.'

Salomé looked around as another man entered the hall. He was large, puffing with the exertion of making his way forward, his bulk working against him. She narrowed her eyes in surprise and rising anger.

Patron Gerrun! I should have known …

Gerrun moved across from her and stood leaning against the railing, conspicuously checking a commtab he had brought with him.

'I object, your honour,' Salomé said.

'You object?' the judge said. 'To what? To the presence of the prosecution?'

'Yes,' Salomé replied. 'This man was present during the interdiction of my ship and is part of this underhanded ploy to disgrace me.'

The judge looked at Gerrun, who shrugged with an expression of baffled innocence.

'Patron Gerrun is not on trial here, Lady Kahina.'

'Patron Gerrun,' Salomé replied. 'Has conjured up this ridiculous charade in combination with others in a deliberate …'

'You have evidence you can provide the court to back up your accusation?' the judge asked.

Gerrun beamed a smile at her. Salomé pursed her lips.

'Rather difficult to gather any evidence when you've been locked up,' Salomé countered.

'You might have been advised in this matter,' the judge replied. 'But you refused legal counsel. We have already established that.'

Salomé rolled her eyes. 'Oh yes, of course we did.'

The judge looked at her. 'Very well, in that case we will proceed to hear the case for the prosecution. Patron Gerrun, please continue.'

'My first witness is Commander Benson, head of station security at Mackenzie Relay.'

Salomé turned and saw a tall thin man in a very sharp Imperial uniform step up from the ranks behind her. He looked drawn and ill, his face grey and his cheeks gaunt.

Someone who has been brow-beaten into submission …

'Identify yourself,' Gerrun instructed.

The commander placed his hand on a panel and a combined DNA and fingerprint analysis confirmed his identity. His holofac representation appeared in the room.

'Commander,' Gerrun began, 'I understand you were on duty during the incident in question.'

'I was.'

'And that you have evidence that Lady Kahina was present in the system at the time.'

'We have flight traces which confirm that Lady Kahina's vessel was within the Cemiess system at points around the dates in question,' he confirmed.

'Is it now illegal to conduct a flight through the Cemiess system?' Salomé queried.

'Silence,' the judge rumbled. 'The defendant will not speak at this time.'

Gerrun ignored her and gestured for the commander to continue.

'In addition, several encrypted transmissions were received from her vessel during that time frame,' the commander continued, not looking at her. 'We have been unable to decode them, but they are short enough that they can only be terse text-based messages.'

'Aimed where?' Gerrun asked.

'Analysis indicates some were beamed at the station and some were broadcast wideband to other systems.'

'Secret text-based transmissions,' Gerrun mused. 'Instructions of some sort, perhaps?'

'Perhaps.'

'And the timing of these transmissions?'

'Received just before and immediately after the incident.'

'Quite astonishing,' Gerrun said. 'Would you care to elucidate the nature of these transmissions, Lady Kahina?'

Salomé looked at the judge.

'You will answer the question,' the judge instructed.

Salomé turned back to Gerrun and fixed him with an icy glare. 'No, I would not. A Lady's private communications are her own business.'

Gerrun nodded and made some notes on his commtab. The commander was dismissed and a second witness was called. This time it was an agent of the Imperial Internal Security Service. Salomé recognised the bland features, nondescript clothing and the odd, completely detached mannerisms. A fragment of rhyme came to her mind.

Double-I, Double-S, no identity, more or less ...

'Identify yourself,' Gerrun asked once more. The agent merely looked at him.

'Ah,' Gerrun said, with a faint smile. 'Of course. My humble apologies ...'

The agent nodded and then looked ahead, his face as blank as ever.

'You were present,' Gerrun began, 'As I understand it, at the attempted assassination itself. You are responsible for saving the life of our Fleet Admiral and for apprehending the individuals directly responsible.'

'I was,' the agent confirmed. 'Though the single survivor had taken excessive doses of the drug hexedit by the time we had secured him.'

'Fatal?' Gerrun queried.

'Extremely,' the agent replied.

'Describe the events just prior to the attempted assassination,' Gerrun prompted.

The agent related a factual description of the attack on Patreus. The fake holofac camera, the destruction of the dais and how Patreus had been hustled to safety. He described how they had cried out the phrase, 'The sun has not set for the Emperor's Dawn.' It transpired that the 'camera crew' had been prepared for failure, quickly applying supplies of hexedit. All four were rendered instantly moribund and died within minutes of their plan coming apart.

'I assume they were searched thoroughly?' Gerrun said.

'Yes,' the agent replied. 'The holofac camera itself was custom built by some kind of rogue engineering outfit, still fully functional, but effectively a high-powered beam laser masquerading as a camera. None of the individuals have been positively identified, none had fingerprints or subcutaneous ID chips, and DNA records do not match any known criminals. However, one was found to be carrying an item.'

'An item?' Gerrun asked.

Salomé saw both Gerrun and Patreus look at her for a brief moment.

Planting evidence! What …

'Yes,' the agent continued. 'A medallion. It is inscribed with a symbol on one side and bears a name on the other.'

The agent gestured and a nearby holofac lit up with a spinning representation. Salomé frowned in surprise.

How did they …

It was hers. A medallion she had been given long ago. A symbol of trust from …

It can't be … how did they get hold of that?

The medallion was engraved with a stylised representation of the Pilots' Federation ranking emblem, Elite rank, surrounded by a fierce reptilian creature, perhaps a dragon or wyvern.

'Have you positively identified the symbol?' Gerrun asked.

'We have,' the agent replied.

Gerrun almost chuckled, clearly amused by the agent's unwillingness to answer anything other than a question asked directly.

'And?'

The agent sighed. 'The symbol belongs to a group, a faction resident in the Shinrarta Dezhra system. A faction calling itself "The Dark Wheel."'

Muted mutterings buzzed around the hall behind her.

'You mentioned a name,' Gerrun prompted.

The agent gestured again and the holofac representation of the medallion spun around. On the back, in clear but calligraphic wording, the medallion bore a signal word. A name.

Salomé.

'Salomé,' Gerrun said, taking his time to study the image. 'Are we familiar with this name?'

'We are,' the agent replied.

Gerrun sighed. 'Would you care to clarify and supply some background detail?'

'Salomé is the name of an itinerant spacecraft commander,' the agent replied. 'She first came to our attention in mid-3300. She has been involved in several obscure missions across the galaxy and was confirmed to have been present in the Distant Worlds Expedition earlier this year. She has been linked with several disaffected minor factions, including the Children of Raxxla, the Phoenix Group, the Dark Wheel and now, the Emperor's Dawn.'

'Is there a point to this?' the judge interjected.

'If you will indulge me for a few moments more …' Gerrun asked smoothly. The judge inclined his head to indicate acquiescence.

'And where did this Salomé come from?' Gerrun asked.

'She comes from here,' the agent replied.

'The Prism system?' Gerrun asked, in mock surprise. 'Could you identify her?'

'She sits before us,' the agent said, pointing at Salomé.

Gerrun turned, his mouth open in carefully orchestrated surprise and disbelief. 'Lady Kahina is this mysterious Commander Salomé?'

'There is no doubt,' the agent said, 'We have scans of her image.'

The agent gestured again and a series of images appeared, replacing the medallion. Salomé examined them. Many were of poor quality, taken from long range or from awkward angles, but it was definitely her.

I knew I would be under surveillance, but these are images taken by those I thought I could trust …

'Remarkable,' Gerrun said.

'There is more,' the agent said. 'We have a recording of Commander Salomé in conversation with one of these disaffected factions from a year ago.'

'If the judge allows …' Gerrun said, with a bow.

'Granted,' the judge said.

The agent gestured a third time and a holofac video feed appeared. Salomé watched in dismay as the events of a year ago played out before her. A choice of words that would do her no favours here …

But there was no one else present, no one! How could they have got hold of this? The only other people who knew where we were …

The medallion, the recording. She had been betrayed.

Again!

The holofac began to play.

Salomé watched in dismay. The spiky-haired woman stood facing two men in some kind of darkened hangar. She took in the small wiry frame, fit and supple, dark eyes, her skin olive. She was dressed in a tight fitting full-length tunic.

Her … Thorn and Lestenio! Did they betray me? Or was it that woman?

Thorn was the taller of the pair, with short dark-brown hair and a goatee without a moustache. He was wearing a navy blue tactical vest over a black shirt with matching cargo pants, finished with black combat boots, apparently fitted with magnetic soles. A pair of optical enhancers concealed his eyes, doubtless providing him with a wealth of telemetry about what he was looking at.

Lestenio was shorter and stockier, with a heavier build. He simply nodded without saying anything. He wore a long grey coat zipped at the front, it ran almost down to the floor. His hands concealed in deep pockets.

'Ah, the Children of Raxxla.' The spiky-haired woman began. 'How sweet. I trust your trip was safe, Commanders?'

'Safe as it can be in this day and age,' replied Thorn.

The woman turned to him.

'You understand who I represent, I assume, Commander Thorn?'

'I've seen you run missions out of Shinrarta Dezhra,' Thorn replied.

'Shinrarta Dezhra?' The woman laughed, her scorn plain to hear. 'You think the Dark Wheel advertises on a station board in plain sight? That we need rookie pilots to drag a couple of tonnes of thrumpberry flavouring across to Hutton Orbital? A trivial ploy to keep the Founders off our backs.'

'I'm gratified to hear it,' Thorn replied. 'You had me worried for a moment.'

'It was a little too obvious,' Lestenio agreed.

'It keeps the treasure seekers and wishful thinkers occupied,' the woman said. 'They believe they are onto something. They have their uses for occasional menial activities. The truth is far more subtle than they will ever suspect. Shinrarta is merely a front.'

'So …?'

'You should not consider the Dark Wheel a single organisation, gentlemen. How could it survive for so long if it were? The Wheel has many levels, many hubs, cogs, gears and spokes. It is more akin to an affiliation of organisations that share certain common goals. Interlocking in purpose. Consider yourselves now spinning on the outermost rim.'

'You promised you would help us,' Lestenio prompted.

'And so I have, my dear Lestenio. I have selected you a leader.'

'We already have a leader …' Thorn said with a frown.

'Trust me, you do not. Nor strength enough for the tasks ahead.'

'We have allies,' Thorn argued.

'You've done well to ally with the Phoenix Group. Commanders Noctivagus and Moore were most complimentary. But you still lack more than you know.'

The woman could be seen beckoning to someone out of sight of the holofac imager. As the courtroom watched, another woman walked into view, cloaked and cowled.

'I'm never adverse to a pretty girl,' Lestenio was heard to say, 'But …'

'Does she have her own voice?' Thorn asked.

'You may call me Salomé,' the woman said, lowering her cowl.

'Pause!'

Gerrun's voice broke the flow of the recording and it stopped, the figures motionless on the holofac display.

'As we can see, Commander Salomé, our Lady Kahina herself, is present with individuals who claim to represent the Children of Raxxla, the Phoenix Group and this mysterious Dark Wheel. All factions known to be associated with low-level criminal activity.'

'Go on,' the judge said.

'We will now learn her true intentions,' Gerrun said. 'Play on!'

The recording began again.

Thorn was talking directly to the unidentified woman with the spiky hair.

'Means nothing to me, I don't know her. This time I need more than just your word to accept a stranger. We have worked hard to get where we are. I will need reassurance that this ... girl ... is as capable as you say she is.'

Salomé saw herself tense on the screen, but she said nothing.

The woman leant forward slightly, pointing a finger towards Thorn's face.

'Oh, but you do know her,' she stated with an amused tone. 'She is Lady Kahina Tijani Loren, until very recently the senator of the Prism system.'

'Pause!' Gerrun called out triumphantly. Once more the holofac stopped. 'And now you see that she has been positively identified by these faction leaders.'

'Agreed,' the judge said, 'Proceed.'

'Play on!' Gerrun called.

There was an audible gasp from Lestenio.

'Senator Loren ...' Lestenio muttered, looking at Salomé with wide eyes. 'Then you're the one who ... Thorn – the Rift! It's her!'

'You want us to bow the knee to an Imperial senator?' Thorn sneered, raising his chin and still ignoring Salomé. 'She's a spoilt prima donna, I've read about her antics ...'

There was a faint sound, a whip of something travelling through the air at high speed. On the holofac, Salomé had drawn her bright-steel Holva blade with remarkable speed, it was resting gently under Thorn's chin. His gaze travelled down the blade to see the hilt held in her right hand.

'Don't believe everything you read on GalNet,' Salomé said. 'Though that bit about the disembowelling?' She smiled thinly. 'That did happen.'

'Enough,' the woman said. 'You may be the Children, but this is no time to be childish. Salomé has been chosen by those above. She is what you need at this stage; more than just a leader, a figurehead and rallying point. She knows the Empire, she knows the Federation and the Alliance. She has the diplomatic contacts you will need. She can open doors that would otherwise remain permanently closed to you. She is acclimatised to power. She can engender loyalty and adulation. When the time comes, you will need more than ships and weapons, you will need charisma, charm and admiration. The masses will follow her, love her and ... if necessary, they will fight and die for her.'

Thorn looked at Lestenio, who nodded. He looked back at Salomé.

'And what do you want from us in return for your … favour?' Thorn asked.

Everyone saw Salomé lick her lips. The holofac zoomed on her unmistakable features.

'For now? A place to hide far from prying eyes. Then, a team capable of carrying out covert operations under the noses of the factions and powers, discovering the secrets we all know are out there. And one day …'

She paused, a flash of anger crossing her features.

'Yes?' Lestenio was heard to ask.

Salomé's mouth was dry, she felt her stomach clench. She knew what the holofac image of herself was about to say.

'Senator Patreus' head on a platter.'

The holofac stopped and faded out. Mutterings filled the hall once more.

Salomé watched as Gerrun turned to her.

'Do you deny this recording as accurate?'

Salomé swallowed. 'No.'

'Do you deny you were present in the Cemiess system at the time of the assassination attempt?'

'No.'

'Do you deny you held a grudge against Fleet Admiral Patreus for his exploitation of the Prism system?'

'Fleet Admiral Patreus …'

'Yes or no, Lady Salomé,' Gerrun interrupted.

'He stepped beyond his remit in annexing my homeworld …' Salomé said.

'Yes or no!' Gerrun bellowed.

'I will not incriminate myself!' Salomé cried. 'Imperial justice demands the truth. If that can't be done in a single word I won't be bullied into a compromise …'

'You had the means, the motive and the opportunity,' Gerrun continued. 'Capitalising on the loyalty of those disaffected by the politics of the core worlds, you sought to use them to carry out your wishes.'

'I did not try to assassinate Patreus!' Salomé snapped. 'Nor did I order it.'

'Do you deny it?'

'Yes!'

Gerrun turned and faced the judge. 'The case for the prosecution rests.'

The judge made his own notes and then turned to Salomé.

'Since you have no representation, you may now present the case for your defence, should you wish.'

Salomé took a deep breath and nodded. She went through the motions of cross-questioning Gerrun's witnesses, but it was clear they had all been bribed, tricked or browbeaten. They would not deviate from the party line. She repeated her denials, but it all felt futile. No one here was interested in justice. Anyone she could have relied upon had been kept well clear.

'I am not guilty of the charges,' she ended.

'There will be a short recess while I consider the verdict,' the judge replied.

'Don't take long to come to your utterly equitable decision,' Salomé said.

Gerrun was the first to leave, followed by the judge and his aides. Many of the attendees in the ranks behind her filed out. The guards alongside her remained. She was not free to move.

She watched as Patreus got up from where he'd been sitting throughout and walked across to her. He paused on the way past, his gaze locked on hers, but didn't say anything.

***

Cuthrick had been notified that another ship was approaching the Prism system. Part of him was reassured that having some of Salomé's companions close by would be a comfort to her, another despaired that despite their presence there was nothing any of them could do.

He cleared the old Cobra for arrival at Leeson City regardless, arranging for the necessary flight approvals and clearances, leaving a message for them to meet him as soon as practically possible.

Once the ship was berthed, it took them only a few short minutes to journey from the spaceport via aircar. Cuthrick met both Luko and Hassan on the steps of the Prism Hall of Justice. He beckoned them in out of the approaching rain.

'We got here as quickly as we could,' Hassan said, ignoring the Imperial traditions of introduction. Cuthrick wasn't offended. Offworlders rarely appreciated the niceties of etiquette. Given the current situation, he could be excused.

'The trial has begun,' Cuthrick said.

He saw Hassan's expression drop in dismay.

'We hoped to arrive in time to wish her well,' Luko said, by means of explanation.

'I'm sure she knew of your intentions,' Cuthrick answered. 'Alas, we are barred from entering the hall by Imperial decree.'

'Is there any hope of justice?' Hassan asked.

'Justice?' Cuthrick replied. 'I think not. All we can hope for is that Imperial law will be upheld.'

'Which means nothing,' Luko said.

'It means process will be followed,' Cuthrick replied. 'Nothing more.'

'What will happen to her?' Hassan asked.

Cuthrick sighed. 'She no longer has the defence of being a senator, Patreus has already seen to that. As a Lady of the Empire she retains certain rights, only the Emperor herself can order an execution.'

'Execution!' Hassan gasped.

'Imperial sanction is harsh,' Cuthrick replied. 'She is accused of attempted murder.'

'But she didn't do it,' Hassan blurted out. 'It's this Patreus …'

Cuthrick saw Luko looking at him intently, a frown growing on his face.

'It is not Patreus?' Luko asked. 'You don't think so?'

Cuthrick beckoned for them to draw closer, his voice dropping to a whisper.

'I fear this is more complex than we can yet see.'

'Who is behind this …?' Hassan breathed. 'We were interdicted by Imperials under command of Patrons Zyair and Gerrun. They have enough reason to hate her.'

'Gerrun is running the prosecution. Both he and Zyair work for Princess Aisling now,' Cuthrick replied.

'The princess?' Luko asked. 'She does this?'

Cuthrick considered it. 'It is not impossible, but I fail to see what Princess Aisling gains from this. They have squabbled, as two young women may, but this plot seems … well … rather beyond her abilities.'

'Prima donna, nothing more,' Luko agreed.

'But who else could it be?' Hassan demanded.

There was a faint notification from behind them. An aide appeared.

'They are in recess, Ambassador. A verdict will be reached in the next session.'

Cuthrick exchanged a worried glance with Luko and Hassan.

***

The delay was short. Salomé stood waiting in the courtroom as the judge, his aides and the rest of the ensemble filtered back in.

The judge thumped his orb three times.

'This court is now in session.'

He looked up.

'Lady Kahina Tijani Loren. It is the judgement of this court that you are guilty of the attempted assassination of Fleet Admiral Patreus in the Cemiess system, having provided individuals belonging to the Emperor's Dawn faction the means and instruction to carry out such an attempt.'

Salomé steeled herself not to react, but her mind was racing with the implications.

'In light of your conduct since and your stature in Imperial society, the death sentence that would typically apply in such cases has been commuted.'

A rumble of muted outrage rustled around the room behind her.

Hoping they would simply bump me off, were you?

The judge continued. 'It is the judgement of this court that you will be stripped of the rank of Lady within the Imperial hierarchy and that you will be subject to life imprisonment at the Imperial penal colony at Koontz Asylum in the Daibo system, there to see out the remainder of your natural life.'

She felt a muscle spasm in her cheek. She clenched her teeth firmly shut, determined to show no emotion.

How dare they ... Life imprisonment!

'Sentence to be carried out immediately. Court dismissed.'

The orb struck three more times, the noise echoing through her mind.

Life imprisonment ...

She looked up to see Patreus looking at her. She stared back. His expression was oddly blank.

As she was pulled away by guards he mouthed a single word to her.

Wait ...

Chapter Sixteen

Location unknown, Pleiades sector

A news vid holofac transmission was playing out in the cockpit of a dark-hued Cobra Mark III. It was hard to see against the darkness of space, its hull painted a deep lustrous black. The glow from the canopy was one of only a few lights that marked its outline.

'No way.'

The pilot had been in the middle of eating a nutri-snack and had stopped mid-chew, leaning forward as the newscaster continued with their narration.

'... Kahina Loren has been sentenced to life imprisonment in Koontz Asylum in the Daibo system. She is to be taken there after due process, sentence is to commence immediately upon arrival. Leaked holofacs from the press room indicated one particularly damning piece of evidence; a feed apparently showing Salomé in conversation with two unidentified men where she demanded the then-Senator Denton Patreus' head "on a platter." Now known simply as Ms. Loren, she has been stripped of her titles and status as a Lady of the Empire. She was bound and led away to a secure holding facility. Princess Aisling Duval was quick to talk to the Imperial Citizen about the trial ...'

Commander Shabooka cast his mind back over the last few months.

He had met Kahina once, or rather Commander Salomé as she had called herself then, on the far side of the galaxy on one of the desolate worlds of Beagle Point. He'd taken part in the famous Distant Worlds Expedition which had charted a course to the far side of the galaxy. She, and members of her adoring troupe of zealous followers, the Children of Raxxla, had dramatically overflown the landing point. He remembered what she had announced at the time.

We are searching the void for the mystery of Raxxla, the secrets of the Rift and whatever else we might find ...

All is not well in the core worlds. Thus, I must soon return. But keep that exploration data safe ... it is far more important than you know ...

Be careful who you sell it to ...

I must depart now. Be safe in the void ... and good luck. You will need it.

The answer will come … soon.

'All is not well in the core worlds,' he muttered to himself. 'Well, you got that right.'

Shabooka was an observer, not for him allegiance to any given cause. He had admired Salomé from afar, watching what she said and what she did. He liked the way she took part in exploration, but he was not a zealot to her cause in the manner of some. Likewise, he found the dogged approach of the Canonn Interstellar Research Group to be laudable, but he was content to follow the clues they unravelled at his own pace and in his own way.

'Looks like the Imps stitched you up good and proper,' he said, finishing off his snack and turning back to the flight controls. 'But you're a player too, more to this than meets the eye.'

But she'd been right. There was trouble in the core worlds. Everyone was talking about war, with the Imperials and the Federals posturing left, right and centre. Now she was being taken out of the game.

Did she miscalculate, or is this part of something bigger?

The holofac flashed up a new message, interrupting the news coverage. *Incoming transmission.*

Shabooka toggled the comms system online and was rewarded with the faces of three familiar colleagues, Commanders Turjan Starstone, Greytest and Josh Hawkins. They, like he, were lone wolf explorers,enjoying the freedom to do things the way they saw fit.

'Guys?' Shabooka asked. The transmission wasn't scheduled, something must be up.

'We've been piggybacking some comms from Canonn Interstellar,' Josh began without preamble. 'They're chasing something down in …'

Greytest interrupted, his accent betraying his origins from a particular part of Old Earth. 'That could mean only one thing. Canonn are looking for something, something big.'

'Unregistered comms beacon,' Turjan added. 'We've followed them to San Tu. The transmission decodes to a series of co-ordinates. They're getting ready to deploy a search.'

'Where?' Shabooka asked.

Josh grinned at him. 'Could be your lucky day, my friend. We're looking for a system with an A and F-class star somewhere near the Pleiades. Not many candidates. We think the best one is HIP 17403.'

Shabooka didn't even need to pull up the star chart.

'I'm almost right on top of it!'

Turjan nodded. 'Why do you think we called you? You can steal a march on those cocky Canonn dudes for once.'

Greytest chuckled. 'That would be very sweet.'

Coded information fed into Shabooka's navcom. Just a handful of jumps.

'You'd better get moving,' Josh advised.

'Gents, I owe you one,' Shabooka said, his hands already flying over the controls and plotting the course.

'More than just one, I think,' Turjan replied. 'Good hunting, Commander!'

'Fly safe,' Greytest added.

The Cobra spun on its axis, twisting around as it simultaneously charged its jump drive.

If I can get there first, a chance to make my mark on these mysteries from the void. Maybe even figure out what is going on …

It didn't take long to reach the system, and only minutes more for Shabooka to triangulate the position based on the data he'd received. He'd been in space a long time and had been exploring for most of that. He had the instincts and the expertise.

The rocky surface of the planet rose up below. It wasn't long before the scanners began to pick up something ahead.

He adjusted speed, careful to watch the increasing g-loading as he approached the surface. The Cobra was an ideal ship for this sort of work. Powerful and agile, but big enough to carry the necessary gear, coupled with an excellent jump range.

He toggled the hull lights and the onboard cameras. He didn't want to miss a moment of this.

Let's hope it's something worthwhile …

A sharp angular shape came into view over the rim of a crater.

His heart sank. It was clearly a wreck, but the overall shape was familiar. This was no alien ship or ancient artefact. The burnt out hull of an Anaconda was all too mundane. The demise of some hapless explorer who must have come out this way years ago. If he ran the hull plate idents he'd probably be able to identify who they'd been.

Damn …

The Cobra rose a little higher as he surveyed the wreck.

Wait a minute …

There was another wreck. Another Anaconda. His hull lights were picking out details in the hull. Scorch marks, blackened and ripped hull panels. This was no crash, there had been a fight, a big one.

Then another. A Type-9 freighter. Smashed and gutted, half of its hull contents splashed across the surface.

And another!

The fourth ship was another Type-9. This one was different, though. It seemed more intact than the others, but its midsection had been ripped open and a … Shabooka struggled to find a word for it – a wing? –had lodged straight through the hull. It was of no design he recognised. It looked vaguely organic, but it clearly had immense strength if it could slice into a hull like that.

Four ships. Some sort of fight to the death out here … and they all crashed in the same place … this doesn't make sense …

But there was something else.

Where there should have been darkness, there was a faint glow. Green against the shadows, it pulsed vaguely in the gloom.

Shabooka swallowed and nudged the Cobra closer. His thumb slipping unconsciously to the trigger, ready to deploy the meagre weapons he had onboard.

Explorers can't fight, they have to run …

A vaguely octagonal object, at least as big as the wreckage of the Type-9s he'd just passed. It dwarfed the Cobra and looked undamaged, other than the impact marks in the ground around it, as if it might suddenly come alive and rise up to face him.

But there was no response. Shabooka observed it for several minutes without seeing any activity at all.

It was visually similar to the crashed alien ships that others had encountered, but this one seemed newer, perhaps a more recent encounter. Further investigation should reveal the answers.

One thing was clear though.

One of these alien ships took down four of ours!

Leeson City, Chione, Prism system, Empire

The mood inside the panelled side room of the Prism Hall of Justice was sombre. Salomé had been escorted out incognito, rather than returning through the main entrance. Cuthrick, Luko and Hassan had seen Patreus, Zyair and Gerrun emerge, along with the court attendees and the judge.

Reporters had surged around them, holofac imagers snapping footage for immediate transmission across the core worlds via the GalNet newsfeeds. Sickened by the media feeding frenzy, they had retreated inside.

'Is there nothing we can do?' Hassan asked.

Cuthrick sighed. 'Short of breaking the law ourselves, no. Justice has run its course.'

'This Koontz Asylum,' Luko asked. 'A prison?'

Cuthrick shook his head. 'In name perhaps, but it is infamous. A place you send people if you want to forget about them. Political prisoners, dissidents, those the authorities find awkward to deal with. No one returns.'

'They intend to kill her then,' Luko said. 'We cannot allow this!'

Cuthrick's comm panel lit up. He acknowledged it, seeing the holofac form of Commander Cornelius appear before him.

'Commander?'

'This travesty has just hit the wideband newsfeeds,' Cornelius reported. 'I've already been told the Children of Raxxla, amongst other groups, are up in arms. No telling what they will do. They're apoplectic.'

'Warn them any action they take may play directly into the hands of those who are holding her,' Cuthrick instructed.

'Already done, Ambassador, for all the good it will do. Feelings are running high. I've half a mind to firebomb Patreus' flagship myself.'

'Keep me apprised,' Cuthrick said. 'I will be exploring all possible diplomatic channels.'

Cornelius nodded and the transmission faded out.

'We can't just sit here,' Hassan said. 'There must be something we can do.'

'Kahina will be under armed guard,' Cuthrick said. 'Protected by a convoy and, most likely, with several decoy convoys set off to make tracing her whereabouts impossible. Even if we did know where she was, a hostile attempt would set us against the jurisdiction of the Empire. She is a convicted criminal in the eyes of the law.'

'Yet we know she is innocent,' Luko said. He looked at the dour faces around him. 'Yes?'

'And we're still no closer to finding out who is behind all this ...' Hassan said, before being interrupted by the holofac comms system again.

Cuthrick signalled for quiet and then looked at the incoming transmission.

No ident.

'Who is it?' Hassan asked.

'I don't know,' Cuthrick answered. Both Luko and Hassan looked at him. For a call to come in with no ID check ... it was supposed to be impossible.

The holofac tone sounded again, insistent.

Cuthrick acknowledged the call.

'This is Ambassador Cuthrick.'

The holofac image was flickering and unclear. There was no image, just a hologrammatic cloud of static. The voice was also disguised, obfuscated by some anti-surveillance technology. Encryption algorithms flickered in the notification window, indicating that the message was being hidden, and routed in a circuitous manner with multiple redundant pathways.

'Ambassador Cuthrick,' the voice said, speaking swiftly, 'We are aware of the condition of your charge, Kahina Tijani Loren. All is not lost. You must send her pilot.'

Cuthrick looked at Luko and Hassan. Both looked back without speaking.

'Who are you? How can I assess the veracity of this information?' Cuthrick demanded.

'My identity is no concern of yours and as far as trust is concerned you have little choice. Simply know I have no ill intentions towards Kahina Tijani Loren. If you wish to save her from what awaits her on Koontz Asylum, I suggest you move quickly. The co-ordinates are attached. Farewell.'

The holofac faded.

'Got to be a trap,' Hassan said. 'They're trying to get rid of all of us.'

Luko shook his head. 'I think not. They ask only for you. They could have killed us whenever they wished. Me, I think this is our clue. We must chase it.'

Cuthrick nodded. 'Only someone very high up in the Empire could have overridden my console in that fashion. The Imperial security service, perhaps, or those in direct line of report to the Emperor herself. Powerful eyes are watching this affair.'

Hassan gulped.

'Will you go?' Cuthrick asked. 'This will doubtless be dangerous. Whilst it would seem Kahina has friends in high places, she has many enemies too.'

Luko looked at Hassan. Hassan nodded.

'I will go.'

Cuthrick steepled his hands together. 'Go then. Fly safe, Commander.'

Deep space, Eotienses system, Empire

Fleet Admiral Patreus' flagship, the *Imperial Freedom*, was holding station in the Eotienses system, several light years away. The Fleet Admiral himself had dispatched the ship, deeming it poor taste for it to be seen in the Prism system whilst the trial was taking place. Flanked by a few escorts and fighter patrols, it sat stationary in the depths of the system.

Aboard, the duty command were at their stations, monitoring the vast vessel and the immediate surrounds. Comms from patrol ships were also being checked, the activity unceasing.

The captain of the ship saw one of his officers scrutinising a readout.

'Problem?'

'One of our wings hasn't reported in.'

The captain moved across the bridge to join him. He toggled the comm circuits.

'Recon Beta Two, this is *Imperial Freedom*, report.'

Static crackled from the return feed. He tried again.

'Recon Beta Two, this is *Imperial Freedom*, report.'

More static.

The pair exchanged a look.

'Scanners to full power,' the captain said. 'Let's see what's going on.'

The scanner holofac dominated the central part of the bridge with a representation of the system around them, and all known moving targets. There were supposed to be four sets of patrols present. One was missing. It had been patrolling their port side.

'Focus scans on the port side. Are they off station?'

'Can't get a lock,' the officer said, tweaking the sensitivity of the scan. 'Wait … there they are.'

Two blips appeared on the edge of the scanner, flickering uncertainly as the computer systems tried to confirm their identity.

'Recon Beta Two, this is *Imperial Freedom*, report.'

There was something this time, but it was garbled.

'Sir …'

The captain focussed back on the scanner. The two blips had been joined by a third. As he watched, a fourth and fifth appeared alongside.

Instinctively, he looked out of the portside window, but there was nothing to see.

On the scanner, the blips increased in number and closed towards them.

'Condition yellow. Secure the centrifuge.'

The bridge crew moved quickly to alert status, bringing the ship to readiness. Shield generators were primed, weapons charged and emergency bulkhead doors secured. Huge flywheels within the structure of the ship absorbed the rotational inertia of the spinning section as it was brought to a halt.

Lights flickered from green to yellow, indicating the heightened security posture of the mammoth vessel.

'All systems report ready, Captain.'

'Transmit on wideband,' the captain instructed.

'Ready, sir.'

'To unidentified vessels. This is Captain Asquith of her Emperor's vessel the *Imperial Freedom*. Do not violate a five-kilometre perimeter around this ship or you will be designated hostile targets. State your intentions.'

More static and a curious warbling noise.

'They're jamming us,' the captain snapped. 'General quarters. Shields up and all weapons hot!'

Ships streaked out of the darkness. There were dozens of them, a collection of privateer vessels by the look of them, ranging from tiny trading vessels to sizeable Anacondas, Cutters and Corvettes.

'Their weapons are deployed, sir ...'

Laser fire crashed against the shields of the *Imperial Freedom* as the ships made their pass, arching above and below. Beam weapons discharged, drawing streaming lines of sparks and flares against the shields of the capital ship.

Missiles, both guided and dumbfire, blasted through space, hurling their violence into the defences of the Imperial vessel.

'Return fire!' the captain yelled.

Huge weapon emplacements mounted on the top, rear and flanks of the mighty capital ship opened up, causing the incoming vessels to scatter and break their formation.

More came on, lasers crackling all around. The *Imperial Freedom* vibrated from the dozens of simultaneous impacts.

'Shields failing on rear flank, sir. They're going for the heat vents!'

They know what they're doing, they're trying to force us to retreat ... why?

'Who the hell are they?'

'Idents scans are running, sir,' the first officer said as the ship rattled again. Alarms went off, signalling some kind of damage.

'Charge the hyperspace drive, be prepared for immediate jump.'

A dark-hued Cutter, flanked by two Anacondas, unleashed a devastating barrage at them, the shields before the bridge flickered and flashed as they struggled to repel the assault.

'Ship markings indicate they are from a faction called ... er ... the Children of Raxxla, sir.'

The captain was none the wiser, he'd never heard of them.

Some local outfit with a grudge? Won't be the first time Patreus has drawn ire ...

'Heat vents malfunctioning, sir!'

'Get us out of here, maximum jump as soon as we're charged.'

Streaming coolant from puncture wounds in her hull, the *Imperial Freedom* turned, orientating itself away from the pale glow of Eotienses' red dwarf.

Space blackened, lightning flickered and the Majestic-class Interdictor ignominiously fled the field of conflict.

Chapter Seventeen

Location unknown, En route to Alioth system

No sooner had the Fuel Rat appeared and transferred the necessary fuel, the ships of the Earth Defence Fleet swung through the system. They noted the departure of the Fuel Rat's ship. It wasn't hard to surmise what it had been up to.

Raan, who had lost no time spooling up his drives and jumping out, knew he had only a small head start. He hoped it was enough. No sign of the main pursuit yet, but there were other marks on the scanner. He spotted a Viper, a Mark IV by the scanner ident. It seemed to be following him too, hanging back from the pack of Earth Defence Fleet Cobras. Raan locked the targeting scanners on it and found that it quickly retreated, eluding his scan, only to reappear again on the edge of range once more a few minutes later.

More than one set of folks following me!

There were plenty of trading vessels about too, which reassured him a little, but his course was taking him through Federal space, towards the border with the Alliance. Out here the Imperial Eagle was an oddity, a rare and unusual ship. It was going to attract attention.

The wrong type of attention.

Raan reviewed the scanners again. Not too many jumps left before his destination, but he had to give these ships the slip.

Easier said than done …

The Imperial Eagle was a tough little fighter, but its jump range was mediocre in the extreme.

Can't run, can't fight!

He toyed with the idea of forcing a mis-jump of the frame shift drive. That would definitely throw them off his tail, but he might end up in interstellar space, light years from anything. No Fuel Rat would be able help him with that.

The scanner pinged again.

More ships!

Raan locked the scanner onto the newcomers and was dismayed to see their faction displays roll up the holofac.

Sirius Corp!

The comms crackled a moment later.

'Raan Corsen, this is Adjudicator Morris of the Sirius Corp. Your vessel is Sirius Corp property. You will stand down and prepare to be boarded. No harm will come to you if you comply.'

Yeah right!

They were ahead of him, closing the distance fast. An Anaconda, flanked by a pair of Vultures. If they caught him he stood no chance whatsoever.

Got to keep running …

It was then that an idea came to him. Running was futile. He was out-gunned all around.

But there is one thing I can do that maybe they can't …

He thumped the hyperdrive controls. Alioth was still multiple jumps away.

Just got to get there first!

Chione orbit space, Prism system, Empire

The *Seven Veils* roared up out of Chione's gravity well. The svelte Clipper was running at full throttle, ensuring it was far from the eyes of any potential observers. Hassan, setting the course and trimming the ship from the pilot's chair, had no intention of letting anyone who might be following them have an easy job of it.

Hassan watched the blue-green moon receding on the monitors. Ahead, the massive blue curve of the bright planet Daedalion loomed large in the cockpit windows. Lightning crackled and flashed on the dark side of the planet, marking the huge storms that wracked it daily.

Satisfied that he was alone in space, he triggered the jump drive.

'Here we go again.'

Frame shift drive charging …

Light flashed in the darkness and the Clipper vanished from view, briefly trailing twin streaks of flux exhaust that slowly dispersed into the vacuum.

Alioth 4a, Alioth system, Alliance

Laser fire flickered around the Anaconda as the Earth Defence Forces engaged the agents of Sirius. The two Vultures peeled off and began to spar with the Cobras. Beam, pulse and the staccato flash of multi-cannon rounds peppered the darkness of space.

Raan took the opportunity. He fired up his ship's systems and powered up the frame shift drive, aiming the little ship squarely at the nearby planet.

Orbital flight engaged.

The drive shuddered into life and propelled the vessel forward. Before him, the arc of the planet grew, levelling out as he descended towards it. The computers automatically compensated for the approach, adjusting the trim.

Glide engaged …

A crackle on the comms told him he'd been noticed, but he'd gained the crucial few seconds head start he needed. The ship creaked and groaned about him as it fell lower into the moon's gravity well, the sombre grey landscape rising up towards him. Six marks glowed on the scanner. Four close by, two further back.

Glide complete.

With a surge of deceleration, the Imperial Eagle burst back into normal space, its main sublight engines thundering up to full power.

'Going to need everything you have now,' Raan muttered.' Let's see what this Imperial showboat can do …

He toggled maximum power to the engines and shunted what was left to the shields and supplementary systems. No weapons. He wasn't going to need them, not for this.

The Imperial Eagle was still descending at breakneck speed as the displays flickered, indicating the other vessels had caught up with him. The scanner seemed covered in traces; they were all trying to catch him. Sirius, the Earth Defence Fleet, even the elusive Viper was probably hanging around at the back somewhere …

Below, the contours of the landscape were drawing closer. Vast chasms, rills and canyons, here and there pockmarked with craters large and small, formed a jagged and pitilessly hostile terrain.

Perfect.

Raan triggered the boost.

The little Eagle might not have the jump range or the weapons, but it had speed and manoeuvrability in abundance.

'Let's see you stay with this!'

The Imperial Eagle blasted into the nearest canyon at over six hundred metres per second, drives flaring, trailing a churning trail of dust and debris in its wake, skimming the canyon floor just a few metres above the ground.

***

Tsu watched as the Imperial Eagle executed a neat half-roll and then turned into the canyon below. From her vantage point she could see its exhaust flux ripping up a wake of dust and gas behind it, the pilot performing a breakneck manoeuvre at a dangerously low altitude.

The Anaconda didn't have a hope of matching that kind of flying, and wisely didn't bother trying. Tsu saw it pull back from the pursuit and return to a position several kilometres above the surface. There was no way it could keep pace and soon dropped off the scanners.

The Cobras and the Vultures were game, though, but she instantly saw the genius in the Eagle pilot's move.

The Cobras were being a lot more circumspect than the Vultures, despite their inherent speed advantage. Say what you would about the old ship, it had lasted because it was good. No other ship packed the Cobra's combination of speed, poise and handling. But here, they were no match for a racing spec Imperial Eagle.

To stay with him the other pilots were having to divert all possible power to their engines, that left them with a choice between shields and weapons.

At six hundred metres per second, I know what I'd choose! There's no way they can hope to fire on him without risking ...

One of the Vulture pilots clearly thought it was a risk worth taking. Tsu saw the intermittent light of twin pulse lasers scything through the darkness of the canyon. They missed the target, but shattered great chunks of the canyon wall which cascaded down in slow motion around the pursuing ships. The Vulture pilot miscalculated the rate of descent.

Don't ...

The Vulture clipped the disintegrating canyon wall, tumbled end over end, its drives flaring brightly as it spun, before impacting half a kilometre further on. The explosion flash-lit the outlines of the canyon in lurid orange light for a brief moment before all that was left was spiralling debris.

Tsu could see the Eagle pilot slowly drawing out a lead, getting a few twists and turns of the canyon between him and his pursuers, having left the hulking Anaconda far behind.

He's good. But what's he going to do next?

***

Raan only need a few brief moments out of sight. The Imperial Eagle pulled a tight turn around a rocky outcrop. Raan saw what he needed, centred the controls, activated the autopilot and then bashed his seat harness, lurching up out of the pilot's seat.

He pulled himself back through the cockpit as fast as he could, chucking himself bodily down the companionway to the lower deck.

There, stored in its compact and foldaway form, was an SRV. Raan pushed himself into the cramped cockpit, swiftly activating its controls and activating the deployment sequence.

The onboard computer immediately queried his commands.

'Warning! Vessel in motion, deployment not advised …'

'Override!'

Below him the bay doors snapped open, giving a dizzying view of the desolate landscape surging past below.

This is madness … don't think just …

He closed his eyes and pulled the emergency release. The bottom dropped out of his world, his heart hammering in his chest and feeling as if it was rising up through his throat.

A moment later the Imperial Eagle was above him, drives burning brightly against the vacuum of space, the SRV falling silently downwards in an accelerating arc.

One chance to get this right …

He placed his trigger finger over the thruster buttons. The SRV didn't have the thrust to hover, even in this low gravity, but the few metres per second of delta-v it could save from his meteoric descent could mean the difference between landing with some damage and being nothing more than a dark stain and a jumble of broken parts on the canyon floor.

The Imperial Eagle pulled abruptly upwards, looping in a high-gee overhead turn and gaining altitude. The Cobras and the Vulture flashed into view, trying to copy the manoeuvre, engine exhausts flaring as their boost mechanisms were engaged to match the Eagle's turn.

He heard his own voice over the comms, prerecorded moments before.

'I'm losing it … I'm losing it!'

The Eagle began to spin, pirouetting and arcing down towards the surface, gaining speed with every moment. As he watched, it passed behind his line of sight, deeper into the nearby chasm.

A moment later there was a bright flash, white and gold, quickly fading to red. Fragments and dust were ejected back from the point of impact.

The Cobras and Vulture swarmed the impact point; two kilometres away from where the SRV was gently falling through the sky.

They haven't seen me …

Now the ground was rising up. Rising up fast.

Hold it … hold it …

He could see the rocks, the big ones … even the small ones. Only a few dozen metres left.

Now!

He mashed the thruster trigger, sinking into his seat as the SRV's miniature engines attempted to slow the descent, the roar building to a crescendo and then …

The impact was hard. Harder than he expected. It jarred his neck and his back, sending a spasm of pain through him. The SRV had landed slightly nose down. Dust splashed against the cockpit windows before settling abruptly in the near vacuum outside. The internal holofac displays flickered for a moment.

'Hull integrity compromised,' the computer announced.

You don't say!

But he was down and relatively intact. He looked at the status readouts. The shields were dead, but he could recharge them.

76% hull. I can live with that.

Now he had to hide. The ships weren't far away. If they suspected that he'd bailed out they would organise a search. If he was caught in the open he was dead. The SRV was no match for a ship.

He spun the SRV on its gimballed wheels. Ahead lay a crater. Luck was with him. The star was at a low angle in the sky, accentuating the deep shadows in the craters ahead. All he had to do was drive down there, cut power and stay put.

Now all I've got to do is drive to Bill Turner's base …

He pushed the throttles forward to their stops and the little vehicle surged forward, its six wheels digging into the powdery surface. He skipped over the edge of the nearest crater and arced through the vacuum for a moment before what little gravity there was exerted its will once more.

The SRV skidded to a halt in the darkness. Raan hit the kill switches and everything went dark, including the life support. Automatically, his Remlok facemask deployed, and a small holofac warning appeared on the helmet display.

Life Support Offline. 20 minutes.

It wasn't a moment too soon. With a rumble of exhaust flux, the remaining Vulture appeared almost directly overhead. It was moving slowly, hull lights casting bright patches of illumination on the ground. It came within twenty-five metres of his position.

Raan held his breath. He could only hope the down blast from three low flying craft had disturbed the surface enough to disguise his tracks.

He'd approached the crater from the opposite rim and had relied on his trajectory to get into the crater shadow. But from his landing point to the moment he'd lost contact with the ground, the SRV would have left its mark on the powdery surface. If the pilots were paying attention …

Don't spot the tracks, don't spot the tracks … Star is pretty low in the sky, tracks might be visible, not sure …

Sweat cooled on his face, chilling him. He didn't dare breathe, somehow holding his breath made it better …

Stupid! It's not like they can hear you …

The Vulture paused, hovering for a moment before turning and moving smoothly away.

The darkness returned.

Raan gasped out loud, closed his eyes, leant back in the SRV chair and then puffed out his cheeks.

Serebrov Terminal, HR 6421 system, Independent

For Commander Erimus, the news was going from bad to worse.

He watched the intel updates flash across his screen with dismay.

This is turning into a disaster! If we don't get a handle on this then the entire galaxy is going to turn on us, Federal and Imperial alike. I don't trust them, but I don't want them beating on us either …

He'd admit they'd made mistakes. Interdicting system authority ships in the Cemiess system had been a poor choice, turning much public opinion against them and giving both superpowers an opportunity to brand them as a terrorist organisation. Many of their pilots had lost their lives in the resulting backlash.

But they snatched her out of our hands, this travesty of a trial …

They'd given Patreus a bloody nose in the Eotienses system over the affair, in the hope that Salomé might be rescued. But there was no sign. She hadn't been aboard Patreus' flagship after all. She was gone and her secrets were lost with her. Forcing the flagship to retreat had given some of the more vociferous and impatient types in his faction something to do, but Erimus had a nagging doubt that the event was being stage managed elsewhere and that the Children of Raxxla had inadvertently played into the hands of whoever it was that was determining the course of events.

Everything we do is making this go south. And we've searched, long and hard. We're still no closer to solving this mystery …

He sat back, watching the intel feeds coming in.

His heart sank lower, crushing into the pit of his stomach as he read the latest updates.

The Feds? But how? How can they possibly know … Karl Devene? That arrogant 'stard from Mars High again!

The information was stark. He scanned it quickly.

The preeminent Astrocartography department of the Federation is seeking a large amount of data regarding particular sectors of the galaxy. Mark Devene, head of AstroCartography on Mars High, explained the request thusly.

'The purpose of this campaign is to gather high quality and systematic information on system configurations, planet types, spectral classes and compositions from zones around the galaxy. What we are looking for is specific data from three distinct zones in order to verify certain hypotheses that are currently postulated regarding these regions.'

'We are looking at these co-ordinates,' Karl Devene continued, 'PLAA AEC IZ-N C20-1, PRU AESCS DL-W C15-37 and EAFOTS EU-R C4-1. Explorers are required to journey to one of these waypoints and then investigate out to a radius of 200 light years. Explorers may be more familiar with the colloquial names for these areas, namely Hawking's Gap, The Conflux and the Formidine Rift.'

Erimus sat back in his chair for a moment, waiting for his heart to stop beating so fiercely.

'My God,' he whispered. 'We've been outflanked …'

Whilst we were busy agonising over Salomé, they've been prepping for a mission into deep space!

Taking a breath he hit the intercom. The answer was immediate. Zenith Ddraiglas was one of his closest associates, a member of the trusted inner circle of the Children of Raxxla.

'Sir?'

'Assemble the consul.'

'Everyone, sir?' Zenith asked. Erimus could hear the surprise in his voice over the commlink. He could well imagine Zenith's dark-hued face crunching into an earnest frown at the unusual request. Zenith Ddraiglas headed up their intelligence team, sifting all the knowledge acquired from clues and hints.

'This is a primary override,' Erimus said. 'The Federation has found out about the Rift and is trying to stake a claim. If they acquire the data ... nothing will ever be found again and Salomé's work will have all been in vain.'

'The Federation?' Zenith asked. 'How ...?'

'Not now,' Erimus snapped. 'Assemble the consul first.'

They were there in minutes, the trusted central membership of the faction. Erimus himself, the current leader, Commanders Eisen, Kron, Zenith, Jellicoe and Tick.

Erimus wasted no time on pleasantries. The group knew each other well.

'Within the last hour,' Erimus began, 'The Federation has launched a massive exploration mission, labelling three specific locations in the galaxy.'

He typed in commands on his commtab and a holofac representation of the galaxy appeared in the air between the group, drawing gasps from some of them.

'Hawking's Gap, the Conflux ...' Jellicoe said, tugging his naval uniform into place. It was a habit others noticed he adopted when he was tense. Too much intrigue in the Federation had driven him out of the core, along with a certain fascination for the mysterious Salomé.

'... And the Rift,' Eisen muttered, his deeper voice rumbling around the room. 'How the hell do they know about that?' He cast his eyes left and right, as if probing those about him. A retired Admiral, he was more than familiar with the capabilities of the Federation, having served them for many long years.

'Those are the areas ...' Zenith began.

'... that Salomé indicated to us before she was abducted,' Eisen finished, his deep voice even more sepulchral than usual. 'If they're going looking, it means the Federation is taking this very seriously indeed.'

Erimus nodded. 'The Federation has indicated some very specific co-ordinates. I suspect that Salomé would have relayed them to us if she'd been able ...'

Three specific points lit up on the galaxy map.

'Long way out,' Kron said, his rasping voice cutting through the air across the table.

Erimus nodded, taking in Kron's grim visage. Erimus didn't know the whole story, but Kron had a troubled past. He was a self-made man who had pulled himself up out of wrenching poverty to stand tall here in the consul. Nothing got in his way.

'The Federation are already mobilising,' Erimus added. 'They've made a call for independent pilots to join their formal expedition.'

'Let me guess,' Jellicoe said. 'That 'stard, Karl Devene.'

'Yes, him again,' Kron said. 'He's been trying to gather all exploration data from remote zones for months and also trying to shut down independent expeditions.'

'If he's calling for help now,' Eisen said. 'The Feds must be desperate. No way they would advertise unless they were worried.'

'Or in a hurry,' Erimus said. 'Best guess is that this secret has been leaked in more than one place and the Federation are trying to gain a monopoly on the data.'

'I don't get the Federal involvement,' Jellicoe said, shaking his head. 'Salomé was taken by the Empire …'

'It doesn't matter how they know,' Zenith said. 'If they find something, they'll adopt their usual scorched earth policy. They'll destroy or embargo anything they find …'

'And whatever it was that Salomé was hoping we'd locate will be lost forever,' Erimus finished. 'And likely any chance of unravelling this mystery.'

'But we can't match the Federation,' Kron said. 'We have a few thousand ships at best. We're outnumbered a hundred to one …'

Erimus nodded. 'We need help.'

'From who?' Kron asked.

'Anyone who will answer the call,' Erimus said. 'Any faction who will come to our aid.'

'This isn't wise,' Jellicoe said. 'If we call for factions loyal to the Federation, we risk bringing their direct attention to our operations.'

'I concur,' Eisen added. 'Asking Federal factions for help is asking for trouble and raising our profile. We'd be running a massive risk.'

'I could say the same for the Imperial factions,' Zenith added. 'After Cemiess, we are not popular with many of our former allies. Some are openly hostile. We risk crystallizing those animosities if we directly confront the Feds. They'll say we are openly trying to cause a war.'

'If we leave them unopposed,' Erimus replied, raising his voice. 'We might as well pack up and go home. We'll be handing the Rift and whatever it is out there directly to the Feds. Salomé told us that this was beyond …'

'Salomé isn't here,' Kron said. 'We don't know where she is! She may even be dead. The most likely explanation is that she's been interrogated, tortured and whatever secret she had is now in the hands of the Federation and the Empire. If we go up against the Federation, they'll simply retaliate and wipe us out.'

'I know we have misgivings about Salomé,' Erimus answered, unable to repress a sigh. 'I share them. But this is the mystery we've been trying to solve for over a year now. Are we really prepared to just leave it to the Feds?'

'Zenith is right,' Eisen said, nodding to Erimus. 'If we don't go, the Feds will wipe out all the details. It'll be back in their databanks.'

'Which is what started all this when Salomé exposed the Imperial data,' Erimus said.

Tick coughed. All eyes turned to him.

'They are likely to wipe us out anyway,' he said. 'We know more than most, even if we know very little.'

'Your point?' Jellicoe asked.

'If we're going down under the Federal jackboot,' Tick said with a grin, 'let's go down knowing the truth.'

Conversation petered out, the group exchanged grim looks with each other.

'This could be our final decision as the consul,' Eisen said. 'If this goes awry, they could well destroy us.'

'I believe we have to try,' Erimus urged.

Slowly, there were nods of agreement.

'It is decided then,' Tick said.

Erimus turned to Zenith.

'Grab the Federation text from the newsfeed and make a counter-offer,' he instructed. 'Give it an Imperial spin and underscore Salomé's plight. Run the text past us prior to sending. Quick as you can.'

'Aye, sir.'

The group got to their feet, making to leave the room.

'There's one more thing,' Tick said. He had remained seated.

'Yes?' Erimus asked.

'You're not going to like it.'

'I don't like any of this,' Erimus snapped. 'Your point?'

'It may not be sufficient simply to match the Federal effort,' Tick said. 'We may need to slow them down.'

The others returned to their seats. Their voices lowered.

'Deliberately sabotage their venture?' Eisen asked. 'Do you know how much pain we would bring down on ourselves? Have you forgotten the backlash over Cemiess and Eotienses?'

'If you want to win, sometimes others have to lose,' Tick said, unrepentant. 'And I'm talking about hired hands, incognito, not being directly involved ourselves.'

'What do you have in mind?' Erimus asked, warily.

'There are those with a reputation for … disruption, piracy … even casual murder. They could be encouraged to bring their influence to bear.'

Eisen frowned, but Erimus shook his head.

'No way. Not them,' Erimus said. 'We are not aligning our interests with those gutter infestations. They are anarchic. They kill without reason or provocation. They are scum, a scourge on the galaxy.'

'Who are you talking about?' Eisen demanded.

Tick raised his eyebrows and gestured to Erimus.

'I'm not even naming them,' Erimus said heavily.

'They will disrupt the Federation …' Tick began.

'By murdering innocent explorers! Some of those people may not agree with our politics, but they are our fellow colleagues – we've worked with them, shared missions. No …'

'They will choose a side regardless of what you think of them,' Tick said. 'We can try to make them work for our benefit … or risk that they will work against us. Any explorer going out there unarmed in the current climate is a fool anyway. The Federation may have already engaged them for all we know. We have to use them to our advantage.'

Erimus rubbed his forehead, pushing at the pain that was growing there. A headache was the least of his worries.

No right answers anywhere. How did this become so complicated?

'More blood on our hands?' Erimus said.

'The Federation are forcing the issue,' Tick said. 'Not us. They must bear the responsibility. This is about maximising the chances of us being successful. If the stakes are as high as we believe them to be, we have to take the difficult path. I will do it if you agree, no need for the rest of the consul to be involved.'

Erimus placed his head in his hands and ran his fingers through his hair, clenching his eyes shut for a long moment.

How do you weigh truth against lives? Make the wrong choice for the right reason? And how many folks will see it that way?

'Do it,' he said. 'We must win.'

'Regardless of cost?' Eisen asked, his voice barely above a whisper. 'Erimus ...'

Erimus nodded. 'Regardless of cost. We are committed, come what may.'

Erimus kept his eyes closed, feverously trying to run through all the possible outcomes of the situation. It felt as if they were on the precipice and the ground was about to crack and break away under foot.

I guess this is when we find out whether those words she spoke were true.

He cast his mind back to the founding moments of the Children of Raxxla, ironically a piece of 'evidence' that had been used against Salomé in the trial.

'She can engender loyalty and adulation ...'

That was true enough ...

'When the time comes, you will need more than ships and weapons, you will need charisma, charm and admiration ...'

Again, true.

'The masses will follow her, love her and ... if necessary, they will fight and die for her ...'

Erimus sighed. He felt a hand on his shoulder and looked up. Jellicoe was standing beside him, looking out at the distant stars.

'You're wondering whether she was telling the truth or not.'

Erimus took a deep breath.

'Dozens of our pilots have died trying to help her, or what we thought would help her,' Erimus said. 'Every move feels like we're stepping forward blindfolded in the dark. What do you think?'

'I think she's honest,' Jellicoe said after a pause. 'But I doubt she's told us the whole truth. Though I'm not convinced she knows herself. If she knew she was going to be tortured ...'

Erimus nodded. 'I'm sure you're right.'

He looked back out into the void.

And now the test of that last statement comes. Will the masses fight for a missing lone woman with a cause, or seek the filthy lucre of easy money with the Federation? I am making a pact with the devil ... will it cost me my soul?

Do they truly love you, Salomé? And was I right to place my trust in you?

Chapter Eighteen

Lombardelli's Legacy, Persephone system, Empire

'No, I don't trust her.'

The voice was subdued, ensuring it wasn't overheard in the noisy hub-bub. The two pilots were sharing a drink in one of the low-gee bars near the station docking rim. Persephone was as good a haunt as any, and this bar served drinks at all hours, making it a favourite stopover for crews on long range hauls or returning from exploration jaunts.

Drew Carnegie downed a shot of Mercurian Flame Liquor and wiped his lips with the back of his hand.

His companion was an older man by the name of Felix Adhock, who had a variety of connections to the Mars High astrocartography department.

'Not to say she isn't quite a diva,' Felix said. 'She caused a stir last year. Did you hear about the boosting episode?'

'No …' Drew replied. 'But I'm guessing you're going to tell me all about it.'

'Got fed up with the delays orchestrated by the docking personnel, so she boosted her ship through the docking slit,' Felix said, smiling at the memory. 'Blew out half of the windows in the orbital and then mocked the crew over the airwaves with her little catchphrase "I don't like to be late."'

'So she has a sense of humour,' Drew replied. 'But she's just another power hungry maniac like all the others. The Feds and Imps are squabbling over the meta-alloys and all the other unknown stuff. She's gunning for whatever it is in the Rift. Ownership and arbitrary lines, same old, same old.'

'She says she's doing it for the sake of everyone.'

Drew shook his head. 'Yeah? And who believes that? Look at the facts. She uses people to her advantage, whether it's companions, fleets, ships or crew. Wars, conflicts, whole moons and systems matter nothing to her – as long as she gets her way. Some of us haven't forgotten the debacle over the Chione moon. Some of those who died served with me.'

'So I take it you're not planning on running support for this … what are they called?'

'Children of Raxxla.'

'Yeah, them.'

Drew grimaced. 'No. I'm not a huge fan of the Feds either, but if it's a choice between them and a messianic maniac, backed by her very own personality cult and personal militia, you'll catch me flying a Fed flag any day. Did you see what they pulled at Cemiess and Eotienses?'

'Yeah, won them no favours. Terrorists by any other name. Sent Patreus' flagship packing though, that's got to count for something. The Fed newsfeeds loved it.'

Drew changed the subject.

'Can you guarantee the Feds will publish what they find, or is this another closed shop routine like before?' he asked.

Felix sighed and took a long slug from his drink.

'In truth?' He shook his head. 'I'm not sure. This isn't just some speculative exploration mission, that's for sure.'

'That's obvious enough.'

Felix licked his lips. 'People have been … discouraged from asking too many questions.'

Drew looked disappointed. 'So the Feds are trying to cover something up.'

'Looks that way.'

'Damn stupid way to do it,' Drew replied. 'Asking for independent commanders to go take a look.'

Felix shrugged. 'Maybe. Maybe not. Search area is pretty big and I'm guessing that whatever is out there needs a lot of data to reveal it. But whatever this secret is, it's leaking out. Nothing is going to stop it now. I'm guessing somebody upstairs wants to put their spin on it before anyone else gets the chance to. Maybe they know it's out there but don't know precisely where. It'll be interesting to see what the Feds do with the data.'

'And the Feds have such a history of being open with their findings.' Drew chuckled and took another pull from his glass.

'You know what the cynics would say … exploration is dangerous,' Felix said, laughing. 'I'll be keeping an eye out for bounty hunters once the data has been turned in. Rumours are they are being paid to selectively remove explorers in certain areas. I heard one called Besieger has already claimed a series of scalps.'

'You're not wrong.'

'You know I'm not.'

'So,' Drew said. 'There's a choice between allowing the Feds to spin the story to their advantage whilst keeping the knowledge to themselves, or giving it over to a mad sociopath with a divinity complex. Can't trust either of them.'

'This Salomé girl is prettier than that flux-stain Karl Devene.'

'And a pretty girl, my friend,' Drew said, pointing a finger at Felix, 'as you know from bitter experience, is a very bad reason to be getting involved in anything.'

Felix laughed again. 'I'm guessing most of their support is because she's sassy. If she were as ugly as sin and as old as Raxxla we probably wouldn't be having this conversation.'

'Did you see her face off with Aisling on the holofac?' Drew asked. 'That was the only time I actually agreed with her. She has a line in invective, I'll give her that.'

'True enough. Time to make up our minds though, my friend. Ships are already en route to Mars and those Raxxla nutters' outpost. Folks are taking sides. They'll be getting underway soon.'

'My choice is between supporting a spoiled brat of an Imperial ex-senator who abdicated her responsibilities to go vacationing off into the void, or supporting a bunch of arrogant Federation flux-stains ...'

'Pretty much.'

'My father told me never to trust a pretty girl.' Drew said. 'So ... Feds it is.'

Felix nodded and raised his glass. 'Here's to the Federation.'

Serebrov Terminal, HR 6421 system, Independent

Erimus took a deep breath. He was acclimatised to public speaking, it had been necessary enough times in the past. One didn't drive the actions of a faction by hiding in the shadows, nor was it a role for the timid.

But this was going to be his sternest test.

They had come.

From across the chart, factions aligned with the Empire had responded to the invitation. The HR 6421 system was buzzing with ships. Comm lines were running at capacity.

Jellicoe and Alessia stood with him, organising the arrivals and the communication backlog. Everything was set. Everyone was here. Alessia had been on the go for more than two days in her role as spokesperson for the Children of Raxxla. Erimus knew she must be exhausted, but no trace of it showed on her features. He was lucky to have Alessia Verdi on his staff.

Representatives of those factions awaited him below. He'd heard of all of them. Some he knew. A few he could trust.

Commander Isaiah Evanson, the representative of Loren's Legion and sent by the revered Commander Cornelius himself, was perhaps the closest ally. The Legion didn't always approve of the Children's actions, but offered support when they felt it was in Salomé's and Prism's interest – though Isaiah always referred to her as Lady Kahina in reverent tones.

Alex Ringess of the League of Star's Pilots was another trusted friend, bringing huge exploration experience. The LOSP were perhaps one of the oldest and longest serving allies of the Children of Raxxla, having worked with them for years.

The others were a mixed bag.

He ran down the list of attendee factions. Some had been indifferent in the past, others he had deliberately vied against. Some wanted to stick up two fingers to the Feds and weren't going to be too choosy how they did it. Others simply wanted to be part of the exploration and the data sharing.

The presence of some of them was concerning, though. Erimus blinked and did a major double take on two of the names.

'Aisling's Angels and the Prismatic Imperium?' he asked. 'Really?'

'You should have seen Zenith's face when they reported in,' Jellicoe said with a grin. 'I swear I saw his fingers twitch on the firing controls.'

Both of those factions were aligned with the People's Princess, Aisling Duval. After the public spat between Salomé and Aisling, their appearance was a mystery.

'Why are they here?' Erimus asked.

'I can only assume they hate the Feds more than they hate us, which must be quite a lot,' Alessia replied.

'Keep them at arm's length.'

'Don't worry, we'll be all over them. If they make a move out of line ...' Jellicoe said.

Erimus reviewed the list one more time. League of Star's Pilots, Spinward Marches Alliance Concern, Paladin Consortium, Loren's Legion, Da Vinci Corp, Winged Hussars, Chapterhouse Inquisition, 9th Legion, Aisling's Angels, Prismatic Imperium and LYR, Exo, the Sovereignty, even a rather motley looking group calling itself the Formidine Rifters ...

Their leaders all awaited him, sensing that something significant was about to take place. They knew that the Federation was already mobilised and would be sending forth ships within hours. But the destinations were thousands of light years distant. They had time, they even had resources already out there.

Just got to convince these people to throw in their lot with us ...

'Hey. You've got this,' Alessia said.

Erimus nodded.

He took a deep breath and then walked assuredly into the conference room. He made no eye contact, but walked down the left side of a long panelled table around which the faction representatives sat. He took his place at the head of the table and fixed them all with what he hoped was an authoritative stare.

Conversation dropped away. All faces turned to him expectantly.

'Welcome to Serebrov Terminal,' he said. 'I trust you are all familiar with each other and that formal introductions are unnecessary. We have little time, so I will cut to the essentials. Earlier this afternoon we received word that the Federation has commissioned a two-week expedition to three particular sectors in the galaxy.'

He gestured and a pre-prepared holofac display lit up, throwing a three-dimensional view of the galaxy above the table. The location of the core worlds was marked, with three parallel tracks leading away from it. One headed towards the centre of the galaxy, one to the right leading to a distant spiral arm, and the third veered to the left crossing a dark abyss towards the edge of the galaxy. As Erimus looked at it, he noticed that the three tracks were tangential to a path in the opposite direction, one that led towards the Pleiades Sector and the Orion arm.

'And just how did the Federation get hold of this data?'

Erimus looked into the light green eyes of a thirty-something woman. He knew of Commander Lyrae of the Chapterhouse Inquisition. It was she who had relayed news of Salomé's capture. Her security expertise had been very much welcomed.

'In truth, we don't know. It matters little at this stage,' Erimus replied. 'The Feds have the data and they are acting upon it in their usual fashion, by throwing a large stash of credits at the problem. We believe they seek to acquire whatever knowledge they can. They will likely destroy all evidence of what they find, and thus whatever it is that is out there will be hidden forever.'

'No doubt about that,' said the woman standing immediately behind Lyrae. Erimus recognised the face of Penny Umbra, she of the Social Eleu Progressive Party. 'Folks always follow the credits.'

Erimus tried to regain the initiative. He raised his voice.

'You know of our leader, Salomé. You know what has transpired. Whatever you think of her actions and motivations, know this. She found something out there, she was guided to it. Powers, whether they be Federal or Imperial, are trying to suppress this knowledge. There is no other explanation for her farce of a trial.'

A large man pointed his finger across the table. Erimus recognised Big Pappa, of the Paladin Consortium. 'Integrity. Honesty. That's what it's all about. Salomé has her faults, but she does at least acknowledge them. Unlike the rest of the Imperial power structure ...'

Another man pushed forward. He was thin and wiry, his eyes darting about suspiciously as he looked about him. Erimus recognised the man known as the Truthsayer, although everyone called him 'DJ' for reasons none could recall.

'The Empire is sick, we of the Sovereignty have said this all along,' DJ said. 'It is rotten to the very core. Our leader, Maiva ...'

'Spare us the self-promotion,' replied a rough looking man from the other side of the conference room. Erimus looked across at Commander Asamith. He'd come representing the Da Vinci Corp. His body language did not look encouraging. His arms were folded and he was leaning back, disconnected from the conversation. 'We all have concerns over the state of the Empire and have had so for a long time.'

'I am more concerned over how the Federation will respond to this competitive stance,' interrupted another man standing to Asamith's left. He was younger, an explorer with an outfit called the Rock Rats, one of the smaller factions present. 'We risk much in supporting the Children of Raxxla. The Empire is not united on this and the Federation remains unbowed. We risk making powerful enemies of them with this alignment.'

'You do not need to renege on your existing relationships to support us,' Erimus countered.

'So just what are you asking us to do?'

Eyes turned towards a figure at the back of the room. He stepped forward into the bright illumination towards the centre.

Here we go ...

Corwin Ryan was the head of the Prismatic Imperium, a powerful political lobby that held the system of Cubeo on behalf of Princess Aisling Duval herself. They were far bigger and more powerful than the Children of Raxxla. They were far bigger and more powerful than most of the other factions combined.

Sway them and I sway this group, lose them and ...

'Good question.'

That rebuke came from another commander, seated in the more dimly lit recesses of the conference room, his face hidden in shadow. 'Answer that one, Erimus.'

Erimus shot him a glare, remembering the pilot's name. Matthias, from a faction called the Winged Hussars. He didn't look like a trustworthy type.

How has it come to this? Consorting with anyone from anywhere ...

'We need you to join us in searching these areas,' Erimus said, focussing back on the conversation and looking directly at Corwin. 'We alone do not have the resources to cover it in the time period allowed. The Federation has the reach, if we're to compete with them ...'

'And what will you do with the data recovered?' Corwin replied. 'The Children of Raxxla don't have the most honest of reputations. Some brand you terrorists. I tend to agree with them. Why should we trust you now? What guarantee can you give us that you will publish the results of research based upon the data retrieved?'

'I can only give you my word,' Erimus said. 'Whatever this is, shadowy forces want it concealed. It's been hidden for decades. This may be our last chance to uncover the mystery. I will personally guarantee you all carte blanche access to whatever we find. We're not the Federation, we couldn't suppress it even if we did want to!'

There was a rumble of approval around the table.

'If you do suppress it, it will be the end of you.' This last warning came from Lance, the representative for Aisling Angels, another faction supporting the People's Princess. 'Corwin and I will see to that.'

'And I want the same assurance from you,' Erimus continued. 'Trust goes both ways. We all deserve this data.'

'If the data is worthless, what then?' Corwin asked. 'We too have chased this mystery for months with nothing to show for our efforts but maps of empty tracks of space. Perhaps it's all an illusion, a deceit, an invention of your so-called leader, Salomé. Perhaps she is space-addled, crazy and truly belongs in that asylum!'

Isaiah from Loren's Legion was on his feet, leaning forward menacingly, his voice rumbling.

'Do not speak ill of Lady Kahina before me.'

The commanders in the room began making space, moving into groups, staking their territories. Erimus saw hands going surreptitiously towards belts and holsters …

'Peace!' Erimus yelled, smashing his fists down on the table.

Conversation stopped.

He flexed his fingers and pursed his lips before speaking.

'We know our leader is both an inspiration to us yet a divisive figure to others. But she is not here. She has been taken from us by force, sentenced in a travesty of justice. Disunity here only suits the agenda of those who pull the strings behind the posturing of the Federation and the Empire. We have been manipulated, we continue to be manipulated. Our choice is between allowing that or aligning ourselves with what she was attempting to do, whether you agreed with her methods or not. Salomé … Kahina … she was trying to uncover the truth. A truth that powerful forces want hidden from us and the masses we represent. We can prove that we are a force to be reckoned with. That the superpowers do not have absolute authority over our affairs.'

Another rumble of approval sounded around him. He stared into eyes that stared back at him, unflinching.

'A pretty speech, but you need to offer more than a dubious moral choice,' Corwin said.

'We can't offer the compensation that the Federals can,' Erimus said, 'But we have enough that we can make decent recompense, rewarding those who commit to us.'

'Even if we all agree to do this, it is not enough.' Lyrae said, running a hand through her short orange hair. 'You need the support of the independents. The legions of solo commanders out there? They only care about the credits. The Federation will win. You can't compete with that.'

'We offer them a choice,' Erimus countered. 'Try to uncover the truth and exonerate an innocent woman, or just pile up more money.'

Lyrae shrugged. 'They'll go with the cash. They always do …'

Erimus played his trump card. He cancelled the holofac display and signalled for the blinds in the conference room to rise.

The light of the HR 6421 star caused all to squint for a moment, but their eyes soon adjusted.

'Dr Kaii. Are you receiving me?'

The comm system crackled for a moment.

'Loud and clear, Commander,' a jaunty voice replied. 'I took the liberty of transmitting your message far and wide.'

Before the station, hundreds upon hundreds of ships were jockeying for position. Hull lights flickered in ordered sequences. Everything from the smallest Eagle to the biggest Cutters and Corvettes could be seen. Disorganised, independent, but an armada none the less.

'And uh, I bring friends …' Dr. Kaii's voice continued. 'We have many pilots from the Earth Defence Fleet with us. In fact, looks to me like pretty much anyone from anywhere is right here.'

The comms crackled again. 'This is Commander Finn McMillan, ready to serve the Children of Raxxla. We await your orders.'

Further comms crackled in an overlap of voices, all reporting their readiness and eagerness to depart.

'The Children of Raxxla called for assistance,' Erimus said, feeling tears forming in his eyes. 'The independents have answered.'

Silence reigned in the conference room for a long moment.

Erimus turned about and faced the people in the room, leaning forward on the conference room table.

'So, what of you?' he demanded, raising his voice and trying to keep the tremble out of it. 'Will you aid us, or will you stand aside and let the Federation dictate the fate of the galaxy?'

'Loren's Legion will see this done,' Isaiah said immediately.

'As will the Sovereignty,' said DJ.

'The LOSP is in,' Alex said, casting a look around the others yet to respond. 'Our loyalty and courage were never in doubt.'

'As are the Rock Rats!'

'And the SEPP!' said Penny.

The cries continued.

'I speak for the Chapterhouse Inquisition when I say we will join you,' Lyrae said, a grin spreading across her features. 'Even if it is a fool's errand, it'll be fun!'

'As will Da Vinci Corp,' Asamith said.

'The Spinward Marches Alliance will support you.'

'And me,' a rough looking pilot at the back lurched forward, pushing through the crowd. Erimus hadn't heard of the faction before today, but knew this pilot represented something called the Formidine Rifters. They appeared to be pretty much a crackpot group of legend seekers.

Can't be choosy, not now, we need everyone we can get …

'Name's Lucky Luke,' the man said, leaning nonchalantly against the table. 'I'll tell you something. Feds, Imperials, Alliance. All liars, every single one. Now I don't know who you fine folks have supported up to now, nor do I much care. But one thing I do know? This Salomé girl? She's right on the money. We've been sold a fake history and we all swallowed it. This is our last chance to figure out what the hell is going on … maybe before it's too late.'

He gestured towards Corwin and Lance.

'So, you guys have a choice,' Lucky Luke drawled. 'This girl is in a heap load of trouble. You gonna do the right thing or not? It's time to give the Feds a bloody nose.'

Eyes turned towards the remaining two individuals in the room. They stood together. The representatives of the Prismatic Imperium and Aisling's Angels. Together, they commanded forces greater than the rest of the representatives combined. Erimus waited, clamping down on his desire to say something, anything, to convince them.

I need you!

Corwin clearly enjoyed his moment. He stepped forward to glare at Erimus across the table.

'This had better be worth it, Erimus of the Children of Raxxla.'

Erimus stared back, struggling to stop his body from shuddering.

Corwin looked over his shoulder at Lance, who nodded. He then looked back at Erimus, his mouth twisting into a wry smile.

'We're in.'

Mars High, Mars, Sol system, Federation

'The explorers are departing,' Exo said, an obfuscated holofac displaying a series of telemetry reports before his eyes. 'It appears that the animosity fostered towards dear Karl Devene and the general suspicion around Federal motives in this matter has prompted them to deploy.'

'Fascinating, really,' Society said, eying the same data. 'How easy it is to manipulate them all.'

'They are convinced that the mission will somehow exonerate their erstwhile leader,' Personnel said. 'So, they go out into the dark willingly.'

'We should not be overconfident,' Infrastructure answered. 'Timing is delicate here. The revelation about the Dynasty expedition is a secret we have long kept. Given that we have set the Federation up to be blamed for the costs involved in that mission, we must anticipate a backlash against them.'

'We have confidence in President Hudson,' Personnel said. 'Complete confidence.'

'Once they return with the mission data,' Finance added, 'With all the necessary Earth-like world locations and so on, surely that is all the exploration data we need.'

Infrastructure nodded. 'Yes indeed.'

'Then our dear ex-senator may step off the stage,' Society said.

'It has already been arranged,' Personnel smiled. 'I have been assured that her time at Koontz Asylum will be quite ... brief. A mercy, really.'

'Excellent,' Infrastructure concluded. 'If we have no further business?'

'Just one item,' Personnel said. 'Our alternative quest.'

'Ah yes,' Infrastructure nodded. 'How are the good Doctor Arcanonn and his motley crew performing?'

'For all their investigations, they don't appear to have made as much progress as we anticipated.'

'Is the poor chap losing his touch?' Infrastructure said with a chuckle.

'I dare say they could use a little fortitude,' Personnel said. 'A measure of luck perhaps ... another clue?'

'Make it encrypted,' Exo said. 'They love that. They must be fully occupied, after all. They have considerable resources at their disposal, which might interfere with our plans.'

'A thorough investigation of the Guardian ruins will occupy them sufficiently,' Society said. 'Eyes diverted there will not be looking closely elsewhere.'

'Agreed,' Infrastructure said. 'Ensure their focus is where we desire it to be.'

Chapter Nineteen

En route to Daibo system, Empire

Salomé was bound by the wrists and led aboard the Imperial Cutter *Diadem* by a cohort of Imperial guards. Within its spacious interior, she was led past the first class accommodation immediately behind the bridge and taken down into the hold. She had not been allowed to speak to anyone, but had been taken directly from the courtroom following the sentence.

Her eyes widened in horror as she took in the view. Chained hand and foot to the bulkheads were tens, no hundreds, of people. Some were slaves, others Imperial citizens of various statures judging by the stained garments that they wore. All looked forlorn and dejected.

A stench reached her nostrils, causing her to flinch, a mix of body odour and human excrement. She struggled then, but there was no escaping the grip the guards had on her.

'No! How dare you treat me this way …'

They roughly forced her up against a bulkhead where a small gap between prisoners remained. There she was pushed down to her knees whilst they tried to secure her wrist restraints to the flooring by a long length of chain.

'You ain't no lady now,' one guard replied. He tried to run a hand across her chest. She stumbled up and wriggled out of the way, kicking at him, catching him in the shin. He cursed and fell back before dealing her a vicious blow across the face. It sent her reeling back against the bulkhead, smacking her head hard against the unforgiving surface. She flopped forward, half stunned with the pain, half with the indignation.

Before she could recover she found herself hoisted up by her neck, the guard having gripped her tightly. She flailed against him, struggling to gain a grip with her legs.

'Upperclass posh bitch,' the first guard said, spitting into her face. 'Finally getting what's been coming to you.'

'They'll knock the feistiness out of her at Koontz soon enough,' the second guard added.

'And stick a few things in her too,' the first replied, with a coarse laugh. 'Some lucky bastard will get to tame her …'

'Captain's coming!'

Salomé found herself dropped back on the floor. She lay gasping for breath for a moment, her head spinning. The sound of the chain being locked into place echoed around her.

'Prisoner secured, sir.'

'Excellent, excellent. Ah yes,' said a new voice. 'Our new passenger. We are most privileged to have someone of your stature ... well, your previous stature ... aboard. It's not often we get to deal with such class.'

Salomé looked up into a fat swarthy face, bedecked by an enormous greying moustache. The rest of the head was bald, with a pair of thin watery eyes peeking out above a rather twisted bulbous nose.

A coward's eyes ...

'Captain Ruskin, of her Emperor's, rather hastily commissioned I might add, prison fleet vessel *Diadem*,' he said with a jovial grin. 'Welcome aboard, Ms. Loren. Patron's Gerrun and Zyair speak so highly of you ...'

Salomé said nothing, but simply glared at him.

'You will want for nothing aboard, during our trip,' Ruskin added. 'Of course, if you don't find the default accommodation to your tastes all manner of niceties can be provided ...'

Salomé heard the guards chuckle and looked aside, staring at the cold metal flooring.

'... upon receipt of certain ... favours.' She looked back and saw Ruskin raise his eyebrows suggestively.

The very thought!

Salomé lurched forward, aiming another kick, but she was brought up short by the restraints around her wrists. They cut into her flesh, bruising and painful.

Ruskin had anticipated her and had stayed just out of range. Then he lunged in, grabbing her by the hair. Now the pain was excruciating, but her movements only made it worse. She scrambled upwards, trying to relieve the pressure. He bent her neck backwards and then cradled her body in his arm as she lost balance. His face leered close, she could smell his breath, rank and foul, alcohol mixed with fast reprocessed food.

'Nothing will be too much trouble for you ...' he whispered. 'Just ask.'

'You'll get nothing from me,' she managed.

'Really?' Ruskin replied. 'I think I'm already owed for the passage. Tolls, taxes and so forth, repairs to the ship. All very costly.'

'Touch me and you'll pay with your life!'

That earned her another blow. Ruskin pushed her forward into the bulkhead, knocking the breath out of her. Before she had a chance to recover, hands had grabbed at her neck. In a moment of horror she realised they were pawing at the clasp on her dress behind her neck. Before she could move, the garment was loose and with a rip of tearing material it had been snatched away.

Whistles of appreciation from the guards and the other prisoners reached her ears. Her cheeks stung with the aftermath of the blow to her face, rage boiling in her at the humiliation. Her temper, only barely in check, burst its bounds. She screeched, managing to break his hold on her and struck out with a high kick, catching Ruskin under the chin and knocking him to the floor. She vaguely heard murmurs of appreciation before orders were yelled.

She saw a baton swing towards her. She blocked it, but the chains hampered her movements. There must have been another …

Pain and spinning dizziness.

'You'll regret that, Ms. Loren …'

Darkness. Void.

***

She woke to frigid cold. Her side was numb, her muscles cramping and stiff, her head a thrumming agony. She tried to move, but the attempt made her head swim sickeningly around her. Bile rose in her throat, burning and bitter. She stopped, focusing on breathing. That hurt too.

A broken rib?

Then came the shivering. It was freezing cold, she could see frost glittering on the corrugated metal of the floor and her breath suspended as a light mist around her as she struggled to rise.

So cold!

Her fingers, hands and arms would barely obey her instructions they were trembling so violently. After several false starts, she managed to move herself and look around.

The cargo hold was only dimly lit now, with a faint blue illumination that only increased the sense of cold. About her, bodies were clustered, huddled close to each other for warmth, wrapped in whatever clothing they had managed to retain after they were brought aboard.

She was still chained to the bulkhead, but she was floating free.

Zero-gee! We're in space.

She found her ankles were chained as well. She couldn't feel her fingers or her toes. They were already blue with cold, the metal clamps leeching the heat out of her body. She braced herself against the floor and tried to assess her situation.

She knew the shivering was a good sign, at least for now.

It's when the shivering stops you have to worry …

She pulled herself upwards. She had nothing but her thin undergarments left, her skin goose-pimpling in the cold air. She rubbed herself as vigorously as she could in an attempt to get a little heat into her body.

Ruskin wouldn't risk his 'cargo.' The temperature was unpleasant, dangerous for long exposure, but she guessed he knew his business. He was simply inflicting maximum discomfort for the journey. If the hold had been completely unheated she wouldn't have woken up; would have frozen to death as she lay unconscious. Away from the heat of stars, space was brutally chill.

Just enough heating to keep us alive, that's all, sadistic 'stard.

She crouched down again, pushing herself against the bulkhead, trying to keep herself as compact as possible. It was coated in some kind of rubber surface, less cold than anything else around her. Now only her feet were exposed to the metal.

She could hear a faint thrumming within the ship. It echoed through the cargo bay.

Hyperspace … we're jumping.

She tried to turn her mind to recent events, to stop her thinking about the immediate future. A fake assassination, a staged trial, Aisling and Patreus playing a game.

But they're only pieces … and so am I, it seems. What is the game, and what are the rules? Is this all that old lady's doing? And if so, why? Why so obscure and complex?

The image of Patreus at the end of the trial swam into her mind.

This was not his doing. He is being forced to play a role against his wishes. What did he mouth at me? Wait? Wait for what?

She was interrupted by a shudder. The hyperspace jump was over. She felt a faint sense of motion as the ship changed course. It was a big vessel, turning slowly, perhaps orientating itself for another jump.

Then a familiar sensation of gravity rose about her. Within moments, she was drifting down to the floor.

Ship is entering a gravity well, our destination? Are we there?

Then she yelped as a cascade of freezing water trickled onto her head. She looked up in surprise and then noticed that all around her the frost had melted. Water, or other liquids she didn't really want to think about, were pooling on the floor about her. Mist was rising like steam from an oven. Warm air … no, hot air! It was wafting all about her.

She welcomed it for a moment before she realised what was happening.

The ship must be scooping fuel. With the environment systems set to barely compensate for ambient temperature, it would soon be roasting within the bay.

Others around her were becoming conscious of the changing temperature. Mumbles and groans accosted her ears as the prisoners about her woke up. The stench, mercifully hidden by the chill, returned with full force. She gagged at the smell, turning her head aside.

Humiliation seems their plan. Gerrun and Zyair must have arranged this!

Alioth 4a, Alioth system, Alliance

Tsu brought the *StarStormer* low across the desolate surface of Alioth 4a. She'd watched the skirmish between the Vultures of Sirius forces and the Cobras of the Earth Defence Fleet with detached interest. It would do her no good to be involved, in fact it was better if she wasn't noticed at all. She'd kept *StarStormer* deliberately cool, with judicious use of its limited stock of heat sinks to mask its visibility on any scanner.

From her perspective, they'd confounded their own objectives. The Eagle had crashed, suddenly losing control over a canyon and slamming into the ground at high speed. She'd seen the crash at range but it was clear there would be very little left of the ship. The impact would have been catastrophic with the Eagle's engines running at full power. She replayed the pilot's last words.

'I'm losing it … I'm losing it!'

She set the *StarStormer* down some distance away and waited, watching as the Vultures and Cobra swooped across the crash site, lights blazing and illuminating the scene below. Her own scanner pinged with their emissions as they repeatedly searched the site, presumably trying to read any data that might have survived the crash. Data units were tough, and often withstood impacts that would pulp any passenger or pilot.

Doubt it would have survived that, though…

Hours passed, but she was patient, knowing she couldn't move in until those ships had retreated.

Eventually they left, their disgruntled comms and message exchanges indicating that they hadn't found what they were looking for. The Eagle was pulverised, the pilot incinerated and the data, whatever it might have been, lost beyond recall.

Tsu shook her head.

Too convenient, but …

Maybe they had shot him down. Three ships on one, all with guns blazing? Tough odds. She rubbed her forehead, thinking it through, pulling up the pilot's profile on the holofac display.

Raan Corsen …

She read it again, noting the series of CQC wins attributed to him as 'Commander Falchion' and wondering how much real flying experience he had. She called up one of the bouts and watched it from beginning to end, checking out the tactics and the guile. He was no rookie; he knew his ship and what it was capable of. It seemed unlikely he'd simply crash.

She frowned. His last match played out on the holofac display.

Suckered Yuri right in … by playing dead … big risk, but what a payoff!

Suckered his opponent in by playing dead, then took him out? But this was different, surely? Could he be hiding somewhere?

It couldn't have been an escape pod, it wouldn't have done him any good as the pods were automated and would have blasted up into orbit in an attempt to return to the nearest station or outpost.

If he intends to keep going, to complete his mission … he must still be out there. But how …

She replayed the telemetry of the Eagle's course as it swept ahead of its pursuers. She saw the telemetry stop for a few brief seconds.

Out of sight …

Then the Eagle reappeared again, following a smooth curve which rolled it up out of the canyon, following a steady arc. As it reached the top the transmission sounded again.

'I'm losing it … I'm losing it!'

Tsu watched as the ship completed its arc and slammed back down onto the moon. The replay ended.

Then she grinned.

'You sneaky 'stard,' she said. 'You weren't even onboard by that point!'

She turned her attention back to the canyon. She'd set *StarStormer* atop the ridge, giving her a panoramic view. She waited, sure her instincts were correct.

Sure enough, a few minutes later, light flickered dimly on the floor of the canyon. She couldn't make out any detail, but she knew what she was looking at.

The faint thruster glow from the articulated wheels of an SRV.

He must have bailed out in the SRV and crashed his ship. He was still trying to complete his own mission. The only obvious target was the Engineer's base some forty clicks to the north-west.

The Engineer's base belonging to a certain Bill Turner ...

Quickly, Tsu jumped into her own SRV and had it lower itself out of the ship. It unfolded around her, its six wheels digging into the powdery terrain.

She ran it forward to the edge of the canyon, looking over.

Not the easiest of descents, but not impossible.

With a couple of hand gestures she sent the 'dismiss' call to her ship, which lifted up under its autopilot control and accelerated swiftly into the blackness above. Moments later, with a brief flash, it was gone.

Tsu turned her attention forwards, pushing her SRV over the canyon edge and into pursuit.

Race on ...

***

The SRV was trundling across the desolate surface of Alioth 4a. Raan hoped the SRV would hold out for the journey. For the first few minutes he'd had a blast driving the machine across the dusty surface, revelling in the thruster-tuned grip from the six articulated wheels and making a few jumps over outcrops and bluffs.

But he'd had to settle down for the journey ahead. According to the scanners, Bill Turner's base was some forty kilometres away. Nothing for a ship, but it was an interminably long distance to drive, particularly over terrain that could change from a flat plain to a bottomless gorge in next to no time.

It wasn't a comfortable ride, either. The landscape was strewn with debris, this was no smooth surface, but a maze of jumbled rock. He had to keep slowing down to pick a safe route through the chaos. He dared not use the SRV's own illumination. It would certainly help him see better, but it would also light him up like a solstice celebration for anyone looking.

A big fat 'here I am' sign …

Each rock jolted the SRV, sending a crashing thump through the machine's framework. It was a tough mechanism, designed for precisely this sort of use, but the experience quickly took a toll on the driver. It wasn't long before Raan was longing for peace, quiet and to be able to lie down anywhere where the room wasn't jolting and vibrating around him all the time.

Can't take it slow though …

Were they still looking for him? If so, an SRV would be very hard to spot from a ship, particularly driven like this, with no lights and in the shadows of mountains and hills. They hadn't felt like the types to gave up without being absolutely sure. He tried to put himself in their position.

What would I do?

He wouldn't waste time and fuel searching for something so hard to find. He would let it come to him. There was little else on Alioth 4a other than Bill Turner's base, and it was by far the closest outpost. If he survived the crash, where else would he go? And what better way to be sure than lookouts around the base waiting for him to turn up?

He toyed with the idea of trying to get a message through to Bill, but that would give away his position just as quickly and he had no guarantee of a positive response. Bill likely wouldn't take the risk. No, it was up to him to find a way in.

He pushed the throttles forward and the SRV trundled across the frozen vacuum-dried surface once more.

***

Tsu, her own SRV half a kilometre behind him, had a far easier job of it. She wasn't running with lights either for similar reasons, but she had one major advantage that Raan did not. She could simply follow his tyre tracks. The ridged markers were easily seen on the powdery surface. She had followed at a discreet distance, keeping a lookout for anyone else. So far it had remained quiet.

Raan was taking a cautious route through the depths of a gorge on his way to Turner's base. It was easy enough to follow his tracks. Tsu decided to return to the top of the gorge to spy out the land ahead. They were down to fifteen kilometres now, the base should be in visual range.

Her SRV's wheels dug into the soft surface, churning up a wake of dust which settled curiously fast in the vacuum outside. Thrusters helped to dig the wheels into the surface, increasing the available grip. The machine surged up the slope and she was rewarded with the sight of the horizon widening out before her.

The landscape looked as desolate as before, but faint lights could be seen in the distance atop a group of buildings. As she watched, a ship departed, thrusting upwards into the sky before disappearing with a flicker of hyperspace energy.

Far below, she could just make out Raan's SRV, still moving cautiously forward, slipping between the shadows. From this vantage point she could follow the gorge all the way up to the base. It would take Raan straight there eventually, despite turns and furrows in the route.

She squinted into the distance, seeing some kind of movement ahead. Perhaps a faint churn of dust.

It was too far away to be sure.

She triggered the turret HUD, not so much for the weapons as they were far out of range, but more for the telescopic display enhancement the targeting systems provided. Now she could zoom in and survey the land ahead.

Damn!

She could make out two SRVs heading away from the base; both were running fast, lights ablaze with no indications of stealth. Both had turned into the gorge and were proceeding along the valley floor at pace. She could see the dust churning in their wakes as they bounced across the landscape, skidding and sliding as they tried to maintain their pace.

Search party?

Raan wouldn't be able to see them until they were on top of him. Then it might be too late.

Tsu stowed the turret and gunned her SRV around. She kicked the throttles and headed back down towards the bottom of the gorge. She triggered the floodlights, ensuring she could see ahead, dodging rocks and boulders as they appeared in her path, any pretence at stealth now abandoned.

***

Raan saw flickers of light ahead of him and slammed the throttles closed. The SRV juddered to a halt.

Something around the next bend!

There was little cover in this part of the gorge; the landscape had been slowly flattening out around him as he neared the base, making it harder and harder to conceal him.

Dust was illuminated by the beams of whatever it was that was approaching. A pair of SRVs by the look of it. Moving fast.

Time to make a run for it!

He had a small chance they wouldn't spot him, but they'd encounter his tyre tracks moments after passing his position, then the game would start.

Light flickered, brightening the brow of a hill ahead. Two SRVs jumped over the top, landing several metres beyond the summit. Their drivers didn't see Raan's SRV, lurking in the shadows to one side, but within seconds they had skidded to a halt as he suspected.

He watched as they stopped. Raan could see the pilots looking about, their figures clearly visible within the plexiglass cockpits of the SRVs. One was gesturing.

Spotted!

Slam! Throttle to its stop and full pips to engines! A forward surge. Just like it was Yuri coming at him again in the Arena. Adrenaline pumped through him as the SRV charged towards the hill.

'Let's see what you've got!'

***

Tsu could see the two other SRVs had located their quarry. The lights of Raan's SRV flickered on and she could see it racing away at full speed, with the other two in pursuit, all three bouncing precariously across the surface. As she watched, tracer fire began to flicker from the pursuing vehicles, churning up bursts of debris and dust from the surface. Raan's SRV began to zigzag in an attempt to throw off their aim.

It would be down to skill now. Driving an SRV at high speed was fraught with peril. It was easy enough to lose control and send the little vehicles into a roll or a spin, but it was the landscape that would kill you. In low-gee the vehicles weren't always able to change course if an errant rock loomed large in the way. An impact at speed was going to hurt, shields or no shields. A deft hand on the thrusters was what you needed.

None of them had any choice in the matter though.

Raan was trying to escape. The pursuers were trying to bring him down. And Tsu was trying to catch all of them.

***

Tracer fire flashed outside the cockpit, the SRV lifting on its portside wheels. Dust and smoke flashed past and were gone. The vehicle tilted erratically before Raan was able to wrestle it back under control.

Hull integrity compromised! Hull 62%.

He spared a glance over his shoulder, seeing the tell-tale streaks of weapons fire blistering from the pursuers; he zigzagged across the surface, trying his best to evade their fire. It felt awfully limiting being confined to the ground, he was used to manoeuvring in three-dimensional space.

Not going to be able to get away …

They were pecking away at his vehicle bit by bit. The shields had put up a valiant defence, but they had failed and there was no way he could spare power to recharge them now. Ahead, the ground was undulating in a series of almost dune-like hills, pockmarked with the occasional crater.

Three-dimensional space? That's an idea!

He pushed all the power available into the engines and then drove directly down into the nearest crater. The SRV gained speed on the down-hill run and then began to ascend the other side. As he reached the rim he triggered the vehicle's retro thrusters.

His SRV lurched into the air. He pulled the control yoke back hard and the SRV flipped over in a graceful curve, his finger still pressed firmly on the thrusters.

He caught sight of the horizon, inverted and still receding. Below, the tracer fire went wide and cut out. His pursuers ground to a halt immediately below him, confounded by the unexpected move.

Raan's SRV reached the top of its trajectory and began heading down again.

My turn!

He triggered the SRV's weapons.

His turrets surged into life, spitting fire at the nearest target below. Caught unprepared, the target's shields collapsed within seconds. His gloved hand remained held fast to the trigger, and the bullets slashed at the unprotected SRV.

The SRV struggled to reverse out of the way, wheels spinning helplessly in the low-gee.

Too late.

The cockpit broke up in a sparkle of glistening shards. He must have hit the power supply too as the stricken SRV abruptly disintegrated with a faint flash and a crackle of discharging energy.

Then the ground was his concern. His own SRV was descending.

Too fast.

He struggled to right the little vessel, triggering the thrusters to slow his descent.

The SRV rang with the impact; it felt as if someone had punched him in the stomach and the face at the same time. His head spun and he clenched his eyes shut against the pain and disorientation. It would have been easy to give into the bliss of unconsciousness.

Hull integrity comprised! Hull 18%. Damage to primary drive!

One of the six wheels had been completely dislodged by the impact. It was still bouncing past the canopy in slow motion.

Move!

He jammed the throttles open again and the SRV struggled forward, crabbing to one side as he tried to wrestle it onto a course. He couldn't see the other SRV. He had to get away …

The vicious sound of fire hitting the exterior thumped around him. Sparks flew in the cockpit as something shorted out. The holofac systems died a moment later and the SRV ground to a halt, then flipped over into a disorienting spin. Raan found himself held firmly upside down in the driver's seat as motion ceased.

He bashed at the restraining harness and gently fell to the floor.

He looked up.

The other SRV was right outside, its guns trained on the cockpit. He could see the figure within. As he watched it gave a jaunty wave.

A single round of fire blistered against his cockpit, followed by another. A crack appeared, spidering its way across the plexiglass in slow motion. Raan heard a faint hiss as pressure began to leak out into the void.

Remlok …

Another burst of fire and the cockpit shattered about him. His protective suit immediately deployed, shielding him from the vacuum of space, but the decompression threw him out of the wreckage to spiral through the darkness before landing with a gentle thump on the dusty surface.

He got to his feet to see the second SRV turning around to face him again.

Gave it my best shot …

Tracer fire lit up the darkness at the base of the crater. Raan flinched, waiting for the brief moment of slashing pain, violent scream of air and then the blissful end of everything.

But it didn't come.

He blinked and stumbled back, the SRV before him blasted over by a torrent of incoming fire from off to his left. As he turned, yet another SRV launched itself from the rim of the crater, its guns pummelling fire into the stationary one before him.

He threw himself backwards as the fire found its mark, ripping into the SRV and smashing it to smithereens. He lost his footing, spiralling out of control above the surface. He only just missed a collision with a sharp-edged rock before he found himself bashing into the surface once more, bouncing a few more times before he came to a halt, lying on his front, his breathing heavy in his ears.

He pushed himself up on his hands. Was his suit damaged? Relief, it seemed intact.

A shadow fell on him and he looked up.

Another suited figure stood over him, silhouetted in the starlight. He could make out little other than the shape of a gun.

The comms unit in his suit crackled. A woman's voice, sharp and business-like.

'Welcome to the Alliance, Mr. Corsen.'

***

He looked battered, bruised and exhausted, but that didn't stop Tsu from taking precautions. She got him to remain where he was while she searched the wreckage of his SRV, quickly locating the data cache he'd been carrying. She took it across to her vehicle and secured it, keeping an eye on him throughout the operation.

He hadn't moved.

'Get in my SRV,' she instructed.

He got to his feet and bounced across to the cockpit, pulling himself into position and strapping himself in. She climbed in the opposite side, pressurising the cockpit. As one, their Remlok systems retracted.

Life support restored.

'Now listen closely,' Tsu said. 'Your suit has less than five minutes of air left in it. Mine has close to twenty. If you try anything I will vent the cockpit to space. All the controls are voice-printed to me. We're still kilometres from any help. You'll have a few minutes to wish you'd not tried something stupid. Understand?'

He nodded. She studied his face for a moment. He wasn't very old, perhaps a similar age to herself. He looked pretty scared, but it might be an act. Dark skinned, with a mop of closely cut hair upon his head. He looked back at her, his breathing still shallow and rapid.

'Who ... who are you? You said Alliance?'

'Alliance Interpol,' Tsu said. 'I've been following you since Chi Orionis.'

He nodded. 'The Viper.'

'You stole something from the MetaDrive company,' Tsu said, matter of fact. 'What is it?'

He hesitated.

'I have the data,' Tsu said. 'I can vent you out of the cockpit. Talk!'

'I don't know what it is,' Raan said. 'I was told to get it out of Chi Orionis by my boss ...'

'Femi Dakarai?' Tsu queried. 'He died ...'

'Died?' Raan replied. 'No way. Sirius had him killed. The whole take-over business was a sham.'

'So Sirius is after this tech,' Tsu said. 'What were you trying to do with it?'

Raan sighed. 'I was told to take it directly to a man by the name of Bill Turner. He has base here.'

Tsu took a deep breath.

So it is all about Bill Turner!

Raan clearly saw the look on her face.

'You know him?'

'I know of him.'

'All I was told was that Bill would know what to do with it,' Raan finished glumly. 'No one told me I would be chased across space and nearly killed for it.'

Tsu pondered for a moment, calling up a view of the data stored in the cache. A brief glance told her it was heavily technical, clearly something to do with hyperspace, but it was data, not a schematic design, a modification recipe or even a blueprint.

'Do you know what this is?'

Raan shook his head. 'MetaDrive was working on top secret hyperdrive research,' Raan said. 'I was only an administrator, not part of R&D. But I'm guessing it's something big, something new. Femi and Bill were collaborating on it in secret …'

The coded transmissions we picked up. The Alliance must have whatever this is, but I need to figure out what Bill's part in all this is too. He's clearly working on this without informing Alliance command!

'That was a neat trick of yours by the way, playing dead,' Tsu said. 'You pulled that before?'

'Kind of a signature piece,' Raan replied. 'Used it in the Arena, beat Yuri Nakamura on the Melee Masters.'

'Close quarters combat?' Tsu asked. 'Not pretend stuff, I mean in real life.'

Raan looked back at her. 'First flight.'

Tsu stared. He had to be kidding her. But something about his fixed expression and pallor gave his words a ring of truth. She shook her head, fired up the engine …

'We'd better move,' she said. 'Could be more Sirius agents about. I'll take you to Bill. Let's go get some answers.'

EAFOTS sector, Formidine Rift, Uninhabited

The beacon co-ordinates continued to pulse on the scanner, the monotonous landscape of the desolate airless moon rolling slowly below. The pilot stretched, looking down through the expansive cockpit of the Asp Explorer. It was a perfect ship for this kind of work, rugged and dependable, if not the last word in aesthetic design. An Asp would never win a beauty competition, but it would always get you home.

Commander Joshua Hales had flown the *Wayfarer* for many years. He was a veteran of exploration, one of the few that had flown to the centre of the galaxy, the infamous super-massive black hole known as Sagittarius A* and gazed upon its fearsome power, a vast maelstrom of gravity bigger than an entire solar system.

A few more passes just to satisfy my curiosity. Doesn't look like anything out here after all. This has got to be the longest and most tortuous wild goose chase ever …

He'd had a chat with a few other pilots out this way, thousands of light years into the void. You had to be a little crazy to do this, the isolation alone took its toll on your mind. Some of these folk had been out here for years, looking for something on the scantiest evidence. Some said they were curious, some said they just wanted out of the core worlds and the endless politics, others seemed to have an almost messianic belief in the words of some strange Imperial woman. Some belonged to factions, some didn't. Collectively they referred to themselves as the 'Rifters.'

But I'm here because it feels like the right place to be …

He looked at the scanner again, the latitude and longitude markers slowly unwinding as the Asp thrusted forward. He was ten kilometres up, eyeballing the surface, looking for anything out of the ordinary. So far there had been nothing, just craters, rills, ridges and valleys on a tarnished beige and otherwise non-descript surface. Some people couldn't cope with this kind of work, he found it relaxing.

Beige, beige, beige …

The system name was listed at the bottom of the display.

EAFOTS LZ-H B10-0. Such a memorable name!

Nothing was showing on the scanners, the shadows were playing havoc with the sharp terrain, hiding much of it in deep blackness. His gaze swept across untold empty kilometres of vacuum-frozen wilderness.

Wait a minute …

There was a smudge on the surface, a mark where there didn't seem to be any relief in the terrain. A faint shadow, but of what?

Worth a look.

Joshua adjusted the Asp's course and pointed the nose of the ungainly ship downwards. Thrusters flared, automatically controlling the ship's descent. The targeting reticle flickered with the revised vector, the altitude monitor counting down as the landscape rose up around him.

He expected a collection of boulders, casting unlikely shadows across the surface, but the shadows didn't soften into rough-hewn shapes as the Asp came down, if anything they got sharp, more delineated, hard-edged … regular …

Damn! There's something down there!

He cautiously flew the Asp in a circle about the location, making a careful note of the co-ordinates. Training and long experience took over. Even in the excitement, there was no excuse for cutting corners. This far from home even a minor mistake could be fatal. He'd heard that several pilots had grown careless out in the deep void. They had been seasoned explorers, but one momentary lack of attention and the blackness had killed them. Space was utterly unforgiving.

With the ship readied for landing he proceeded; the Asp lowering itself to barely a kilometre above.

It's some kind of base ...

He could make out structures; antenna masts, inflatable biodomes, the marks of vehicles still showing in the thin dust. It wasn't huge, but it was big enough that it must have been deployed from a sizable ship, something Anaconda-class or thereabouts.

So someone has been out here before!

He toggled the comms. He didn't expect an answer, but he thought he ought to try. There was no response to his hail.

He landed half a kilometre away and readied his SRV, taking only a few moments to climb into its snug cockpit. The vehicle dropped out from the Asp's hull and thumped onto the surface.

Drive assist off.

The SRV always deployed facing in the opposite direction of the ship. Joshua accelerated out, the SRV bouncing a little in the low gravity, its wheels being dug into the surface using onboard thrusters. He gave his ship a wide berth and then steered around, driving towards the buildings.

They were eerie, unlit and covered with a thin film of dust. There was no sign of movement, no sign of power. The bigger units looked like hydroponic bays of some sort. Joshua could just make out rows upon rows of plants, all dead, frozen long ago when whatever powered the base had succumbed to failure. It was clear the place had been abandoned for years, maybe even decades.

There was something, though. The SRV scanner revealed a faint trace. Joshua steered towards it.

Some kind of data node. Can it still be functioning after all this time?

It was. A solid state memory with a radioisotope backup transmitter – still working. It was easy enough to download the data. There was a file, encrypted, but the technology was ancient and easily circumvented by the modern software built into the onboard computers in the SRV. They made short work of deciphering the code and a holofac video flickered into life. Joshua could see a man, sitting in a functional cabin, leaning in close to the imager. He didn't introduce himself, simply started talking. A timer at the bottom of the image gave a date.

Expedition Log: 30/08/3270

Wow... that's like... more than thirty years ago!

'Been travelling for weeks. Passed this amazing twin nebula just recently, about the only interesting sight on this whole trip. We are a long way out now, I don't think anyone else has been this far. Still, pay is good!'

The video crackled and stopped for a moment before resuming.

Expedition Log: 12/09/3270

Now the man looked visibly more nervous, looking one way and then the other as if to check he wasn't being overhead.

'Stars have thinned out and we've started dropping our cargo. Looks like some kind of long-range beacons to me. It's all hush-hush, no questions asked stuff. Heard some of the senior bods talking about a Dynasty project. Careless talk and all that ...'

Expedition Log: 18/09/3270

The man now had his head in his hands, a few days stubble showing on his face.

'Nothing prepared me for the boredom. It's very dark out here, really dark, darker than normal space. There's hardly any stars ahead of us, it's just blackness ... the void.'

Joshua recoiled at the next image, the man looked like he'd aged a decade. There were dark rings around his eyes, and they were bloodshot and staring.

Expedition Log: 01/10/3270

'Picked up some kind of signal yesterday and it looks like the crew weren't expecting it. Got them proper rattled. There's definitely something very strange about this area of space. Won't be sad to turn around and head home.'

Expedition Log: 11/11/3270

'Last batch of cargo due today, but the hyperdrive has malfunctioned. We tried jumping and got yanked straight back out. So we're stuck here, Randomius knows where ...'

Now the man was slumped forward, not even looking at the imager.

Expedition Log: 29/11/3270

'We can't fix it. Hyperdrive is dead. Lucky we're in a system with a habitable world. We've sent a distress call, who knows if anyone will ever hear it. We're going to abandon ship. If anyone finds this, we're in ...'

The image faded out abruptly, leaving just a series of words at the bottom of the display.

Automated telemetry report: Power Failure.

Joshua sat back, trembling.

What the hell was I watching?

Chapter Twenty

Daibo system, Empire

A gloved hand acknowledged the holofac. Secure encryption messages flickered for brief moments as the system established communication.

'It is time for our little interception.'

The incoming voice was masked, but retained enough of its original form to be made out as belonging to a woman.

'Everything is prepared.' The man's tone was firm and controlled, the voice of one used to authority.

'Excellent, proceed,' was her response. 'Let's see if we can wrest their plans awry. It is vital she is recovered.'

The holofac faded to be replaced by another one, this time showing the view of a ship with Imperial officers dressed in military uniforms.

He held up his gloved hand to stop the inevitable deference.

'I will excuse the formalities this time, Captain. The less we transmit the better. Proceed with the plan immediately.'

On the holofac the captain nodded, barking orders to his subordinates.

'Interdict the *Diadem*, now. Flank speed, weapons to disable modules only.'

'Bring her to us the moment she is secured,' the glove-handed man said.

'It will be done.'

The communication was completed and a third began.

More encrypted preamble was undertaken before a new display flickered into life.

The figure at the other end was shrouded, but the face in profile revealed enough to indicate a hideous disfiguration.

Besieger ... a bounty hunter ... we cannot afford to be associated with whatever the outcome may be ...

'A time is coming when your services may be required at short notice,' the glove-handed man said.

The returning voice was gravelly, distorted. Whether that was by design or by accident was impossible to tell.

'You name the target, I'll name the price.'

'I will do so when I am ready, that moment is not yet upon us. All I require for now is that you be prepared.'

Dawes Hub, Achenar system, Empire

The holofac recorders in the first-class suite of the *Diadem* were providing an interactive display of Salomé's misfortunes. Gerrun was chuckling at the expression on Salomé's face as she watched in horror at the behaviour of her fellow prisoners. Both he and Zyair were secured in comfortable low-gee armchairs within a private suite at Dawes' Hub, many light years away.

'Not exactly sophisticated entertainment,' Zyair said, disapprovingly. 'I was content to see her stripped of her titles and banished from Imperial society.' He shuddered as he watched the holofac, considering how he himself would react to such adversity.

'Come, come, my friend,' Gerrun said. 'Our little victory is at hand. Let us at least enjoy the show. It is a pure unadulterated delight to watch her suffer for what she brought upon us.'

Zyair raised an eyebrow.

'You seem to have a rather sordid streak to your preferred titillations.'

Gerrun favoured him with a look. 'I will admit that I do find her state of undress rather stimulating. Perhaps it's the chains or the underwear. I'm not entirely sure. It merits further study.'

'Your base instincts come to the fore, I see,' Zyair said, sparing Salomé's image a glance. 'Are there not enough strange vices and all sorts of exotic temptresses across the core worlds to satisfy your desires? Surely you can have any female acquaintance you desire given a price.'

Gerrun waggled a finger at him. 'But that's the trick, is it not? The price. This ...' He gestured to Salomé on the holofac. 'This is beyond price.' Gerrun's face was split by a wide grin.

Zyair looked again. Salomé could be seen mopping her brow with the back of her arm, handicapped as she was by the wrist restraints. Her body was glistening with sweat, smeared with dirt, her hair bedraggled. Gerrun continued to stare at the image in fascination.

A faint tone sounded and another image overlaid the view of Salomé.

'Accept,' Zyair called, welcoming the distraction.

The secondary image flickered for a moment and then Captain Ruskin appeared, grinning jovially at them.

'Ah, our good Captain,' Zyair said. 'I trust everything is in order.'

'Indeed it is,' the captain replied. 'We have just completed refuelling at the Kumod system and will shortly be jumping onwards to our destination. I'm afraid I cannot make the journey last any longer, good patrons. We have tarried long enough.'

Gerrun gestured, holding up a zero-gee adapted decanter of wine. 'You have done us proud, proud! I only wish you could join us in a cele-bratory tipple. Our soupçon of retribution against our erstwhile mistress of torment.'

Ruskin grinned. 'Next time I am back on Achenar I'm sure you can oblige.'

'We look forward to it,' Gerrun assured him.

Ruskin looked sideways from their perspective, casting an eye on his own monitors. 'A shame really, she could be put to much better use, you know.'

'Too recognisable,' Gerrun countered. 'But you are right. A shame to waste a talent such as hers. However, I prefer to think of it as rather like a fine wine. Drink deeply and enjoy, rather than lament the fast approaching end of the bottle.'

'She will live on within the asylum, no?' Zyair queried.

Gerrun and Ruskin shared a chuckle.

'Care to share the joke?' Zyair asked.

'There is a word in an ancient language I forget the name of,' Gerrun said. 'Ah yes ... Oubliette.'

'Oubliette?' Zyair asked.

'It means a place of forgetting, or somewhere you abandon those you do not wish to recall. Koontz Asylum serves such a purpose for those within the Imperial echelons whose presence ... is no longer required.'

'No one ever returns from Koontz,' Ruskin said. 'And those that arrive there do not leave.'

'What will happen to her?'

'Imperial research projects that innovate beyond the restrictive bound-aries of legal control often require subjects upon which to validate and hone their theories,' Gerrun said. 'She will continue to further the interests of the Empire ... for a short time at any rate.'

Zyair nodded. 'As long as we get rid of her. That's all that matters. I'd prefer a neater and more efficient solution, myself.'

'You needn't worry,' Ruskin's voice crackled over the holofac trans-mission, laced with a flutter of static. 'She won't last long, the famous ones never do ...'

The transmission broke up. The view of Salomé flickered and intermittently froze and corrupted.

Gerrun frowned and leant forward. 'Ruskin?'

Ruskin could be seen barking orders to someone out of line of sight of the camera, the illumination around him changing to a bright crimson. The image vibrated and then abruptly cut out, followed a moment later by Salomé's holofac.

Words floated above the holofac transmitter as Gerrun and Zyair exchanged worried looks.

Transmission terminated at source.

'I trust you have a plan B?' Zyair demanded.

Daibo system, Empire

The heat had faded once more. Salomé could tell the hold was rapidly cooling down and would soon be heading for a deep chill once more.

How many jumps was it between Prism and Daibo? It can't be that far … and how long was I unconscious?

Then came the faint thrum. The hyperspace subsystems were spooling up again. Salomé listened to it as the humming throb vibrated through the ship. It was familiar enough to her after long journeys in the void.

Can't be long now … wait, what's that?

The ship lurched underneath her, causing the chains that bound her to rattle. She was flung to one side. Other prisoners around her looked up at the strange interruption to the tedium of their transit. All looked worried and scared, unaware of what it meant.

Salomé knew though, she'd experienced it before.

Interdiction! Someone is trying to rip us out of supercruise!

There was a thump and then the cargo bay seemed to be spinning around her. She was almost glad of the chains now, they kept her in position as the ship gyrated. It must be spinning.

Another lurch, this time in the opposite direction, those on the bridge must be trying to wrestle the ship under control. Interdiction always threw the orientation out …

The structure of the ship groaned and flexed about them. Around Salomé, the prisoners whimpered with fear, clutching at each other. Then came a screech of tortured machinery and the bass thrum of the main engines cycling up to power. Everyone within the hold was rolled towards the rear of the ship. Salomé found herself dangling painfully by the wrist binders and struggled to get a firm purchase on the floor. Everything that was not bolted down slid rearwards, bouncing off the walls, floor and ceiling in wildly fluctuating inertia. Salomé ducked down as a collection of loose objects bounced towards her, fluttering through the air.

Another sound; a mixture of buzzing and crackling, sweeping around the ship.

Laser fire. Someone is attacking us!

The battle, if that's what it was, was short. The noise of the drives faded with a stutter and weightlessness returned. Faint scrapes of noise, metallic and deep, could be heard from somewhere outside.

Another ship alongside?

A bright light from the rear of the cargo bay, sharp blue and actinic. Salomé squinted into it, unable to see anything else in the glare. A light that was slowly moving.

Cutting into the hull …

Whoever they were, they were efficient. A section of the bulkhead was cut away in under a minute and was pushed aside, slowly rotating, its edges still glowing red hot. Two figures stood in the gap, silhouetted against a brightly illuminated backdrop. They moved forward and Salomé could just make out they were dressed in combateer flight uniforms, helmeted and both bearing weapons and portable scanners.

They were equipped with mag-boots and paced forward into the hold, searching. The scanner was pointed in her direction and Salomé heard a distinct beep of confirmation.

Someone else wants me, who is it this time?

The figures turned bright torches onto her, causing her to squint further. She tried to move back, but there was nowhere to retreat to.

'There she is.'

Their voices were muffled by their masks, but she could make out the words. The intruders stomped across to her.

'Who are you?' she demanded as they pulled her upright. Neither responded, but both pulled out what appeared to be weapons. For a moment, she thought they were going to kill her there and then.

Why go to all this trouble …?

The weapons were used on the chains that held her captive, making short work of them. She was pulled aside and towards the cutaway in the cargo bay bulkhead.

She let herself be taken, there was nothing she could do in zero-gee to resist them. She found herself bundled unceremoniously through the gap and then into a connecting docking umbilical that had been strung from another ship. She could make out a massive outline through the small windows in the walls.

Majestic-class …

Then she was in an airlock, listening to the sounds of air cycling in sequence. The outer door had closed and there was a brief pause before the inner one opened.

She was escorted into a plush reception area that would not have looked out of place in the grand hotels of the Empire. Everything was shades of red and purple, overlain with gold highlights, plush drapes and Imperial insignia. Salomé immediately recognised the colour scheme.

Behind her a clunk signalled that they had detached from the *Diadem*. A group of people marched up to her. Medical staff, she thought. Within moments she was covered in warm blankets and given a preliminary check.

One, a doctor by the look of him, touched an earpiece and spoke.

'We have her.'

Salomé couldn't hear the reply.

'Yes, she's not badly hurt, but in a poor state of …'

Something hissed against her arm and everything went blurry.

***

It didn't take long for reporters and investigators to flood the system. The rise and fall of Lady Kahina Loren had been covered by most Imperial news outlets, and quite a few of the Federal ones too. Many had been in the general vicinity hoping to cover her arrival at Koontz Asylum, either to mourn her imprisonment or revel in her ultimate humiliation.

What none had expected was a distress call.

Camera-equipped news vessels vied with ships from the local system authorities and Imperial jurisdiction as they attempted to determine what had happened.

There was little to go on. All that had been found was a spiralling field of debris.

GalNet buzzed with the news.

A prisoner convoy en route to Koontz Asylum in the Daibo system has been interdicted and destroyed. Wreckage was found in system and has been positively identified as belonging to the Imperial Cutter 'Diadem' and the accompanying four Imperial Clippers 'Cypripedium', 'Velum', 'Monile' and 'Vestimenta' in the formation.

It would seem that the Loren name will always be associated with controversy.

***

She recognised the layout of an Imperial Majestic-class Interdictor, she'd been a guest aboard Admiral Brice's vessel often enough to know them well. After the doctors had finished their checks she was once again taken in hand by the flight-suited figures and moved into a lift.

It rose and twisted in a peculiar away, as if spinning around. After a moment of dizziness and disorientation, Salomé felt herself being pressed onto the floor, feeling the carpet give beneath her shoes.

Gravity …

They had allowed her to shower and to change. Smart, semi-formal attire had been provided, along with all the finery and frippery associated with the finest Imperial tastes. Once ready, she had been led through to the central section of the enormous vessel. Now they were entering the habitation ring, a vast, spinning toroid elegantly engineered into the midst of the Interdictor-class ships, providing a simulated gravity comparable with life planet-side. These parts of the ship were usually reserved for dignitaries or statespersons. They represented the most prestigious accommodations available in space.

The lift doors snapped back to reveal the interior. It was even more glamorous than she expected. Chandeliers hung from a gently curving roofline that swept away in an elegant arc above her. The floor also curved upwards to her right and left, ending at dark wood-panelled walls to either side. The walls themselves were hung with actual paintings, bound in gilt-edged frames and separated by rich and opulent curtains, shades and drapes. Tapestries, ancient weapons, busts and statues competed for attention. The history of the Empire was arrayed before her.

The room seemed to be unoccupied; though its central space was finished with a plush selection of comfortable looking chairs and antique tables, chaise longues, stools and footrests.

In the middle was a fireplace, with an actual fire blazing away within its hearth. Salomé blinked in surprise. Whoever had furnished this place had very old-fashioned tastes. It had her longing for comfort and relaxation after the brutality of the prison ship. Settling into to one of those chairs ...

Don't even think about it. It won't last, it never does ...

'You may approach, Kahina Loren.'

Salomé looked up at the voice. It had come from a high-backed chair placed near the fire, facing it, obscuring the owner.

Her!

Only an arm was visible, thin, with delicate and long fingers extending from the hand, gently clasping the arm of the chair.

At the words, the two flight-suited figures stepped back into the lift. The doors closed, leaving Salomé alone.

The warmth of the fire was welcome.

Red and purple ...

Salomé stepped forward. As she came close, the hand gestured to another high-backed chair adjacent.

'I apologise for the unorthodox method of rescuing you, and that the rescue could not be accomplished any sooner. Timing had to be precise, I am afraid.'

Salomé swallowed, looking down into the face of the woman before her.

It was a hard face, acclimatised to difficult decisions, stern and fierce. Neatly styled brown hair framed it, with a hint of grey at the temples.

Salomé immediately curtseyed.

The woman nodded, apparently satisfied.

'We have much to discuss.'

'Yes, your Imperial and Royal Majesty.'

Salomé bowed low as was correct and proper for Imperial protocol. Even had she retained the rank of Lady and of Senator she would have still bowed as reverently. Nothing less would be expected in the presence of the Emperor herself.

Emperor Arissa Lavigny-Duval!

'You may sit,' Arissa instructed.

Salomé did as she was told.

Arissa held herself with practised grace, her posture and bearing beyond reproach, conveying a calm and measured air of dignity.

'I have watched your antics with quite some interest,' Arissa said. Her voice was clear and distinct, her inflection spoke of breeding and long being familiar with power and status. 'You have upset many, not least our dear People's Princess.'

'I have done what I thought best,' Salomé said carefully.

'Have you indeed,' Arissa replied, one eyebrow raised. She snapped her fingers and a slave appeared, as if from nowhere. 'Anlian Gin?' Arissa asked, inclining her head to Salomé who nodded and was quickly provided with a glass, filled with dark purple liquid.

Not glass, Anlian Gin dissolves glass. This must be pure crystal ...

'To the Empire,' Arissa said, raising the crystal as the slave retreated out of sight. Salomé raised hers in response.

Arissa took a delicate sip and then set her drink down on a small and beautifully carved wooden table alongside her chair.

'So much more sophisticated than Lavian Brandy, I find,' Arissa continued. 'Don't you agree?'

'I have always found the brandy rather rough,' Salomé admitted. 'And the gin is less ostentatious than Leestian Evil Juice.'

'That is a drink for the less than erudite,' Arissa agreed.

Salomé took her own sip. The warm liquid swirled around her mouth, lighting it with a subtle but fiery flavour. She closed her eyes for a moment, half expecting her rescue to be some witch-space induced delusion and to find herself back in chains aboard the prison ship.

But no, this is real ...

'So,' Arissa asked. 'Should I continue to refer to you as Kahina Loren, or the mysterious Salomé? I have studied my ancient history too, you know.'

'It is a convenient travelling name,' Salomé answered. 'A little mystery can go a long way.'

'You have become adept at it,' Arissa said. 'Nonetheless, you have me to thank for your salvation this time. I have followed your style, I hope you approve of the manner of your rescue.'

Salomé bowed her head. 'And I do thank you for it.'

'Well you might,' Arissa said. 'They had a rather ... unsavoury ... agenda planned for you at Koontz Asylum.'

Salomé shuddered at the thought.

'They?' she asked.

Arissa smiled. 'Yes, a good question. One I hope to find an answer to. But let us not jump ahead of ourselves.'

'I am in your debt,' Salomé replied. 'I remain a citizen of the Empire, a servant, your majesty.'

'Enough with the formalities,' Arissa said. 'They serve only to slow down our discourse.'

Salomé nodded once more. A log shifted in the fire, drawing Salomé's attention to it for a moment. Sparks flickered and died, the red coals glowing brightly.

'I have been watching your progress with interest,' Arissa went on, 'and I was curious to see whether you might succeed in flushing out the secrets hidden in the darkness. You have come closer than most, I think.'

Salomé sighed. 'I have endangered many and have little to show for my efforts.'

Arissa's eyes flashed. 'Not so little. They have tried to do away with you, which means they are scared of you. Those who flock to your banner have defied the Federation in the depths of space and won a round. You have those who love you and those who hate you scattered across the entire expanse of the core worlds. There are few who haven't heard the name of "Salomé." It has become a rallying call for the disaffected, the disillusioned and the desperate. You have started something that is bigger than you know.'

Salomé looked up with a frown.

'You have power, Salomé,' Arissa said. 'If you call, they will answer. You have influence greater than you know. It makes you significant … and dangerous. Aisling's interest in you was no accident.'

'I have not sought power,' Salomé answered. 'I wanted only to expunge the grief and remorse of what I inflicted upon my home. The deaths … yet everywhere I go, more death follows me. I do not wish people to fight and die for me …'

'But they do,' Arissa replied. 'They do. Willingly, reverently, even gratefully. What you intended is, by now, quite irrelevant. You are the leader many have looked for. The plain fact that you have not sought ultimate power is precisely why they look to you for guidance, for inspiration and leadership. They do not trust what they are told, what they read, what they see. Who can blame them? Misdirection and obfuscation is the way of things today. Only you have gone beyond the veil.'

Arissa took a sip of her gin.

Salomé sighed. 'I had no choice once I began to follow this wretched mystery.'

Arissa smiled. 'The old lady. Yes, I know of her.'

'Then you know more than I do,' Salomé replied. 'I have been played by her, enticed into a mystery and then exploited, along with many others, to chase half-truths, puzzles and no end of dead ends in the depths of space!'

'She was quite the enigma,' Arissa agreed.

'She told me something,' Salomé continued. 'She said there was a key and a location to search. My people are looking for it ...'

Arissa abruptly held up a hand. 'Do not tell me more. The fewer who know the details, the better. If your people find it, they are putting themselves in great danger. I believe this secret may be about to be revealed ...'

'But what secret!' Salomé cried. 'This is maddening. I should never have gone looking for this ... that old lady ...'

'... has marked you out as her protégé,' Arissa said with a chuckle.

'A singular honour I could have done without!'

'Perhaps she chose more wisely than you suspect.'

'I do not know what she intended,' Salomé replied. 'If I am to carry out some mission, why it is not clear? Why assign me such a task and then omit to tell me what to do?'

'I have some insight, at least,' Arissa replied. 'The Empire, contrary to what we impress daily upon our loyal citizens, is not all powerful. Neither is the Federation or the Alliance. There are those who work behind the scenes, brokering power, influencing markets, corporations and whole systems, steering humanity along a path they determine. Exactly how far their influence extends is not clear to me, but it has great depth and breadth.'

'I have heard this speech before, though not from you,' Salomé replied. 'Clandestine organisations, hidden beyond sight, working behind the scenes ...'

Arissa smiled again. 'A shadowy revolution, it would seem ...'

Their eyes met. Salomé swallowed. 'A corps of ruthless, power-crazed elitists hiding behind the scenes. Myths and romantic stories filtering back from the darkness, planets lost in the void. Exaggerated nonsense, surely?'

Arissa chuckled. 'Tall tales must start somewhere, no?'

Salomé frowned, 'You believe in ... Raxxla?'

'No, I don't,' Arissa replied. 'But I believe in the power of misdirection, confusion and obfuscation. Myths and legends are inhabited by those who want to direct attention elsewhere. They take the dreamers and the romantics and use them.'

'A cloak ...'

'Yes, and these people are certainly well cloaked,' Arissa agreed. 'We believe they may have been active for centuries.'

'If so, they will be everywhere ...'

'And I cannot trust many of those highest in the Empire,' Arissa said.

'With any influence comes the possibility of extortion and compromise. These people may work with the fortunes of the Empire and then work against them. It is impossible to reveal them. But this time, I hope I have confounded their plans.'

You can't trust those highest in the Empire? Can I trust you? Do I even have a choice?

'By rescuing me.'

Arissa nodded. 'I believe they genuinely intended to kill you this time. Which means you are close to success. They have made great efforts to drag your name through the refuse, sully your reputation, cast aspersions upon your character. They have tried to associate you with criminals and terrorists, and sow the seeds of discontent amongst those who follow you. And they have tried to disgrace you.'

'They succeeded,' Salomé said. 'Patreus …'

Arissa leant forward. 'Dear Denton? Did you not think it was odd that he was not consumed with rage over his attempted assassination?'

'He tried to convince me to trust him. I do not trust his motives,' Salomé answered. 'His loyalty is unclear …'

No more than I trust you right now!

Arissa chuckled. 'He might seem to be the strutting popinjay, but that is by design. It was by my orders and his skill that you weren't immediately sentenced to death. He has worked long and hard to keep the Empire safe. It was not by his doing that you were abducted in Cemiess, others were involved. I trust him and so should you.'

Salomé didn't answer. Arissa was looking at her expectantly.

'You're asking yourself whether you can trust me,' Arissa said. 'A valid question. You must judge my own integrity.'

'You could have rescued me before I was subjected to that …'

The doors to the room snapped open. Salomé turned, her eyes widening in surprise as she took in the sight of a figure striding boldly into the room. She gasped in surprise as he stepped into the subdued lighting and his features were revealed.

'Patreus …'

'At your service,' Patreus said, with a brief nod. 'You are a difficult person to rescue, if you don't mind me saying. Third time is the charm, though.'

'Rescue?' Salomé asked, her mouth falling open.

'Dear Denton has been working very hard on your behalf,' Arissa said with a touch of amusement. 'You turned down his help, do you not remember?'

Patreus strode across, poured himself a gin and took a seat adjacent to the two women.

'Your health,' he said, with a grin.

'I don't understand,' Salomé said, looking between him and Arissa.

'Denton revealed to me that he had been contacted by persons unknown,' Arissa said. 'In an attempt to discredit you and remove you from circulation. It seems they thought the animosity between the pair of you was genuine.'

'And we took the opportunity to try and flush out who is behind all this scheming,' Patreus said. 'By playing along. They were clearly worried that you were getting close to … whatever this is all about.'

'The trial …'

'I rather enjoyed playing the injured party,' Patreus said. 'Though I was trying to ensure it didn't take place. You are a very determined young woman. Your dogged determination not to compromise is admirable, but it did mean that we had to come up with this rather unorthodox way of securing you.'

Salomé half got to her feet. 'Then why didn't you tell me the truth?'

Patreus shrugged. 'We were on Achenar, there was no way for us not to be overheard. I tried to indicate my intentions, but you still believed that I was the warmongering fool I am forced to portray. I could have stopped the trial, but you were determined. Thus, I had to curtail the sentence.'

Salomé looked from Arissa to Patreus and back again. Their expressions were open and expectant, clearly watching her to see how she would react.

Can I trust them? Really?

She sank back into her chair.

'But if it isn't you …' Salomé began. 'Who is it?'

'A very good question,' Arissa said. 'These people, whoever they are, are extremely circumspect and careful. But they have let their guard slip on occasion. People previously close to you have been embroiled …'

'Gerrun and Zyair betrayed me,' Salomé said, thinking it through. 'But they are mere patrons …'

'And they were in the pay of…?' Patreus prompted.

'Princess Aisling?' Salomé asked in disbelief. 'Really?'

'Jealousy can be a powerful motivator,' Arissa said. 'More than enough reason for her to take a dislike to you. You have achieved by accident what she believes is hers by right. The love and dedication of willing followers. She truly is vacuous in the extreme, but we believe she is a compromised and powerful figurehead through which this group can influence and shape the Empire. I doubt she knows she's their tool, but that in no way detracts from her abilities.'

'But why?' Salomé exclaimed in exasperation. 'What are they trying to achieve? You say this mysterious "they" have been operating for centuries, but what possible reason can they have?'

Arissa leant back in her chair, steepling her fingers. She paused for a long moment.

'I will tell you what we know. Few in the Empire are aware of this, the knowledge is too dangerous to reveal. It oft leads to death. You seem to have been chosen for some reason or another, whether it is by whim, or by selection or by chance I know not. After all that has transpired, we have no choice but to tell you.'

Salomé swallowed.

'There is a pattern in events,' Arissa said. 'It is hard to see, but it is there. New technologies are suddenly introduced, major breakthroughs occur. Frequently it is just before some strange new calamity impacts the core worlds. Economic activity fluctuates, sometimes in favour of big corporations, sometimes against. People are put in positions of power without having much evidence of ability. Others stumble across secrets or unexpectedly go missing.'

'Like Halsey …' Salomé whispered.

'Palin's abduction,' Patreus added. 'And numerous others beyond count.'

Arissa nodded. 'It is not just within the Empire. I have contacts across the core. The same happens within the confines of the Alliance and the Federation. We are all being manipulated behind the scenes. Some of us know we're being manipulated, some of us don't.'

'But for what?'

Arissa smiled. 'That, of course, is the question. I am not sure. But consider this. If you were working behind the scenes to influence the course of humanity, perhaps in response to some great knowledge of an overwhelming threat perhaps, or some other major societal change, how would you do it?'

'I would leverage the people in power …' Salomé began and then stopped. 'A threat to humanity? What could possibly be so devastating that they would need the combined might of all humanity to deal with it?'

'A very cogent question indeed,' Patreus said.

***

Hassan watched as the *Seven Veils* emerged from hyperspace. The ship decelerated, the glowing sphere of starlight ahead swelling to fill the view in moments. He rolled the Clipper about its centre axis and pitched the ship away before the fuel scoops had a chance to engage. He had reached his destination.

There's a beacon … and a set of co-ordinates. Looks like I'm expected.

He typed away on the keyboard within the cockpit and the data skittered across to the main nav panel.

Threat level 5!

He adjusted the flight systems, diverting power to engines.

If this goes south, my only choice will be to run …

Hassan touched the control that would drop the *Seven Veils* out of frame shift and back into normal space.

The ship slowed, blue and violet light swirling about it as the drives aboard discharged their astonishing energies. A rising rumble from behind them made the ship vibrate as the main drive units flared up to full power.

The shocking abruptness of a vast vessel hung in space above them. Hassan recoiled instinctively and rolled the Clipper away from a collision course.

'Woah! An Imperial Interdictor!'

He locked the ident computer onto the huge vessel and information flashed up on the displays.

The Imperial Honour.

It was huge, a white expanse of Imperial architecture stretching out before him, sleek yet intimidating. He ran a scan on the name. The onboard computers buzzed as they searched for an answer.

But that ship belongs to …

The comms system crackled into life.

'Gutamaya Hotel, Alpha, Sierra. Proceed to dock in Bay 4. Do not deviate from supplied flight corridor.'

Hassan toggled the comms and responded.

'Acknowledged, *Imperial Honour*.' He raised his eyebrows and closed the comms.

The computer finished its ident query and flashed up a response. Hassan gulped as he saw the identification, unconsciously running a hand through his hair.

'Best to look smart, eh? Going to meet the Emperor herself!'

***

Arissa gestured with her fingers and a holofac display appeared in the air between them. 'I cannot be sure, but history gives us some possibilities.'

A grainy video appeared. It was remarkably crude, two-dimensional, a series of simulated wire-frame objects revolving on a monochrome screen. Salomé could make out primitive status displays, crosshairs …

Some kind of telemetry… it must be ancient.

Arissa was watching her as she studied the display.

'Yes, it's very old,' she confirmed. 'It dates back around two hundred years. Ships then didn't have the sophisticated scanning capabilities we take for granted now. Only very basic information was recorded. But it's enough. Watch.'

Within the video a disc rolled into view, a representation of a world. The word 'Hyperspace' appeared in blocky text, followed by a countdown. There was a flicker, a series of concentric rings, expanding past the frame of reference at a dizzying speed.

Then another phrase appeared.

Hyperdrive Malfunction.

The rings disappeared, replaced with a stark view of empty space, punctuated only with the occasional trace of a star. Salomé saw the status indicators showing abrupt pitch and roll, clearly the commander of the ship was attempting to understand the situation they'd found themselves in and regain control of their vessel.

In the lower third of the video was an ovoid. Belatedly, Salomé realised it was a simplified form of scanner information. There were marks on the scanner, lots of marks. The ship must have been turning, as those marks rolled around on the scanner, moving into the forward quadrant.

On the main display more wire-frame representations appeared. Salomé frowned as four curious looking objects were rendered. They were octagonal, eight-sided shapes with chamfered sides, turning and orienting themselves towards the perspective of the recording. More lines appeared, emanating from those curious shapes. The status indicators changed, indicators dropping abruptly. She saw the beleaguered ship return fire …

The recording stopped.

'What was that?' Salomé asked.

Arissa smiled. 'That was the first known altercation with an alien race. Sometime prior to the year 3125, a hapless commander found their ship pulled out of hyperspace and set upon by an overwhelming force of powerful, and hitherto unknown, vessels. You may have heard of them. They became known as the Thargoids.'

Salomé blinked.

She'd heard the word, of course. Thargoids were the stuff of children's tales, aliens who lived on the edge of space, some even said in witch-space itself, the default explanation for anyone who went missing in the void. Hell-bent on destruction and chaos, they were the evil unseen, the product of humanity turning its fear of the unknown into a tangible form. No one believed those stories …

'Are you saying they're real?'

Arissa nodded. 'There is plenty of evidence available, I assure you. There is little doubt of that.'

'But we've heard nothing …'

'Nothing official, there have been rumours. Mostly hearsay of course, but certainly enough for our own intelligence services to take it seriously. There is much we don't know. The Alliance certainly had some interactions with them. There was a sustained conflict for several decades and then …'

'Yes?'

'They retreated and haven't been heard from since.'

'They might be coming back?' Salomé felt her stomach clench. 'This group … are they helping them … are they already here? Why have there been no warnings?'

Arissa nodded, gesturing with her fingers again. The holofac faded. 'Good questions. We don't know. Perhaps the impact is considered too great. The idea of an alien threat would cause mass panic, riots, economic turmoil.'

Salomé thought that through for a moment. 'It would be chaos …'

'Agreed,' Arissa said. 'And what would this group need? Technical knowledge, vast economic influence and wealth. The control of those in positions of power. The removal of any who might dare to expose their plans. Exploration data …'

'Exploration data …' Salomé said.

'Where you come in, I think,' Arissa said. 'This is only supposition on my part, but I don't believe I am too wide of the mark. Other indications confirm my view. Whilst the Empire and the Federation play their games of war, the Alliance stays mute. Those with power across the galaxy consolidate their gains, new technologies are researched and developed in secret. These so-called Engineers, for instance, is it not strange that you can have a ship enhanced by such a dramatic degree in so little time? Why should this be occurring now, in just the last few years?'

Salomé shook her head.

Arissa gestured again and a new holofac appeared, a press article, lamenting the death of some corporate executive.

'We've been watching this one for some time,' Arissa said. 'Femi Dakarai died recently.'

Salomé shrugged. 'And he was?'

'The chairman of a small company called MetaDrive. It was due to be acquired by Sirius. His death coincided with their takeover. A super corporation that takes what it wants by means fair and foul. They were working on some kind of hyperdrive technology, the data for which went mysteriously missing the moment Femi died. Our spies report that both the Alliance and the Federation are involved. Encrypted communications were detected, originating from a base in the Alioth system. We've traced it to one of these Engineers, a fellow by the name of Bill Turner.'

Salomé watched as the holofac changed to a representation of the Alioth system, the heart of Alliance territory. A place she had never been to.

'Perhaps you do not recognise his name?' Arissa asked.

Salomé shook her head.

'The Turners have quite a place in the historical records,' Arissa explained. 'The Alliance had the last known contact with the Thargoids in the 3250s … and the Turners, for good or ill, were heavily involved.'

'You think this Bill Turner has something to do with these … Thargoids? Today?'

Arissa nodded.

The Alliance and the Thargoids! Is he in contact with them, working for them or against them? How is the Alliance involved? This is why they need me!

'So,' Salomé said, 'my rescue does come with strings attached.'

'I told you she was clever,' Patreus said, with a grin.

Arissa smiled. 'I will admit it feels rather sordid to require such conditions, but you are right of course. I need you to undertake some tasks for me, for us. You're in a unique position.'

'You're dead, you see,' Patreus said, his grin breaking into a chuckle. *And not for the first time …*

'And if I refuse, you will send me back to Koontz Asylum.'

'Something like that,' Arissa said with a nod. 'Our delightful justice system has convicted you as a criminal; it would not look good for either of us to be seen to be defying our own laws. If undisturbed, these shadowy figures will doubtless continue with their plan. I would prefer the Empire knew what it was and could take a more active role. I do not appreciate being kept in the dark. Right now, you are my best route to finding out.'

'It seems I have little choice but to continue with this affair,' Salomé replied. 'What precisely is it that you ask of me?'

Arissa leant back in her chair, taking another sip of her gin.

'Two things,' Arissa said, placing the drink back down again.

'Two?'

'Just two,' Arissa said. 'The Federation is as concerned as we are. They do not like the idea of being manipulated from within and without either. They seek answers. Like us, they do not know who to trust. We struggle against each other of course; you've seen the posturing and the childish taunts and insults. Fear not, it is all agreed by diplomats months in advance. But they do not trust us and we do not trust them. Another communication route is required.'

I haven't had much luck trusting anyone thus far …

'Me? You want me to go to the Federation?'

'You have earned their respect, it would seem,' Arissa replied. 'The tour you undertook a year ago gained you many admirers and, I'm told, they consider you a worthy adversary. Given how your loyal factions confounded their exploration activities in recent weeks, I can see their point. They respect you. In fact, they have asked for you by name.'

'But how do they know I am still alive?'

Arissa laughed. 'My dear, there are many in the Federation I trust more than those of high rank in the Empire. Politics knows no real boundaries. They know because I have told them. Thus, they want you.'

'And who am I going to meet?'

'You will be informed when required,' Arissa said.

'To do what?'

'Exchange views.'

'Views?'

'Neither side can meet in an official capacity. I cannot go without causing untold repercussions, even if I were free to. But, incognito, you can represent my interests. We all know the Federation and the Empire are being spurred towards war. We do not want it, they do not want it, but neither of us can resist it. I need you to explain my theory about the Alliance to the Federation. In turn, they will relate their thinking back to us, via you.'

'You said there were two tasks …'

Arissa paused before continuing.

'One item at a time. Your mission to Earth will be your probation, shall we say. After that, we will discuss what to do about the Alliance.'

Salomé thought it through. 'And if I'm successful?'

'You will be pardoned,' Arissa said. 'Your position restored, others dealt with as you see fit. I will see to that.' She winked at Salomé. 'I still have a little influence, you know.'

Salomé took a deep breath. Arissa regarded her.

'So, Salomé. Will you serve your Emperor?'

Arissa's gaze had never left hers. She was still awaiting an answer. Salomé looked back at the steady grey eyes.

Can I trust her? I have no higher authority to go to. If I can't trust the Emperor at the very pinnacle of the Empire that bore and raised me, who can I trust? She wouldn't have rescued me otherwise!

Salomé nodded.

'I remain an Imperial citizen. I will serve you, your Imperial and Royal Majesty.'

Arissa got to her feet and extended a hand. Salomé rose to meet her and took Arissa's hand in hers. The touch was cool but firm, confident and self-controlled.

'Let us hope we can expose this conspiracy,' Arissa said. 'Denton, if you please?'

'Of course,' Denton said, standing up. He reached behind him and drew out a sword. A familiar sword. 'I am sad at having to return this, it is rare and valuable. Not unlike its owner.'

Salomé looked from one to the other.

'I thought you might like your personal effects returned to you,' Arissa said. 'This blade has much history associated with it. Somehow, I feel it will have some more before long. Wear it well.'

Salomé took the weapon reverently.

My family's heirloom. Our Holva blade, handed down through so many generations of Lorens. It has been used for good and ill …

'I trust I will use it wisely.'

Arissa nodded. 'I hope so. You have quite the reputation with it, so I have heard.'

'Thank you for this,' Salomé said. 'It means much.'

Arissa smiled. 'I have another gift for you. Something you value even more, perhaps.'

Salomé frowned at the evasive comment. Arissa gestured to the doors through which she had entered the room. They snapped back with a faint hiss.

A man stood there.

'Hassan!'

Salomé ran to him, embracing him closely, exchanging greetings and mutual concern for the other's well-being. She could see he was battered and bruised.

At Zyair's and Gerrun's hand. There will be retribution for the injury they have caused!

'Are you all right?' he asked. Salomé nodded.

'I was rescued by …'

'Good friends are perhaps the most valuable resource of all,' Arissa said, her voice loud enough to grab their attention. 'Something to be treasured and fought for.'

Salomé released Hassan from her embrace.

'What do you mean?'

Arissa smiled. 'I trust you, my dear, but events required me to have certain assurances. Your friend will remain here until such time as you return from Earth. I will take no risks. You must earn that trust.'

'You don't need to do this,' Salomé answered. 'I will serve you regardless. I will not let you down.'

'I believe you,' Arissa said. 'But your friend will remain in my care, until you return. Trust must be earned, even here.'

Salomé walked back to her, standing barely a metre away.

'I will do as you command,' she said, her voice low. 'I hold you responsible for his safety. If harm of any kind should befall …'

'I am quite aware of your vindictiveness and passion,' Arissa said, unfazed. 'It is your conduct that will determine his fate, not mine.'

The two women stared at each other for a long moment. Patreus watched them, with a wry smile on his face.

Biggs Colony, Altair, Federation

'There has been a complication.' Infrastructure turned to Personnel.

'Kahina Tijani Loren's prison convoy was attacked and destroyed.' Personnel answered. 'She has been presumed killed.'

'Do we really believe that?' Exo demanded, leaning forward in alarm.

'Of course not,' Infrastructure said. 'Please continue, my dear.'

'The escort ships for the convoy were commissioned through standard commercial negotiations at Hiram's Anchorage in the Prism system,' Personnel said. 'Or so it appeared. The names of the ships provided indicate that whosoever procured their services knew they would be attacked.'

'How exactly?' Exo demanded.

'The names of the ships were quite telling,' Personnel said. 'The lead ship was the *Diadem* and the accompanying four Clippers were *Cypripedium*, *Velum*, *Monile* and *Vestimenta*.'

'I don't understand …'

'They mean "Crown," "A pair of lady's slippers", a "Covering," a "Collar" and "Clothing."'

'Somebody is sending a message,' Society said.

'Yes. It does have that rather mystical flavour to it,' Infrastructure agreed. 'Have we been able to ascertain precisely what happened?'

'Whoever intercepted the convoy was extremely thorough, presupposing that they are partially aware of our activities,' Personnel said. 'All the ships were obliterated, down to the black boxes, recorders and escape pods. There were no survivors left at the scene.'

'Someone is being careful,' Exo said. 'And now they have her … what do they intend to do with a tried and convicted terrorist?'

Personnel smiled.

'You already know?'

'It seems that Earth is receiving an unofficial visit from a mysterious Imperial negotiator on behalf of Emperor Arissa Lavigny-Duval,' Personnel answered.

Infrastructure chuckled. 'Well now. I wonder who that could be?'

'It appears our errant Senator has found a way to stay on the stage a little longer,' Exo said.

'Has our man been briefed?' Infrastructure asked.

'He has,' Personnel said. 'He knows what is expected of him. He will do as he is directed, he knows what is at stake.'

'An interesting development,' Infrastructure said, 'Please keep us all informed. It would seem that a few surprises still lie ahead. We must continue to pay close attention to the details.'

Medupe City, Cubeo system, Empire

Princess Aisling Duval smiled demurely at the massed ranks of senators, patrons and notable citizens arrayed before her. She had given a short speech regarding the oppression of slaves on the outer borders of the Empire. The applause, as expected and arranged in advance, was rapturous. She looked appropriately abashed, as if embarrassed by all the attention, held up a hand as if to resist the adoration bestowed upon her.

Holofac imagers were placed around her, with some reporters holding their own devices for a personal shot. She made sure she was looking in the right direction at the right time to favour those who favoured her, delighting that her perfectly prepared visage was being broadcast across the galaxy to billions of watchers.

'Beautifully put, Your Highness,' said the chief editor of the Imperial Citizen. 'Majestic and supreme. Your eloquence and poise were a wonder to behold.'

'Why thank you,' she responded. The Imperial Citizen was often invited to her functions and had been granted a number of exclusives with the princess. Coincidently, they tended to publish articles and editorials on her affairs which portrayed her in a positive light.

Today was no different. The chief editor was allowed into her private reception to watch the post-speech coverage. Occasionally, the princess liked to offer her own opinions on what the analysts were saying and they usually saw the wisdom in agreeing with her.

Newscasters began their own analysis of her speech without pause. She settled into a plush chair in the reception, curling herself demurely and affecting an air of unconcern and disinterest as her image appeared from dozens of different angles about her. Only after a pause did she look up to watch them.

'… Princess Aisling, courting controversy once again with her stance on slavery. Some accuse her of pandering to political popularity, others that this is her cause célèbre and she genuinely has a heart for the mistreatment of slaves in the outlying jurisdictions of our glorious Empire. She can rightly claim ...'

'... Princess Aisling pushes for the plight of the oppressed to be high-lighted in the highest echelons once more. She risks driving against the hard-liners in Imperial society, but her youth, vigour and determination will be her staunchest allies in the tough battle that awaits her ...'

'... So wonderful to see the Princess stand up for the rights of those abused by our centuries-old tradition. Some say that traditions should be maintained, but we must do as the Princess commands, throw off the shackles of the old and embrace the new ...'

Aisling turned to the chief editor.

'Numbers?'

'Slaves, Your Highness?' he queried.

'No, not slaves!' she snapped. 'Popularity ratings. Coverage share, unique mentions ...'

'Initial indications are supremely positive,' he replied, rapidly tapping queries into his commtab. 'Above our expectations across the board. All the major Imperial broadcasts are covering it, well, save one ...'

Aisling's eyes narrowed. 'The Imperial Herald. And what are they broadcasting that they think is more important than my speech?'

The chief editor looked distinctly uncomfortable. Aisling didn't care.

'They are covering, well ...'

'What?'

'With your permission, Your Highness ...?'

'Yes, yes! Get on with it. What can possibly be more significant than my speech about ...' she stopped for a moment.

'The institutional exploitation of slaves in the outer territories?' the chief editor prompted.

'Yes, that.'

The chief editor gestured to one of the holofacs, muting the rest. It flickered and then its image changed to a view of tumbling debris adrift in space. A reporter's excited tones could be heard talking over the display.

'A prisoner convoy en route to Koontz Asylum in the Daibo system has been interdicted and destroyed. Wreckage was found in system and has been positively identified as belonging to the Imperial Cutter *Diadem* and the accompanying four Imperial Clippers *Cypripedium*, *Velum*, *Monile* and *Vestimenta* in the formation. We spoke to one pilot who signalled the location of the destruction.'

The holofac image shifted to a young, but unshaven and rough-looking space pilot.

'Completely wiped out, by the time I arrived there was nothing but floating debris. That convoy was heavily protected, but someone really wanted to make sure these ships were taken out. We even found debris from escape pods. Someone took the trouble to make sure there were absolutely no survivors. Even the black boxes have been blasted.'

The image faded back to more footage of the tumbling debris field.

'It has been confirmed that the convoy was carrying various political dissidents, convicted murderers and terrorists. Amongst them was the, now infamous, Ms. Kahina Loren, recently found guilty of the attempted assassination of Fleet Admiral Denton Patreus.'

An image of a young dark-haired woman with dark grey eyes and a fierce haughty expression appeared and slowly rotated.

'Her!' Aisling snapped. 'How dare she interrupt my speech coverage.'

'I doubt she planned to be killed precisely on schedule,' the chief editor said, deadpan.

Aisling was oblivious to his comment.

'She was supposed to go to be tortured and taught a lesson!'

The holofac feed switched to a view of a planetary surface.

'Reaction in Loren's home system of Prism was muted, but officials led by Ambassador Cuthrick Delaney indicated that a service of remembrance would be held in the Leeson Piazza to mark her passing ...'

'They want a service, for her?' Aisling said, her voice a harpy-like screech. 'She was a murderer, a convicted felon! Her name should be struck from the record and never spoken again. What next, a bloody statue?'

Chapter Twenty-One

Cambridge, Earth, Sol system, Federation

Salomé watched as the Beluga liner descended. It was winter in the northern hemisphere, but despite this the air was clear and blue, with only the faintest wisps of cloud trailing backwards as the liner made its descent.

She had enjoyed the complete attention of the onboard crew. It appeared she was the only passenger aboard. The staff had been polite to a fault, not reacting to her obvious Imperial accent. If they had an issue with her presence, it was impossible to detect.

The trip had been uneventful and the luxury aboard the vessel a welcome relief after the trials and tribulations of the last few days, but she felt tense as she watched the planet come into view below.

The sky was bright, the star in the system pouring down a bright illumination around the ship as it dropped down towards the ground.

Earth …

She had been here before, but hadn't tarried long. She had been whisked southwards, escorted by Ambassador Waite, to the rebuilt City of London, on account of business with Chancellor Blaine.

… not London this time.

Earth was the planet of everyone's common origin. Before the Alliance, before the Empire, before even the Federation, before humankind had even thought about voyaging to the stars, Earth had been home. Salomé looked around her, trying to imagine the whole of humanity confined to a single planet.

The starlight, no … it was sunlight in this system, had a curious yellow hue to it, making everything look oddly warmer and softer than the sharper and bluer light she was used to living under.

This is where we evolved. Where history began …

Earth had seen its fair share of destruction, much of it wrought at the hands of humans. Her history told her of countless wars fought over its resources, but she struggled to imagine why anyone would fight over a planet and risk its destruction when you had nowhere else to go. It seemed like madness …

Yet I suppose our own conflicts will look as pedestrian to historians of the future. Perhaps one day we will call the universe our home and the affairs of a mere hundred star systems will seem as nothing …

Much of Earth's history had been destroyed in those early wars. Little of what the tourists came to see was genuinely historic, much of it was recreations from archive footage or blueprints, little originality remained. Earth had been badly tainted and then cleaned up. Its atmosphere scrubbed, its gardens manicured and its scars healed, much to the lament of some of the archaeologists.

There were exceptions though.

This meeting …

Unlike the rigid and organised structure of cities built or rebuilt since those long ago wars, the city below her couldn't have been more disorganised. She looked at it in surprise. The pilot of the Beluga was clearly taking a sweeping turn about the place to ensure she got a good view. She made a mental note to thank him.

They call it Cambridge … what a strange name.

It was only one of a few cities on Earth that had recovered pretty much intact from the wars of the 21st century, in which much of the planet had been lain waste in a terrifying nuclear holocaust in what historians called, 'The Energy War,' a dark period of history prior to Earth's factional corporations coming together and forming the seeds of what would later be the Federation.

Part of the reason for the city's name was obvious. A bright clear blue stretch of river meandered aimlessly through the centre of the town. Around it, Salomé could make out archaic spires, buildings made out of some curiously earthen-like material. The entire layout was haphazard, unplanned and uncoordinated.

She'd reviewed the holofac data on the flight in. The oldest surviving buildings dated back to an almost impossibly ancient time more than two thousand years before, when humanity had looked up at the stars without even knowing what they were, let alone been considering travelling amongst them.

To protect this remarkable historic legacy from the continued ravages of time, the entire old city was enclosed in a protective energy dome, ensuring that no precipitation could fall upon it, or any winds disturb it. No aircraft or spacecraft were permitted entry to ensure noise levels were kept to a minimum. Thus it remained a macrocosm, a preserved environment, one of the oldest and best kept examples of humanity's legacy from a time long gone. A museum unlike any other.

As such, very few people were permitted entry. Archaeologists at the top of their fields might gain admittance to study the relics contained within the historic buildings. Cambridge boasted the only surviving collection of books that pre-dated the wars of the 21st century. Public tours were organised, but they were exceedingly expensive and did not provide access to the most prestigious buildings.

Only those with certain connections could bypass the rules and regulations. Whoever it was that she was going to meet on behalf of the Federation was clearly somebody with some significant influence.

Ambassador Waite presumably, just like last time.

The historic city fell behind the viewports as the Beluga liner adjusted its course and lowered itself gently into a landing bay at the spaceport, a few kilometres beyond.

Salomé walked to the lower decks, finding the boarding ramp already deployed. Chill air greeted her. She sniffed and then breathed in; it was thicker than she was used to.

A transport awaited her at the bottom of the ramp. A single uniformed guard stood alongside. The transport's side access door was already open and swung outwards. The guard swept his arm towards it, indicating she could board. There was no one else nearby. In fact, as she walked down the stairs of the ramp, it was clear that no other ships were nearby, either.

'Ma'am,' the guard said, gesturing again.

She entered the transport, the door swung down and she was whisked away.

There was no pilot; the car was under some kind of automatic control. It accelerated away from the spaceport, effortlessly reaching a dizzying speed before gently slowing as it approached an access port.

Salomé watched in fascination as the transport proceeded through a series of airlocks that opened and closed before and after the transport. It then entered a tunnel before arriving at a final gateway, pausing there for a moment.

The gateway opened and the transport moved slowly forwards.

Salomé stared in surprise. Gone was the high-tech roadway, the gantries, the navigation lights and holofac adverts. They were replaced by streets composed of what looked like shaped rocks, impossibly ancient buildings, carefully preserved trees and flower beds.

The transport slowed and came to a halt. Salomé found herself deposited on the edge of what she first took to be a strangely even rocky outcrop.

Only belatedly did she realise it was a wall, also constructed out of stones, shaped and fitted together.

Above her, she could hear birds calling to each other in the trees. The trees themselves were almost bare, the ground covered in orange-brown leaves. Only the faint shimmer of a distant force field hundreds of metres above spoiled the illusion of having been magically transported back in time.

'You should visit us in the spring,' said a voice. 'The birds are even more delightful then.'

It was tutored and refined, almost unpleasantly so. Salomé instantly recognised the tone of an academic, studious and polished.

She turned to see a man dressed in the most unfamiliar garments. He wore a black jacket and matching trousers, severely cut and decorated with circular buttons. Around his neck he wore a band of coloured material, tied in a knot and draped down his front. But it was the hat, if that's what it was, that drew her attention.

It looked like a black skullcap, neatly fitting onto his scalp, atop of which was a square board, also black. From this was hung a purple tassel.

She tried not to react visibly to his peculiar appearance. He looked at her for a long moment.

'You must be Kahina Tijani Loren,' he said.

Salomé nodded.

'Though I understand you also go by the name of Salomé. Quite fascinating.'

'Fascinating?' she asked.

'Oh yes,' the man replied. 'The etymology of your name is rather ap-ropos to the air of mystery which surrounds the arrangements which I have had to put in place at such short notice to accommodate your arrival. Doubtless you will draw the veil aside and elucidate for me.'

She tried a smile. 'There are many veils.'

'Awfully remiss of me,' he volunteered, extending his hand. Salomé recognised the Federal habit of exchanging a handshake as a sign of peace and trust. She took it, being rewarded with a firm grip. 'I am St. John Gregory Smythe, Master of Jesus College, Cambridge. I am at your service.'

'I am pleased to meet you, Sinjun Gregory Smythe,' Salomé answered, hoping she had the pronunciation correct. It seemed it was close enough.

'Just Sinjun will serve,' he replied. 'Shall we?'

He gestured to a small pathway that led through the wall.

'Your first visit to our wonderful city of Cambridge?' he inquired, as they walked.

'I have been here before,' she answered. 'But only to the spaceport. I went to London.'

'Yes,' he replied with obvious distaste. 'Well, that often can't be helped. I shan't hold it against you. I was forced to go there once myself. Awful place, awful.'

Salomé considered it wisest not to respond.

After a short walk up an uneven stone clad pathway, flanked by cobbled stones and walls made out of ancient red-coloured blocks in a regular formation, they reached a gatehouse. Salomé studied it in surprise.

It was made of stone, the doors themselves being made of wood.

'More than two thousand years old,' Sinjun said. 'Please don't touch them.'

There was a sign to her left which bore the inscription – 'No bicycles, dogs, radios or picnics allowed.'

Bicycles? Picnics? What is a picnic?

Sinjun offered no explanation and led her through into a courtyard.

By Imperial standards it was laughably small, enclosed on three sides, with a blaze of green grass in the middle somehow striped forwards and back across its length. In the very centre stood the statue of a large four-legged creature Salomé did not recognise.

Some of the buildings were festooned with vegetation, the entrances marked with curious heraldic emblems. Other than their footsteps and the faint call of the birds, there was no other sound. It left her with an eerie feeling of having stepped back to some long forgotten age.

Sinjun turned to his right and led her through a sequence of low-ceilinged rooms and corridors. Exposed beams and wooden flooring caught her eye as they moved on through and then emerged into the open once more. There seemed to be no logical organisation to the buildings at all.

'Is it far?' Salomé asked.

'Not in the slightest,' he replied. 'Merely a stroll.'

They ambled along a covered walkway with alcoves overlooking the landscaped gardens.

The master paused at an entrance.

'The cloisters,' he announced, and gestured for her to go ahead up a flight of stairs. They too were ancient and creaked in the most alarming way as she moved up them, carefully placing one foot in front of the other.

A strange smell greeted her at the top. She couldn't place it. Something like the aroma that cleaning robots left in their wake as they serviced rooms. It was most peculiar.

The walls, floor and ceiling were panelled with wood. Her footsteps echoed on the polished floorboards. Narrow-framed windows looked out upon the greenery outside. But the most remarkable feature of the room drew a gasp from her.

Books. Hundreds of them, perhaps thousands, all stacked in endless wooden frames. Here and there were antique chairs, presumably from the same period in time.

'Yes,' said Sinjun, evidently pleased with her response. 'It is rather impressive upon first glance, I will admit.'

'Books?' Salomé said.

'Around nine thousand of them in total,' Sinjun said. 'The only surviving works of some of the great authors of times long ago, you understand. I'm sure I don't need to tell you not to touch them. They are all priceless antiques.'

'Of course not …' Salomé said, thankful for the reminder.

Sinjun turned to go.

'Wait,' Salomé said. 'Who is meeting me?'

'I am unaware of their identity, I'm afraid,' Sinjun replied. 'You are to wait here. I'm sure your interlocutor will be along presently.'

And with that he was gone, slowly making his way down the rickety stairway.

Salomé frowned and then walked forward, hearing the floorboards creak under her feet. She reached the end of the corridor, taking a moment to peer at the remarkable collection of books, when she became aware of another presence. She turned down an aisle to see a man sitting comfortably in one of the antique wooden chairs. He was gazing back at her with a quizzical look, one of the books open in his hands.

She recognised him instantly. She'd never seen him without a frown upon his face. The high forehead and swept back dark hair framed a chiselled face with high cheekbones, a prominent nose and steel grey eyes. Even so, she couldn't repress a short gasp.

The president!

'Ah, precisely on time,' he said. 'I heard you were a stickler for promptness. I approve. Welcome to Cambridge, Kahina Tijani Loren. Or should I call you Salomé? My instructions weren't entirely clear.'

'Either is acceptable,' Salomé managed to answer.

He rose to meet her, extending a hand in the Federal manner. Salomé took it and was surprised to find he took her gently by the palm and kissed her hand in the Imperial manner.

'I hope my knowledge of Imperial greetings is sufficient,' he said, keeping his gaze locked on hers throughout.

'Quite sufficient,' she replied.

'It seems you wear many masks,' he said. 'Come, sit with me. There is much to discuss.'

He gestured to another chair, adjacent to his. She sat down, never taking her eyes off him either.

'I apologise for the theatrics,' he said. 'We in the Federation are rather obsessed with surveillance. There are times, such as this, that call for a little more discretion.'

Salomé nodded and swallowed. 'How may I help you, President Hudson?'

He smiled. 'Please, call me Zachary.'

She nodded.

'I requested you specifically,' he said. 'Should it be required to announce your presence, you are well regarded here on Earth, for an Imperial anyway.' He chuckled at the look on her face. 'Oh, of course, you're currently dead, aren't you? For the second time, I believe. You may start a religious cult with all this rising from the grave. Your little soiree last year did much to endear you to the Federal populace. As a result, I can offer you much.'

'Such as?'

'For a start, political asylum should you wish it,' Zachary said. 'You might consider defecting.'

'That would require me to be a loyal Imperial in the first place,' Salomé replied. 'I remain a criminal in the eyes of most of my people at present.'

'You stood up against Patreus and Aisling,' Zachary said. 'The Federal media enjoyed that immensely, even if we all knew it was a show for the holofac feeds. Such guile would only elevate you further in the eyes of the Federation. You have committed no crimes against us, other than that little ruckus at Mars High.'

'Somehow, I do not think my future lies here,' Salomé replied, with a faint smile.

Zachary chuckled. 'Perhaps not. But you are in a unique position. Poorly treated at the hands of your own, I would trust your words where

I have no time for the legions of ambassadors sent to me by your Empire. Tell me, Kahina, does the Empire truly want a war?'

Salomé blinked.

'A war? Of course not.'

'Truth be told, neither does the Federation. Peace is desired by both sides, yet we seem to be locked in an ever-spiralling cycle of conflict. When one advances, the other must too, anything else is an admission of weakness. That path has only one ending.'

'Then perhaps you should honour the boundaries of Imperial jurisdiction,' Salomé answered simply.

'Merely that,' Zachary said with a smile. 'In the same way you did in the Prism system?'

'We had a prior claim,' Salomé said, her voice dropping.

'Did it justify the actions of Admiral Brice?' Zachary said. 'Did a mining claim justify genocide? Truly? The slaughter of thousands of innocents to secure a claim to a mineral?'

Salomé was silent.

'And the glorious battle of Chione? Was it so glorious?'

Salomé's eyes were haunted. She shook her head.

'That story plays out once more,' Zachary continued. 'Prism, Mu Koji, Maia. Claim and counterclaim, blame, anger, retribution and reprisal. It's the same story, over and over again. A cycle of anger and hate that pushes us ever closer to war. It will take but a single flashpoint for it to erupt into something more powerful, and far more dangerous.'

Salomé looked up.

'So if we both collectively do not desire a war, what then?'

'Diplomatic relations between our powers are at a low ebb. Official channels are stymied. Unless something changes, war is inevitable.'

'I truly don't see what I can do.'

'I can no longer be seen to be negotiating directly with Emperor Arissa,' Zachary said. 'The political situation in the Federation no longer allows it. Your Fleet Admiral Patreus threw the London Treaty back in our faces.'

But Patreus is playing a more complex game …

Zachary continued, '… I am forced to take a strong line. I can show no weakness or my own people will take away my office.'

'So this is all about you?'

Zachary raised his eyebrows, his face crinkling into a smile. 'In part.

But if I fall the Federation goes back to squabbling over leadership. That is not in the Federation's interest at this time, nor the Empire's.'

'So your solution is to negotiate with the Empire behind closed doors.'

'In a manner of speaking. I must make progress, but in public I must be seen to be defending the interests of the Federation. Arissa still supports Patreus as she can do nothing else, Patreus has wronged us, Arissa is thus our foe. Perception is everything.'

'And what is it you want us to perceive?'

Zachary smiled and leant forward. Salomé heard his ancient chair creak with the movement. 'I want you to be defeated, on behalf of the Empire.'

'Defeated?' Salomé exclaimed in surprise. 'Me?'

'Allow me to claim a resounding victory over Imperial arrogance,' Zachary said. 'It will be told that, in private negotiation with Arissa's un-named envoy, I force the Empire's hand. A few speeches filled with purple prose will satisfy those that bay at my door here in the Federation. The Empire backs down, we talk about reinstating the London Treaty. We both appear to move towards the peace we desire.'

'You make it sound simple.'

'It is. I just need to be seen to get the upper hand. My reputation for fierce negotiations and driving a hard bargain remains intact. The Empire becomes less confident. Patreus is undermined.'

'And me?'

'Simply take my proposal back to Arissa. We will back down from our military stance in exchange for this perception. They back down from theirs. We co-ordinate a few well-chosen speeches, some choice insults. Everything will be as it once was.'

'Our eternal cold war,' Salomé said.

'It has kept the peace for decades,' Zachary said. 'Surely that is better than the alternative?'

Salomé sighed and nodded. 'I see the wisdom in it.'

Salomé became conscious of birdsong outside the window. She looked up as she listened to the unfamiliar sound. The world outside seemed peaceful and content. She turned her attention inwards again.

'By the way,' Zachary said. 'I must thank you for your assistance in removing Karl Devene from his position.'

'Karl Devene?' Salomé queried, confused.

'Astrocartography on Mars High,' Zachary responded. 'Quite an insufferable man. In fact, the entire staff at Mars High could do with being rotated.'

'I recall their welcome being less than enthusiastic,' Salomé said.

'Your interactions with them last year were widely reported in the media,' Zachary said. 'I think you did more in those few short weeks to further Federal and Imperial relations than legions of polite diplomats have done in years. Which reminds me ...'

Zachary smiled. Salomé waited expectantly.

'These Children of Raxxla folk, searching out in the darkness at your whim. May I ask what they have found?'

Salomé smiled in return. 'You may ask. In truth, I do not know. I have no way to contact them at present without revealing I am alive.'

'Then can I speak candidly about our mutual mystery?' Zachary said. 'Arissa and I have discussed it; this shadowy manipulation of all our worlds in the interest of some unseen overarching power structure.'

'The Emperor believes it's to do with the Thargoids,' Salomé said, carefully watching his expression.

Zachary merely nodded. 'An alien species out of the past, hell-bent on our destruction? I've listened to the theory. I suspect it may be a little more mundane.'

'And your thinking is?'

'I believe it is wholly concerned with the Alliance. I think they are interfering with our industry. Keeping the Federation and the Empire on the brink of war, our mutual resources tied up and thus our attention focussed elsewhere serves their purposes well. If we do go to war, they can watch while we both weaken each other and then step in and mop up what remains. They know they couldn't tackle us in a traditional confrontation. There's no need for a fantastic alien invasion, it's a simple territory grab. Economic warfare.'

Salomé thought about it. It made sense.

'Then Sirius ...'

'The Alliance were involved in that little affair,' Zachary said. 'Communications between a small company and the Alliance? Secrets stolen just as Sirius tries to step in? Sirius are being accused of all sorts of unsavoury things in the press, not least the murder of the chairman ...'

'You think the Alliance killed him?'

'MetaDrive were working on some secret hyperspace technology,'

Zachary said. 'They ran into financial trouble. Sirius bailed them out. Shortly after Femi's death, an employee left the Chi Orionis system with an Alliance vessel in escort. Both headed directly for Alioth with the only copy of the data relating to the technology. Sirius may not be the most up-standing corporation within our sphere of influence, but they're innocent of that particular crime.'

'No aliens, then?' Salomé asked.

Zachary chuckled. 'The Alliance did have altercations with something long ago. It makes for a good myth. There are many claims of advanced technology being reverse engineered from strange discoveries out in the void. We have seen vague stories of crashed alien ships far out in the dark-ness. Are we really convinced an implacable alien force lies on our door-step? Explorers have been to the far side of the galaxy and found no such signs. I don't believe it's beyond the bounds of possibility that all this has been manufactured by the Alliance, they have the resources and the skill. Doubtless, Arissa has asked you to investigate.'

'I'm not at liberty to say.'

Zachary laughed. 'Which tells me all I need to know.'

Salomé smiled.

'You see, my dear,' Zachary continued, 'the Empire and the Federation have similar problems. We are stale, almost moribund. Yes, we have great assets, our respective territories are huge, but we rot from within. Little altercations such as the fracas in your home system signalled the problem. Our governments, our systems, our processes, our legislature are all based on hyperspace technology that required weeks of planning to deploy a major naval force. In the last decade all that has changed and we, with our vast administrative structures, have been slow to adapt. The Alliance has remained quiet, unobtrusive, lurking in the background, hardly taking part in current affairs at all ...'

'You believe they are consolidating a technological power base and will then sweep forth and overrun us all?'

Zachary smiled. 'Not just technological, political and societal too. You cannot deny that many worlds in both our realms are unhappy with their lot under the free market conditions of the Federation or the authoritarian control of the Empire. The Alliance is playing a long and cunning game, waiting for the Federation and the Empire to grow weak enough to chal-lenge. That moment may be closer than we all realise.'

'And this new hyperdrive technology then ...'

'Another link in a long chain. The Alliance has stolen it from the Federation. Naturally, I want it back. If you can assist me in that, it would do much for relations between our two superpowers, and put the Alliance back where they should be.'

'I will take your message back to the Emperor.'

Zachary rubbed his chin. 'Well, you must decide how you're going to approach this. Caution is to be advised.'

'Obviously. I trust hardly anyone,' Salomé replied, with a brief laugh.

'What about Arissa?'

Salomé paused for a moment. 'I have no doubts about her.'

Zachary looked surprised. 'Really? I would say her conduct was highly suspect. I don't trust her.'

'The Federation giving me advice on whom I should trust in the Empire?' Salomé said, a smile forming on her features. 'Forgive me if I pay little attention.'

Zachary shrugged. 'You must decide for yourself. I think she's been manipulated by someone else.'

'Do you trust me?' Salomé asked.

It was his turn to smile.

'I might, given time.'

'I could say the same of you.'

He nodded.

'I think we're done here, mysterious Salomé, emissary of the Empire. You'll have to forgive me …'

'Pressing matters of state,' Salomé replied. 'Yes, I understand.'

'Indeed. And you must return to Arissa.'

They stood, Salomé taking his hand in a firm shake. He looked into her eyes as she stared back at him.

'It has been a pleasure,' Zachary said.

'Likewise.'

The master returned to the library and escorted her out.

Zachary remained where he was, until the Imperial woman was gone, thinking for long moments.

'Handled with your customary tact and discretion,' said a voice from behind him. 'She will return to Arissa having completed her task and being received as a trustworthy emissary. Arissa will doubtless send her onwards to rendezvous with Bill Turner. We have arranged that she makes that rendezvous. In return, we will ensure your presidency continues … with enthusiastic support. A job well done.'

Zachary didn't turn around. It was not wise, nor would it reveal anything of the identity of his companion.

'And Arissa will continue to entrust her with what she knows,' Zachary replied.

'For now, it is imperative that this woman be allowed to continue this quest,' the voice said.

'Why?'

'Thanks to your effective endorsement, she has the confidence to continue,' the voice said. 'The Federation retains the upper hand. You will expose the Alliance's involvement and triumph over the Empire. As it should be.'

Zachary smiled grimly. 'Such an outcome would cement my popularity, certainly. And when she completes this quest and you have what you want? What then?'

The voice was unfazed. 'She will be terminated immediately. Those who complete their tasks either gain their reward, or disappear into the void.'

Zachary didn't move, but the words echoed in his mind regardless.

Kolmogorov Hub, Leesti system, Independent

Scarlet was waiting for her when she stepped off the transport. Saffron pulled her into a long close hug.

'Woah, girl,' Scarlet said. 'Folks are going to start talking …'

'I was looking over my shoulder the whole time on the flight,' Saffron said. 'I thought that any minute someone was going to interdict us and blow me away.'

'Let's get inside my ship,' Scarlet suggested. 'Talk a bit more freely in there.'

Scarlet led Saffron over to an adjacent pad where the *Umbral Whisper* sat, nestled on the docking platform. A ramp unfolded from the Federal Assault Ship with a metallic clunk as they approached and the pair proceeded inside, the airlock locking in place behind them.

Scarlet led her into the cramped cockpit, gesturing to a seat. Saffron sank into it gratefully.

'So … what's this all about?' she demanded.

'A cover-up, I reckon,' Scarlet said. 'There's something that links all this stuff together. Here's the latest weirdness. There's something big going on.'

She gestured and a holofac display lit up with a galactic plot.

Saffron scrutinised it.

'What am I supposed to be seeing?'

'The locations of Wreaken's construction outposts,' Scarlet said. 'I've been checking them out. See this? Splashed across the core worlds, but they aren't far from all the conflict points between the Federation and the Empire.'

'So?'

Scarlet gave her a look. 'Don't you see? Federation and Empire.' She emphasised the *and*. 'Lots of clandestine comms, ships ferrying stuff about. Gearing up for something, I would say ...'

'What do you think they are doing?' Saffron asked.

'Don't know, but there's got to be a story, right? What do your reporter's instincts say?'

'That they're hiding something. Not being honest with their shareholders, maybe something illegal, political stuff, something they don't want people to see ...'

Scarlet pointed at one particular mark on the galactic map. 'And this one isn't even listed on their official brochures. I did a little digging and it's listed as a "business continuity facility".'

'But it's out in the middle of nowhere. What use is it out there?'

Scarlet nodded. 'Exactly.'

'We need to find out. Can you get me there? This could be the scoop of the century! Imagine, exposing a cover-up of this scale ...'

'You sure? This is dangerous stuff,' Scarlet said. 'Last I heard, Wreaken bases were guarded by ships and warnings were issued with laser fire.'

Saffron patted her shoulder. 'Then you need to come up with one of your nefarious and underhanded plans. I'm not letting this one go.'

Chapter Twenty-Two

Deep space, Daibo system, Empire

Arissa met Kahina within the grand reception rooms of Imperial Interdictor *Imperial Honour* once more. The Emperor was dressed in her Imperial robes of state. Kahina curtseyed as she approached, as decorum required. Patreus was also present. He inclined his head to her, but said nothing.

'You have done well, Kahina,' Arissa said, with a smile. 'Forgive my attire, a broadcast to the populace, state occasions demand it.'

'Where is Hassan?' Kahina demanded.

'You think of your friends first,' Arissa said, giving a small gesture. 'A strength I think, though some would call it a weakness. Be careful of that.'

'Promises made should be promises kept,' Salomé returned, conscious that Patreus had a smile on his face at her words. 'The demands of honour.'

Arissa inclined her head. The doors to the suite opened. Hassan walked in, unescorted and unharmed. He was dressed in Imperial attire, looking a little uncomfortable in the severe styling.

'You're all right?' Salomé demanded.

'I'm fine,' Hassan replied, his voice easy going and relaxed. 'It's been quite an experience. I can see the attractions of high Imperial society, you know …'

Salomé embraced him. He whispered in her ear.

'I'm really ok, they treated me well.'

'That is good to hear,' she whispered back and then released him. He looked a lot better than before.

'The president was very complimentary of your approach,' Arissa added, her voice raised a touch. 'Perhaps you have a career ahead of you as a diplomat.'

Hassan stifled a laugh.

'Or perhaps not,' Arissa said, unperturbed. 'Regardless, you have served me well and proved your integrity. Now, the president must have left you with a message, yes?'

Salomé nodded. 'He believes this is all an Alliance plot. That they seek to undermine the Federation and the Empire, by fanning the flames of war between us.'

'That may be true enough,' Arissa said.

'He does not believe in these Thargoids,' Salomé continued. 'All he desires is the new hyperdrive technology. He wants it shared between the Empire and the Federation.'

'So the cold war continues as ever it was,' Arissa said, thoughtfully. 'Everything is equal once again.'

Salomé nodded.

'Which brings us to our ongoing business,' Arissa said. 'I have been making what enquiries I can. It seems that many take an interest in your affairs.

'I believe I was arrested for the exploration data,' Salomé said. She clenched her hand and then opened it again, turning it over to look at her palm.

And whatever it was that the old lady hid here!

'Perhaps,' Arissa said. 'Perhaps not. There are many things being sought.'

Salomé frowned. 'Such as?'

'The Federals have indeed lost track of some secret hyperdrive research,' Arissa said. 'A thief by the name of Raan Corsen.'

'I don't know him,' Salomé replied.

'I wouldn't expect you to,' said Arissa. 'He was an inconsequential employee of a small Federal corporation until recently. Perhaps you have heard of them though. MetaDrive.'

'MetaDrive … yes,' Salomé said. 'President Hudson said there had been a theft … this Raan Corsen?'

'Most suspicious,' Arissa continued. 'Though the Federals made light of it as they usually do. The Sirius Corporation has been trying to acquire all sorts of technological innovation recently. Even my contacts in the Federation are unable to penetrate their organisation.'

'You said they'd lost it, though?' Salomé asked.

Arissa nodded. 'Stolen from MetaDrive before it was acquired. This Raan Corsen fellow is still at large, pursued by their agents.'

'Where is he going?' Hassan asked.

'The thief has fled into Alliance space, reportedly. Alliance operatives are already following the lead closely. Our last reports had him bound for the Alioth system. We believe it all leads back to the same individual.'

'Bill Turner,' Hassan said.

Arissa looked at him sharply. 'You know of him?'

'Most pilots do,' Hassan replied. 'He is one of these … eh, Engineers. They tinker with ships. Make them faster, tougher. It takes a lot of time and money. But Bill doesn't usually work on hyperdrives from what I've heard …'

'It's not the only thing he doesn't usually work on, reputedly,' Arissa finished. 'The name Turner has a long history in the Alliance worlds, dating back many decades.'

'So the Alliance is involved? I don't see how we can help,' Salomé replied. 'We can't catch this thief …'

Hassan looked at Arissa. 'Bill won't talk to you, will he?'

'No,' Arissa said. 'Not directly. He seems very well informed but does not have a great love for the Empire. However, he is a practical man and is open to negotiation.'

'Negotiation for what?'

Arissa smiled. 'Tantalum.'

Salomé shivered at the mention of the word.

Tantalum.

The presence of that semi-rare metal had started the events that had upheaved her life, caused the death of colonists, her family, and untold others since. Tantalum was an essential component in the manufacture of the frame shift drive. With the current situation, demand for the commodity had only continued to increase.

'He needs that resource and in industrial quantities.'

'So that's why you really wanted me,' Salomé said.

'The Prism system is well known as a bulk source, of course,' Arissa said. 'But you can personally vouch for it.'

'You want me to broker a conversation with this "Turner?"' Salomé asked.

'Exactly. A straight exchange. tantalum for the hyperdrive technology. It must be secured for the Empire.'

'Our informants tell us that tantalum is in short supply in the worlds of the Alliance,' Patreus explained. 'And we know that his work requires industrial quantities of the metal. We have taken the liberty of asking Ambassador Cuthrick to arrange a shipment you can take as a gesture of goodwill. Your homeworld is well known as a major exporter of tantalum; that gives you credibility.'

'But … I'm dead,' Salomé countered. 'And a convicted felon! I have no credibility.'

'Only in public,' Patreus said. 'Everyone who we trust and is in a position of power will know you have our confidence.'

'And what about Bill Turner?'

'It will be a pleasant surprise for him,' Patreus answered. 'Judging by his reputation, he will be quite used to subterfuge.'

'You can guarantee further shipments,' Arissa added. 'We want you to win his confidence and negotiate for this hyperdrive technology and, if you can, expose the the truth of the Alliance involvement in this subterfuge.'

Just that!

'Your servant, your Imperial Majesty,' Salomé said.

Arissa nodded.

'One last thing,' she said.

Salomé looked back. 'Yes?'

'If things do not turn out the way we hope,' Arissa said. 'We cannot intervene. The reach of this organisation is long. If we are to retain the ability to expose them, we cannot be associated with you.'

Salomé nodded. 'I understand.'

'A safe trip,' Patreus said, stepping up behind Arissa. Salomé spared them both a glance before looking at Hassan.

'Let's go then.'

Leeson City, Chione moon, Prism system, Empire

Cuthrick Delaney, Cornelius and Luko watched as the Imperial Clipper descended through the rain. Wind whipped at their clothing, flapping it around them as they stood on the exposed landing pad at the Leeson City complex. These were private areas, only for visiting dignitaries and others who required, and paid for, a certain level of discretion.

The Clipper settled rapidly, water cascading down its sleek form in great sheets. All three waited until the deluge had subsided enough for them to walk, with hurried steps, to the boarding ramp that folded out from the ship's undercarriage.

Two more cloaked figures emerged. After brief embraces, Cuthrick gestured towards the plexiglass building immediately before them. All five hurried across, intent on getting out of the rain as quickly as they could.

'So good to have you back home, my Lady,' Cornelius said.

Salomé smiled at him. 'It is good to be back; a short visit I fear. We are in haste as usual. You received our transmission?'

'Everything is already in place,' Cuthrick said. 'The mines are running at full production, but it won't be enough for the demand. We've taken the liberty of putting a call out for more. Hundreds of independent pilots have responded. I believe it will be sufficient.'

Salomé nodded. 'We are late to the party, our gift must be all the more impressive. We need huge quanitites, perhaps a million tonnes, all told.'

Cornelius whistled. 'That will be quite an ask, my Lady.'

'It must be done,' Salomé answered.

'I am wary of this Turner fellow,' Cuthrick said. 'What do we know of him?'

'An Engineer,' Luko volunteered.

Salomé ignored him, turning instead towards Hassan. 'Yes, an Engineer …'

'Engineer?' Cuthrick replied. 'I don't understand …'

'A rather special type of Engineer,' Hassan said. 'These folks are specialist individuals, having acquired massive wealth and influence. Some rival many major governments in their reach. They offer upgrades and enhancements to those who have the means.'

'And Bill Turner needs tantalum,' Salomé continued. 'Huge quantities of it. Our best quality. In order to gain his favour, I need to take a shipment to him immediately, with the promise of more to follow.'

'May we ask why?' Cornelius asked.

'The Emperor believes he has some new type of hyperspace device,' Salomé answered. 'Stolen from under the noses of the Federation. Something quite powerful. Something that could perhaps shift the balance between the superpowers in favour of the Alliance. I have been asked to bargain for it on behalf of the Empire and the Federation.'

'The Federation …?' Cornelius asked in surprise.

'The Emperor has asked you to do this?' Cuthrick asked.

Salomé nodded. 'Directly. It was she who arranged for my transport to be interdicted en route to that asylum. The usual political channels are closed …'

Cuthrick nodded. 'There is more news in this regard. There has been a massive increase in demand for all manner of metallurgy and equipment provision from many industrial facilities in the last week. It's unprecedented. I haven't seen anything like it before.'

'Contruction firms, yes?' Luko asked. 'Heavy industry I am guessing.'

Cuthrick noticed the glare Salomé aimed in Luko's direction. There was a moment of uncomfortable silence before Cuthrick decided to proceed.

'Wreaken Construction features often in the procurement lists. Yes.'

Luko nodded. 'They are building ships, is my guess. Molto ships. Big ships.'

'With the London Treaty in tatters,' Cornelius added, 'The escalations in Mu Koji and Maia ...'

'Building up for a war,' Cuthrick said. 'If what you say about the Alliance is true, they will be fanning the flames of war between the Federation and the Empire, hoping each is weakened.'

Salomé nodded. 'The Emperor and President Hudson's concern exactly. And if the Empire doesn't have the necessary advantage in hyperspace ...'

'Whoever gets this new technology up and running first is going to launch a preemptive strike,' Cornelius said. 'Classic tactics if you have an advantage over a well-matched opponent.'

'There is more,' Cuthrick said. 'We have received word from your friends, the explorers of the Children of Raxxla.'

Salomé looked up. 'Yes?'

'They, with assistance from many others, have discovered something out in the darkness, a series of curious beacons and abandoned settlements in the sectors you asked them to search. It appears there was a mission of some kind, more than thirty years ago. I've uploaded the logs into your commtab so you can review them on the trip. They have yet to discover their precise purpose, but ...'

'I knew it!' Salomé cried. 'I knew there was a clue out there! Perhaps the old lady has not led me astray after all.'

And perhaps this clue will unlock whatever it is that the old lady placed in my palm!

'It would seem the threads of this mystery are pulling tighter at last,' Cornelius said.

'I must depart as soon as possible,' Salomé said. 'Have my ship loaded with the tantalum as fast as it can be arranged.'

Cuthrick bowed. 'With our utmost alacrity, my Lady.'

'I will arrange for an escort to the Alliance borders,' Cornelius said. 'Loren's Legion will be pleased to be able to assist you once again.'

'Your escort will be very welcome,' Salomé replied. 'I am still a felon in the eyes of officialdom. This must be discreet and low key.'

'And we will encourage and guard any and all traders who will run the gauntlet into our system. All tantalum shipments will be protected to the best of our abilities.'

Salomé stepped aside, looking at Luko.

'You and I need to talk.'

The others looked at her. She didn't move.

'In private,' she said.

'Ah …' Cuthrick said. 'Of course. Gentlemen, this way.'

***

The meadow was peaceful, a far cry from the turmoil of the spaceport or even the pedestrianised streets of Leeson City. They had flown several hundred kilometres further south into the unspoilt beauty of Chione, until all the signs of civilisation were left behind.

The *Bella Principessa* descended gently amidst the green grass, flowing river and scenic mountains that formed a backdrop to its presence. It settled between the trees, looking a little incongruous in the midst of nature. Animals scattered by its arrival peeked out from behind foliage as the noise of its engines subsided. The background sounds of the wilderness resumed.

A slow whine emanated from the ship as the docking ramp descended. A woman in a flowing green dress was first, followed by a man in grey-brown flight overalls. The woman stepped down quickly, striding out into the grass, the man slower, pausing at the base of the ramp, watching her. It was clear she was angry and he was trying to explain something.

Salomé turned about.

'You knew,' she said. 'And you didn't tell me.'

Luko's gaze was impassive. 'Signorina?'

No games! No more …

'Don't start with the charm offensive,' Salomé replied, her eyes flashing. 'The old lady at Tionisla, she knew you. So you must know her. Who was she, and who are you? How are you mixed up in this?'

Luko sighed and walked out into the grass. He looked up to the planet Daedalion, a huge crescent almost overhead.

'Come with me,' he said. 'I tell you what I know.'

Salomé followed him down to the bank of the river, its water slowly flowing past, glittering in the light of Chione's closest star, Prism itself. Water trickled over rocks, a calming sound which did little to soften her mood.

He sat down by the water's edge and gestured for her to join him. After a moment, she did so.

'Well?' she asked.

'When I tell you long ago that … I just a simple trader,' Luko began. 'Perhaps, I not tell you all the truth.'

He looked out across the picturesque landscape, a deep sigh escaping from him.

'Really,' Salomé replied. 'You do surprise me. You're quite the actor.'

'Everyone has secrets, signorina,' Luko said. 'I am no different. They asked me to be your … pastore …'

'Pastore?'

'Shepherd,' Luko replied. 'To look after you …'

'Who are they that you speak of?'

Luko looked at her. 'Truthfully, I do not really know. They are very mysterious. I was asked to wait for you on that desert planet … LTT 8740 it was … to steer you away from …'

'Steer me away?' Salomé said, her voice rising in anger. 'So you were lying, you weren't marooned at all! That was all a fabrication too? It was too convenient you were there …'

'They are very powerful people, signorina. You do not say no to them. My instructions were to keep you safe from …'

'From?' Salomé demanded. 'From who?'

'Octavia Quinton,' Luko said.

'What?'

Salomé paused, remembering. Octavia had been a brutal crime lord with a cybernetically enhanced body, a fearsome grip on dozens of star systems in the Prism vicinity and wealth beyond the imaginings of most. She had tried to possess Salomé's body, and only Hassan's accidental intervention had stopped her. She had almost succeeded, twice.

'I suppose you knew her too, despite your denials at the time, simple trader Luko.'

'I knew of her, yes. Only later did I discover why she was after you.'

Salomé frowned. 'She was connected to all of this?'

Luko nodded.

'You'd better start at the beginning,' Salomé said. 'Explain yourself.'

'She gave you a word, yes?' Luko asked. 'The old lady, hmmm?'

Salomé nodded, casting her mind back. 'Cuculidae…'

Luko nodded.

'It means cuckoo. It is a bird from old Earth, I believe.'

Salomé frowned. 'What does that mean? I don't understand.'

Luko sighed.

'The Cuckoo was famed ... it laid its eggs in the nests of other birds,' he said. 'The egg would hatch, the parents would feed the chick. They believed it was their own, yes? As it grew, it would push the other chicks out ...'

Salomé looked at him, a wave of memories and thoughts crackling around her, flooding in and threatening to overwhelm her mind.

'You are one such cuckoo,' Luko said heavily.

Dark hair, in a family of blondes. Her intelligence and stamina, so different from the waif-like fragility of her sisters. Her defiance, her arrogance ... the adventures that had transpired from the events set off here on the Chione moon ...

Can't be, that's just ridiculous ... and yet ...

'You are not quite who you think you are,' Luko said softly. 'You never were. There were only two true daughters of Algreb.'

Her breath caught in her throat. She gasped, trying to draw air into her lungs, but it was as if she was suffocating. Luko reached out towards her but she angrily batted him away.

'No, this is lies ...'

She stood up, walking a few paces away, trying to control her breathing. 'It cannot be.'

'They placed you in the Loren family,' Luko said, standing up and following her. 'A phantom pregnancy. Molto clever. You were to grow there in hiding, until such time as they could put their plan into action.'

'And what is this plan? Who are they?'

'They have no name,' Luko answered, 'They work always in secret, passing knowledge down a line in codes and hidden memories. You are next.'

'Next?' Her voice cracked with anger. 'Next for what?'

'It was not supposed to be you,' Luko said sadly. 'But the one before you betrayed their trust, broke the connection. You were to replace her.'

'The one before ...' Salomé's eyes widened. 'Octavia!'

'Octavia found out about you,' Luko said. 'That is why she pursued you. You were a genetic match ... you are all ...' he looked downcast. 'Genetic matches ...'

Salomé stared at him. 'All?' She frowned, her eyes darting from side to side. 'The old lady ... the spiky-haired woman ... What are you saying? Genetic matches? What does that mean?'

Luko swallowed and looked up at her.

'Salomé, you are a clone.'

She couldn't answer. No words would come. She simply stood there, her mouth hanging open, shock, outrage and surprise fighting for control of her emotions.

A clone, of who? The spiky-haired woman? The old lady? Octavia? Are they one and the same? How many? No …

Her head was spinning, emotions flashing from anger to disbelief. She felt her feet going numb and nearly fell, sitting down just in time, still unable to say a word.

'I do not know all of the story,' Luko said. 'But it started with a woman called Elyssia. She was a pilot, who flew with a commander by the name of Ryder. She learnt many secrets that the powers did not want her to know. She tried to reveal them, but there are those that want that truth hidden. She tried for decades, extended her life with cybernetics and genetics to give herself more time. She recruited the old lady to help her. For years they worked, trying to disclose the truth. They had to conceal their memories and knowledge, even from themselves, to stop it falling into the wrong hands. Secrets buried in such a way they could be found if one knew where to look.'

Salomé stood, her whole body vibrating with emotion, unable to answer.

'Octavia was … created,' Luko said. 'Designed to carry on with the task they had started when they no longer could but … it went wrong … she used what they had given her and turned it against them. Using the abilities she had to build her own fortunes. So they tried again … a different way …'

Salomé looked up. Tears now streaking her face.

'Me,' she said, swallowing hard. 'They made me …'

Luko nodded. 'Octavia found out about it and knew she could possess your body.'

'So it was no accident the old lady was waiting for me in that hospital,' Salomé said. 'They were following me everywhere. The message in the Imperial databanks …'

Luko nodded. 'All arranged.'

'And how much of what I've done is me?' Salomé asked. 'Am I just programmed to think what they wanted? Just some mindless vessel which they control?'

Luko shook his head. 'You are your own woman, signorina. They gave you great intelligence, great strength, but you determine what you do with it. It is no accident that people follow you and love you …'

'So my life is a sham,' Salomé replied, shaking her head. 'I am nothing more than a figurehead for someone else's whim and fancy.'

Luko grabbed her by the shoulder.

'Salomé,' he said. 'This mystery they chased. It is molto important. They fought so hard to reveal it, trying for decades. The powers out there do not want this revealed. They have tried to suppress it. The galaxy deserves the truth … you can show them …'

Salomé shrugged off his grip and walked a pace forward.

'I will not do this …'

She took long deep breaths, her hands clenching and unclenching several times. Finally, she turned to look at him.

'And you,' she whispered, her voice tight and her lips trembling. 'You lied. You've always lied, all along …'

'Salomé …'

'How dare you even speak to me! You called yourself my friend, but it's lies … all lies!'

'Please …'

'No!' she said, her voice sharp and perfunctory, with just the faintest broken edge to it. 'Our … this is at an end. You will take me back to Leeson City, trader Giovanni. I depart for Alioth immediately. Now, if you please.'

'Signorina …'

Her gaze was firm, only her voice betrayed the rage that boiled within. 'Now.'

Chapter Twenty-Three

Engineering base, Alioth 4a, Alioth system, Alliance

Tsu drove the SRV up the boarding ramp at the engineering base. It automatically slotted itself into a matching receptacle and bolted itself fast against the interior bulkheads. She pulled out her laser sidearm as the pressure equalised, pointing the business end directly at Raan's head.

'You first,' she said, gesturing with the gun.

Raan waited until Tsu keyed in the escape code for the SRV airlock and a hatchway slid aside. He stepped out, Tsu immediately behind him.

'Forward, slowly,' Tsu said.

The hatchway led into a standard airlock, with another hatch at the other end. Tsu jabbed the cycle controls and waited while the automated sequence ran its course. With a faint chime, the hatchway ahead slid across out of the way.

Someone stood on the other side.

'You can step out now.'

It was an older man's voice. Gritty and worn. Someone who had been exposed to vacuum at least once in his life, if she was any judge.

Tsu looked carefully, but in the glare of spotlights beyond the hatchway it was hard to make out more than the figure's outline. She shoved Raan through, keeping the gun jammed directly in his back.

'There's no need to hold him hostage,' the figure said, stepping forward.

'Don't move,' Tsu called. 'I know you want him.'

'Want him?' the figure said. 'I don't want him at all. He's just the messenger boy ...'

Tsu frowned. The figure stepped out of the light. Tsu caught sight of a tall, but stoutly built man, with a shock of grey hair upon his head.

'... And you are out of your depth, Alliance girl.'

'Stand your ground, I have a gun. I will use it ...'

'Standard issue Voidmaster 3c, typical for Alliance intelligence operatives,' the man replied. 'Multishot capability, auto tracking, with a quick recharge powerpack. Disabled, naturally.'

Tsu spared a look at her gun, seeing a faint red illuminator on it.

Discharged ... but how?

'I do take precautions,' the man said with a grin. 'After all, it could have been one of those Sirius goons. It was difficult to tell who won that little altercation from here.'

'You were watching?' Raan asked.

'Ever since you left Chi Orionis,' the man said. 'Femi seemed to think you were the right guy for the gig. Since you did make it, it looks like he was right. Now …'

He turned his attention back to Tsu.

'Your weapon has been electronically disabled, but this one,' he drew out a much older looking mechanical contraption with a surprisingly large calibre. Tsu watched as his thumb pulled back on a heavy looking hammer at the rear of the weapon. It snapped into place with a thick click. 'Is immune to the process. Less is sometimes more.' He pointed it directly at her face. 'So, unless you want your pretty face splashed all over the bulkhead, I suggest you let him go, Alliance girl.'

Tsu thought about it for a moment, but knew she had no choice. No amount of martial arts expertise had ever conquered a bullet to the brain.

She dropped her gun and kicked it through the airlock, releasing her grip on Raan at the same time. He stepped alongside the newcomer.

'Bill Turner,' she said, a sneer curling her lip. 'You're supposed to be working for the Alliance, but you're betraying us to the Feds, aren't you? Sold out. What was it? Money, power?'

Turner waited for her to finish.

'You may wish to give me the benefit of the doubt,' Bill said. 'Until you know a little more about what is going on.'

'I know what's going on!'

Bill laughed at her. 'Trust me, you know nothing.'

'I know that you're a traitor!' Tsu snapped. 'You've betrayed the Alliance …'

She stepped back at the look of rage that suddenly suffused his face. He pushed past Raan and shoved the barrel of the gun into her face, forcing her up against the bulkhead. Tsu found herself pinned against it, the muzzle of the gun pressing against her cheekbone.

'Traitor?' he whispered. She felt his warm breath on her face. He was only centimetres from her, staring into her eyes. 'If I thought you knew what you were talking about I'd end you now …'

'Then explain,' Tsu managed to gasp. 'This tech you've developed …'

Out of the corner of her eye Tsu saw Raan edge away from her and Turner, staying out of the way against the bulkhead wall.

'Your precious Alliance government tried to sell me out. Tried to denigrate the name of Turner, bury the truth like they always do. Then they come crawling over my operation demanding this and that, they can't have it both ways.'

'You should give them whatever you have developed,' Tsu replied. 'Not barter it with the Federation …'

'It's the Feds who ended up financing this for me,' Turner replied. 'Oh, I tried to get funding from the Alliance. Guess what the answer was?'

'They would have given you the money …'

'And demanded I work on their terms, their rules? Not acceptable, Alliance girl. Not acceptable. I don't trust them anyway. Not after what they did to my family …'

'And you trust the Feds?'

Turner laughed, pulling the gun away. Tsu propped herself up, rubbing her face to ease the pressure on her cheek.

'Of course I don't trust the Feds,' he said. 'There's much more to all this than meets the eye. I don't trust any of them, but they all have their uses. You won't trust them after this is over.'

A buzz of commlink communication interrupted them.

'Boss,' came a gruff voice.

'I'm here,' Turner answered, the aim of his gun not wavering.

'Your Imperial guests are leaving soon. What do you want done with them when they arrive?'

'Send them down to the archive. I'll meet them there.'

Tsu frowned.

'Imperials?' she asked with distaste.

'Fun, eh?' Turner said with a grin. He stepped back, still pointing the gun at her. 'Now. You have a choice. You can hear me out, or I can kill you where you stand. Don't try to escape; I've already keyed the internal security system to your ident.'

Tsu shrugged. 'That's not a choice.'

Turner grinned. 'I suppose not. This way, both of you …'

He gestured with the gun. Raan stumbled forward out of the way and Tsu followed.

Leeson City, Prism system, Empire

Hassan watched Salomé board the *Seven Veils*. She said nothing, but buckled herself into the co-pilot's seat, stabbing at the controls, her lips pursed.

'We're heading to Alioth?' he asked. 'Cuthrick has made contact with this Bill Turner chap. He'll be expecting us.'

She nodded once.

Hassan busied himself with plotting the course and prepping the ship for launch. After a few minutes of silence and with the ship beginning its first jump, he turned to look at her. She was staring out of the canopy.

'I'm guessing Luko isn't coming,' he said.

Her glare intensified, a cold look fixed upon her face. She held his gaze for a moment. Intimidated, he turned back to the controls.

Guess not …

'Is there anything …'

'No.'

'Salomé, you're upset, I …'

'I do not want to discuss it.'

Her voice was sharp and angry, her lips pursed in fury. He saw her cheek muscles clench. He turned back to the controls.

Engineering base, Alioth 4a, Alioth system, Alliance

Tsu trudged silently as she and Raan were led down a series of corridors and into what she took for some kind of meeting room. It was blandly decorated, a conference table centred around a large holofac projector, with a series of chairs under it. The illumination was subdued. Clearly some kind of presentation had been prepped. She took a chair, seeing Raan sit down across from her. Turner retreated and the door slid closed behind him. Tsu heard it lock into place.

They sat without speaking for long moments.

'Imperials,' Raan said, breaking the silence. 'Why Imperials?'

Tsu was thinking it through.

'Enjoying the real world now?' she asked. 'Not quite the same as the Arena, is it?'

Raan shook his head, but she could see his face was pale.

Looks like he was telling the truth after all. Considering this is his first time outside of a game he's doing better than I'd expect …

'That traitor must be planning to sell this technology to the highest bidder,' Tsu replied. She shook her head. 'He won't get away with this. Trying to sell the Alliance out from under their noses! I must find a way to report back home …'

'Fat chance of that in here,' Raan replied. 'Do you think he will let us go?'

Tsu didn't reply for a moment. Logically, Turner's best move was simply to kill her straight away. He could easily dispose of her body. Officially, nobody knew she was here other than Edmund Mahon, and his position of Prime Minister of the Alliance meant that he'd never admit it. No, Turner wanted her to see something, maybe take a message back.

A ransom demand, I guess … money for the hyperdrive tech …

'He hasn't killed us yet,' Tsu replied.

'Us?' Raan answered. 'He's got no beef with me.'

Tsu laughed. 'You know how he acquired this data from a Federation company. You know Sirius killed the chairman. I don't think he's going to be all that keen on witnesses hanging around.'

She was gratified to see Raan's face go even paler.

But it doesn't make sense. With the data cache he doesn't need us … And these Imperials? Why Imperials?

The door clicked and then retracted. Two people entered, escorted by conspicuously armed guards who walked onwards and stood, alert, in the corners of the room. The man looked like a pilot. He wore an Imperial-style flight suit. Tsu didn't recognise him.

She'd seen the other woman before, though. Her face was familiar to anyone with a passing interest in the newsfeeds.

The Imperial stateswoman who was accused of trying to murder Fleet Admiral Patreus!

'That's …' Raan stuttered, from across the table.

'Kahina Loren,' Tsu finished for him, aware that both their mouths hung open. 'Otherwise known as Commander Salomé …'

'Who are these individuals?' Salomé demanded. Tsu watched her as she took in the confines of the room, assessing it and its contents. Tsu disliked her voice, it was full of Imperial arrogance, along with a peculiar lilting accent. 'This was intended to be a private negotiation …'

'Not anymore,' Turner said, entering the room behind them. 'I'll make it easy for you. I need ten million tonnes, delivered over the next year.'

Ten million tonnes! Of what?

Tsu saw Hassan look across at Salomé. She looked completely unconcerned.

'Within the year?' she replied, disinterested. 'You will guarantee market rates?'

'Don't worry about your precious tantalum, you'll get your price,' Turner answered. 'I have something far more important to discuss with all of you.'

'I don't understand,' Salomé said.

'Join the club,' Raan replied.

'And who are … you?' Salomé demanded, looking at Raan and Tsu.

'Allow me,' Turner said. 'Tsu Annabelle Singh, an Alliance operative charged with investigating me under the direct orders of Edmund Mahon. Raan Corsen, ex-employee of MetaDrive Inc., currently on the run from Sirius Corporation.'

Tsu saw Salomé look at Raan as if she recognised him from somewhere.

Turner grinned. 'You were set up too, you know.'

Raan's mouth dropped open.

'And this, of course, is Kahina Tijani Loren,' Bill concluded, 'Disgraced senator to the Prism system, given a mission to come here on behalf of Emperor Arissa Lavigny-Duval.'

'I go by the name of Salomé now.'

'I …' Tsu began. She saw the man who accompanied Salomé grin. 'And who is he?'

'I'm just the pilot,' the man replied. 'I'm tagging along for the ride. Name's Hassan.'

'You have brought me here under false pretences …' Salomé began.

'Yes, I have,' Turner replied.

'I demand …'

Turner pointed his gun at her, cocking the hammer.

'Quiet.'

Tsu saw Salomé tilt her head up slightly, but she didn't flinch.

She's had guns pointed at her before.

'Typical Imperial,' Turner continued. 'I hold the cards. Sit down. It is time for all three of you to listen.'

Everyone held their breath for a moment. No one moved. Salomé's only response was a raised eyebrow.

'Or I can shoot you,' Turner said, with a grin.

Without a word, Salomé took a seat a few places up from Raan, with Hassan sitting beside her.

'Federals, Imperials and Alliance,' Turner said, walking around to the head of the table. 'Good. I require your full attention. This will not take long, but I think you'll find it most interesting.'

Location unknown, COL 70 sector, Uninhabited

Saffron sucked in her breath through the Remlok mask and then watched as the moisture from her exhalations condensed briefly on the inside of the faceplate, before being cleansed by the atmospheric processor. A neat piece of kit, the Remlok, notwithstanding its ubiquitousness across the void. It sustained life in the vacuum and must have saved millions of lives over the decades it had been in use.

Its designers probably hadn't expected it to be used in this fashion, though. Sometimes you had to do crazy stuff to get the scoop you were looking for.

Saffron hadn't liked Scarlet's plan, but had gone along with it. She had smuggled herself inside a cargo canister.

There was no life support inside, hence the Remlok mask. The canister was listed as carrying dehydrated protein.

Which isn't too far from the truth. Lucky I'm not claustrophobic!

She'd been riding, if that was the right word, inside for several hours now, waiting for the ship to reach its destination.

She'd tried to find a way in before, but had been rebuffed, forcibly. A direct approach had been turned down. Flying a private ship into the area had been discouraged.

Discouraged with pulse lasers and multi-cannons!

So now she was here, stuck inside a cargo canister, trying to find a way in.

Investigative reporting at its best ... should get danger pay for this!

She had a lead; something was clearly going on out here that someone didn't want to become public knowledge. She intended to find out what it was.

Her patience was finally rewarded. A thump jolted her inside the canister. She could just make out the sounds of the ship settling down on a pad. The faint whirrings of the massive machinery that jockeyed arriving and departing ships into position rumbled around her before echoing into silence.

The ship was docked.

Minutes passed without further noise. Saffron guessed the ship was being refuelled prior to offloading, which was a sensible precaution. You never knew when something might go wrong, it paid to be cautious.

Then the much louder sound of cargo bay doors opening reached her ears and shortly afterwards the canister lurched as it was hoisted by an automech. She braced herself against the interior walls, waiting for the unpredictable motion to stop.

Still zero-gee, so we're not planet-side.

With a final clunk, the canister seemed to be in position. She pressed her ear to the interior wall and listened intently, hearing the noise of the automechs retreating. She gave it another few minutes to ensure there was no one else about.

She pressed the toggle.

The forward end of the canister irised open, giving her a view of another canister. They were stacked far enough apart that the automechs could move between them, making it easy for her to slip out.

The Remlok, detecting a compatible atmosphere, flipped back and folded itself away neatly in the lapels of her suit. Her mag-boots clicked into place on the floor and she took a look around.

The ship was a tatty-looking Type-7 freighter, listing very slightly to one side on a stained and tarnished undercarriage. It was sitting on a large pad just below the level of whatever docking bay they had arrived in. She could see two individuals standing below it, gesturing up at the hull and pointing, before making notes on a commtab.

She grinned. Their black jumpsuits were a match for hers. She'd done her research well.

Let's hope the fake ID works.

She looked down at her clothing, with its stylised logo and the words 'Wreaken Construction.'

There was a service elevator behind her and she walked across to it, tapping her ID against the access port. The doors slid open without complaint.

Yes!

The lift took her back up to the docking level. She gasped as the doors opened and she stepped out, momentarily overwhelmed with the view.

The landing area was unlike anything she'd seen before, a flat expanse that easily stretched for several kilometres before her and certainly at least a kilometre wide. The area around her was pressurised, with a flickering blue force field several hundred metres above her head. Ships big and small were arriving, loading or unloading cargo and then departing. All of them were large-scale freighters, with food supplies or raw materials. She could see fighter escorts holding station beyond the perimeter, waiting to ensure the safety of vessels setting out from the facility.

ELITE DANGEROUS: PREMONITION

She'd expected one of the industrial space stations, probably a Coriolis, maybe one of the Orbis structures, but not this ... this was ...

She walked forward a few hundred metres, squinting into the distance. Beyond the landing zone, the structure of the facility quickly broke up into huge pens, kilometres long, stretching away both up and down from her perspective. She could see huge numerical markers on each one, themselves probably a hundred metres in size. Within the pens lurked huge objects, the skeletal internals of massive outlines in various states of assembly. Faint lights flashed around them and small vessels, dwarfed by the scale of the behemoths, flitted in between the vast array, delivering parts, tools and equipment. Saffron could just make out a few spacesuited individuals, attached by tethers to some of the nearer ones.

Further away, she could see the constructs had more form, some had full structures, some had internal compartments fitted, others were partially covered with hull plating. As she watched, a massive pair of engines were towed into place by two Asp Explorers.

The pens further from her vantage point gave the game away.

I was right!

Down the left side of the facility spread a line of vessels in various stages of construction, growing from skeletal outlines to fully finished, their bright paintwork sparkling in the starlight, completed and ready for departure.

She looked down the right side to see the same pattern repeated, but a different design of ship. The ships on the left were the largest, with an aggressive low profile and a cleft structure, the ship's centre line being hollowed out with a vast cavity. The ships on the right were completely different, with smooth flowing lines and an enormous carousel, already rotating on the final vessel, its centre just ahead of the rear quarter. She recognised both ships immediately.

Wreaken are constructing ships for both the Federation and the Empire ... simultaneously!

A complete series of Federal and Imperial battlecruisers.

Prepping for a war, or something else?

A pre-arranged mental command activated the camera feed from her eyes. An overlay appeared in her eyesight and she panned the view across, ensuring she got coverage of the facility and the ships' construction.

Wait until this gets out on the feeds. They've been denying this for months. The galaxy will go ballistic!

But she had to get out with the information. That meant another vessel.

Time to go …

She headed towards the lift, trying to act casual. A few other workers and technicians milled about, but none spared her more than an idle glance.

Relief at reaching the lift was shattered as the doors snapped open. Two burly-looking guards emerged, hands moving swiftly towards their belts …

Guns!

Instinctively, she dove to the right, sprinting down a stack of containers. Booted feet thundered behind her. In panic, she ducked between two canisters, pushing herself up against the cold metal, her heart pounding in her chest.

Shit.

Silence. She chanced a look around the edge of the canister.

For a moment she could see nothing, but leaning out a little further revealed one of the guards cautiously moving up the aisle between the stacks.

He caught sight of her and raised his gun.

Saffron expected him to call out and demand she give herself up, but instead he took aim and fired.

She jolted back as some kind of electric blast ricocheted off the metal before her in a shower of sparks.

'I … I surrender!' she yelled, her voice catching in her throat. 'I'll come quietly!'

'No you won't, sweetie!' came the gruff reply.

What?

She chanced another look. Two more shots followed, the noise terrifyingly loud, making her ears ring. She ducked back down.

They're going to kill me!

Panic rose. No one had ever fired at her before. Barely knowing what she was doing, she fled. Then she was scrambling through a maze of haphazardly jumbled canisters, some floating in the zero-gee, held only loosely with tethers. Something had come adrift. She could only feel thankful as she clambered underneath into the opportunist hidey hole.

She pulled out a small firearm. It wasn't much. Five, maybe six rounds of high voltage stun-fire. All she'd been able to get at short notice. She was a reporter, not a commando.

Her only way out now was to snatch a ship. At least she knew how to fly. It would mean doubling back to the lift, getting into the docking area and seeing what she could find.

How had they known?

No time for figuring that. She had to get out of here.

She looked around her. On second glance it wasn't such a great place. She couldn't see out clearly and she had no idea where the two guards were. She tried her best to still her rapid breathing and then concentrated on listening.

All around her were vague creaks and groans, noises she had ignored before, but now might mean life or death. Something rattled off to her left and she turned, seeing a shadow slide across one of the far canisters.

Sneaking up the side!

She lowered herself down and found a crawl space under the cargo storage. She was thin enough that she could just slip through, so she wriggled in, concentrating on keeping every move silent.

Footsteps reached her ears, followed by low voices.

'Where'd she go?'

'She's here somewhere, got stun packs?'

'Yeah, loaded. Not spacing her?'

'Boss wants this to look like an accident.'

Saffron could see two pairs of mag-boots shifting position. She'd been lucky, the two guards had dropped down right behind where she'd been hiding. Anywhere else and they'd have spotted her for sure.

Don't look down, don't look down!

She continued crawling away, struggling with grip in the zero-gee with her mag-boots off the floor. She had to brace against the canister she was under. It shifted slightly under the pressure.

'What was that?'

The guards moved, their mag-boots snapping rhythmically on the flooring as they walked back down the aisles. Saffron saw them move past her and decided to retreat. Oddly enough, going backwards was much easier.

'Nah, nothing. She's hiding out. Stay put here, I'll try to flush her out.'

One of the guards was moving back to her hiding place.

This isn't going to work … unless …

She inched forwards, making no sound, watching the mag-boots that were all she could see of the guard.

Carefully, she pulled herself along and then squeezed out from underneath the canister on the opposite side. She touched a pad on her mag-boots, deactivating them before they could clamp to the floor.

Unsecured, she was free to move anywhere she liked, but she'd have to be cautious. One misstep and she'd be drifting away from the facility. She looked up, seeing the flickering blue force field that kept the area pressurised.

Don't fancy that.

She pulled herself up and over the canister, ensuring she didn't travel too fast. A deft move had her on top of the canister and she pulled herself along its length using the securing straps draped around it.

Peering over the edge, she saw she was above the guard. He was looking to his left and right, with his gun out ...

Got you.

She took aim and fired. The electrical stun burst caught him directly in the head. He gave a strangled yelp and then went limp. He looked odd like that. She'd expected him to fall down, but he was still secured in his mag-boots, so he just gently rocked back and forth despite being unconscious.

The click-clack of mag-boots sounded behind her and she pulled herself flat as the other guard appeared. He saw her and fired, a blast of energy sizzling past so close that she felt the heat. She chanced a blind shot over the edge, but heard nothing as her weapon discharged. She shoved the gun back into its holster.

Then there was a clank. Footsteps, coming up the side of the canister!

It's zero-gee, girl! No up in space!

The guard appeared at right angles on the side of the canister and then stepped over onto the top, unfazed by the ninety-degree change of direction. Saffron fumbled for her gun, but with one foot secured, the guard kicked out at her.

'No trespassers,' the guard said, with an unpleasant grin. He aimed his gun at her, his finger on the trigger.

She didn't think, there was no time for that. She jabbed her own boots down on the canister's roof and then launched herself at him.

There's no weight in zero-gee, but there is mass and inertia. That bit of physics doesn't change.

Whatever the guard expected her to do, that wasn't it. His own mag-boots were ripped from their connection and both of them tumbled end over end, flailing desperately.

Saffron glimpsed a grab handle and snatched at it. Her outstretched fingers caught hold. Then she was floating upside down, tethered by one hand. Her forward motion was arrested with a jolt that tugged through her arm. Then came a massive jerk on her leg.

She looked down her body; the guard had grabbed her by the ankle. She felt his fingers clasp as he tried to pull himself further in, his gun still clasped in his other hand.

She still had her gun too.

She brought it round.

She saw his eyes widen.

'No, shit ... no!'

She had no hesitation in pulling the trigger.

Hired scum!

The electric fire spat out once more, catching him in the chest. A residual shock coursed up her leg, causing her to yell out in pain. She struggled to hold onto the grab handle, tensing her hand to ensure she wasn't dislodged.

When her vision cleared, she could see the guard floating away above her. Somehow he was still conscious, tumbling end over end and yelling curses once he realised he was spiralling upwards towards the force field perhaps a hundred metres above them.

His cries became screeches of terror. Saffron turned away, not wanting to look.

She didn't see the bolt of blaster fire that hit her. She was only dimly aware of the electric shock that shattered through her body.

There was just enough consciousness left for her to watch her grip on the handle loosen and come free, and for her to see the metal horizon of the facility begin to gently spin around her.

There was little pain, her nervous system almost completely paralysed by the guard's final shot of revenge.

Two bodies drifted slowly upwards. The first impacted against the force field at high speed, ripped to shreds by the fierce energy that held back a full atmosphere of pressure.

The second hit at a slower velocity. Cascades of current and fierce radiation shocked across it, spinning it around and directing it back down towards the facility flooring. By this time it had been spotted by others, who made arrangements for its recovery.

But it was unrecognisable.

Engineering base, Alioth 4a, Alioth system, Alliance

'It's no accident that you're all here,' Bill said. 'I don't expect you to trust me, or each other, but I know you are all embroiled in something which is far bigger than anyone else out there realises, save those who sent you. You've all been chasing mysteries, got caught in plots, or been given strange assignments that don't make any sense.'

Salomé, Tsu, Raan and Hassan exchanged a look, but none of them said anything.

'Mysteries in deep space,' Bill prompted, looking at Salomé. 'Strange clues left in the Imperial databanks? The Formidine Rift? A strange old lady giving you clues?'

Salomé's eyes narrowed. 'How do you know about that?'

Bill smiled, but then turned away to look at Raan.

'Femi placed you in MetaDrive as an insurance policy. Used you to expose what Sirius was up to,' Bill said. 'You're one of the best pilots to be found. Do you think that whole Arena combat thing was down to chance? He planned it all, set you up. Got you to do what he needed you to do.'

Bill turned to Tsu. 'You were assigned to check me out, based on tailing him.' Bill gestured back at Raan. 'All your normal procedures bypassed. All on your own, quite an honour for a junior member of the team, eh? Ever ask why?'

'They needed my expertise,' Tsu said.

'And you're unique in having that expertise, are you?' Bill asked. Tsu didn't reply. She didn't need to.

'It's all part of a plan,' Bill said, and folded his arms.

'Who's plan?' Hassan asked. 'Yours?'

Bill smiled. 'No, not mine. Your leaders have set you on this path to uncover something, something they can't investigate themselves, because they don't know who to trust. They've chosen a disgraced aristocrat, a junior staff member and a lucky hot shot as their eyes and ears. That's because you're all expendable.'

'How do you know this?' Tsu demanded.

'I've been following the patterns. I get a lot of visitors here, with a lot of data. I store it, process it … archive it. I've been watching for a long long time and I have certain information at my disposal which helps me take a long view of events.'

Bill gestured to the holofac, which illuminated with a map of the galaxy. Its vastness was familiar, but the untold thousands of light years it represented were still overwhelming.

'You're all here because your respective authorities believe a conspiracy is taking place. A conspiracy which is manipulating all of us, our homes, our systems, our territories. Whoever these people are, they act sometimes in the shadows, sometimes in plain view. Their people are everywhere, at all levels in society. Those who get too close or find out too much are dealt with, bought off or encouraged to retire unexpectedly early.'

'To what end?' Salomé demanded. 'What is this grand purpose?'

Bill shook his head. 'No one knows, we can only see facets, but your combined experiences shine a light on what it might be.' He gestured at Salomé. 'You, with your people chasing clues in the darkness, have un-covered some kind of strange historic mission out in the void based on an obscure message hidden in an Imperial vault. Dozens of ships, deploying strange beacons in the depths of space, all in secret. But why?'

Salomé narrowed her eyes, but didn't respond.

Bill turned to Tsu. 'The Alliance has the best technicians in the galaxy, and yet we never turn that to military or economic advantage. We invented frame shift technology and everything associated with it. We could have kept that to ourselves and brought the Federation and the Empire to their knees before us. We didn't. Why?

'Edmund believes peace is the ...'

Bill snorted. 'Edmund is a master politician. He could have used that leverage for the good of the Alliance, instead he threw the advantage away and now everyone has that technology. Again, why?'

Tsu didn't answer.

'And the Federation,' Bill said. 'Still the mightiest force in the stars, yet it is content with static borders and posturing against the Empire. Minor skirmishes on the edges of its domain, yet it seems to lack the courage to be bold and deal with its ancient opponents. The Empire was severely weakened after the power struggle for the Emperor's seat; the Federation could have taken advantage of that. It did not. Why?'

Raan didn't answer either.

'Here's something else,' Bill said. He toggled an overlay onto the galaxy map. Various sectors appeared in coloured blobs across the map, some bigger, some smaller, with a group surprisingly close to the core worlds themselves.

'What are these?' Tsu asked.

'Permit locked regions,' Bill replied. 'Areas of the galaxy which you can't access without the proper permission.'

'Nothing unusual there,' Raan said, 'Plenty of systems require you to earn a level of trust outside before they'll let you in ...'

'I'm not talking about sightseeing in Sol,' Bill snapped. 'These are far reaching areas, and they shift and move. This one here ...' he pointed at an area of the map and it zoomed in. 'Is new, it used to be open for shipping. Now it's locked.'

The galaxy map slowed its zoom and stars appeared, they all had a common sector name.

COL 70. Unknown Permit Required.

'Unknown permit ...?'

'These areas have been deliberately blocked, you can't travel to them, your hyperdrive can't establish a lock. It's been tried.'

'Who is blocking them?' Tsu asked.

'The Pilots' Federation,' Raan said. 'Has to be, they control the ...'

'The obvious answer,' Bill said, 'and thus the wrong one. They certainly enforce certain system permits, but these ones? No. This is something else. It's a convenient fiction that the Pilots' Federation manages this.'

'But if it's not them, who is it?' Tsu asked again.

Bill shrugged. 'It's a mystery, but consider this ...'

The GalNet logo appeared; a spinning animation that then faded to reveal one of their articles.

An unidentified individual has been found dead at a Wreaken Construction site in the COL 70 sector. The body was disfigured as a result of radiation exposure, and identification has so far not been possible. System authorities are conducting an investigation.

A representative of Wreaken Construction responded to the discovery with a statement:

'There have been several incidents of individuals trying to break into our facilities. This is an unfortunate event, but frankly the victim brought this accident on themselves. Our facilities are secured for a reason – manufacturing is a dangerous business.'

Meanwhile, independent pilots have reported that Wreaken Construction sites are heavily guarded, and that approaching ships have been aggressively warned away by Wreaken-owned vessels.

'Wreaken are contractors,' Salomé said, 'Large-scale industrial, they helped build Hiram's Anchorage in my home system as subcontractors to Mastopolis Mining.'

'And here they are on the edge of a mysteriously locked sector, doing something they don't want anyone to see.'

'And you think this is all connected?' Hassan asked.

'Everything is connected,' Bill replied. 'Tied together by unseen threads …'

'And you believe somebody is pulling all the strings,' Salomé added.

Bill nodded. 'I believe there is another power structure, subtly, or not so subtly, manipulating events behind the scenes. A core of ruthless individuals operating out of sight, with more power in their collective grasp than anything the Empire, the Federation or the Alliance can wield. I call them "The Club."'

'And what does this have to do with you?' Tsu asked. 'And why are you telling us?'

'My hyperdrive research,' Bill explained. 'I hold a legacy of information from the Turners, secrets which, if researched, could reveal their actions. I've operated in secret for as long as can, but now they know what I'm doing. This hyperdrive modification will change the balance of power once again, just like the introduction of the frame shift drive changed the modus operandi of the powers. They intend to acquire it.'

'What does this thing do then?' Raan asked.

'I'll show you.'

Bill stood and gestured to the doorway, leading them out of the conference room.

'Ten million tonnes?' Hassan whispered to Salomé.

'Shhh!' Salomé hissed. 'Not now!'

'But …'

'Cuthrick and Cornelius will find a way …'

Bill gestured down the corridor to where a pair of doors could be seen recessed in the bulkhead. They trudged down to them, and they opened to reveal an internal transport pod. All five filed inside. The pod dropped away.

***

Tsu quickly lost count of the floors they descended. The base had to be enormous, the above ground buildings just a tiny fraction of the overall volume of the facility. The others started talking, she turned her attention to them.

'Femi said I could trust you,' Raan said. 'And that you would know what to do with …'

'The data he gave you,' Bill replied. 'Yes. Femi was going to bring it himself, only time ran out.'

'What data is this?' Salomé asked.

'Configuration data,' Bill answered, 'Required for the calibration and setup of this device. Highly prized data …'

'Sirius,' Raan said.

'Sirius,' Bill repeated. 'Purveyors of humdrum and common hyperdrive mechanisms across the whole galaxy. Pretty much a monopoly. Not a very pleasant organisation in any respect.'

'Are any Federal corporations?' Salomé asked.

Bill ignored her.

'We license their tech,' Tsu said. 'They provide the hardware, what's the problem?'

'Where do you think that tech comes from, Alliance girl?' Bill snapped. 'Sirius doesn't innovate, never has. It buys, it acquires, it steals … it takes every new idea and assimilates it, passing it off as its own. Profits, only profits. The stinking Alliance government didn't have the balls to realise it was being licensed its own technology. We made most of the hyperdrive breakthroughs in recent years, but no … we buy it from Sirius.'

Tsu frowned. Bill's words were charged with an emotional undercurrent.

'Your stinking Alliance government won't cause a ruckus,' Bill said. 'Peace above all, fair trade and commerce with the other powers.'

Tsu grimaced at his disparaging tone. 'The Alliance is stronger for peace. Edmund …'

Bill snorted. 'Edmund is no fool. We could have brought both the Feds and the Empire to their knees with the expertise we have. We have the best technical minds in all the stars. Our hyperdrive tech outclassed theirs. But we threw it all away in the name of peace; at least, that's what we're supposed to believe. So I took it underground.'

'MetaDrive …' Raan whispered.

'Yes, MetaDrive,' Bill replied. 'I had the reference material, Femi had the expertise and the funding, together we were working on something pretty damned important.'

'Sirius found out?' Raan asked.

'You should know,' Bill replied. 'Femi had his suspicions, but you dug it out.'

'The MetaDrive board …!'

'Sirius compromised them in the usual way,' Bill said, 'Bribes, blackmail, the details don't matter. They were after the hyperdrive tech we've been working on.'

'And what does it do?' Tsu demanded.

The lift slowed, sliding to a smooth halt. The doors snapped open.

Bill grinned and gestured to the door.

They stepped out into what appeared to be a massive automated shop floor. A gantry led through the midst of it, suspended in the air. Tsu stepped out in front. She spared a glance upwards and staggered to one side. The others joined her, staring upwards, around and down at the enormous internal space. The echoing clank of machinery droned all about them, a cacophony of whirs, thumps and hisses as countless mechanisms undertook the work assigned to them. Robotic arms spun and turned, sparks flew, monstrous machine mechanisms rotated and hummed.

'Sorry about the noise,' Bill called, indicating they should proceed along the walkway. Tsu went first.

Above her rose a superstructure of massive girders, repeating every few dozen metres up to a height beyond her vision. Locked in the framework were pieces of equipment stretching up and outwards. Some were clearly whole ships locked into place, classic designs stretching back into antiquity. She saw old Cobras, a Mamba, even a Merlin lay tilted sideways and partially dismantled. She squinted at the name plate, it was tarnished with several laser burned scorch marks, clearly it had its own history and tales to tell.

Escape ... velocity?

Another antiquated design caught her eye, a severely elongated vessel with what looked like two jutting weapons on either side.

Is that a Krait? I've only seen those in the history books ...

There were other ships she didn't recognise as they continued to walk along. One was huge, its engine nacelles disconnected. Wherever it had been it had suffered some pretty intense action. The hull was scarred, the metal burnt and blackened by some kind of weapons fire, it almost looked as if it had been dipped in acid. The name plate was half missing, but a few of the letters remained visible.

Something ... Quest.

Surrounding the vessels was a jumble of machine parts, technology and other objects. Tsu could identify some of them, but the collection was vast, stretching out up down and to the sides as far as the eye could see. The noise reduced as they continued, slowly dropping away to a level that was comfortable.

'Welcome to my … archive,' Bill said. 'And that's why we're called Engineers.'

They came to another pressure door, which snapped open on their approach, leading into what appeared to be some kind of clean room or laboratory. As the doors closed behind them the sound abruptly cut off, much to Tsu's relief.

Tsu moved further in. Raan followed, with Salomé and Hassan bringing up the rear. A smooth orb one-third filled with bubbling brown liquid caught her eye on the left-hand side as they walked past. She peered into it, seeing a collection of roots, leaves and thick branches. It looked as if some kind of tree was being preserved inside. She stopped.

'Have a look,' Bill suggested.

She approached it and touched the plexiglass exterior. It was warm under her fingers. She rubbed at it, trying to see.

Something moved, quicker than she could see, smashing against the glass with a dull thump.

She jolted back, staggering against a nearby railing to steady herself.

A ghastly face was crushed against the glass. It was all eyes and teeth, a grey rubbery visage surrounded by tentacles and claws. It writhed angrily, the teeth and claws scraping at the glass, impotently.

Bill was laughing at her reaction. Tsu turned to glare at him, noticing Raan also looked pale, his eyes wide. Salomé looked unmoved, but Hassan was chuckling again.

'What is that … thing?' she demanded.

'Cute, ain't it?' Bill said. 'The historians say they're extinct, but there are quite a few still about if you know where to look. Don't listen to what the academics say. We'll bring 'em back eventually, when the market is right and we can guarantee the environment is secure. Those fools on Ashoria are a little short of cash right now, unfortunately.'

The creature shuffled around against the glass and then, apparently bored, disappeared within once more, leaving a mucus-like stain behind it.

'Somebody will pay for that?' Tsu asked. 'It's the most disgusting thing I've ever seen.'

'We're wasting time,' Salomé said.

'Lavian Tree Grub,' Bill said, ignoring Salomé. 'An acquired taste I'll agree, bit like the planet it comes from and the people who live there.'

'I thought they couldn't be bred in captivity?' Raan asked.

Bill coughed. 'A convenient fiction aimed at retaining exclusivity. Don't believe everything you read in those gazetteers. Keep moving.'

They continued on, finally arriving at a cleared open space where the gantries came together. It was brightly lit, featuring a series of raised table tops sporting a variety of high-tech diagnostic, manufacturing and repair equipment.

Pride of place in the middle sat a device. It was clearly designed to be plumbed into a vessel. Tsu could see the power, cooling and telemetry connections. They were all plugged into static delivery mechanisms beneath the table. It was a curious mix of metal and non-metal components. Parts of it looked vaguely organic. Holofac schematics floated about the device, recording or reporting on telemetry. It was some kind of test environment.

'Don't touch,' Bill said, with a grin.

Tsu looked it over, examining the holofac displays with interest.

'What is it?' Raan demanded. 'Some kind of weapon?'

'Something a little more subtle than that ...' Bill began.

'Some kind of hyperdrive modulator,' Tsu replied, continuing to look over the schematics and the readouts. 'Fine tuning for greater range, faster transit maybe?'

Bill stopped and looked at her for a moment. 'Not bad, Alliance girl.'

She glared at him. 'I have a name.'

'Tsu Annabelle Singh,' Bill replied. 'Class of '96. Graduated with honours. Specialist in encryption and covert surveillance. I know who you are.'

'Is she right?' Salomé asked.

'No,' Bill replied. 'But you'd have to be a hyperdrive specialist to do much better. This is all about wake concealment.'

Tsu saw Bill look at Raan.

'You can hide your transit?' Raan asked.

Bill nodded.

'With this on your ship, no one will be able to track you when you jump.'

Tsu thought about that for a moment. Such a technology would allow ships to move through territories undetected. Even if they were spotted, no one would be able to determine where they had gone. It would give any military force a massive tactical advantage.

'Then I see why Sirius wanted it,' Raan said, giving a low whistle.

'Worth killing for,' Bill agreed.

'The Empire will meet your demands,' Salomé said. 'Assuming it works.'

'Does it work?' Tsu said. She had been looking over the readouts, many of which were marked with red status indicators.

'I like that you all cut to the chase,' Bill said. 'I can see why they sent you for this job. To answer your question, no. At least, not yet. That's where the data comes in.' He pointed to Raan. 'If you please.'

Raan gestured towards a holofac display and summoned up a link to the data cache aboard Tsu's SRV. It prompted him for Femi's codes. He jabbed them in with his fingers.

More schematics appeared in the air about them, with several streams of data flowing upwards in their midst.

'Femi did all the simulations,' Bill said. 'All the theoretical stuff. Let's see. It helped me understand what we had found.'

'Found?' Tsu echoed.

Bill gestured to the test device.

'Does that look human to you?'

Raan stepped forward. 'You mean …?'

'Such elegance, not so much designed as grown to a pattern…' Bill said, his eyes narrowing in appreciation.

'You're reverse engineering alien technology?' Tsu said.

'Yes.'

Tsu's mouth dropped open, but she couldn't figure out what she wanted to say.

'Most of the interesting advancements in recent years have come from studying them,' Bill said.

Salomé stepped forward. 'Wait … them? Who is them?'

'You probably know them as the Thargoids,' Bill said, matter of fact.

'Thargoids?' Raan's mouth was hanging open too.

'So … they're actually real,' Salomé murmured.

'Strictly speaking they are the Oresrians, at least, that's what they call themselves, as near as we can render it in our language. Thargoid is a crass term we humans came up with.'

'This is a Thargoid hyperdrive system?' Raan said, stumbling back and falling onto his backside. 'What if it … I don't know … does something? I mean, how do you know this thing is safe?'

'The whole point is to make it do something,' Bill said. 'Don't concern yourself. I've been studying their tech for decades. We know a lot about it.'

'And?' Salomé demanded.

'We do not have time for a detailed explanation,' Bill said. 'Suffice to say they have a different technology base to humanity. Where we create designs and fabricate machines, they grow and refine organic structures with comparable properties. Where we experiment and evaluate, they approach and embrace …'

Tsu ran her tongue around the inside of her mouth. 'How did you get hold of this?'

'A whole bunch of their ships were captured in the war,' Bill explained.

'War?' Raan asked. 'What war?'

Bill chuckled. 'The war against the Thargoids. Yeah, I know, it's not in the history recs. That's because they don't want folks to know …'

'And yet …'

'The Alliance recovered dozens of alien vessels. You think our capabilities in hyperspace were down to us being smart?'

'There's nothing in the Alliance databanks about this!' Tsu said.

'Funny that.'

Bill strode over to the table, quickly making adjustments to the displays about him. A series of indicators appeared: sliders, rotating status indicators, graphs and metrics. They seemed to move randomly for a few moments before settling down.

'That's it?' Raan asked.

'That's it,' Bill said. 'Now it needs testing.'

Everyone else in the room exchanged a look. Bill walked across to a hatchway, typed in an access code and then removed a cube of metallic-looking material, it had a faint rainbow sheen to it, reflecting the lights above in a curious way.

'Meta-alloy,' Hassan whispered.

Salomé and the others looked at him.

'I've seen some of this stuff being traded,' he continued. 'Ultra-strong, ultra-light and ultra-rare. They're created by those bizarre things they found out in the Pleiades …'

'Barnacles,' Bill added, returning to the hyperdrive system on the table. He busied himself installing the cube of material into the mechanism. After a few moments he stepped back.

The mechanism gave off a faint low pitched hum. Tsu could feel it more through her feet than her ears. She got the impression that the mechanism was trying to power itself up but was somehow struggling, throbbing with potential, but somehow constrained. Bill adjusted some of the holofac displays, but indicators began moving into red zones. It was clear something wasn't right.

Bill touched a control and the power failed.

'Damn,' he said.

'So it doesn't work,' Salomé said.

Tsu walked across to take a closer look. Bill was extracting the meta-alloy sample from within the mechanism. He held it up for inspection, it was blackened and tarnished, partly disintegrated along one side. He applied pressure and it broke into fragments.

'I don't understand the properties of this stuff well enough and I can't manufacture it.'

'Do you have more?' Raan asked.

Bill shook his head.

'Then how ...'

'We need a decent supply of meta-alloys to fine tune this device and ensure it works,' Bill replied.

'You can't just wander into dock and demand a consignment of meta-alloys,' Raan said. 'They're strictly rationed. Everyone knows that.'

'What about the Barnacle sites?' Salomé asked.

Hassan shook his head, 'They're guarded by Federation and Imperial warships, everyone wants them. There is no way anyone could sneak past those.'

Bill nodded.

'But you have a way?' Salomé asked, looking at him.

Bill straightened. 'Yes, one of the reasons I need your help. A heist.'

Tsu's eyes narrowed as she thought it through. 'There's only one place in the galaxy with a guaranteed supply of meta-alloys. Darnielle's Progress ...'

Bill nodded. 'You got it.'

'Getting in there will be easy,' Tsu said. 'But they won't sell in bulk as Raan pointed out ...'

'There are ways around that problem,' Hassan said with a grin.

'Oh yes?' Tsu demanded. Hassan's grin remained in place, but he offered no further explanation.

'Getting out again is the trick,' Bill said. 'And we can't come back here either, too obvious. But I have another installation, out in the HIP 16497 system. It will serve.'

'But thieving meta-alloys. If only this wake concealer was working ...' Raan said.

Hassan looked at Salomé. 'We know someone who can get us out of there incognito.'

Salomé shook her head. 'No. That's not an option.'

Raan, Tsu and Bill looked at them both.

'Who?' Bill demanded.

Hassan grinned. 'A friend of hers. A wily old trader by the name of Luko. Let's say he knows his way around. Only ...'

'What?' Tsu asked.

'They had words,' Hassan said, softly.

Bill grinned at her. 'Then, dear Imperial Lady, you are going to have to eat humble pie, beg, grovel and apologise.'

Salomé glared at him.

Bill leant back against the defunct hyperdrive mechanism, unconcerned. 'And given you're an Imperial girl, that will be fun to watch.'

***

Raan checked his messages, there were dozens of them, each more insistent than the last. Most he ignored, but there was one he needed, so he dug it out.

Yes, he's online!

Raan initiated the call, ensuring the crypto was on at its maximum setting.

'Raan!' came the surprised voice at the other end. 'Where the hell have you ... where are you? You're calling me crypto. I've been trying to reach you for days after all that stuff broke out in Chi Orionis ... your name is everywhere, they're saying you're a criminal!'

'I'm ok ...' Raan replied. 'Got to keep this short. Just listen, you know you wanted to do something significant?'

'Er ... yeah?' Yuri's voice was excited and nervous all at once.

'Time may be soon my friend, time may be soon. We're going to need pilots and you're on my list.'

'To do what?'

'The fight of your life, buddy. You up for that?'

'Hell yes!'

'Won't be a milk run. This could get proper serious, I'm talking life and death. Not kidding.'

'I'm still in.'

'Gotta go. Keep online as often as you can. I may not be able to give much notice.'

'Copy that … you sure you're ok? Are you really mixed up in …'

'Dude, you wouldn't believe me even if I could tell you, but this is important stuff. Seriously … speak soon.'

Raan cancelled the call.

Chapter Twenty-Four
3303 AD
En route to Maia system, Aries dark region, Uninhabited

The bridge of the Federal Corvette *Dauntless* never failed to impress upon entry. The ship was not one for the shy or retiring commander. Unashamedly a military vessel, even in its basic configuration, it could be built into a veritable warship that even local militias or smaller governments would hesitate to take on.

Commander David Paul 'DP' Sayre couldn't help but feel a flush of pride every time his mag-boots clamped onto the decking. He didn't let it show in his face, that wouldn't have been the correct decorum, but he allowed himself a flash of pride. He figured he deserved it.

It had taken years to acquire the ship, and longer to upgrade it into the premier fighting machine it had now become. A brief glance over the status consoles would have drawn admiring glances from any spacer who knew their ships.

Its internal componentry had been fully fitted, A-class throughout, at not insignificant expense. It was fair to say that billions of credits had been lavished on the outfitting, but that was only the start. A tactical relationship with the Empire in the service of Princess Aisling Duval had provided access to prismatic shield technology, along with engineered triple regenerative beam lasers. The main weaponry consisted of heavy duty multi-cannons and a few other surprises not directly obvious from the hull hatches. DP had taken the ship to many of the Engineers, upgrading componentry far beyond its original design specs.

The result was a ship that had never, not once, been disabled in combat.

The *Dauntless* was a war machine, plain and simple. Its only limitation was a shorter than average jump radius; a reasonable trade-off against the sheer power of the ship.

Professor Palin's engineering outfit was the last on the list, the only remaining way for DP to squeeze a little more devastation out of the vessel. A few more percentage points. Palin's base was in the Maia star system, part of the Pleiades star cluster, some four hundred and fifty light years from the core worlds. It was a long trip for the *Dauntless*, marked only by a few bounty hunters who quickly learnt that taking on a massively engineered Corvette was a fool's errand.

The fights were short, brutal ... and meaningful.

He'd long since forgotten the last time he'd come across an adversary that put his ship to the test.

DP allowed himself a small grin on his otherwise grizzled features.

I like it that way, but a challenge might be refreshing once in a while ...

The galactic holofac chart glowed in the centre of the bridge. He studied it for a long moment.

Sure is a long haul.

The *Dauntless* was traversing the Aries Dark Region before entering the vicinity of the Pleiades Nebula itself. Space here was unremarkable for the most part, just slightly heavier in dust particles than anywhere immediately close by, dimming the starlight, giving the region its name.

He toggled the food dispenser, requesting an Opala Beer. Moments later it was in a 'squeeze' pack in his hand. Carbonated drinks didn't mix well with zero-gee. He took a long pull from it and settled himself down into the pilot's command chair at the very centre of the expansive bridge.

System automation ran the vessel for the most part, but he enjoyed the experience of flying the vessel directly. It was not an agile fighter, but with its onboard weaponry and system sophistication, anything that got within a firing arc soon found its existence to be short lived.

But the scanners were blank. There was nothing of interest, just the faint humming of the frame shift drive as it pushed the vessel away from the local star. Refuelling was complete, there was no reason to hang around further.

'Commence jump,' he instructed, taking another pull on the beer.

'Frame shift drive, charging,' the computer intoned. The hum grew to a crescendo, there was a faint surge of acceleration, and then the ship was in that other realm.

Witch-space ...

He'd often wondered about the lights during the hyperspace transit. Some held they were stars, but that was nonsense, there were too many, and they flashed past too quickly. There were other shapes too, nebulae? Same objection. Sometimes he could swear he saw faces in the strange patterns.

That's just a warning you've been out in the void too long ...

His senses were attuned to his ship. Countless voyages in the dark tended to do that to a commander. DP felt something wasn't right with the transit before the computer flashed up a diagnostic. A rumbling echo that vibrated through the decking.

'What the …?'

Warning! Hyperspace conduit unstable!

He stared at the diagnostic readout in surprise. He'd never seen such an error before, never even heard of a pilot suffering such a failure …

He was jolted in his seat, the *Dauntless* creaking and groaning around him. Nausea took him, his senses confused by the unexpected pitch and roll. He grabbed the control yokes instinctively, but there was no response. The *Dauntless* was impotent, lit only by the eerie glow of witch-space. The illumination flashed in tandem with the erratic rotation, sparks of light spinning around the interior of the bridge.

The strain of systems being pushed beyond their designs echoed through the hull, a rending mechanical sound of distress. He could almost feel the pressures mashing against his ship. A lesser vessel might have broken up under the strain.

Before him, the familiar muted hues of hyperspace transformed into a whirling maelstrom of angry blazes of light, rolling and pitching about him. The holofac HUD indicators flickered, their displays showing meaningless data.

'… the hell is going on!'

With a shocking surge, the hyperspace transit collapsed, the *Dauntless* splashing back into real space. DP felt the flight harness cut into his shoulders as he was thrown forward.

Just as well I always buckle up …

The *Dauntless* steadied, but as he tried to reorient the ship the power plant hum crackled and failed, the holofac emitters flickered and died.

Frame shift drive malfunction!

'DP Sayre to Ryder's Rangers, come in. Uh, guys? I've just been pulled out of witch-space …'

There was brief crackle on the comms, a chuckle.

'Yeah right …'

Static buzzed for a moment and the comms faded out.

Then the internal illumination, with a final brief gasp of power, failed completely. There was nothing but the faint glow of distant stars and the milky band of the galaxy bisecting the forward canopy.

'System reboot,' DP said, ruthlessly squashing the tides of panic he felt rising inside.

Just a systems malfunction, probably overdue for some maintenance ... even if the module health shows 100% ...

The onboard automation didn't respond. No power, no scanners, no holofac. Nothing. Dead in space!

He prodded the controls, looking around the bridge.

Nothing? But the backup systems should have kicked in by now, multiple redundant power systems across the board, all tested, all designed for exactly this scenario ...

Then there was something else.

DP had seen the scanner trace before it had gone offline. Nothing present in the system.

The *Dauntless* rocked gently, as if it had crossed the wake of another ship. He looked up, to the sides and around.

The faintest of vibrations buzzed through the deck. He'd experienced something like it once before, when he'd flown a ship through the exhaust flux of a capital vessel during an attack back in the Empire.

But out here ...

A shadow eclipsed the stars above him. He looked up.

His hands fell limply away from the controls. The shadow grew, an irregular line of darkness blocking out the distant light.

Whatever it was, it was turning, rotating, pulsing. He tried to assimilate what he was seeing. A massive, slowly spinning pinwheel, grey-green, flecked with trails of red, moving slowly away from the *Dauntless*, like an impossible space-borne flower.

Its size was impossible to estimate. DP had no range information, but he got the impression it was considerably bigger than his own ship. His mind ran through possibilities automatically, quickly discarding each one in favour of the next until he was left with only the most outlandish of conclusions.

Not human ...

It was turning, altering its course.

It's coming about!

Adrenaline flushed through him, DP pulled at the controls, jabbing buttons in a frenzy, trying to elicit any response from his beleaguered ship, but it was to no avail. The *Dauntless* was stricken, helpless in the face of the unknown intruder. His mighty ship brought low without even a shot being fired. He couldn't even record a log.

The alien vessel gracefully completed a turn. He studied it harder, trying to get a measure of it. Green lights pulsed and flickered on the extremities of its 'petals.' He counted them.

Eight …

He felt his stomach twist.

Eight-sided alien ships ripping people out of witch-space …

Every spacer knew the legends. They were the butt of many jokes, many wild stories, told and retold in a million bars across a thousand worlds. But no one truly believed them, no one really took them seriously.

Can't be …

The ship had completed its turn and was now moving towards him at a measured pace. Streams of red material wove and drifted away from it. The output of its motive power perhaps, or something else, it was impossible to say.

The green lights pulsed, brightening, accompanied by a deathly groaning wail that shuddered through the *Dauntless*, setting DP's teeth on edge. He was grateful for his knuckle-white grip on the deadened flight controls, they were stopping him from shaking too much.

His mind was numb with fear now, but he had enough presence of mind to wonder whether it was some form of communication, a message, a warning, a preamble to conversation, an overture to weapons being unleashed …

But I have no way to respond!

The alien vessel seemed to twitch, visibly distorting to his eyes, waves of something seemed to pass before it, as if he was looking at it through running water. The whole vessel seemed to be animated, each part moving or articulated in some way, as if …

Organic …

He was just pondering this when it struck.

Fierce yellow light flickered, tendrils of energy writhed out of the darkness, crashing against the ship's hull. A strange rending grind echoed around him. DP was thrown forward in his restraints as the *Dauntless* careened backwards, locked in some kind of energy from the intruder. Vibrations made it difficult to see, but it seemed as if the ship was travelling at supercruise speeds.

He gritted his teeth through the disorientation, trying to take in any details. His heart pounded in his chest.

DP fully expected the ship to come apart around him within moments, but before he had a chance to think about resisting, the light was snatched off and both he and the alien vessel hung motionless against the starry backdrop once more.

Somehow the silence was worse than the noise and confusion.

The alien seemed to contract, more of the strange interference rippling over its features. There was a central orb, a cockpit …

Or an eye? First contact … what I do here might set the tone for …

The alien ship moved aside, swiftly turning and sweeping past the canopy. There was a rough jolt as the *Dauntless* nudged against something, but it wasn't the alien itself. The *Dauntless* yawed slowly around, still powerless. DP craned his neck to watch as the alien retreated, accelerating at an unprecedented rate for something so huge.

A rising hum signalled the return of power, holofac emitters flickered back into life unsteadily. The computer came online, and greeted him a few moments later.

Auto stabilisation in progress. System reboot initiated.

The thrusters!

He grabbed the controls and the *Dauntless* belatedly came about, seemingly no worse the wear for the strange encounter.

Shields, weapons, systems a-ok …

The alien vessel was already some distance away. DP squinted, it looked as if it were spinning rapidly. As he watched a faint green glow expanded around the receding ship.

He tried to focus the scanners on it, only then thinking of pursuit and pushing the throttles up to give chase.

Then, with a flash, the alien ship was gone.

DP realised he'd been holding his breath and let it out with a gasp, struggling to breathe for long moments. His pulse was way over safe limits, he could hear blood surging in his ears, a thumping rhythm echoed in his chest.

It was a while before he could pull his grip off the flight controls. He had to make a mental effort to get his fingers to release their claw-like hold.

He looked at the scanner information. It had completed its analysis. But the computer had little to tell him that he didn't already know.

Unknown Wake.

He sat for long minutes, waiting for the adrenaline to purge from his system. He didn't trust himself to fly the ship. He looked out across the distant vista of space. Somewhere out there were the core worlds, the little bubble of space humanity called home.

'These aliens, we don't know anything about them,' he said to himself, not really knowing where the words were coming from. 'We're up shit creek without a paddle. We're going to have to stop beating ourselves up over petty, little things ... really come together ... focus as a human race to deal with this. Or we're dead.'

Schnieder Colony, Liaedin system, Independent

'An extraordinary meeting,' Infrastructure said. 'Apologies for the lack of due process, but we all were aware this moment was coming and now it is upon us.'

'Overdue, if anything,' Exo replied. 'Which begs its own question, why the delay?'

'We have benefitted from the additional time,' Finance said. 'With explorers and commentators tied up with archaeological ruins and mysteries in the depths of space, far fewer ships were in that particular vicinity.'

'That won't last long,' Exo said. 'You know what they're like, they'll swarm in that direction in days.'

'It's already occurring,' Society confirmed. 'Crackpots, independents, various minor factions all see this as a way to gain advantage, whether financial or otherwise. Since there is no way to predict where these encounters will take place, there's no way to police the outcome.'

'Have we gained any new information that we were not aware of?' Personnel asked.

'Very little,' Infrastructure replied. 'Size, capability and intention match very closely all previous records. Current activity is consistent with reconnaissance.'

Exo nodded. 'We can confirm that the current sightings match with scout ship configurations encountered before.'

'The vanguard approaches,' Personnel said, softly.

'What little we can detect of it,' Exo said.

'Our communications plan?' Infrastructure prompted.

'To be implemented shortly,' Society said. 'We have ensured that various news outlets are briefed with the appropriate material and our illustrious leaders are currently putting together statements on the event for public disclosure.'

'Suitably vague, one assumes,' Exo said.

Society nodded. 'We will throw doubt upon their extraterrestrial origin, roll out the clichés of being prepared and talk about the need for further study, so on and so forth. It will quickly degenerate into a slanging match between the Empire and the Federation, with the Alliance appearing to take a high-minded stance.'

'The same as ever then …' Infrastructure beamed.

'What of the independent pilots actively trying to start conflicts by firing on them?' Personnel demanded.

Exo appeared relaxed. 'Based upon our visitors' previous modus operandi, they will either be ignored or destroyed. They will remember that we do not operate as a unified presence and discount individual behaviour …'

Finance chuckled. 'Of course, those who are destroyed won't report back.'

'Excellent. The exploration data?'

'Likewise,' Exo replied. 'Whilst embarrassing for the Federation, the overwhelming support of the mission by the collection of minor factions rallying to the Children of Raxxla banner has played to our requirements precisely. Almost all the Dynasty expedition material has been recovered and the explorers remain completely unaware they have been manipulated into retrieving it. Quite a coup for us, I would say.'

'Masterfully arranged,' Infrastructure added.

'We were quite delighted,' Exo said. 'What with that and the revelations about the Guardian sites we have kept them all successfully occupied.'

'Is our insurance in place?' Society asked.

Personnel nodded. 'Yes, it is.'

Arcanonn Headquarters, Thompson Dock, Varati, Independent

Dr. Arcanonn was reviewing the footage of the alien vessel. He watched it over and over again on a repeating loop, allowing his subconscious to process the images without his thoughts getting in the way. It was a technique he used to analyse events – not forcing it, but allowing his mind the time to spot the incongruities and the inconsistencies. It wasn't a foolproof method, but it had often allowed him to identify the frauds and the fakes.

But not here.

The alien ship seemed compelling, authentic. It had already been subject to intense forensic examination by his own teams and they had revealed nothing that shed any doubt on it whatsoever.

The holofac newsfeed was displaying messages from the worthies across the core worlds. They were typically irrelevant and ambiguous, neither confirming nor denying anything.

So they don't really know either, or they're not prepared to say …

He rubbed his chin.

Probes, artefacts, transmissions, scans, Barnacles … and now this …

He looked at the deployment of his teams, most still occupied with the enduring mystery of the Guardian ruins. Some progress had been made there, but it was slow and painstaking work.

And those ruins are older than anything humanity has left on Earth …

He sighed, placing his head in both his hands as he thought it through.

We've been deliberately diverted away from this. Teased aside … Yes, the Guardians are important archaeologically … but this … this is happening now …

If the alien ships were truly alien …

Someone has been keeping us occupied! Until now … until the secret was out … but who? And why?

Chapter Twenty-Five

Alioth 4a, Alioth system, Alliance

Two ships lifted off from the engineering base. One a multi-purpose Imperial Clipper bearing the name plate *Seven Veils*, the other a titanium grey Viper Mark IV with the tag of *StarStormer*. Both accelerated quickly upwards before disappearing into the darkness.

'Course set,' Tsu's voice crackled across the comms. 'I have your wing beacon. I'll follow your lead.'

'We've got the course to HIP 16497 plotted,' Hassan replied, checking the controls on the *Seven Veils*. 'Here it is.'

'Received,' Tsu said.

Hassan could see her ship on the scanner, marked by a blue square. Her holofac image was showing in a vid feed, with Raan sitting in the Viper's second seat.

'Ready for jump,' Hassan said, looking around at Salomé and Bill in the rear. 'Here goes nothing.'

Frame shift drive charging ...

'It's a fair way out there,' Bill said, from behind the pilot's chair, holding himself in place by bracing against the bulkhead. 'But we should make it in half a day.'

'Getting in is easy,' Hassan said. 'And I can reprogramme the automechs to bypass the restriction on cargo quantities for the meta-alloys, but getting out again ...'

'That's where you come in,' Bill said, turning to Salomé.

She was sitting, looking rather forlorn, in the portside seat of the Clipper's bridge. She looked upon hearing her name and took a deep breath.

'Yes, I must make arrangements.'

The *Seven Veils* flashed into hyperspace, the strange lights of witchspace casting coloured patterns across her face. She undid the flight harness and stood up, looking out at the spiralling vista for a few moments before turning on her heel and walking off the bridge.

'Is she going to be able to convince this guy to help us?' Bill asked.

Hassan smiled. 'If she can't, no one can.'

***

Salomé paused in her quarters, taking several deep breaths.

What am I going to say?

She activated the holofac transceiver and typed in a code, her fingers poised for a moment over the transmit toggle, before she tapped it decisively.

The holofac display indicated it was attempting to make a connection, and then the image of a man appeared.

He looked around at the display and frowned in recognition.

'Signorina, a pleasure always.' His voice was the same strange broken accent she was familiar with.

'Are you sure?' Salomé replied. 'I was a little … short with you last time we spoke.'

'I am used to your ways now. You would call me, this I knew.'

'Are you going to make me apologise?'

Luko rubbed his chin in an exaggerated fashion.

'Yes, I think so.' He looked at her. 'Yes.'

Salomé sighed.

'Is it such a hard thing for one such as you?' His expression was serious now.

'I am … not familiar with it.'

'Then some practice you need, signorina.'

Salomé glared at him, but he simply folded his arms and waited.

'I … I regret what I said before,' Salomé began. 'It was a shock. I was … I couldn't take it all in. I didn't mean to offend you.'

Luko regarded her, but didn't speak.

'I'm sorry for what I did,' Salomé said, her voice faltering.

Still Luko did not move.

Salomé's anger flared.

'All right then! I'll beg. I want you to be my friend again! Is that good enough for you? Please, Luko! I'm sorry, I said hurtful things and I didn't mean it. You truly were looking out for me and I threw it all back in your …'

'Peace, signorina,' Luko said, with a smile.

She glared at him.

'You enjoyed that, didn't you?' she demanded.

He shook his head, an expression of mock surprise on his face. It was quickly replaced by a grin and a nod.

'Molto. The great Imperial, Lady Kahina, grovels before me, just a humble trader …'

'You are not just a humble trader.'

'Hmmm, perhaps no.' He grew serious. 'Salomé, I was telling the truth when last we spoke. I would have told you before, but …'

'She wouldn't let you,' Salomé finished. 'Not until …'

'She passed away,' Luko finished. 'My job, protect you, this is true. Protect you from knowledge, too.' He looked up at her, his image flickering for a moment. 'Is still true, yes?'

Salomé nodded. 'I need your help, your expertise.'

He turned his head to one side, but his gaze was still locked upon her. 'Will you do as she wished?'

Salomé nodded. 'I will solve this mystery. That is why I'm calling you. Long story, but we need a shipment of meta-alloys, a decent quantity, but …'

'They are not sold in bulk. You plan a heist. Illegal, eh?'

'I like to think of it as just circumventing trading restrictions,' Salomé answered. 'We can get in easily enough and Hassan knows how to repro-gramme the automechs without being discovered. Getting out …'

'Requires tact and discretion,' Luko finished for her. 'This I do best.'

'And I need the best,' Salomé said, her voice soft. 'Will you help me, trader Luko?'

Luko grinned. 'I can never resist a lady in distress, signorina. I will always defend you.'

Salomé nodded her thanks.

'We're en route to HIP 16497 now, can you meet us there?'

Luko looked aside for a moment.

'Yes. Darnielle's Progress is not far from there. But I think only one ship to go. The *Bella Principessa* will arouse less suspicion.'

Salomé nodded. 'It will be good to see you again.'

'Likewise, signorina.'

She smiled. 'Thanks Luko. I mean it.'

Luko nodded and the transmission faded out.

Salomé found tears in her eyes and wiped them aside. She wasn't sure if they were happiness or relief, or a mixture of both.

***

The glorious arc of Barnard's Loop wasn't truly visible to the naked eye, but its majesty was revealed by the enhanced vision provided by the cockpit canopy. The constellation of Orion was quite distorted now, but still recognisable to seasoned space travellers.

HIP 16497 was a hot white A-type star, burning through its supply of hydrogen at a far faster rate than the dim red dwarfs that surrounded it, or even the brighter yellow stars so familiar to humanity. Its light was of a hotter hue, sharp, harsh and unforgiving.

A dark spot was moving swiftly across its surface. At first glance an observer could be forgiven for taking it as a starspot, a wrenching twist of powerful magnetic fields bigger than many planets, but the star was otherwise devoid of blemishes. Yet this spot remained.

Closer examination would have revealed it was slightly irregular in shape, slowly rotating end over end. Not a spot, but an object cast in silhouette by the fierce fusion glow.

The doors at the rear of the bridge slid open. Hassan turned to see Salomé walk in. He could see her eyes were puffy, but as usual, her face revealed little of what she was thinking.

'So …'

'He's coming,' Salomé answered. 'He will meet us here.' She changed the subject. 'Where is here, by the way? And where's Bill?'

'He's below decks,' Hassan answered. 'And according to the navcom his base is just ahead. Transmit the code, let's see if it opens up.'

Salomé touched the controls for the comms system and they listened as a curious warble filled the cockpit, ending in a high-pitched tone.

After a pause, a voice answered out of the darkness. It was metallic and monotone, clearly an automated system.

'Gutamaya Hotel Alpha Sierra. Docking clearance is granted. Proceed to pad zero-eight at your discretion.'

Hassan adjusted course and decided on a curved intercept, bringing the object away from the glare of the star so they could get a better view of it.

'An asteroid,' Hassan said, squinting against the light of the star. 'Has he got some kind of surface installation on it?'

Salomé was examining the sensor readouts, having locked the computer on.

'I think the asteroid is the base, look.'

Hassan could now see a series of lights, aerials, transmission arrays alongside a gaping entrance way. It had been dark moments before, shrouded in the shadowed side of the enormous rock. Now it was illuminated.

'It's hollow,' Hassan whispered.

Salomé nodded. 'Our friend isn't short of credits, is he?'

'No kidding.'

Their Clipper was dwarfed by the sheer enormity of the asteroid as they approached. Hassan expertly rotated the ship and they passed the entrance, noticing that the external illumination quickly faded once they were inside. Clearly it was set not to draw any unnecessary attention to itself. Behind them, Tsu's Viper followed them in, having also received clearance.

Inside the base, the surface was superficially much the same as the interior of the familiar Coriolis stations. Only here, between the pads made available for arriving ships, solid rock walls were the main features, laboriously carved out from the interior of the asteroid by vast industrial machines. Some were still at work at the rear of the cavern. They could see sparks flying beyond a series of precarious-looking gantries that formed a fragile barrier at the far end. Below them, most of the pads seemed to either be under construction themselves, or playing host to the carcases of old and partially dismantled spacecraft.

'Looks like another graveyard,' Hassan said, looking about him. 'What's with all these derelict ships, anyway?'

'I have no idea,' Salomé answered. 'Set us down, and don't let anything start taking my ship apart!'

The Clipper landed gently on the pad, surrounded by the haphazard collection of materials and ship parts.

By the time they had made their way back to the exit ramp in the low gravity, Bill was already waiting for them. Beyond, they could see Tsu's Viper making its descent to an adjacent pad.

'Welcome to the *Versteck*,' Bill said. 'My home from home.'

'It's a junkyard,' Hassan said, looking about him.'

'Spare storage area,' Bill said. 'I can't keep everything on Alioth. Here's where I keep some of the more interesting bits, or anything I am working on as a long-term project. Hardly anyone comes out this far and it provides a certain degree of anonymity. Follow me, there's plenty of food and drink available.' He looked at Salomé. 'Is your man on his way?'

Salomé nodded. 'He is, yes.'

'Then we have a raid to plan. Let's get busy.'

Chapter Twenty-Six

Location unknown, HIP 16497 system, Uninhabited

'It is going to be cramped, we must … make do, best we can.'

It was two hours later. Salomé's friend, Luko, had just arrived. His ship the *Bella Principessa* looked tiny and insignificant in the vastness of the asteroid cavern. And now Tsu found herself crammed into its compact bridge, along with Salomé, Raan, Bill and Hassan.

'Wow,' Bill said, a note of admiration in his voice. 'I haven't seen anything like this in years.'

Luko was clearly proud of his ship.

'A Campaign model from 3120. Very few original Cowell and MgRath Cobras still flying. This one? The best left for sure.'

Tsu looked around the interior of the Cobra's bridge, chatting inconsequentially with the enigmatic trader. The ship looked very strange to her, ancient and unfamiliar. There was nothing that she recognised at all. The instruments were vintage. There were no holofac displays, the vitals of the ship being monitored by physical gauges, dials, controls and flat-screened information panels.

Belongs in a museum. I can't believe we're going to use this!

It was in good condition, she had to give credit there. Everything was burnished metal, chrome, brass and … could it be … real leather?

'Gentlemen?' Salomé asked, with just the right amount of impatience. Tsu smiled and Raan laughed.

'Ah yes, time to talk later, perhaps,' Luko said, looking around. 'Speed is of the essence. Cargo bay is fitted for maximum capacity.'

'And what about us?' Tsu asked. 'There are no passenger cabins …'

Luko smiled and winked at her. 'Ah, old school ship, old school solutions. Come.'

He led the group through the doors of the bridge into a connecting space above the cargo bay. It was narrow between the panels of equipment, but it opened out into an area that must have been just above the engines. There were a series of horizontal lockers in the bulkhead. Luko pressed his hand against one and it slid smoothly out.

It was a small bed, almost cocoon-like, filled with an aquamarine gel of some kind.

'What is this?' Tsu demanded.

'Well, well,' Bill said, pushing past and looking closely. 'Silastoplaston acceleration couch. I haven't seen one of these for a few years. Does it still work?'

Luko nodded.

'You got the Stardreamer tech, too?'

Luko nodded again. Bill laughed. 'Awesome.'

Raan looked at Tsu. 'Same question as her, please.'

'This is how long duration travel was done back in the day,' Hassan said from behind them. 'You strap yourself in, lie back and enjoy the trip.'

'In there?' Tsu said, recoiling. 'No way.'

'It's perfectly safe,' Hassan said.

'It might have been back then,' Tsu retorted. 'How old is this stuff? Did you say 3120? That's near as damn it two hundred years ago!'

Luko shook his head. 'This is much newer, signorina. Not so old.'

'Oh, ok.' Tsu said. She felt suspicious, Luko's answer was too quick and easy. 'How old is not so old?'

Luko shrugged and raised his hands. 'Fifty years, maybe a hundred.'

Tsu swallowed. 'A hundred …'

'Time is pressing,' Salomé interrupted. 'If Luko says it will work, it will work. Or you can stay behind. Make your choice.'

No way!

'I'm not letting any of you out of my sight,' Tsu glared at Salomé.

'Then get in the couch,' Salomé replied, her gaze equally stern. 'We're leaving now.'

Tsu thought about replying but only watched as Salomé jumped up and pulled herself into position on the nearest couch. She lay back, allowing the gel to ease up around her. Luko stepped forward and placed a clip around her forehead and put a mouthpiece across her face.

'Relax, signorina.'

Faint lights on the clip flickered on and off. Salomé's expression became dreamy, her eyes rolled up in her head and her body went slack. The gel smothered her. As Tsu watched, Luko checked a few readouts and then pushed the couch back into the bulkhead.

'Who is next?'

Darnielle's Progress, Maia system, Pleaides sector

Darnielle's Progress was an average starport. Much of it was underground, hewn out of the solid rock of the planet it was built upon. Trading vessels came and went regularly, many often coming in for repair work. Outposts were scarce in this part of the galaxy, and there were plenty of pirates and anarchists preying on unsuspecting ships.

A small wedge-shaped vessel was making its approach to the starport, slotting into place in the traffic queues and awaiting clearance. One of the smaller pads illuminated in readiness and the ship made its way towards it.

'Easy does it,' Hassan said, watching the approaching base from the *Bella Principessa's* cockpit canopy. He gripped his flight chair. The Cobra was coming in quickly and rotating around all three axes as it did so. 'Flight assist …'

Luko tutted and shook his head. 'No computers, not for real pilots. Flight assist? Drive assist? Rotational correction? Pah!'

The Cobra yawed, slowed and came to a halt on the landing pad with a barely perceptible jolt.

The local SysCon's voice crackled over the commlink.

'Docking complete. Engines disengaged. Damn, Commander! That was the best piece of flying I've seen in years.'

'Show off,' Hassan said.

Luko had a look of mock indignation on his face, then it cracked into a smile. 'Maybe a little.'

The ship was lowered into the hangar below and came to a halt after being shuffled into a vacant storage slot. The hum of the engines faded away as they unbuckled themselves from the pilots' chairs. The gravity was faint but welcome, lending a little more stability to their movements as they made their way aft.

'Let's get our friends out,' Hassan said. 'My grandfather always said Stardreamer made him puke.'

Luko nodded and set about securing the ship. Hassan made his way aft to the midsection and opened the Stardreamer couches.

***

Six figures stood in the docking bay of the Cobra, watching as the ramp was lowered.

Tsu, Salomé and Raan had a distinctly grey tinge to their pallors. Bill seemed unaffected.

'I am not doing that again,' Tsu said, grasping at the cargo ramp's hydraulic strut to steady herself. 'That was ghastly. It was like spinning through a sped up recording of spaceflight.'

'You're supposed to keep your eyes closed,' Bill said. 'Not look at the monitor.'

'Now you tell me.'

'The plan?' Salomé asked.

'Refuelling first,' Luko said. 'Then ready to go if needs be. Credits for the meta-alloys next. Best you all stay inside, mustn't be spotted.'

They nodded in agreement. Every experienced spacer had the same routine. *Always be ready to run; fuel, repair, cargo … in that order.*

Salomé, Raan and Tsu retreated away from the ramp.

'You can only requisition a tonne of meta-alloys,' Bill said. 'How you getting around that …'

'This is a problem,' Luko acknowledged.

'And?' Bill asked.

'Watch and learn,' Hassan said as one of the wheeled automechs emerged from the side of the hangar, a cargo canister clenched in its articulated manipulators.

The three men stepped out of the way as the automech trundled up the ramp, securing the cargo canister in place within the *Bella Principessa's* hold. Hassan pulled a device out of his pocket as the automech began to retreat.

'What is that?' Bill asked.

'Cargo 'crypter,' Hassan said, pointing at the canister. 'Cost me a fortune, but it has its uses.'

The device buzzed and then Hassan called out to the automech.

'Hey, you've delivered the wrong cargo!'

The automech paused, turned on its wheels and returned.

'Delivered cargo canister ID BP1-MA1 as requested,' the automech said tonelessly.

Hassan shook his head. 'You made a mistake, check it.'

The automech moved back to the canister.

'This is cargo canister ID BP1-FS13,' the automech replied. 'Apologies for the error. It will be removed immediately.'

'Don't bother,' Hassan replied. 'I'll take this too, put it on the account. Just hurry up with the requisition please.'

The automech reversed, rotated and made its way off.

Bill chuckled. 'I like it.'

'Automechs are dumb,' Hassan said. 'I learnt this trick from the Trader's Guild out near Ferenchia. The stupid thing will debit the other inventories based on the code I input. It will look like we filled up the ship with a mix of stuff. Don't know why they don't give them a bit of intelligence ...'

'There's a lot of history on AI getting a little ahead of itself,' Bill said, rubbing his chin. 'Some of the advanced sentient stuff caused a lot of trouble years ago. Nasty business, very nasty indeed. The law keeps it pretty simple nowadays.'

'What happened?'

'Story for another time,' Bill said. 'Look, here it comes again.'

The automech trundled up the boarding ramp and deposited a second cargo canister. Hassan went through the process again and, oblivious, the automech unit trundled off, none the wiser.

'So we still only buy one tonne of meta-alloys,' Luko said, with a grin. 'We're not lying.'

Hassan nodded. 'We just get it delivered over and over again!'

***

One of the station supervisors frowned at his instruments.

The Cobra on pad zero-four had caught his attention. It was an older ship, properly old in fact, pretty much a museum piece as these things went. That was the first odd thing.

The second was that, for short moments, there was a group of three people hanging around at the exit ramp. He zoomed in the security camera. They all looked fairly ordinary. As he watched, one of the men retreated inside the ship.

The third strange thing was the odd way they were loading cargo. They seemed to be buying it one canister at a time.

He called up the purchase history and studied it for a moment. It was an odd collection of requisitions. Foodstuffs, textiles, industrial materials, machinery and medicines. Out of curiosity, he reviewed the known history of the vessel.

Bella Principessa.

It wasn't tagged as wanted anywhere, in fact the history was remarkably clean, with only a few minor docking violations to the record. The owner was listed as one Luciano Prestigio Giovanni. All checks and repairs were up to date.

Something didn't feel quite right. He called up a small recon drone and set it to take a surreptitious look at the ship.

***

Hassan had given the 'crypter to Luko and retreated within the *Bella Principessa,* making his way to the cockpit. He closed the door behind him, seating himself in the second pilot's chair. With a brief toggle of the comms system, he typed in a complex code, watching as a progress metre moved quickly up on the displays.

Communication established.

'Ah, my young friend.' The voice was rich and mellifluous. 'We are gratified to hear from you once again. You have a location for us?'

'Bill Turner has a hideout in the HIP 16497 system. An asteroid ...'

'We will find it. You are departing soon?'

'Yes, within the hour.'

'Then it won't be long before you have your reward,' the voice replied. 'Our mistress will be pleased, and as for the lady in question ... she will be yours.'

Hassan swallowed.

Best for me, best for her ...

***

The occupants of the ship were gratefully stretching their legs in the cargo bay whilst the automechs were at work. They watched as the canisters were slotted into place in the racks, their clamps securing the cargo, each in turn.

'Can't believe it's this easy,' Raan said.

'Too much faith in automation,' Tsu said. 'Everyone just trusts the machines and the readouts nowadays.'

Salomé remained quiet, watching the operation proceed canister by canister. Tsu busied herself with checking the inventory, holding up her own scanner and examining the canisters.

'What are you doing?' Salomé asked.

'Taking the opportunity to watch criminals at work,' Tsu answered. 'Might not get the chance again. What your friend is doing is illegal, and it's supposed to be impossible. I want to know how that 'crypter device of his works.'

Tsu raised the scanner a little higher and then frowned at the display. The scanner beeped and she turned around, clearly looking for something.

'What is it?' Raan demanded. He heard a faint buzz sound in his ears and saw something small retreat out of the cargo bay, moving outside the ship and disappearing. 'Was that ...'

Tsu swore and then ran to the cargo ramp.

'Hurry it up, they just sent a bug to scan us! I've jammed it, but no telling what they got!'

'Bug?' Salomé demanded.

'Tiny little flying camera,' Tsu said. 'Fed tech for surveillance. Somebody is taking an interest in what we're doing. They might identify us!'

Luko and Bill ran up the cargo ramp.

'We are ready,' Luko said. 'Time to go I think!'

'Back in the couches for us,' Raan said. Tsu pulled a face but caught the urgency of their situation and joined the others in a sprint for the confined space above the engines.

***

It appeared that the Cobra had finished its loading operation. The supervisor reviewed the purchases. There was still nothing odd about the detail. Thirty-four tonnes of requisitions, the last being a tonne of the meta-alloys that Darnielle's Progress had become famous for. There was nothing particularly unusual about it.

The drone he'd sent was reporting in. He toggled the view camera.

From the drone's perspective he could see two men now at the base of the ramp. They appeared to be watching the automech's loading procedure. That made little sense either, it was completely automated, they didn't have to do anything.

Let's see what's going on in here.

He directed the drone inside and the image of the Cobra's internal bulkheads appeared on the viewer. He saw nothing immediately out of place, just the expected racks of cargo stretching out within the Cobra's bay.

Three other people were standing by the internal hatch that led to the bridge area. Two of them were clearly women, the other a darker skinned man.

'Hello.'

He set the drone to record, making sure he got a detailed scan of the individuals in question.

As he did so, one of the women turned and directed some kind of device directly towards the drone's point of view. He saw her frown.

Spotted!

He typed the command for the drone to return to base. A moment later, the drone's camera failed, the image being replaced with static.

Definitely hiding something, but what …?

He checked the Cobra's loadout. It had a shielding system, a fuel scoop and a collection of discovery scanners listed on its manifest.

How are they transporting five or six people on that thing?

Thirty-four tonnes meant that the Cobra must have been full of cargo racks, the ship simply wasn't big enough to accommodate passenger cabins as well.

A glance at the camera feeds showed that the ship was preparing to leave. The cargo ramp was sealed and the hull illumination had been activated. As he watched, the ship was shuttled forward by the docking mechanisms, moved into place on the pad and then hefted upwards, ready to depart.

Got to have something concrete to stop them with …

He ran a check on the Cobra's inventory again, seeing nothing out of place. To cross check, he compared it with the station's own supply records. The computer systems came back with an unexpected answer.

'Error. Mismatch detected in inventory records. Excess inventory recorded.'

The supervisor gestured for more detail and the system dutifully responded.

'Excess inventory as follows: 1x Food Cartridges, 1x Clothing, 1x Ceramic Composites, 1x Atmospheric Processors, 1x Progenitor Cells …'

'Cancel,' he said, looking at the readout in confusion. 'When this did excess inventory appear?'

'Records indicate that excess inventory has been present within the last thirty minutes.'

The supervisor frowned. 'This doesn't make any sense. Is anything missing?'

The computer systems paused for a moment before responding.

'Thirty-three tonnes of meta-alloys are not present in assigned storage locations.'

'What?'

'Thirty-three tonnes ...'

'I heard you,' the supervisor snapped, quickly typing the codes for the port authority.

The comms system buzzed as he waited for the operation staff at the other end to respond.

'Flight operations.'

'There's a Cobra on pad zero-four,' the supervisor blurted. 'I think they're stealing cargo. Do not provide them with clearance.'

A rumble vibrated through the office. From the window the supervisor saw the bright blue exhaust flux of the Cobra as it lifted vertically off the pad. He saw the undercarriage retract and then the ship accelerated with a blast of red-tinged fire from its main engines, the roar loud enough to stop him hearing what the flight operator was trying to tell him.

'Tag that ship!' the supervisor yelled over the din. 'Bring it back!'

***

'Cowell and MgRath Lima Uniform Charlie, your clearance has been revoked. Please return to pad zero-four immediately and submit to inspection.'

Hassan looked over to Luko. 'I'm guessing they're on to us.'

'I think you right,' Luko replied.

'Just out of interest,' Hassan said. 'How are you going to evade them?'

Luko smiled. 'Now time you learn.'

On the *Bella Principessa's* scanner, several markers could be seen. Hassan didn't need to ID them to know they would be a mix of Vipers crewed by the local system authority pilots.

'Cowell and MgRath Lima Uniform Charlie, you are not cleared for departure. Return to pad zero-four immediately. Failure to comply will be met by lethal force.'

'Play hard around these parts,' Hassan mumbled.

'Frontier justice,' Luko agreed. 'Very severe.'

The *Bella Principessa* was roaring upwards. Hassan could see the HUD showing their angle at close to forty-five degrees, the ship gaining altitude, but also moving swiftly away from the base. The other ships were now a cluster of traces towards the rear.

Laser fire flickered around the cockpit and the threat warning indicators flickered on the dashboard.

'Missile lock ...' Hassan breathed. 'We can't trigger the frame shift with all that mass behind us!'

Luko seemed relaxed. Hassan saw his fingers touch an auxiliary control. 'Hang on,' he said.

A noise Hassan recognised as a heat sink dump swirled about the cockpit. At the same time, every instrument in the *Bella Principessa* went dark. The noise of the engines, the instruments, even the life support systems. It all went offline in a moment.

Hassan assumed they had been hit, but Luko did not react as the ship failed about him.

Without engines, the *Bella Principessa* began describing a ballistic trajectory. Hassan felt himself go weightless as the ship reached its maximum altitude and then began falling. He could see the ground below, growing closer with ever increasing speed.

We're going to pancake on the surface. There won't be a piece big enough to hold in two hands ...

Luko remained poised, one hand on the flight controls and another hovering over whatever it was he'd switched off.

Hassan pressed back in his chair as the ship plummeted downwards. He could see every crater, the rills running across the barren surface, free standing rocks with hard edges ...

'Luko ...!'

Luko's hand came down on the control. The *Bella Principessa* roared to life. Luko wrenched back and the ship rotated skywards, the ferocious roar of the engines at full boost thumping through the cockpit.

The altimeter was still counting down.

One hundred metres, fifty, twenty-five ... ten!

Dust surged past the windows.

'Ci abbiamo fatta!' Luko yelled. 'No catch me now!'

The ship nosed downwards until the landscape came back into view. The Cobra was running at maximum velocity, still only just above the surface.

The scanner was blank.

'You lost them,' Hassan gasped, his voice shaky. 'What the hell kind of move was that?'

Luko grinned. 'Kill switch.'

Location unknown, Formidine Rift, Uninhabited

The Formidine Rifters had no central authority, no real co-ordination. Some of them were members of minor factions such as the Children of Raxxla, others distrusted any authority or power and were lone wolves, exploring at their own behest. They had one thing in common, a willingness, or perhaps craziness was a better word, to go looking for secrets in the darkness.

Commander Joshua Hales had synched up with them via long range comms. He hadn't been the only one to stumble upon derelict outposts deep in the void. He suppressed a shudder as he remembered the voice he'd listened to from an expedition log from 3270.

We've sent a distress call, who knows if anyone will ever hear it ... Automated telemetry report: Power Failure ...

He looked down the list of names. Some were straightforward, others merely coded words that revealed little about the individual in question. These people were paranoid, and rightly so.

Commanders Raktavijan, Britain, Lyrae, Baton, Robbie, Tick, Sajime, Goliat, Eadghe and AvvieXB1 ... a long list ...

Joshua reviewed it. It was voice comms only, no one was risking anything more. Everyone seemed to be using vocal obfuscators too.

I don't trust them and they don't trust me.

No one had said anything, it looked like it was going to be up to him.

'I called this meeting to give us the opportunity to compare notes on what we've found,' Joshua began. 'We've been out in the dark for weeks. We all know the clues that led us here, the community mandate from the Federation and the call to compete from the Children of Raxxla. Together, we have found evidence of this strange mission more than thirty years ago.'

'The Dynasty mission,' Lyrae said. Joshua could tell it was a female voice, but that was all.

'Yes. Something sent out years ago, leaving these bases behind.'

It was as if a dam had been breached. Voices now competed to say their piece and add to the discussion.

'My people have done a search across all known data silos back in the core,' Tick volunteered. 'There is no record of any Dynasty expedition. Whatever this was, it was conducted in absolute secrecy.'

'Judging from the comms we've recovered,' Sajime said. 'It looks like the crews involved didn't return home ...'

'Some were lost in space,' Goliat interrupted. 'But some seem to have been successful in achieving their aims.'

'Yet no one has ever heard of them,' Eadghe said. 'This was a massive coordinated effort, it would have taken months to plan and prepare and yet nothing. A cover-up by the Feds, the Imps and the Alliance. They must have all been in on it.'

'Or some other force as yet unseen,' Britain said.

'One at a time please,' Joshua interjected. 'We have enough tinfoil already without adding more.' He hoped a little mirth might calm them and wouldn't be lost in the voice coding.

'All I'm saying is that we know none of the factions are being straight with us. There's way more to this than meets the eye,' Britain replied.

'And we still don't know what the hell they were trying to achieve out here, or even who bankrolled it,' Raktavijan said. 'So we have abandoned bases, clearly this was a long term investment. We have beacons, we have instructions about Earth-like worlds. Did they succeed, or did it all go wrong and they died out here? What was it for? What was the point of it all?'

'Three different and completely unrelated sectors of the galaxy,' Robbie agreed. 'Their locations on the map are virtually ninety degrees apart, thousands of light years between them, so far from the core worlds to be inaccessible to most. Why?'

'It has to be something to do with these alien encounters we're seeing in the Pleaides,' Baton said. 'The descriptions in the logs are too similar. Ships being ripped out of witch-space, unidentified ships, power losses. We're all thinking it, I'm just going to say it. Thargoids. Gotta be.'

'Thirty years ago,' Goliat said. 'Who's to say where they are now, what they're capable of ...'

'So, do we keep looking?' Lyrae asked. 'Or are we done? We found this stuff, how do we go about figuring out what it all means?'

'We need more clues,' Sajime said. Her sigh was obvious, even over dozens of light years. 'Maybe some of the Earth-like worlds will reveal something new ...'

One of the commanders had been silent up until now. A brief cough for attention sounded across the comms system. Joshua looked at the ID, it was showing the unlikely moniker of AvvieXB1.

'Listen up,' Joshua interrupted. 'Avvie has something to say ...'

'I may have pertinent information.' The voice was soft and heavily disguised. 'I was responsible for cataloguing the Delta settlement in the Formidine Rift. I have found one entry that I do not understand.'

There was a pause. No one spoke.

'Can you transmit it?' Joshua asked.

'I can,' Avvie replied. 'It's from the third mission log. Here it is.'

The comms crackled for a moment, before another voice spoke, clear and unchanged. It was a woman's voice, ordinary, rough, chatty and untutored. It sounded like just another crew member.

'Expedition log, September eighteenth, 3270. My job is the EVA. Taking out one of our two Sidewinders and dropping beacons out in the void and then making sure they're activated. Not sure what these things are for. Who needs a beacon this far out anyway? Weird, they all have this code in their BIOS – Exodus. Still, at least I now have something to do. The journey was so dull! Months of travel to get out here.'

The recording stopped with a brief crackle of static.

'Exodus,' Britain said. 'What does that mean?'

'Code word of some kind,' Baton replied. 'We know these beacons are in standby mode, maybe this activates them?'

'Tried transmitting the code word at them,' Avvie replied. 'There was no response.'

'I think it's something else,' Lyrae said. 'That's an old word, pre-spaceflight vintage stuff. It means something …'

'I've just looked it up,' Sajime replied. 'It's from an ancient old Earth language called Greek, whatever that is. It means …'

'What?' Half a dozen voices clamoured into the pause.

'Departure,' Sajime said slowly. 'Exit, leaving … a mass evacuation of people.'

For the first time since Joshua had opened the link, no one tried to speak. Only static crackled across the comms out in the darkness between stars.

Chapter Twenty-Seven

Location unknown, HIP 16497 system, Uninhabited

The *Bella Principessa* was once more safely docked in the relative safety of the Versteck asteroid base. Automechs had taken care of unloading the cargo of stolen meta-alloys and Bill had overseen the transfer of the material into the engineering deck below the main docking receptacles.

The other five were together in a refectory overlooking the docking area, with their ships visible below. Bill was overseeing the installation of the prototype wake suppressors into their ships after having satisfied himself with some preliminary tests. Before long, all of them would be ready to leave. Bill had arranged for Raan to take possession of a Fer-de-Lance heavy fighter in lieu of the crashed Eagle that Femi had given him.

'It's probably the best fighter in the void,' Bill had said before leaving to enter the engineering section. 'You'll need that kind of defence. The Clipper is all very well, but that Imperial girl has built it for speed, not offence – and I don't think a Cobra and a Viper will last long in a heavy furball. You'd better be as good as your Arena rep suggests. You're going to need to be.'

Raan had swallowed, but thanked him. Bill nodded and left. Raan rejoined the others.

'So,' Tsu said. 'We have the raw materials. Bill will provide the modifications to the hyperdrive system so we can sneak about with impunity, but we still don't know where we are going. You said you had the answer? So where is it?'

Raan watched as Salomé held out her hand. 'It's in here. Some kind of subcutaneous DNA trace.'

Tsu frowned. 'I've heard of them, but they're rare. Illegal in most places, difficult to detect.'

'I was given this bio-trace by …' Salomé looked at Luko. 'Well. About time you explained.'

Luko's smile was faint. 'I will tell what I know. It is not a short story.'

Raan took his cue from Tsu, who showed no surprise and simply waited. Hassan glanced at Salomé, who was looking unusually subdued.

'Looks like we have the time,' Hassan said.

'Centuries ago,' Luko began. 'A group of Elite combateers, they founded a group. They not happy with the politics of the galaxy, not happy with the Pilots' Federation, or the superpowers. They became their own faction, their own authority. They, how you say, make it their business to learn the mysteries of space. Learn secrets and keep them.

'Sometimes they were successful, sometimes not so much. They had power, molto power, built up over many many years. They knew more than any others about our history and our destiny, but they worked in the shadows, in hiding, subtle and hard to see. You could not join their movement, if they wanted you they found you.

'They became so powerful that they could influence the course of civilisation, a crisis here, a disaster there, an economic collapse. They not just watch history, they change its course. No one knows who they are, some must be powerful people in high positions, others would be a surprise to all. None are known for sure. Power is passed on – generation to generation, always in secret, always in hiding, always in the shadows. They operate out of sight, out of mind, beyond laws and jurisdiction.

'I do not know their aims, what they seek, or what they intend. All I know is that one of them contacted me.'

'One of them contacted you?' Tsu said, her face showing disbelief. 'Why you? You're just a ...'

'Simple trader,' Luko said. 'Ah yes, that is what I am.'

'If you believe that, you'll believe anything,' Salomé said. Luko spared her a look. Raan felt out of his depth and said nothing.

'I have ... travelled the galaxy for many years,' Luko went on. 'I have seen molto things. She was looking for someone with ... certain characteristics.'

'And who was she?'

Luko shrugged. 'She was old, but she was part of this mysterious group. They had called her too and she had served them for decades. But she had grown apart from them. She no longer believed they had the best interests of the galaxy as their core concern. They used people for their own ends, for money and for power. Humanity was their plaything, and they were keeping secrets, secrets that should be known.'

'Above and beyond,' Salomé said. 'A law unto themselves.'

'She worked in secret, still loyal to the group, so they thought. She played her part without suspicion or question. And then she found it, a conspiracy, great enough to signal the end of everything.'

Raan watched Tsu shake her head before saying. 'The end of everything? There's no way something of that magnitude could be kept secret from the populace. Any threat big enough to be that dangerous … you couldn't hide it. With all those pilots out in the void, secrets would be found, everything would be known.'

Luko chuckled. 'People go where they are led. These people can set a trail and we will walk it, we will not even realise.'

'You'll be telling me Raxxla is real next,' Tsu scoffed.

Luko shrugged. 'This I do not know, but I think it is more likely to be real than not. These people, they claimed to know …'

'Wait,' Raan couldn't hold back. 'Raxxla is a fairy story for children, what you're talking about is those crazy stories about the Dark Wheel …'

'Not the same.' Luko shook his head. 'Not the same at all. They need no names, no identification. They just are. As for Raxxla, what better way to hide it than make it out to be a myth? Only the crazy ones go looking …'

'And what is this conspiracy, then?' Tsu demanded. 'What is this big secret your contact is supposed to have uncovered? And why can't she just tell you, and tell us?'

'We don't know,' Salomé answered. 'I have been looking for over a year, and she went looking long before that.'

'And who is this mysterious *she*?' Tsu asked.

'I do not know her name,' Luko answered. 'Secrecy is too important.'

Tsu held up her hands in exasperation. 'Is this the best you have? Vague conspiracy theories and nonsense about mythical legends from long ago? And your contact doesn't even have a name? If she …'

'She's dead,' Luko said. 'We are all that remains. Everyone else was killed along the way, tortured, drugged …'

'And she told you what to do?' Tsu demanded. 'In clear unambiguous detail? No? You do surprise me. And for what?'

'For what is in this bio-trace,' Salomé answered.

'Then let me take a look at it,' Tsu snapped. 'Give me your hand.'

Raan watched wide-eyed as Salomé held out her hand. Tsu examined it briefly and then pulled out her portable scanner, training it on Salomé's outstretched palm.

'Nothing there,' Tsu said, after a moment.

'Not that easy,' Luko said with a grin. 'Or the secret would already be known. The old lady was no fool. You need to think about it.'

Raan saw Tsu's characteristic glare once more.

'Explain.'

'Hidden in plain sight, so not to appear on a trace,' Luko said.

'Bio …' Tsu said. 'Medical checks?'

Luko shrugged. Tsu adjusted her scanner and took another reading. 'Nothing there either …'

'DNA …' Luko prompted.

Tsu adjusted the scanner a third time.

'Wait … some kind of redundant nucleotide sequencing …' Raan caught the note of excitement in her voice. 'There's definitely something here, a massive data block. It's heavily encrypted.'

'Can you decode it?' Raan asked.

'Not with this. It looks … I'm not sure … I've not seen anything like it. I'm not sure it's decodable. It's going to need a key.' She ran the scanner across Salomé's hand once more and studied the readout. 'A key combined with your DNA trace. That's what we need. Do you have the key?'

'Not yet,' Salomé said. 'But I have people working on it.'

'Working where?'

'The clues are out there. We know they are.'

Tsu sighed. 'Out there somewhere? You mean one of these crazy expeditions into the void. Why does anyone even bother?'

'They haven't let me down yet,' Salomé said. 'They will find it.'

'Do not underestimate explorers,' Luko chided. 'They will reveal the secrets of the galaxy in time, whatever happens. It is the timescale that seems to be important. This group, they will kill those who get in their way. They are catching up with us, and they will stop us if we threaten their position, have no doubt of that.'

The holofac projector in the room buzzed for attention. Relieved to be able to turn to something he could understand, Raan checked the ID. 'It's for you, Salomé,' he said.

Salomé looked surprised.

'Could be a trick,' Tsu said. 'A ruse to flush out your location.'

Salomé shook her head as she examined the call details.

'It's Ambassador Cuthrick, we can trust him.'

She waved at the accept sensor.

Cuthrick's form appeared in their midst, flickering and indeterminate.

'Apologies for the unannounced entry,' Cuthrick said, his demure tones unaffected by the transmission. 'And for the necessary brevity. Cornelius assures me that this transmission cannot be intercepted or traced, but I see no need in taking risks.'

'It is good to see you, Ambassador,' Salomé said.

Cuthrick bowed in his customary manner. 'My missive is of both glad tidings and misfortune. News of your exploits at Darnielle's Progress has become public knowledge. You, along with your companions Tsu Annabella Singh and Raan Corsen have been positively identified as being responsible for the theft.'

Raan's heart did a backflip.

'The drone!' Tsu said.

'Holofac evidence has been seen and submitted,' Cuthrick continued. 'It has caused quite a stir, needless to say. I have been fielding off countless requests for a statement from tedious media types since the news broke. Whilst many are glad to discover that you are not dead, others are quite ... well, put out. Of those, one in particular seems to have taken it as a personal affront.'

Salomé smiled. 'Let me guess. Princess Aisling Duval.'

Cuthrick nodded. 'Indeed.'

'At least she's consistent,' Salomé said. 'What has she done?'

'She has reiterated the crimes you were found guilty of and has been present on most of the premier newsfeeds, calling for you to be, as she puts it, dealt with once and for all,' Cuthrick said. 'She has persuaded Imperial authorities to issue a bounty on you.'

'Something appropriate, I hope?' Salomé asked.

'Five million credits,' Cuthrick said. 'Such an amount is worthy of Elite combateers, so I'm told. Clearly you are considered a threat. Bounty hunters have been warned to consider you armed and dangerous. They are also advised not to communicate but to kill on sight. I think you have them ruffled, my dear.'

'They're scared,' Salomé said.

'They're scared?' Hassan echoed. Raan turned as Hassan repeated Salomé's words. Had that been a guilty expression flashing across the man's features? His next words chased the thought away. 'I would be too. That kind of bounty will have everyone in the galaxy looking for you.'

'There is more ill news, alas,' Cuthrick continued. 'A bounty has also been placed on your companions.'

Raan could only stare at the holofac.

'Both of them,' Cuthrick said gravely. 'To the tune of two million each.'

Two million credits!

'They're trying to sweep it all away,' Salomé said. 'They must know that we're the only ones who know anything now ... You mentioned some good news? We could do with it.'

Cuthrick nodded. 'Loren's Legion have received a transmission from the Children of Raxxla organisation. A discovery has been made out in the Formidine Rift location, ratified by a certain Commander Erimus of your acquaintance. They have found a code word.'

'Which is?'

'The word is surprisingly simple, buried in the bios of probes found in those remote locations. Exodus.'

Raan heard Hassan say, 'What does that mean?'

'It is a word from an ancient Earth language,' Cuthrick said. 'It implies a mass movement of people, an evacuation or some such, according to our resources. The context eludes me, though. It is all we have …'

'That may be all we need, Ambassador,' Salomé replied.

'Do you have any further instructions for me?' Cuthrick asked.

Salomé took a deep breath. 'We are going to attempt to locate this … whatever it is. With this bounty raised, many will seek to kill us. I hesitate to ask, but I must call upon the Children of Raxxla, Loren's Legion and any others who will help us to organise an escort in case we need to ...'

Cuthrick licked his lips. 'With the greatest respect, my Lady, the Children of Raxxla are explorers and Loren's Legion is not a mighty force when measured against …'

'It is what I ask,' Salomé said. 'There are few I can trust. They have proven themselves to be loyal factions.'

Cuthrick paused. 'My Lady. I would counsel this is not wise. The ramifications, the potential for conflict … with the galaxy teetering on the edge of war, this could be the spark …'

'I am committed now,' Salomé said, her voice hardening. 'I have asked, will you see it done?'

Cuthrick closed his eyes and bowed his head. Moments passed before he looked up.

'I will discuss the matter immediately with Commanders Erimus and Cornelius. You and your friends will be protected.'

Raan saw Salomé swallow, but her expression had relaxed a little.

'I can always depend upon you, dear Ambassador.'

'I will begin arrangements,' Cuthrick said.

'My gratitude as always.'

'I will endeavour to keep you abreast of events here, my Lady,' Cuthrick replied. 'I have some diplomatic channels to pursue as well, but I must be cautious not be seen to be working against Imperial diktats. We will do our level best to confound their efforts from this end. Good fortune ...'

'And to you, Ambassador.'

Salomé inclined her head and Cuthrick bowed once more. The holofac faded.

'A bounty on us!' Tsu said. 'I've never even had so much as a docking violation and now everyone wants to kill me.'

Raan swallowed, fighting an urge to reach up and disconnect his headset. It was a habit, there was nothing there. This was no game.

'We're involved. It was always going to come down to this.'

Luko smiled. 'We simply be one step ahead of bounty hunters.'

Salomé held out her hand to Tsu.

'A code word,' she said. 'Now you have one, try again.'

Tsu took out her scanner, typing in the word Cuthrick had provided. Salomé watched as her DNA sequence was analysed and used within the decryption process.

'Yes,' she said, her voice rising half an octave with excitement. 'It's working. There's ...'

The scanner buzzed angrily.

'And?' Raan demanded, desperate to hear something that made sense.

'Too much data here,' Tsu said. 'Dozens of petabytes of it. We need something more sophisticated than a scanner or even shipboard computers to make sense of this in a decent time frame. If we were back on Alioth I could do it easily, but out here ...'

'What do you need?'

The five turned to see Bill Turner standing behind them.

'A distributed system network with multi-dimensional processing capability,' Tsu said. 'I don't suppose you have one of those knocking around, do you?'

Bill grinned. 'No, but I know someone who does.'

He walked into their midst and gestured at the holofac display. It illuminated once again, this time showing a view of the familiar galactic map.

'A fellow Engineer,' he said. 'And she specialises in exploration data. She probably has the biggest and most powerful data processing capability in the galaxy, outside of the government and big corporate installations.'

'Who is she?' Raan asked.

'Elvira Martuuk. In the Khun system, it's not too far away. She'll be able to analyse it, guaranteed.'

'Can we trust her?' Salomé said.

'I can broker an introduction. She'll be interested in our new stealth technology. With that, you can negotiate safe passage.'

'That wasn't a yes,' Hassan muttered.

Bill smiled. 'Oh, there's one other thing.'

They looked at him expectantly.

'She has … an eye for menfolk,' he said, giving Hassan a hearty thump on the back. 'That may help you, if you're her type.'

A siren sounded, echoing through the cavernous space within the Versteck station. Bill gestured for the holofac to show a scanner display. Flickering marks were visible on the perimeter.

'Company,' Bill said, with a frown.

'They've found us?' Tsu said, the colour in her face draining away.

'Looks that way.' Bill summoned a visual feed from external cameras. A series of points of light could be seen moving against the backdrop of space. The camera zoomed, revealing the curved shapes of Imperial vessels.

'Cutters!' Salomé said, recognising them immediately. 'A task force …'

As they watched, space crackled behind the points of light, darkness writhed and lightning flashed …

'Capital ship!' Bill barked. 'Move! You've got to get out of here.'

Raan was on his feet along with Tsu, Hassan and Luko. He was aware of Salomé behind them, stopping to look at Bill.

'Wait, what about you?' he heard her say.

He glanced back at Bill and saw him grin. 'Someone has got to delay them.'

Salomé shook her head. 'We're not splitting up, not now.'

'You're the one they're after, not me,' Bill said with a wink. 'Besides, somebody has to give you a chance to get free. Get to Elvira, decode whatever this is and tell the galaxy …'

'Bill …'

'Move!' Bill's voice was stern. 'Otherwise all those sacrifices will have been in vain.'

Raan saw Luko grab Salomé's arm, saw her resist for a moment, then allow herself to be pulled away.

'Get to your ships,' Bill yelled. 'I'll cover you for as long as I can. Once you're in hyperspace they won't be able to track you …'

***

Four ships hurriedly vacated their pads. Luko's *Bella Principessa* was in the lead, followed by Tsu's *StarStormer* and the *Seven Veils,* flown by Hassan with Salomé alongside. Raan brought up the rear with the fearsome Fer-de-Lance, the *Rivincita.*

Versteck station was oriented so that the entrance was facing away from the approaching Imperial ships and they weren't immediately visible. All four vessels were fleeing with shields down and had been rigged for silent running.

Aboard the *Seven Veils*, Salomé was watching the approach of the Imperial ships on a vid feed being relayed from Versteck station. They were still too far away for any markings to be identified.

But how did they get here so fast? Could it have been Cuthrick's transmission?

The local wideband comms crackled with the preamble to a message.

'Outpost Versteck,' said an authoritarian voice. 'Please be advised that this system is now in lock-down in the name of Her Imperial Majesty. No ships are authorised to arrive or depart. Stand ready to receive a boarding party.'

Salomé saw Hassan looking at her.

'What's he going to do?' he asked.

Salomé looked back at the slowly receding station. She was saved from answering by Bill's voice.

'This is Versteck. Unless the Empire has annexed this system in the last day or so and my systems haven't caught up, I don't recognise Imperial authority here. I'm not obligated to answer to your demands and if you try to board this facility you will be fired upon. Back off.'

The Imperial ships didn't slow or change course. Salomé could see they were heading straight for the asteroid base.

Bill's voice crackled across the link again, this time on the narrowband comms.

'Make good your escape, I'll hold them as long as I can.'

'They'll detect us the moment we engage the jumpdrives …' Hassan said.

'You should be far enough away by that point,' Bill replied.

'But what about …' Hassan stopped as Salomé placed one of her hands on his. She shook her head.

'Outpost Versteck. You are suspected of playing host to known criminals. You will submit to boarding or you will be destroyed. This is your last warning.'

Salomé glanced at the console as the asteroid continued to recede.

Still mass locked. We have to creep away … it's taking too long.

Bill's voice sounded on the wideband once more, sounding oddly light-hearted and placatory.

'This is Versteck. We are a mere research outpost. We're unarmed. We are not harbouring anyone …'

Laser fire crackled around the edges of the base. Bits of rock and debris broke off, spiralling away into the darkness, thrown by their inertia as they lost connection with the surface of the asteroid. Defensive fire flickered back, faint and attenuated by the distance. Salomé could see ships swarming around Versteck station. Imperial fighters …

Only moments before …

There was a crackle of encoded transmissions and the fighters started heading their way.

'They've seen us!' Salomé called. 'Abort silent running, all power to engines!'

They were sitting ducks now, silent running meant their shield power was zero, it would take minutes to recharge them. Time they didn't have.

Drives, cool and red, flared across the four ships to a bright white. Plumes of flux exhaust streaked away behind them. A trail that was too easy to follow.

'Mass lock is clear,' Hassan said. 'All ships, engage jump.'

Large vessels had now rounded the edge of Versteck station, guided by the fighters, attempting to close in on the fleeing ships. Laser fire from the swift interceptors was flickering closer.

Frame shift drive charging …

Hits registered on the hull. Salomé saw the integrity status dropping. The rising hum of the hyperspace drive was strained.

Too much mass close by …

'Do we fight?' Raan shouted over the comms.

'We won't stand a chance!' Tsu answered, her voice high pitched. 'We're almost …'

'Good luck, my friends,' Bill's voice said. It was oddly composed. 'Got a last little surprise for our Imperial friends …'

'Bill, wait …' Salomé replied, but the connection had already dropped.

A blast of light blistered out around them. The remote camera systems showed nothing but an intense glare, a wall of whiteness. All four ships were buffeted by an expanding sphere of detonation, superheated plasma raging past at an incomprehensible speed. Hassan wrestled with the controls, trying to steady the ship. Salomé grasped the restraints in her own seat as the ship bucked and heaved around them.

'What was …' Hassan asked.

Salomé was watching the remote cameras. The light faded, leaving sparkling debris tumbling in the darkness of space.

Versteck was gone.

The nearby ships were gone too, the fighters and the other ships that had been in close proximity.

Bill!

Aboard the fleeing ships no one spoke. There was no time to assimilate what they were seeing.

4 … 3 … 2 … 1 … Engage.

***

The holofac newsfeed glowed brightly, casting a warm orange glow on the five faces that sat around it, watching the GalNet newsfeed play out.

Remarkable footage has emerged from the Maia system, following analysis of security recordings from Darnielle's Progress outpost.

It shows five individuals who allegedly took part in the heist and three of them have been positively identified. Most remarkable of all, one of the individuals has been confirmed as none other than Commander Salomé, also known as the disgraced senator of the Prism system, Kahina Tijani Loren.

Ms. Loren was sentenced to life imprisonment in the Koontz Asylum last year, but her convoy was destroyed en route with the loss of all hands. It was assumed she also perished in the attack.

Imperial authorities took the unprecedented move of issuing a galaxy-wide bounty on Commander Salomé to the tune of five million credits.

Princess Aisling Duval also took the opportunity to comment.

'Commander Salomé is a disgraced senator, liar, convicted murderer, felon and terrorist. She has evaded just punishment for her crimes and has undermined the stability of the galaxy, inciting violence wherever she goes. For the safety of us all she must be stopped. I urge all those loyal to the Empire to deal with this criminal once and for all."

The two other individuals have been identified as ex-MetaDrive employee Raan Corsen, previously believed killed in the Alioth system, and former junior Alliance Operative Tsu Annabelle Singh. Both have been as-signed sizable bounties as well.

The following advice was issued to pilots by Imperial military intelligence sources.

'Consider them all armed and dangerous. Do not engage in communica-tions. Show no mercy. Kill them on sight. Holofac evidence of the destruction of the vessels will guarantee the bounty.'

Commander Salomé's current location is unknown, but it is believed she has fled the core worlds in response to the statement and associated bounty.

Infrastructure raised his eyebrows in mock surprise.

'Well, that should get everyone's attention.'

'So ... a bounty issued,' Finance said. 'Galactic terrorism is not accept-able. It must be crushed out of existence, wouldn't you agree?'

'Absolutely,' Exo said. 'Now we have what we need, it's time to tidy up loose ends. This should ensure her swift liquidation.'

'I might even try myself,' Infrastructure said with a chuckle. The others joined in. The idea of Infrastructure wedging his significant frame into the confines of a spacecraft and becoming a bounty hunter was farcical. It wasn't as if he needed the money, either.

Finance was less pleased.

'This shouldn't have been necessary,' she said. 'If the job in HIP 16497 had been done correctly ...'

'Oh ... I don't know,' Infrastructure said. 'It was always going to be difficult to track the ship if the technology worked. And our errant protégé and her friends have proved that it does. We have a working hyperspace wake-concealment prototype. I think that counts as a result.'

'But it's not under our control,' Finance objected.

'We have measures in place,' Personnel assured her. 'This Salomé will be stopped, one way or the other.'

'What do we believe she intends to do?' Exo asked.

'I would imagine,' Infrastructure said. 'That she will attempt to pene-trate the COL 70 sector. It may be that she doesn't survive that experience. We will be waiting for her regardless.'

'So, either she dies in the encounter, is caught and killed upon her return, or ...' Exo said.

'We put our other contingency into operation,' Personnel said. 'Her fate is certain, one way ... or another.'

Chapter Twenty-Eight

Long Sight base, Khun 5, Khun system, Independent

The *Seven Veils* began its descent to the surface, the seemingly barren moon slowly growing in the forward display. Alongside, Luko's *Bella Principessa* matched course and speed, descending towards the desolate surface. Raan's *Rivincita* and Tsu's *StarStormer* were not far behind.

'I have the beacon,' Hassan said. 'Should be on the ground in five minutes.'

'Copy,' Luko's voice echoed out of the comms system.

Salomé watched as the ground rose up to meet them, slowly flattening from an obvious sphere to a landscape. There was the faint hint of mist on the surface, diming distant starlight as they approached.

'Gutamaya Hotel Alpha Sierra, please approach to within seven thousand five hundred metres and request docking clearance.'

Hassan adjusted the controls and the *Seven Veils* turned aside slightly, giving them a better view of the sprawling base they were approaching.

'These Engineers sure have some money,' he said.

Salomé nodded. 'Rich beyond count, by the look of things. Most of them seem to have an interesting past.'

'What do we know of this Elvira woman?'

'She's an explorer,' Salomé said. 'At least, she used to be. Doesn't explain how she came by all this. She did something else beforehand, it's not clear what it was.'

'Paid well, though.'

Salomé agreed, but didn't say anything. Hassan was right, you didn't get this rich by heading off into the black and scanning a few neutron stars. This sort of facility was properly financed, which spoke of inherited wealth or some significantly different career in the past.

The gruff voice of the autodock sequence sounded through the cockpit again.

'Gutamaya Hotel Alpha Sierra, you are cleared for approach to pad one-six. Please observe speed restrictions in the vicinity.'

'Copy that,' Hassan replied and nosed the *Seven Veils* into a descent vector. The ship came to rest on the appropriate pad, settling down with

DREW WAGAR

a gentle sigh of thrusters, kicking up a little dust which fell back to the ground quickly in the vacuum. Salomé looked to her left and saw Luko's Cobra settling down on an adjacent pad. The other ships were already docked.

Salomé toggled the comms system onto narrowband.

'Luko and Raan stay here,' Salomé said. 'Be ready for a quick departure. If we're not back in half an hour …'

'We come and rescue you,' Luko answered, 'Never fear, signorina.'

In her mind's eye, Salomé could see the wry grin on his face.

'Thanks, Luko.'

The doors to the bridge opened and Tsu walked in. Salomé could see she had a svelte weapon strapped to her hip.

'Expecting trouble?' Salomé asked.

'Always.' Tsu's expression was impassive.

Salomé nodded, reaching for her family's sword and slipping it into the scabbard strapped around her waist. Tsu was giving her a look, but said nothing. Hassan had a bulkier weapon at his waist, his trusty Cowell '55.

'Let's go.'

***

Elvira's base was unlike Bill's. Where his had been a haphazard and completely disorganised mess, Elvira's was clean, tidy and ordered. Bright illumination festooned the ceilings, walls and bulkheads. Maintenance bots and automechs vied with humans for space in the corridors, scuttling to and fro with equipment, cargo transfers and other technical assignments. Ships were housed in huge underground bunkers, some in the process of being dismantled, fixed, repainted or having new modules crafted into their infrastructure. Hundreds of technicians swarmed through the vast hangars, working quickly and efficiently.

Salomé, Hassan and Tsu watched this from an observation deck that overlooked the vast apron where the ships were docked.

'Quite an operation,' Hassan said, his eyes wide.

'Why thank you,' said a voice behind them.

They turned, hands going to weapons instinctively.

A woman stood behind them, tall, athletic and wiry, her physique strong and her stance poised. She had short cropped hair in the manner of most spacers, but her eyes twinkled with amusement and intelligence.

She wore a sword at her side and a gun buckled just above it. Salomé's eyes narrowed as she took in the pair of weapons.

Ornamental, or does she know how to use them? So few carry a sword nowadays … especially outside the Empire.

'I do my best,' the woman said. 'There is quite some competition out there now, but pilots know where to come if they want the best possible results …'

'Ms. Martuuk,' Salomé began.

'Elvira, please. You Imperials are so formal, aren't you?'

Salomé blinked in surprise.

'Oh, I know all about you and your little quests,' Elvira said, seeing the look on Salomé's face. 'You've been causing quite the stir on your travels. Many of your followers have passed through my establishment, looking to upgrade their vessels.'

She walked across to them, her hips swaying with an exaggerated gait.

'Your companions though …?'

'Tsu,' Tsu said in her clipped short voice.

'From Alioth I would guess, judging by that accent,' Elvira said, looking her up and down.

'You are correct,' Tsu replied.

'Which explains the connection to Bill, I suppose. He did let me know you'd be coming.' She turned on her heel and looked towards Hassan. 'And what do we have here?'

'My name is Hassan …'

Elvira sighed deep in her throat. 'Hmmm. I love your voice, so soft and smooth, and what do you do, my silver-tongued friend?'

Salomé saw Elvira lick her lips.

Hassan blinked in surprise. 'I … I'm …'

'He's my pilot,' Salomé said, cutting across him. 'We don't have much time …'

'Oh.' Elvira looked back at Salomé. 'He's yours, is he? Perhaps we can trade?'

Salomé exchanged a look with Hassan.

Elvira laughed. 'Come now, I'm only teasing. We have much to discuss it seems.'

She took Hassan by the arm and led him away, with Salomé and Tsu following behind.

***

'Yes,' Elvira said. 'I can decode it. I've seen this sort of thing before. A subcutaneous DNA print. Very neat and very expensive. Where did you get it?'

'That is a long story,' Salomé replied. 'And those who gave it to me are dead.'

'You live an interesting life,' Elvira said. 'Now, let's talk payment. Bill's wake suppression technology. I want a blueprint.'

Tsu held up a commtab. 'It's all here. Blueprints, requirements, schematics.'

'Show me.'

Tsu tapped a command on the surface of the commtab and then directed it towards the holofac transmitter on a nearby table. It lit up, casting a complex representation of the mechanism in the space above, slowly rotating. She passed it to Salomé.

'Fascinating,' Elvira said, giving the display a cursory glance. 'Trade?'

Salomé pressed her hand down on the holofac system, confirming her unlock code. Elvira did the same beside her.

'And here's your data.'

The holofac display of the wake suppressor faded away and was replaced with a short series of characters.

46 Eridani.

'That's it?' Hassan asked.

'This is a trick,' Tsu said.

Elvira shook her head. 'No trick. There's vast amounts of padding around the data, but this is the only actual record contained within. That and a small private message …'

'Message?' Salomé demanded.

'Addressed to you,' Elvira said. 'From someone called … ah … Rebecca.'

Salomé stared at Elvira.

'I don't understand …'

'Well don't ask me, it's your message. It's coded not to play unless you're alone, so you'll have to review it in private.'

'This system, 46 Eridani …' Tsu asked.

Elvira nodded. 'About eight hundred light years from here. Blue supergiant star. Right on the border of the …'

'COL 70 sector,' Salomé whispered, looking around at Tsu and Hassan.

They looked back at her and nodded.

'That's where they're hiding whatever it is that's behind all this ...' Tsu said.

'And that's where we have to go,' Salomé said. 'My thanks ...'

Elvira smiled. 'Oh, it's my pleasure.'

Without warning, she pulled the gun from her side. Electric blue fire splashed across the room, catching Tsu in the chest and throwing her backwards. She fell with a screech and lay still on the floor.

Hassan went for his own gun, but Elvira's warning stopped him.

'I wouldn't do that if I were you,' she said. The gun was aimed directly at him.

Salomé stepped in the way.

Elvira smiled and lowered the gun.

'You murderer,' Salomé whispered, her hands clenching.

'Oh, she's not dead,' Elvira replied. 'The bounty is much more generous if she's alive. You on the other hand ... there are those who really want you dead. Your body will suffice.'

'Bill said we could trust you.'

'He's such a dear,' Elvira said. 'So trusting, these geeky types, don't you find? A little favour or indulgence here and there and you've got them wrapped around your finger ... Don't tell me you don't do the same. This is just as much a game for you as it is for me ...'

Hassan stepped to one side. Salomé gestured for him to remain in place. 'Don't ...'

'You see?' Elvira replied, with a pout. 'So loyal, look ... he will die for the lovely Salomé. Men falling at your feet to serve. Tell me you don't take advantage of them. I know a player when I see one.'

'Leave her alone,' Hassan cried.

Elvira turned her gun on him. 'There's no bounty on you, little boy,' she said. 'I can dispose of you if I so choose. Though I might just keep you around for some amusement. Your brain doesn't have to be intact for what I have in mind ...'

She pulled the trigger and the electric charge shot across the room, cracking into Hassan and throwing him backwards with a yell. He lay on the floor, unmoving.

Salomé rushed to check on him, but heard the sound of Elvira returning her gun to its holster. She looked up in surprise.

'Do you know what I did before I went exploring?' Elvira asked. 'No, I suppose you don't, it was my secret.'

She smiled and drew a sword from the scabbard buckled at her side. It was a Katana-style blade.

'I was an assassin,' Elvira said. 'I made quite a healthy living out of it before ... well, let's just say one assignment had political ramifications that were less than desirable. I had to flee the core worlds for a long time. All thanks to your glorious Empire.'

'My Empire?' Salomé returned. 'Hardly mine.'

'You Imperials value your honour, so it's said,' Elvira continued. 'I plan on putting that to the test. You are rumoured to be a swordswoman, there are so few who know those arts today. I saw how you dispatched your patron on Prism. I will make your end a fitting one for an Imperial dignitary.'

'And if I best you?'

Elvira smiled. 'Not an eventuality I am concerned with.'

Salomé watched as Elvira thrust out with her sword. The woman's stance and bearing told her she was dealing with an expert. The sword was a modern design, formed of bright-steel with illuminated highlights at the tip and hilt, glowing with a fierce blue energy.

'Defend yourself,' Elvira said.

Salomé stepped back and drew her own sword. Her antique Holva blade, its bright-steel surface reflecting the light around her. She raised it vertically and then pointed it towards Elvira in the traditional manner.

'Taught by an old master, I see,' Elvira said.

'Taught by many masters,' Salomé replied, and lunged.

The blades crossed, striking back and forth repeatedly, the blue lighting of Elvira's sword describing momentary arcs of colour in the air. The women circled each other, their footwork timed and precise, swords trading blows in a rhythmic and almost choreographed manner.

'All good so far,' Elvira said, the blue light of her sword giving her face an eerie look. 'But let's take it up a step, shall we?'

She pushed Salomé back and came at her with a whirlwind of feints and strikes, alternating between attacking and defending herself. The blade flashed in a spinning arc of lethal blue. Salomé found herself backing away in confusion at the unorthodox technique.

The flat of Elvira's blade came out of nowhere, striking her on the wrist. Salomé yelled and almost dropped her sword, staggering out of range.

'Not so confident now?' Elvira said, straightening and watching as Salomé regained her composure.

Salomé lunged again, but found her sword arm twisted from a swift move by the woman before her. In a moment Elvira's sword sliced across towards her. Salomé gasped as it caught her left shoulder.

Hot blood, running down her arm. She could see rivulets of red on her skin.

She struck again, trying to regain the initiative. Elvira retreated out of reach and then came back with a dizzying assault that Salomé only just managed to deflect.

Then somehow Elvira managed to trip her. Salomé felt her feet go from underneath her, and she fell, rolling away, scrabbling to hold her sword up to deflect a blow that would have sliced her midriff open.

'At least you pay attention,' Elvira said, stepping back.

Salomé climbed warily back to her feet. She attacked again, seeking to land a strike on the woman before her. A further flurry of blows and counterblows. Salomé ducked one and let loose a punch which connected directly with Elvira's jaw, sending the other woman stumbling back.

Salomé kept her sword poised and ready.

'A rather low trick for an Imperial,' Elvira said, rubbing her jaw with her left hand. 'Where did you learn that one?'

'Even the Federation has some worthwhile lessons,' Salomé replied.

Elvira spun around and lashed out. Salomé backpedalled, but found her sword arm pinned to her side. Salomé felt herself spun around, pain shot up her arm as it was cruelly twisted and she found Elvira's sword at her throat.

'Just playing with you, Imperial girl,' Elvira whispered in her ear. 'A worthy fight, but you aren't the challenge I was looking for. Now ... a little souvenir of your visit here ...'

Elvira's sword pressed against Salomé's cheek. It was only the lightest of touches, but it stung like fury. Salomé felt blood on her face, hot and burning, dripping down onto her neck.

She thrust her other elbow back, catching Elvira in the stomach. The other woman fell away with a cry. Salomé, now free, spun around, her sword describing a sweeping arc through the air, snapping with ferocity.

It was blocked just before it would have decapitated Elvira, who was already back on her feet, sword raised in defence.

'Full of surprises, I see,' Elvira said. 'But only a short reprieve.'

Salomé was panting hard, her breath short and gasping, unable to respond.

Elvira came at her again, with a speed and skill that had Salomé scrambling back, desperately trying to defend herself.

A stinging pain to her arm. She heard herself cry out. Felt her sword wrenched from her grip. Saw it clatter uselessly to the floor.

Elvira was close now, her sword not quite pressed against Salomé's neck, her face lit by the blue highlights. Salomé stared into the dark eyes, seeing death there.

'I admire you, you know,' Elvira said. 'Your courage, your spirit and your swordsmanship. A shame you fell foul of politics in this way.'

Elvira smiled.

'But I am being well paid for this,' she continued. 'Into the void for you, Kahina Loren of Prism.'

There was a whirl of motion. Elvira shrieked. Salomé jerked back in shock. A violent push and she found herself sprawling on the ground. She fought to turn, to see what had happened.

Somehow Tsu was standing there. She had grabbed Salomé's blade and was circling around Elvira, her stance alert and tense.

'How did you …' Elvira began, shaking her head and staggering slightly.

'Maybe you aren't the shooter you think you are,' Tsu growled. She raised the sword above her head using her left hand, poised in a strange fashion that looked nothing like any en guard stance Salomé had ever seen. 'I hope you handle a sword better.'

'But you're Alliance,' Elvira said, looking confused. 'There is no duelling tradition in the Alliance …'

Tsu smiled.

'Yeah, you're right.'

She went for the gun still holstered at her waist and trained it on Elvira.

'But our operatives do wear suits capable of withstanding stun attacks. Maybe you should have done your research a little better.'

'No …'

Tsu pulled the trigger and her gun spat a crackle of energy which flung Elvira against the bulkhead. She yelled out in pain and crumpled to her knees, struggling to get regain her feet.

'Not very nice, is it?' Tsu said and fired again.

Elvira was flung back and now lay spread-eagled on the floor, still twitching.

'Not nice at all.'

Tsu fired a third time and Elvira crumpled to one side and lay still.

Tsu looked across to Salomé.

'Swords? Really? In this day and age? Just shoot the damn 'stards!'

Salomé smiled and Tsu helped her to her feet.

'You have a point …'

'Let's get Hassan back to the ship and get the hell out of here,' Tsu said. 'And get you fixed up…'

'I'll be all right.'

'Do you Imperials like suffering?' Tsu demanded. 'We have medpacks for this sort of thing. Or will that impugn your honour or something?'

Salomé grinned. 'Medpacks will be fine.'

Serebrov Terminal, HR 6421 system, Independent

Commander Erimus could feel his hands trembling. Before him stood the head of Loren's Legion, Commander Cornelius Gendymion himself, arms folded in front of him, his uniform pristine and authoritative. Erimus' heart pounded. He felt short of breath, his head spun. He reached out to steady himself against the conference room table.

'She wants what?'

Cornelius repeated his statement without emotion.

'An escort, prepared to defend her and her co-conspirators, from the COL 70 sector to the core worlds. I came in person to discuss how this might be achieved.'

Erimus sat down. 'But … that's nearly a thousand light years! With a bounty on their heads … it's a suicide mission. We're explorers, not fighters. We don't stand a chance, we'll be killed in the first five minutes. You know this, it's futile!'

'That is the received wisdom,' Cornelius agreed.

'Why can't she just transmit what she knows from …' Cornelius's look stopped Erimus mid-flow. The answer was obvious, comms could be monitored, adjusted, changed, jammed. Erimus jumped to the next question.

'So where is she wanting to go?'

Cornelius shrugged. 'Somewhere in the Old Worlds is the best bet, we're not sure yet …'

Erimus frowned.

'Wait a minute … The graveyard, of course …'

Cornelius looked at him expectantly.

'Yes, old ships …' Erimus said, his excitement rising. 'That's where the last clue came from. A ship in the Tionisla graveyard … it had a transmitter …'

'Tionisla? A gong to be sounded when the time is right?'

'Perhaps ...'

Erimus gestured and called up the holofac galaxy map before him, quickly plotting the two points on the chart. A thousand light years wasn't much against the scale of the galaxy, but it looked like an impassable gulf of desolate empty space from here.

He shook his head.

'It's impossible. Bounty hunters are already swarming the edge of the COL 70 sector looking for her since that bounty was issued. We can't stand up against that kind of firepower and might.'

Cornelius didn't say anything.

Erimus looked up.

'Can we?'

Cornelius smiled. 'No. You're completely correct, there's no way to fight that. Any attempt would be foolish in the extreme. One does not engage a bounty hunter. They are masters of their craft.'

'Then ...'

'Salomé had tactical training,' Cornelius said. 'I knew her original mentor. A man by the named of Dalk Torgen. A formidable strategist. Salomé isn't asking this by whim, she requested me to help. I know what she wants.'

'And what is that?'

'The best way to avoid a punch,' Cornelius said. 'Is simply not to be there.'

Erimus frowned. 'Evasion? Stealth?'

'All that,' Cornelius said. 'Diversion, decoys, misinformation ... and above all ... speed. I have contacts. With a mix of information both accurate and ... otherwise ... we can build an allied coalition. We can flood the zone with ships, issue contrary directives, cause confusion and anarchy. Through that she can make a run, escorted by an inner core of trustworthy pilots.'

Erimus looked back at the holofac chart. The galaxy glowed before him, serene and peaceful. He toggled a comms link.

'Alessia?'

The answer was swift. 'Yes, Erimus?'

'Assemble the consul for me,' he replied. 'We're going to need some comms sent out at short notice.'

'I'll be ready,' Alessia replied. 'Just tell me what to send and when.'

'Thanks,' Erimus said, closing the call and turning back to Cornelius. 'I assume you already have a plan.'

'It's what I do,' Cornelius said. 'I will provide a guide to the necessary ship loadouts. Much must be procured in a short time.'

'And then?'

'Loren's Legion will drill you. It will not be fun. It will be brutal and exhausting. But we will make you explorers into hardened combat veterans capable of serving her needs.'

Cornelius reached out his hand.

'You're actually enjoying this, aren't you?' Erimus said as he took it and gave it a firm shake.

Cornelius smiled. 'I like a challenge.'

Long Sight base, Khun 5, Khun system, Independent

Four starships, one white and elegant, one sleek and elongated, one an arrow head, the last blocky and wedge-shaped, took off from the engineering base, pushed up to full throttle and boosted away from the rugged surface. Within a minute they were tiny receding shapes in the overhead blackness, before disappearing into faint streaks of light which quickly faded from view.

'How many jumps?' Salomé asked.

'Looks like thirty to forty or thereabouts,' Hassan replied, reviewing the course as it plotted itself on the holofac galaxy display. 'It's not far, well, not by our standards. But check this out …'

Salomé looked across. Hassan was scrutinising a section of the chart, grouped in a three-dimensional blob on the display.

'This whole sector just beyond 46 Eridani, COL 70, it's completely locked off. Just as Bill showed us. Unknown permit required.'

'But what does that mean?'

Hassan shrugged. 'Most think it's the Pilots' Federation keeping sectors of the galaxy locked off for reasons only they know.'

'Why would they do that?'

'Secrets, special trade deals, unexploited mineral resources,' Hassan said. 'Who knows? I'm not convinced it's them, though.'

'Who else could lock off the sectors?'

Hassan grinned at her. 'Well, that's the question, isn't it? But there is something out there that someone doesn't want us to see. This system is right on the boundary.'

Salomé took a deep breath.

'Let's find out what this secret is then. We must be quick.'

Hassan triggered the jump sequence and the *Seven Veils* spooled up its frame shift drive for another leap across the stars.

4 … 3 … 2 … 1 … Engage.

The flickering lights of witch-space cast ghostly shadows off of the paintwork of the vessels as they slipped between dimensions, heading out of the core worlds once again.

***

Elvira winced as she activated the holofac system and requested a pre-arranged channel. The answer was swift. The figure at the other end was obscured other than a pair of gloved hands which moved quickly out of scanner reception.

'You made it look convincing,' the glove-handed figure said.

'I think they might have escaped regardless,' Elvira replied. 'Rarely have I met anyone who can handle a sword in that manner.'

'You have the location?'

Elvira smiled. 'You have the compensation as arranged?'

'It will be delivered.'

'It better be. The target is 46 Eridani.'

The glove-handed figure moved aside slightly, relaying the information somewhere else.

'Excellent.'

'Your next move …'

'… is not your concern. Suffice to say that location will be effectively … besieged.'

'There's something else,' Elvira said. 'There was a private message for your Imperial girl. Couldn't grab the content, only the person who recorded it. Someone by the name of Rebecca …'

There was a pause at the other end and then a sigh.

'That woman.'

***

Salomé retired to her quarters, tagging the holofac to receive the data from the subcutaneous DNA trace that Elvira had helped them unlock.

An image appeared, a woman, old and instantly familiar. She spoke in smug, assured tones.

Salomé staggered back and steadied herself against the nearby bulkhead as the message was relayed, not sure what to make of what she was hearing.

'… and now it's your turn. When the time is right you can unlock it – your choice. It's been hidden in plain sight all this time. The core of the problem. You know me by now, I like a little misdirection. These people are smart, I had to be smarter. Good luck. You're going to need it.'

Tionisla …

Syreadie sector, Formidine Rift, Uninhabited

The mammoth vessel hung in the darkness, sombre and desolate, only dim navigation lights shining from its hull. The telemetry system indicated a downlink was still working.

A dark skinned man, with long lanky hair was staring into the imager. His face was haggard, drawn with fear. The accent was sharp and unfamiliar, the voice cracking with terror as he spoke. A time stamp appeared at the bottom of the image. Behind him, a blurred view of what looked like a mess hall could be seen, though there was no one else about.

Data – Log Entry – 01/10/3270

'We managed to overpower the 'stards, but not before they took out the main reactor. We're dead in space, with twenty minutes of life support left. Got nothing out of them before they died, but clearly it was all planned. They took a drug which killed them. Doc says it's nicknamed 'hexedit;' first it kills your memories, then it kills you. Neat and tidy.

'So we're dead, just waiting for the end. This will be the last log from the *Zurara*. Some of the crew have already killed themselves. Others are praying to whatever deity they believe might help them. A few are drinking themselves into oblivion. Not sure what will get us first, the lack of oxygen or the cold. Battery power is about to die.

'Me? I'm leaving this log. This far out I doubt anyone will ever read it, but well, what the hell, eh?

'We all signed up for the promise of big payouts, a year of your life in exchange for enough to retire on. Should have looked a bit closer at it, but you would have probably done the same. No need to work again, right? What's clear now is whoever was behind this mission never intended for any of us to come back.

'Damn, it's cold in here now.

'The folks managing the cargo, they were all psychos. The moment we completed the mission they just 'snapped.' Killed the ship and killed themselves. Some kind of mental conditioning Doc said. We tried to get word to the other vessels when we found out. We got a signal out, but don't know if anyone received it. It will probably freak them out, I don't think they know we're here.

'We dropped a series of beacons out here, all targeted around Earth-like or terraformable worlds. We prepped some of the terraform candidates with seeders and biofilters. No one can figure out why it was necessary, but that was the mission. Just as we were turning back, boom, those cargo-handlers went nuts.

'So that's it. We don't even know why we've been killed. But someone out there knows, someone out there has blood on their hands, a lot of it. If you figure it out, give them a message from us. You know what I mean.

'Funny. We were told there was something bad out here, that it was haunted by ghosts ...

'Never figured it would be us doing the haunting ...'

The video stopped, static replacing the display for long moments before the image stabilised once more. This time the scene had changed. The man had been replaced by an old, but still striking, woman. One hand brushed through simply cut grey-brown hair, revealing a narrow, attractive but otherwise commonplace face, unadorned with any form of make-up or jewellery; no earrings, no bangles, no piercings. Only her eyes were remarkable, a deep brown with a hard, cold and distant look to them; eyes that had seen too many things.

The woman grinned at the imager. In the background, the bulkhead of an old ship could be seen, an old-style Cobra, perhaps. The words 'Apocalypse Engineering' could just be made out on a support beam. She spoke quickly, her voice sharp and to the point. The time stamp had shifted.

Data – Additional Log – 21/08/3273

'So this is what they were hiding. I'm leaving the old logs for reference. I might need to come back this way again and re-educate myself. Chances are my memory will get zapped again. If I don't make it I'll have to leave clues for others to follow. So, if you're reading this and you're not me, here's the deal.

'Found this mega ship. Took me years. This is the evidence. Nothing inside but void-frozen cadavers, perfectly preserved, some with drinks still in their hands. But the log. They sent these poor souls out here because they needed waypoints, all prepped for every eventuality. Three different zones it would seem.

'There's a conspiracy. Guess you figured that out already, but it goes way up, way beyond the Feds, the Imps and the Alliance. Something is coming, don't know what it is, but it's bad and it's all being hidden. All this weird stuff far out in the void? It's some kind of contingency plan. The answer to why and who is back in the core, not out here. That's where I'm going next. Wish me luck.'

Location unknown, Col 70 sector

Hassan attempted to plot the course again. The galactic mapping tool refused to accept the co-ordinates.

'Still no joy,' he reported.

'And you won't have,' Luko called over the narrowband. 'Too new. All these new fangled ships. Old is the best way. Not so much automation, real flying …'

Hassan rolled his eyes and Salomé smiled.

'Key to my frame shift,' Luko instructed. 'Engage wing.'

Console indicators flickered as the ships linked their communications and telemetry systems.

'I will engage the jump,' Luko instructed. 'Do not be alarmed if anything goes wrong …'

'Don't be alarmed …' Tsu's said, across the link. 'What is that supposed to mean?'

'It will be ok,' Raan's voice said. 'Just another jump, right?'

'This is an old way of making a jump,' Luko replied. 'Must be very precise, prone to error. Why you think they don't do this anymore?'

'Dead reckoning,' Hassan said. 'With the emphasis on dead.'

'Let's just go, shall we?' Salomé said.

'Signorina says we go,' Luko said. 'Then we go.'

At Luko's command, all four ships charged their drives simultaneously.

Heat vents rose as tremendous energies were channelled into one enormous outburst of concentrated power.

'Full thrusters now!'

The ship leapt ahead, became brief streaks of light, and then vanished into the darkness.

Chapter Twenty-Nine

Location unknown, COL 70 sector, Uninhabited

Warning! Hyperspace conduit unstable!

'What does that …?' Salomé began, before a wrenching jolt threw them both hard in their harnesses. Nausea rose in her throat as the familiar view of witch-space was abruptly twisting and rolling before her, tinged with angry red and orange. She tasted bile and had to close her eyes, bracing herself as the ship spiralled out of control.

'Something's wrong with the jump,' Hassan cried, over the screaming sound of the frame shift drive. 'Never seen anything like this before …'

The transit was suddenly over, the *Seven Veils* was spat out into normal space, yawing and tumbling end over end. Salomé saw Hassan wrestle with the ship, it seemed to be sluggish, the holofac displays around them crashing with static.

And then they faded out.

'Lost power,' Hassan said, yanking on the defunct controls. 'No power, no thrust … nothing.'

Life support failure.

Before them, another ship flashed into view. They could see Luko's Cobra, the hull plates proudly bearing the name *Bella Principessa*. It too was tumbling end over end, its engines flickering.

'Where are Tsu and Raan?' Salomé demanded, looking at the scanner readouts as they flickered. The displays were unclear, but only Luko's ship was intermittently registering. The *Seven Veils* steadied and began drifting.

'No idea, they must have made the jump successfully or been thrown clear …'

Hassan unclipped his harness and pulled himself down below the console, looking for the auxiliary power controls. Salomé tensed as she watched him. Would he be able to engage the emergency battery systems? The scanners faded out completely, followed by the sounds of the life support system.

Salomé tried the comms, but it was spewing static. At least it seemed to be functional.

'Luko? Luko! Can you hear me?'

The Cobra was likewise drifting away outside.

'Any luck?' Hassan heard her ask as he resurfaced from below.

'The ship won't restart!' he yelled, jabbing at the unresponsive controls. 'Nothing's working! Something has disabled us …'

Salomé didn't answer. Hassan looked up to see her staring out of the canopy window, her mouth slack and her features gaunt.

'What are you …?'

She pointed. Hassan pulled himself up above the console so he could see … and gaped.

'Oh shit!'

Outside, shapes were moving in the darkness. Twisting, turning, unfurling. Malevolent petals that were spinning and rotating, glowing with a faint greenish hue. Moving … moving towards them. Hundreds of ships, massed ranks of them, organised …

An armada!

They were turning. An intercept course. Weapons flickered in readiness, lighting up the darkness.

'Where did they come from?'

'Move!' Salomé yelled, her voice abrupt and stark in the silence.

'Without engines?' he yelled back. 'What do you expect me to do? Get outside and push?'

The comms crackled. Somehow they were still working. Luko's voice, laced with static, was just audible.

'Signorina! Move!'

'We can't, they've disabled our systems. Hassan is trying the reboot sequence but …'

'No time,' Luko replied. 'You must leave now. Charge frame shift the moment you can.'

Salomé looked at Hassan, confused. 'What's he talking about? We can't leave without power …'

Hassan felt as bewildered as she looked.

A blast of engine flux splashed across the canopy, causing the *Seven Veils* to rock in the wake. They made out the twin engines and triangular outrigger thrusts of Luko's Cobra as it spun around before them.

'Luko? What are you …' Salomé began. 'How is his ship still operational?'

The Cobra accelerated away, exhaust flux flashing red as the boosters engaged. The *Seven Veils* shuddered.

'Maybe because it's an older vessel … he had this kill switch, perhaps he shut down before he was disabled … I don't …'

The Cobra was on a direct intercept course, arrowing away from them and towards the alien vessels.

'Luko …' Salomé called, repeatedly hammering the comms circuit. 'Luko … what are you doing? Luko! Answer me!'

***

Luko flexed his back muscles as the abrupt acceleration forced him into his flight chair. He braced himself against the controls. All the instruments showed the Cobra to be operating at full power, its mighty engines still giving their all after almost two hundred years. It was a veteran of space, having fought and survived more battles than most ships would ever know. It had known its share of close escapes and daring escapades. It had been damaged, smashed and buckled, but always repaired. It had known dozens of owners and brought them all safely home.

Luko thumbed the weapons deployment triggers and watched as twin beam lasers snapped into place on the forward hardpoints. A corresponding thump from below decks indicated the matching multi-cannon weapons were ready, too.

Twin shield generators pushed power fore and aft, buzzing with fierce energy. The ship was poised and lethal, a clenched fist ready to strike. Engines roared, the ship vibrating with its own reckless speed, striking forth and rearing up over its enemies like the old Earth creature it took its name from.

When a Cobra bites …

The comms crackled again, buzzing for attention.

'… what are you doing? Luko! Answer me!'

He toggled the comms. 'Signorina, I am molto sorry I lied to you …'

'No … don't you dare. Don't do this. Stop … there's got to be another way …'

'You must get away, you must warn the galaxy of this threat, this is what they were hiding …'

The response was a shrieking cry. Luko couldn't tell whether it was rage or grief. Maybe it was both.

'I forbid this! Luko! Come back …'

'We all have our parts to play,' Luko said softly. 'We step on the stage, we say our lines, we step off.'

'No …'

'Despedida, bella signorina.'

He toggled the comms off. He wouldn't be needing it anymore.

Before him, the alien spacecraft were turning. Harsh yellow light probed the darkness, beams of intense energy flashing out and sparkling off the Cobra's dark hull plates.

Luko yanked hard on the flight controls and the *Bella Principessa* spun and yawed violently out of the way, evading the lattice of illumination.

'Try to stop my friends, eh? I not think so.'

His fingers closed on the weapons triggers as he diverted all available power to their systems.

A Cobra's venom ...

Scintillating beams of energy struck out, impaling the nearest vessel. It shivered in space, whirling away from the point of impact and retreating, unable to withstand the fierce energy assault at such close range. A flickering glow marked its own defences, struggling to repel the attack.

Another trigger, more weapons adding their fury. The staccato rhythm of multi-cannon fire joined the fray. Defences crumbled, and the cold hard metal of primitive but effective human ordnance found its mark.

The delicate petals of the alien tore and ripped under the devastating barrage. The Cobra's antique weapons seemed beneath their acknowledgement and it was too late for them to appreciate their unique effectiveness. The alien shuddered, the petals folding in an attempt to defend the stricken vessel from this barbaric and unexpected attack.

But it was to no avail. The slugs of burning metal rained down upon it, shredding membranes and shattering the delicate organic traceries that served as it's life-blood.

A moment later it disintegrated entirely. Green-tinged debris shattered and spiralled through space.

'Now you learn ...'

The other vessels all retreated, in concert as if by some unspoken signal. Luko had a moment to see them all orient themselves towards him before their own unearthly weapons struck.

Corruscating green and yellow flares erupted about the *Bella Principessa*. The star field spun out of control, engines screamed in protest, with the computers flashing imminent warnings of overload and doom across the console.

Luko retained just enough presence of mind to divert power to the shields when ...

Shields offline!

The energy banks were completely drained. Smoke and crackling sparks burst out from somewhere behind him.

Module Malfunction!

His hand tightened on the controls and the *Bella Principessa* steadied, arcing around, trailing leaking plasma and fuel from more than one breach in its hull.

The beam lasers struck out again.

The yellow-green fire was swift in retaliation.

Multi-cannons barked with fury, discharging into the darkness, shredding more of the delicate alien exteriors.

The *Bella Principessa* survived another pass, another of the alien warships torn asunder and spiralling away in the blackness.

Luko triggered the boost, turning his ship in a lazy loop away from the dark-hued aliens. They turned in pursuit, rapidly closing the gap as the old Cobra's energy reserves began to fail.

'Come to me,' Luko said, grinning. 'Yes. This is the way …'

The *Bella Principessa* turned, impaled by yellow-green fire as it did so. One beam laser was wrenched clean from the hull as the arc swept across it, blistering up the hull plates and narrowly missing the cockpit.

Luko pulled the triggers one last time, but there was no response. The throttles were jammed open, one engine flickering uncertainly, causing the ship to crab drastically to one side. He yawed it back the other way, compensating without thinking.

The two closest vessels loomed large in the canopy. As he watched, a crack snaked across the plexiglass, accompanied by the hiss of escaping air. Far beyond, he could see the glowing white lines of Salomé's stricken ship, still immobile in the distance.

Warning! Canopy Compromised.

Well, he wasn't going to have to worry about that.

He reached down to the lower console, past the old chronometer that had marked his time aboard the vessel and many commanders before him. He could just hear the old mechanism ticking away.

Time's up …

His fingers grasped a short lever. He pulled it hard.

Self-destruct sequence initiated.

The alien ships were still closing, probing the damaged vessel, trying to ascertain whether it remained a threat.

The ascending whine of power systems on overload.

The shadow of a snake. A Cobra … Rising over them …

The alien ships were close. Too close. The deadly discharge of the *Bella Principessa's* final fury eviscerated them in an instant.

* * *

Tears glistened on her face, the fierce flash of brief light from the demise of the *Bella Principessa* lit grey eyes stricken with grief. Tumbling debris spiralled in the darkness.

'Luko …'

Hassan could see her fingers had lost their grip on the controls. Power hummed around him. To his surprise, the ship's systems flickered and came back online.

'We have power … Salomé …'

She still didn't respond, still staring out of the forward canopy in silent grief.

'He gave us a way out!' Hassan yelled, grabbing at her. 'We can escape …'

She didn't respond. Hassan reached across her, toggling the hyperspace mapping systems and bringing up the nearest destination.

Get us back … 46 Eridani …

Hassan toggled the hyperdrive actuator and a rising hum signalled the activation of the drive. He pushed the throttles forward to their stops and pulled the ship around.

Faint flickering traces appeared on the scanner in the rear quadrant.

'They're coming back …'

Frame shift inhibited by factor of 40. Disruptive mass.

Hassan willed the drive to charge. He redirected all available power into the engines, the sleek Clipper thrusting away from the incoming vessels at maximum velocity. With the capacitor taking every available scrap of power, it was possible to boost the engines even further.

'Now …'

4 … 3 … 2 … 1 … Engage.

The *Seven Veils* dropped out of the universe of traditional physics and flung itself into the whirling maelstrom of witch-space. The Clipper flashed through the darkness.

They lurched out of the ethereal dimensions between space, crashing back into the world of suns and stars and spacecraft ...

Hassan recognised a ship ahead.

They're here. It's time.

Salomé was still shaking, her hands white on the seat grips, tears welling up in her eyes. A frown crossed her face as she saw the lines of a large vessel she didn't recognise. It wasn't alien though, this definitely had its origins in human space.

'Get us out of here,' she said. 'Someone must have known we were ...'

Hassan unbuckled and then braced himself against the pilot's chair.

I did this once before to save my life. This time I'm saving hers ...

'Hassan?'

The blow was practised and effective. Salomé slumped in her harness.

Hassan buckled himself back in place, toggling the comms system.

'I have her.'

'Excellent news, my dear fellow,' came a guttural but amicable sounding voice. 'You are just in time.'

Chapter Thirty

Location unknown, Col 70 sector, Uninhabited

Consciousness returned and with it her memory.

Someone had hit her.

Hassan?

Her head was pounding, her vision blurry. She blinked, trying to see. She was still in the co-pilot's chair. Something was moving above her. A ship, moving close by.

She couldn't see what had caught them. A vessel hung above, eclipsing the light of the faraway star and shrouding the *Seven Veils* in darkness. A shadow fell across her.

She tried to move but found she was bound and restrained by some kind of clasp around her ankles, wrists and neck. She tried to move again, but could not get free.

She was gagged too, a piece of fabric pulled tight across her face. She tried to yell, but heard only a muffled moan.

Around her, the *Seven Veils* jolted. She could make out the interior of some kind of docking clamp, the ship had been seized and must have been grabbed by the larger vessel. For long minutes there was nothing but the sound of her own feeble attempts to free herself.

Then the doors to the bridge snapped open.

The sound of mag-boots on the metal decking.

'Princess Aisling will be pleased,' said a voice. Salomé recognised it and scowled.

Gerrun!

At some remote command her seat rotated in place, turning her to face her captors. Her eyes widened as she took in the sight of Hassan standing with a gun trained on her, flanked by her erstwhile patrons, Zyair and Gerrun. She struggled in her seat, wrestling against the bonds that secured her, the edges cutting into her skin.

'As feisty as ever,' Gerrun commented. 'Quite the challenge, isn't she?'

Hassan moved forward and pulled the gag away from her face.

'Don't you dare touch me,' she snarled, jerking away from him. 'You're in league with them? How could you!'

'Hassan has been in our pay for quite some time,' Zyair said. 'Keeping tabs on you, shall we say. It was useful to know where you were, particularly when it appeared you were dead.'

Salomé tried to stare at Hassan, but he refused to look at her.

'You'd work with them?' she demanded.

He didn't answer, but typed some commands into a nearby console.

'What was your price?' Salomé yelled. 'What would they give you so that you'd betray me? Money, fame, riches? What? How did they buy you, Hassan? I thought you were …'

She caught a sideways flick of his eyes towards her. His gaze quickly dropped.

'Oh, something far beyond money,' Gerrun said, his face a mask of smugness. 'Something beyond price, beyond his station, beyond his wildest dreams …'

Salomé frowned and turned to Gerrun.

He smiled.

'We promised him … you.'

Salomé's next breath caught in her throat. The glances, the asides, the furtive looks. She had known his infatuation and ignored it. So many men reacted in such a manner she had become immune to the admiration. She had used it, turned it to her advantage, teased and tantalised to get her way …

Her expression hardened. She was no one's property. That many loved and admired her was not her fault, she was her own person.

'He can't have me,' she snapped. She glared in Hassan's direction. 'Do you hear that? I am not yours, not anyone's!'

'Oh, but you are, sweet little Imperial girl,' Zyair said. 'Or at least, you will be, with a little … modification.'

Salomé's fists clenched. 'Never … no. Hassan, how could you do this to me?'

'Do this … to you?'

His voice was a whisper, but he turned to face her. His face a mask of pain and anguish.

'For years I have followed you,' he said. 'Stepped aside as you conducted your business, taken you to the edge of the galaxy and back. I have given up everything for you, served you, run your errands. You have taken every-thing I had and it's never enough! You have burned me, spurned me, cast me out with not a thought for my feelings as you chase your myths around the cosmos. I have given my life for you ... I love you ...'

Salomé shook her head. 'No Hassan. You do not love me, you love a dream. A lust! A fantasy which cannot be.'

He shook his head. 'No, it can ...'

Salomé's gaze was hard as the icy void.

'If you do this, know I will hate you with every fibre of my being. You can take my body, perhaps even my mind.' She shook her head. 'But you cannot take my soul and the echo of your treachery will scald you every day you look upon me.'

Hassan retreated from her.

Gerrun moved forward. 'Quite the orator still, I see. It is no avail to you, my dear. He is a coward at heart. It's compliance with our wishes or it's his life. He can ... do the math, as they say.'

'Don't do this ...' Salomé pleaded at Hassan. 'You're better than this. If you truly love me as you say, you would not let them!'

'Enough of this,' Zyair interrupted. 'If you want that bounty, it's time to claim it.'

'Hassan, no!' Salomé cried. 'Those ships we saw ... you know what happened to Luko ...'

Hassan ignored her, gesturing with the gun whilst pressing a control on the console. The restraints unlocked with a snapping click, retracting into the pilot's chair behind her.

Zyair also had a weapon pointed at her. Hassan moved across and tied another restraint around her wrists, locking her arms in front of her and pulling her to her feet.

'After you, my dear,' Gerrun said, pulling out his own weapon and carefully aiming it at her. 'To the airlock, if you please.'

She took one more glance around and then stepped forward. Gerrun, Zyair and Hassan fell in place behind her.

There was no opportunity to escape. She might have been able to overpower them had they been unarmed and she was free, but even then fighting in zero-gee was a clumsy affair. She walked onwards, her heart hammering with apprehension and betrayal.

The expansive midsection of the *Seven Veils* opened before her and she walked through the midst of its Imperial opulence, turning to head down a central staircase that led to the lower deck. She could see the starboard side airlock had already irised open and light was streaming in from some-where beyond.

Another ship.

As she came closer she could make out a shadow, a figure was standing there, silhouetted in the light of the exit. She squinted, trying to make it out. It was familiar, tall and bulky, the shadow of another gun held poised.

'Bill Turner!' she said. 'But you're …'

'Dead?' Bill answered. 'You of all people should know nothing is ever quite so neat and tidy.'

'You betrayed me too?' she demanded.

'I was never working for you,' he replied.

He gestured with his gun. Salomé found herself ushered down a short corridor. The airlock cycled closed behind her. Zyair and Gerrun had re-mained on the other side. She was left with Bill and Hassan.

The styling of the vessel was austere and functional, but it lacked the military flavour that signalled Federal capital ship design.

Alliance, perhaps? But why …

She was led into an anteroom, circular in overall appearance, domi-nated by a holofac projector in the centre. Otherwise it was empty, other than a series of concentric seats arranged in rows all facing in. The forceful push of a muzzle in her back made her stumble forwards.

'What is this?' she demanded.

Bill stepped forward, typing commands and codes into the holofac sys-tem. It illuminated with a brief flicker, casting a green glow into the room. Salomé could make out five figures on the other end of the transmission, shrouded and thrown into silhouette by the lighting. She could make out no features, only their overall shape.

'Greetings Salomé, or perhaps Kahina Tijani Loren is more appropri-ate,' said the man in the middle. He was bulky and overweight based on what she could see, his voice flabby yet energetic.

'Who are you?' Salomé demanded.

'Our identities are not your concern,' said a thin man to his immediate right.

'Come now,' said the fat man in the middle. 'I see no reason to be quite so secretive with one condemned. You may refer to me as Infrastructure.' He gestured to the others. 'This is Finance, Exo, Personnel and Society …'

'Then what do you want with me?' Salomé asked.

The woman, Finance, sitting on the bulky man's left side answered her.

'You have caused us much strife and difficulty,' she said, her voice sharp and irritable.

'You are here to complete the final part of the puzzle for us,' Exo finished.

Salomé tried to withdraw, but the muzzle of Bill's gun was firmly pushed into her back once more.

'Elvira Martuuk's data analysis,' said Personnel. She was small, seated on the far right of the five. 'Well, Mr. Turner?'

The pressure from the gun disappeared. Salomé found herself shoved forward. She staggered, trying to regain her balance as her mag-boots skittered across the metal flooring. She turned to see Bill holding up a commtab.

'Here,' he said, activating the commtab and holding it out to her. 'Unlock it.'

Salomé shook her head.

'No,' she replied. 'I won't help you.'

Bill turned and grabbed her, dealing her a blow to the back of the head. She cried out and flailed back, half stunned, but still upright in the zero-gee.

'Unlock it,' Bill said, staring at her. 'Or I will take you apart piece by piece in front of your eyes.'

Salomé didn't move for a long moment. Bill aimed the gun towards her leg. Salomé saw his finger tightening on the trigger.

No odds in resistance now. If I am to escape I cannot be injured …

'Wait. I'll do it.'

Bill smiled. 'Glad you can see reason.' He held the holofac out to her and she jabbed the unlock code into it, struggling with the bonds that still tied her wrists. The display flickered and activated.

Bill took the commtab and interfaced it with the holofac system. 'All her exploration data, and the secret transmission from the Children of Raxxla. Every Earth-like world in the vicinity of the Rift, the Conflux and Hawking's Gap.'

'And the wake concealment technology?' said the man identified as Society. He wasn't as large as the first man, but he was also somewhat overweight, his voice jovial and upbeat. 'We don't want to forget that now, do we?'

'The prototype was installed aboard her ship,' Bill replied. 'My engineers are removing it now. We will have the blueprints and necessary construction details transferred in the next few hours.'

'Excellent, excellent,' Infrastructure said with a chuckle. 'It appears we have reached the end of our little chase. Only a few little details to tidy up.'

Salomé's heart thumped in her chest, she felt sweat chill across her skin.

'Kill me and you will heap misfortune upon yourselves.'

Infrastructure laughed uproariously. 'Perhaps you are referring to your little assemblage of loyal followers. Nothing more than a loose collection of warring tribes come together because of your undoubtable charisma, my dear. We have been monitoring their activities. But with you gone, they will fade into the darkness of the void. They cannot help you.'

'The people of the galaxy deserve to know the truth about all this,' Salomé cried. 'Why do you hide the facts? These aliens … they are massing!'

'Not just any aliens,' the woman named Personal said. 'Surely you know better than that.'

Salomé cast her mind back.

Arissa's suspicions, those ancient encounters …

'You mean, they're really … Thargoids?' she whispered.

'That is the colloquial term,' Exo said with a sneer. 'And as such, is most painfully imprecise. A collective noun for their kind we imposed. There are two distinct cultural groups, or dynasties if you will.'

Dynasties? Dynasty. Project Dynasty!

Society chuckled. 'Putting two and two together now, I see. Yes, we have two distinct dynasties of the Thargoids. One known as the Oresrians, the other as the Klaxians. Unfortunately, both are heading in the direction of the core worlds. A conflict is already taking place, a civil war between their kinds. The Oresrians appear to be losing, falling back. From their perspective, they're retreating, using our worlds as mere cover in their bid to escape their foes.'

'These … Oresrians are what we've been seeing? The reports …'

'Yes,' Exo said. 'They intend to carve a path through our civilisation and leave us cast down on either side. What was once called a "bullet-shield" in military parlance, I believe. They only mean to escape. Humanity will merely serve as a convenient way to delay their pursuers.'

Salomé gasped, a frown creasing her features.

'Wait. You've known they were coming?' she said in disbelief. 'And you've told no one?'

'Of course not,' Infrastructure gestured expansively. 'What do you think all this was about? The clandestine technology acquisition aimed at ensuring that necessary advances took place according to a certain timetable, fanning the flames of war between the Federation and the Empire to ensure humanity has a fleet that has a chance in the coming battle. The encouragement of the space-faring masses to grow their skills in the Arena and weaponise their ships courtesy of those oh-so-convenient "Engineers." We don't intend to allow humanity to be cannon fodder in someone else's war.'

'Then my exploration data …'

Exo leant forward, looming large on the holofac, his features still invisible.

'Yes, your precious itinerate commanders who chased dreams in the deep void, cataloguing systems as they went. Locating every useful resource so that we didn't have to.'

'But the beacons and the abandoned bases they found …'

'A previous expedition we sent out to establish waypoints,' Personnel said. 'Ready in case it became necessary …'

'Necessary?' Salomé echoed.

'You've not yet seen the full capabilities of the Thargoids,' Exo continued. 'It is quite possible that, despite all our work, humanity may not fare too well against this threat. That original mission and the combined efforts of your intrepid collection of explorers have ensured we have three viable escape routes. Four, if you count that ridiculous so-called utopia of Colonia.'

'Routes … out of the core worlds. The Rift, the Gap …'

'And the Conflux, yes. Those Earth-like worlds?' Exo said. 'The secret couldn't be kept forever.'

'But no one came back from those missions,' Salomé said. 'All that expense, all those lives?'

'Weighed against the trillions within the core worlds?' Personnel said. 'A trivial price to pay in order to cover all eventualities.'

Salomé shook her head, trying to take it all in.

'You see, you and everyone else have been guided all along,' Infrastructure chuckled. 'Whilst chasing mysteries, you and your sordid teams of spacers have furnished us with all the exploration data we needed. We have the combined fleets of all major powers at our disposal. We have new hyperspace technology. Thousands of vessels have been augmented with engineering modifications, we have lists of the top bounty hunters in the galaxy. We have the finance and the production capability given our investment in Wreaken Construction and the reach of the Sirius

Corporation. There are many others, of course, but I won't bore you with the details. In short, we are now ready.'

'You're going to tell the galaxy?'

Infrastructure looked over to Society.

'Our organisation has been looking after humanity for centuries,' Society said, airily. 'This is nothing new. We are the shepherds. We do not scare the sheep needlessly. We must be responsible, after all. That knowledge would cause mass panic. That is not conducive to us ensuring the maximum possible survival rate.'

'Survival rate,' Salomé said, shaking her head. 'I once caused the deaths of thousands because I didn't care for individual lives …'

'We are above such petty considerations. The big picture, you see. Do not accuse us of being callous and uncaring. We do this for the greater good of all. Such knowledge and its promulgation remains our business.'

'And your part in this is at an end,' Finance said. 'We're wasting time. Kill them both. I've never understood the point of explaining the tedious details to the condemned.'

'My dear, indulge us,' Infrastructure said. 'There's a certain satisfaction in the telling … but you're quite right. Enough is enough.'

'We get such little credit for the good we do,' Personnel said.

Bill stepped back and pointed his gun at Hassan. She heard Hassan gasp in alarm.

'No, you promised …'

'Nothing personal, you understand,' Bill said, with a brief nod.

Salomé tensed, poised, but there was nothing she could do …

There was a thump from the corridor behind them. The airlock was cycling.

In that moment, Hassan leapt forward. He lurched across the room, knocking Bill aside. The gun fired, the bullet ricocheting off the interior walls of the anteroom. Salomé ran forward, but somehow Tsu had emerged from the corridor, cannoning into Bill and knocking both him and Hassan through the air.

For a moment all three wrestled clumsily in the zero-gee, trying to gain control of the gun.

Tsu managed to secure herself against the floor with one mag-boot and punched down on Bill. He yelled.

The gun fired again. A stream of blood in the zero-gee, pooling into tiny spheres. Tsu punched again and Bill floated away unconscious, the gun spiralling out of his grasp. Tsu grabbed it and tucked it into her belt.

For a moment Salomé thought she had been hit herself, but the blood was not hers.

'Hassan!'

His body recoiled back towards her. She caught it, trying to steady both of them.

More blood, from his lips. Coughing, his voice catching on words.

'Salomé, I'm sorry … for my part … I was a fool …'

'Stop it, we need to get you to medical …'

Hassan coughed, choking on more blood, his body convulsing in her arms. Salomé looked desperately up at Tsu, who had moved in to help her. Tsu shook her head. Bill's aim had been good, the bullet had torn through Hassan's chest.

'Salomé … I did love you …'

Salomé pulled him close, smoothing the long lanky hair out of his face, kissing his forehead.

'I forgive you,' she whispered. His body shook in her grasp and then was still. Tears pooled in her eyes, but could not fall. She wiped them away with the back of her hand, slowly standing back to her feet.

Her hands clenched and fury was etched on her face.

The holofac, with its five enigmatic figures, was still flickering at the rear of the room. Whoever they were, they were still watching.

Salomé turned to face them, her face drawn in a ferocious snarl.

'I know of intrigue and scheming. I know the value of life. I have learnt it in dust and ashes and war and death. You have taken the blood of the innocent, the blameless. Used thousands, millions, for your schemes! Your consciences have rotted as you've comforted yourselves that you do all this for the greater good!'

She pointed at Hassan, her hand trembling with rage.

'His life, you have murdered it. This is what you have become. You are not the arbiters of humanity's destiny, you are not the guardians of forever. You are monsters, playing games with the lives of the people you claim to protect! You are the evil you sought to protect us from and …' she paused for a gasping breath. 'I defy you. I will reveal your secrets to the galaxy. I will expose you, castigate you with my last breath.' She gestured to Tsu. 'Give me the gun.'

'Salomé …'

'The gun! Now!'

Tsu handed it to her. She took it, raising it swiftly.

'Your time is coming to a close,' she said. 'She outwitted you. Yes, you know who I mean. Rebecca. She frustrated your plans at every stage … and she has one little surprise left.'

She fired at the holofac images and watched in satisfaction as the figures flinched despite not being present. She saw the looks of consternation on their faces and laughed hysterically.

'You've lost!'

Her next shot was to the holofac projector itself. It sparked and crackled. The image faded.

She turned the gun on Bill's motionless body. Her fingers closed on the trigger. She blinked through eyes that were thick with tears.

The gun came loose from her fingers and she crumpled to the floor, the energy of her anger deserting her. Sobs broke through and she embraced Hassan once more.

'Salomé, we can't wait,' Tsu urged. 'We don't know what other ships may be incoming. Raan and I were able to track you, others might be able to do the same. The wake suppressors, they're not reliable. Maybe Bill sabotaged them. Those patrons might have alerted …'

Salomé's sobs stopped abruptly and she looked up. Tsu recoiled at the hatred on her face.

'Gerrun and Zyair,' she said, stumbling to her feet, madness in her eyes.

Tsu followed her as she stalked from the anteroom.

***

Raan had both of the patrons at gunpoint, preventing them from leaving. Salomé had wasted no time. He saw her stride towards them. Somehow she'd retrieved her sword, the scabbard was clenched in her hand. He could see her knuckles were white from the grip.

She returned to them, gesturing for Raan to move aside. Her face was streaked with tears, her grey eyes cold and bereft.

'Now you suffer for your intrigue,' Salomé said, her jaw taut. 'I will leave a message for your mistress. I take from those who take from me. You used Hassan, you will pay for that misdeed.'

– 426 –

Zyair and Gerrun backed down the corridor as Salomé advanced. She saw their faces blanch as she drew her sword from its ornate scabbard.

'No,' Zyair said. 'We meant no lasting offence, we were only ...'

'Trying to save your own worthless hides!' Salomé cried. She swung the Holva blade with precision, in a deft, practised move.

Zyair staggered in front of her, his hands going to his midriff, a bright red stain spreading over them, droplets of red spurting out and sparkling in the overhead lights. He looked up in shock and gave a strangled yelp, horror spreading across his features before his eyes rolled up in his head and his body went limp, blood spraying in all directions from his disembowelled stomach, splashing against the bulkheads in the zero-gee. Her next lunge was straight and true, between the fourth and fifth rib. Straight to the heart. Zyair gave a ghastly gurgle.

Behind him, Gerrun staggered back in alarm, holding his hands up in a vain attempt to hold her at bay. Salomé stepped past Zyair's twitching corpse, not heeding the blood that coated her hands, face and clothes.

'My dear Lady Kahina, can we not discuss a mutually beneficial arrangement?' Gerrun said, his voice rising in panic, 'For old time's sake if nothing else, there is much I could do on your ...'

'You chose Aisling over me,' Salomé said, her face twisting with hatred. 'You followed the wrong woman.'

She lunged. Gerrun's voice turned into a spluttering choke. Her sword had lanced through his neck, blood sprayed out in an arc, splattering off the bulkhead walls in a plume of crimson. She twisted the sword cruelly. Gerrun flailed before her in a ghastly manner, but she stared into his eyes as the light began to fade from them.

'I recognised your handiwork. You were the mastermind behind this sordid plot,' she said, her voice just above a whisper. 'Just rewards for your loyal service to me, Patron Gerrun.'

She withdrew the sword, grabbed the floating bloodstained cloth of Zyair's robes and cleaned the blade. Then she replaced it in her scabbard and turned, striding away from the tableaux of slaughter without a backwards glance.

'With me,' she snapped at the horrified Tsu and Raan, wiping the blood carelessly from her face. 'We go to expose this. The galaxy deserves the truth. I intend to tell them. Tionisla, now!'

'Tionisla?' Tsu asked. 'What's in Tionisla?'

'The truth,' Salomé answered. 'We go to unveil the truth.'

Deep space, Location unknown

Raan flipped on the comms link, calling up a secure channel.

'Been waiting,' said the voice on the other end. 'Dude, you have a bounty on you! Two million credits, man. What the …'

'Can't speak for long,' Raan replied. 'Yuri, this is big, galaxy-changing stuff. If you ever wanted that fight, now is the time.'

'What's the deal?' Yuri replied.

'Alien ships, man, the truth. We're going to reveal it. That Imperial woman, the one on the news?'

'Loren something …?'

'Yeah …'

'It's a massive cover-up. She's got the info, but we need to get it across the charts. We're running decoy for her, least that's the plan at the moment. Could do with another pilot.'

'There's bounty hunters everywhere on the edge of the COL 70 sector, they're all looking for her, you and some Alliance girl …'

'Stakes are high,' Raan said. 'Won't think less of you if you don't want in. But you did say you wanted to do something significant … This is the real deal.'

'I'm in, just tell me where.'

'Buddy, you'll likely get a bounty too. Real people trying to kill you.'

'I want a challenge,' Yuri replied. 'I'm ready.'

Raan tapped a quick transponder code. 'Meet me here. Owe you one …'

***

'You will find considerable resistance,' the glove-handed figure said. 'She has many followers, alongside those that travel with her. Her influence is not to be underestimated, Besieger.'

The bounty hunter smiled, his lips just visible on the holofac display.

'The Children of Raxxla?' Besieger replied. 'I know all about them, their allies in Loren's Legion and the disarray they call their "allied coalition." Your wish?'

The glove-handed man paused before letting out a heavy sigh. He gave a terse instruction.

The holofac flickered and shut down.

***

The *Seven Veils* detached from the hull of an unmarked Type-9 heavy freighter, turned about and fell into formation with the *StarStormer* and the *Rivincita*. Encrypted wideband calls went out. Across the borders of the core worlds and out towards the Col 70 sector, ships assembled, convoys moved and every spacer with a concern turned their attention to the void.

Imperial broadcasts immediately re-issued their message.

Commanders Salomé, Tsu Annabelle Singh, Raan Corsen and Yuri Nakamura are to be considered extremely dangerous. Do not open communication channels. Shoot on sight.

Chapter Thirty-One

Deep space, 46 Eridani system, Uninhabited

A rendezvous point had been set. It was the only viable alternative. Strategy determined it. If you were to hide you had to retreat from the star. Hide in the darkness.

Incoming ships always arrived alongside a given star system's centre of mass, the primary object, usually the central star. It was the easiest and most obvious place to look and thus the place to avoid.

Comms buzzed through the vacuum. Sleek vessels hung together in the void, poised and ready to run.

Salomé smiled grimly at the deception. Before her were three vessels, each visually identical to her own, even down to the name plates. Bright white Imperial Clippers, a phalanx of *Seven Veils* drifting in the darkness, thousands of light seconds from the blue-white glare of 46 Eridani.

Erimus had sent her a quick overview of their strategy. Run, hide, evade, flee and disorientate. It was the only way to get to the core worlds and evade the bounty hunters. Fighting was the very last resort when all others were exhausted. The ships were built for speed and stealth. The Children of Raxxla and Loren's Legion had called for assistance. Thousands had responded, individuals, groups and factions. More than could be counted.

Others had not, but had laid their own plans in secret.

Pilots had volunteered to fly other seemingly identical ships, with commander profiles set to emulate her own, a ploy to divert attention away and spread the bounty hunters out more thinly. Fewer eyes on the primary target, fewer chances. Similar ploys had been arranged for Raan, Tsu and Raan's friend, Yuri. Salomé had not been pleased about endangering another life, but Yuri's record spoke for itself and the Children of Raxxla vouched for his prowess based on his Arena reputation. Raan had told her she could trust him. The more targets there were, the less likely any particular target was to get selected.

Commander Zenith Ddraiglas had been assigned by Erimus to be her wing leader, accompanied by the most trusted and capable pilots, Commanders Eisen and Isaiah Evanson. Similar arrangements had been made for Tsu and Yuri. Commanders Adurnis, Chriswoo and Mesa Falcon were to protect the Alliance woman; Commanders Red Ryderr, Azrael Dirge and Stephen were set to escort Yuri.

Decoys …

The decoys were planning to jump around erratically, to lead bounty hunters on a merry chase. A campaign of disorientation and confusion through which they might slip unseen and reach their objective.

Her grip on the flight yoke was tight. She let go, flexing her fingers and wiping away the sweat. She could fly, but she did not relish it.

I am asking so much … and they have answered.

Tears formed in her eyes. She brushed them aside, taking a moment to compose herself. She toggled the comms, running her tongue around her mouth to moisten it.

'Before we run,' she said. 'Know this. By continuing to associate with me you put your lives at grave risk. I would not be angered if you chose to leave now; it may be the wisest move. What we must do is fraught with danger and likely futile. We cannot win, we can only expose.

'We're in this until the bitter end,' Eisen said.

'Your courage is a tonic to me in these dark times,' Salomé said. 'So what must we do? Our mysterious old lady, Rebecca. She planned meticulously over so many years. Those who wish to suppress the truth will try to stop me. Others may try to kill me for the bounty the Empire has placed upon my head. Those in authority that might help … their hands are tied …

'Rebecca's ship, in Tionisla. At the beacon there, her ship rests. If I or my friends can reach it, we can activate its systems and reveal her secret. Thus, we must fight our way there against the odds.

'Everyone knows where we are, but they do not know where we are bound. It is time for us to flee – and … as you know… I don't like to be late.'

'Let's get the hell out of here then. Plot the first jump, long range, FSD inject 3,' Zenith said.

'Roger that.' Isaiah confirmed.

'That'll get us out of the blockade they've probably got set around this area,' Eisen said. 'With those permits locks this is a dead end. Jump system is Synuefe OT-V B20-0.'

'Engage, go!' Zenith commanded.

Salomé engaged the drive. The ships accelerated forwards into the darkness and disappeared into the night.

***

The strategy was multi-layered. Not only were the escorts employing their evasive moves, but wings of other pilots were driving ahead and following behind. 'Shield' wings flew ahead of the groups, engaging other pilots who were attempting to blockade their path. 'Dagger' wings flew behind, interdicting any unknown or hostile pilots in pursuit. 'Reapers' claimed the lives of any bounty hunters that attempted to get too close. Waypoints had been established for all four. Coalition fleets were spread across the stars in an attempt to keep the waypoints clear. Friendly and hostile forces were converging. A battle was inevitable.

***

Raan was escorted by commanders formed into a dedicated 'Cobra Wing.' They, in turn, were supported by a faction known as Adle's Armada. Their allegiance lay with the Federation, but believed strongly in truth and openness. Their leadership had been in a quandary over whether to support Salomé or not. Initially, they had dismissed it as Imperial politics that they didn't need to be concerned about. Salomé's reputation as a terrorist was another reason for ignoring her.

But the debacle over Karl Devene and the exploration deep into the galaxy had soured their view of authority. Ultimately, they decided that whatever it was Salomé had discovered deserved exposure. Their leader, Tyllerius Adle, issued a proclamation that the Armada stood on Salomé's side. They offered their assistance. The safety of Raan, being of Federal origin, became their concern. Raan and his escorts fled into the darkness between the stars.

***

Tsu checked the systems in her Viper Mark IV once again. She'd only done it six times already. She had three commanders in her wing too, Adurnis, Chriswoo and MesaFalcon. All seemed as nervous as she was.

Allied coalition comms buzzed around her, a cacophony of noise and confusion. How anyone was making sense of it all was beyond her …

Maybe that's the plan. If we don't know what the hell is going on, how is anyone else going to figure it out?

She had been trying to follow the organisation of the coalition without success. The overlapping factions, admiral, lieutenants and the often con-flicting orders seemed impenetrable, obtuse and disorganised.

Just focus on what you have got to do. One of us has got to make it to Tionisla. Just one, that's it. Then we expose …

'Salomé is jumping,' Adurnis called. 'Ready when you are.'

Tsu puffed out her cheeks. 'Let's do this.'

She shoved the throttles forward to their stop and engaged the frame shift drive. The Viper and its escorts vanished into the blackness.

***

Yuri watched from the cockpit of his Imperial Courier, the *Sword of Damocles*. About him, the escort had formed. Red's Federal Assault Ship, the *ENV Black Bess*, Az with his Fer-de-Lance, the *ENV Redhead Lass*, all backed up by Stephen's Anaconda, the *Star Gypsy*. The escort was ready, bolstered by the combined forces of fuel tankers and military militia which had lent its aid.

Yuri had been impressed by the swift mobilisation of forces. The scale of the operation was overwhelming, he couldn't keep half of it in his head. He focussed on Raan's instructions.

Tionisla, we make for Tionisla. There's a beacon …

'She's running!' came the communique from the Children of Raxxla. 'Time to go.'

Excitement, nervousness, terror. He wasn't sure what the outcome was going to be, but he wouldn't have missed it for the universe. He felt alive.

***

The first few jumps seemed easy. A few friendly commanders exchanged brief words of encouragement before moving onto their assigned tasks. The system names became a blur of meaningless numbers. Their progress had been rapid.

Twenty minutes! Seems like a lifetime already!

Somewhere in the depths of the Synuefe sector, hostile forces made their move.

Salomé saw the scanner light up with dozens of unknown ships.

'Evasive,' she said, pulling her Clipper into a steep turn. Voice crackled between Eisen, Zenith and Isaiah so quickly she couldn't make out who was talking. The surprise and dismay in their voices told her all she needed to know.

'They're going for Salomé!'

'We've got contacts everywhere!'

'Pulling around.'

'They are on top of us …'

'Go … engage engage!'

A blue light flickered around the cockpit as she activated the hyperspace jump.

Interdiction!

The FSD charged and the *Seven Veils* threw itself into hyperspace.

Escaped, but only just …

Now it really was a chase.

***

Yuri's flight made good time. Not far ahead was their second waypoint.

'We have bounty hunters, closing in on the flanks,' Az reported. 'Some nutter called Ultra. Big rep, best we avoid him.'

Yuri acknowledged the intel. 'Jump for the Hixkaryk system.'

The four ships pulled together as their wing emerged from hyperspace. The star was close. Fuel scooping around it, the four ships encountered dozens of hostile vessels.

'Emergency hyperspace jump …'

'We'll cook …'

'No choice! Jump!'

***

More ships, more pursuers.

'I can't refuel, I can't evade,' Salomé called. 'Not enough time …'

'Fly as close to the sun as you can,' Zenith called.

'I'll burn up!' Salomé replied.

'Fine, then you burn,' Zenith replied. 'When you get the charge, jump!'

She triggered the jump. Hot air blasted her, the *Seven Veils'* cooling systems overloaded far beyond their design limitations. The ship was on the verge of a catastrophic meltdown.

120% Heat!

Smoke was billowing out of the console. Something crackled. Sparks showered her from above. She winced as something burnt her skin.

Module damage!

Ship's systems would be hit. There was no alternative. Run hot, run long …

***

The battle reports to Adle's Armada HQ were coming in faster than they could be dealt with. Hundreds of pitched battles were being fought across the galactic chart. Operators were running backwards and forwards as screens crashed with information overload. Orders were barked, the sense of barely contained chaos pervading the entire organisation.

'She's got the whole damn galaxy at each other's throats!'

'Where's our man?'

'Doing well, we have our target two-thirds of the way to the final destination. Estimates are that twenty, perhaps thirty attackers already dispatched. It's a complete interdiction fest out there. Utter chaos on all comm channels. Pitched battles are raging at the waypoints. Hundreds reported killed.'

The supervisor shook his head. 'This better be worth it …'

'We've got some other contacts coming in!'

'Who are they?' the supervisor demanded.

'IDs are Earth Defence Fleet ships, Commanders Jaiotu and Moonweb in command.'

'What do we have on these folks?' the supervisor demanded.

'Operating out of Chi Orionis, sir. Claiming to be friendlies, Federal aligned …'

'We could do with their help. Assign them a wing, but keep on eye on them!'

***

They crossed the border from the Synuefe sector as they passed HIP 22692. The wing jumped in. Zenith heard Salomé's distressed message over the narrowband comms.

'I have a very strange … I'm on my own … I'm surround …' Salomé's voice washed out in a squeal of static.

'No eyes on the VIP!' Eisen called.

'Separated!' Isaiah confirmed. The wing linking capabilities were supposed to prevent the ships losing track of each other, but nothing was flawless.

She's not here ... she's alone ...

'Drop out!' Zenith called. 'Emergency cut out!'

Only static returned.

'Salomé, do you copy? Emergency drop ... confirm!'

More static, punctuated only by the faint warble of a background hum.

What is going on?

Zenith could see from his HUD that Salomé's ship was reporting it was intact with shields up.

Telemetry still good ... lost contact and voice comms! Nothing on the scanner. Where is she?

More static and then, blessed relief, her voice.

'I'm ok,' Salomé said, her voice high pitched but steady. 'Emergency drop worked but it broke a few onboard systems. Boosting away from drop position ... I think I'm clear. No contacts.'

Zenith let out the breath he was holding. 'Wing form up. She's still there. Salomé, activate your wing beacon and we'll come get you.'

'Missed you guys, don't leave me like that ...'

***

'FSD malfunction!' Yuri called. 'Can't keep the ship cool enough, taking module damage ...'

'We can't afford to hang around,' Red replied.

'If we wait, they'll catch us,' Az added.

'I'm burning up bit by bit,' Yuri said. 'Not sure my ship can take much more of this. It's not the damn hostiles, it's just the heat ...'

'Contact!' Stephen called, interrupting the conversation. 'Target closing from behind. I'm breaking formation to deal with him. You guys run, I'll interdict him.'

'Stephen ...'

'Do it, I've got the biggest slowest ship. Follow through on the mission!'

And then there were three.

***

Tsu had similar problems. Her wing had split up and rejoined. The battle became a strange type of strategic jockeying based around who could interdict who and when. Weapons were hardly ever used. Everything was a delaying tactic. To get away meant taking risks, taking heat … taking damage.

Ships were everywhere, the scanners a mess of conflicting information. It was almost impossible to tell who was friend or foe. Through the midst of it, four ships continued their flight, burning, their shipboard systems cracking and bursting under the load.

Heat damage is killing us …

'Keep jumping! Just go, jump, jump, jump! No time to wait!'

Next stop is Tionisla …

Tsu gripped the controls hard as her ship was wrenched out of hyperspace one last time.

We're here!

***

Another system. Salomé glanced at the scanner as she arrived. Ships everywhere. She had never seen a scanner so full. A bewildering array of flickering marks in all directions.

Surrounded, no matter what route we try. Just too many of them …

'Contacts!' Eisen called. 'Swarming everywhere.'

'I'm low on fuel,' Salomé called. 'Got to dive past the sun.'

'Don't get too close. Just fly as we taught you,' Isaiah added. 'Dive in and out, don't fly in a gentle curve around the corona.'

'I hear you.' Salomé adjusted course.

The *Seven Veils* lurched. Blue flickering light flashed outside the canopy.

Interdiction!

She tried to pull the ship towards a flashing point on the HUD, the escape vector. If she could maintain course she might not get caught. Zenith's words echoed in her head …

Interdiction is death …

Whatever was pursuing her was nimble, more so than her ship. Try as she might, the status indicators for the stability of her frame shift drive dropped lower and lower until …

'He's got me!'

'We have an Asp Explorer,' Eisen called.

'I'm on him,' Isaiah said. 'Right behind you.'

'Salomé, boost, run and jump,' Zenith called. 'Full power to shields.'

Laser fire flickered outside the canopy, the shields repelling it. The *Seven Veils* shuddered but held its course.

'It's a Commander Malticfarm,' Isaiah said. 'Definitely hostile! I have guns on him …'

Flashes from behind left brief shadows in the cockpit. Salomé didn't dare look, she concentrated on the jump controls, that was all that mattered.

The laser fire stopped.

'Killed him!' Isaiah yelled triumphantly.

'You're clear,' Zenith said. 'Jump, Salomé. Just keep going …'

***

Raan's *Rivincita* burst out into the Tionisla system, still trailing plasma from the star he'd just left. The ship was scorched and frazzled, its hull plates blackened and warped from the heat.

I'm here, I made it …

'Now what?'

He scanned space ahead of him, glad to see it seemed mercifully free of any vessels. He plotted the course to the beacon.

Got to find that ship!

***

'Still got bounty hunters on our six. They're getting closer, according to fleet intel,' Az said.

'Fleet reports they're doing their best to clear the course ahead,' Red reported.

Yuri shook his head. They'd changed course, diverted for repairs, slowed down, speeded up. Nothing was shaking their attackers.

'Persistant buggers.' Yuri muttered. 'We're buckyballing now. Just a straight chase to the finish. Let's move! Not far out now …'

***

'He's made it!' The Adle Armada supervisor called. 'Confirmation Raan's at Tionisla! Tsu has made it through as well. Fabulous work, everyone.'

'Now what?'

'He does whatever that Imperial prima donna told him to,' the supervisor replied. 'Get our groups into the surrounding systems and clear them out. Get word through to the Children of Raxxla that we've got a successful outcome. Divert the wing to assist Salomé, sounds like she needs all the help she can get ...'

***

Tsu saw Raan's Fer-de-Lance appear as a marker on her scanner. She flipped on the toggle for her wing beacon.

'Where's Yuri?' she gasped as Raan's holofac image appeared on her console.

'He's still good, just a few jumps behind. His wing is intact. Some heavy fire on the later waypoints, but he's ok.'

'And ... what's next?'

'Haven't heard,' Raan said. 'We proceed with the plan. We've made it, she said that was all that counted.'

'Do you have the co-ordinates?' Tsu asked.

'Locked in. Let's find this ship.'

***

The battle had given Salomé and her wing a brief respite. The pursuers seemed to have fallen back, perhaps to regroup or refine their own strategies. The void seemed oddly peaceful, the light of a nondescript red dwarf star lit the surroundings as the four Clippers hung in formation.

'Lots of damage,' Salomé reported. Zenith looked over the assessment. The hull of the real *Seven Veils* was holding up well enough, but he could see sporadic module damage throughout. The weapons and the frame shift drive appeared to have taken the brunt of it.

'We need to fix this,' Eisen said.

'Can we afford to wait?' Isaiah asked. 'Our location will have been transmitted across the galaxy by now. Everyone with hostile intent will be converging on this position.

'Can't be helped,' Zenith said. 'Salomé's ship is close to being crippled. Activate your AFMU ...'

Zenith watched as the shields flickered out on Salomé's vessel.

Great ... even more exposed now!

They couldn't risk a run to a station for repairs. That would only confirm their location.

Salomé's voice crackled across the narrowband comms.

'I did say you'd have your moment in the sun,' she said. 'Though perhaps this isn't quite what I meant.'

Resilient and hopeful, even after all this ...

Zenith's face crinkled into a smile.

The ships hung in the void for long minutes as Salomé's ship repaired itself. Finally, the shields were engaged once more.

We've got this. They said it was impossible, we've proven it can be done. We're more than halfway ... We're going to make it!

The chase resumed.

***

With a flash of light, two ships appeared in the darkness. Moments later a third joined them. They flew close, tracking quickly across the void to where a sparkling collection of objects nestled in a wide orbit about a blue-green planet.

The graveyard ...

As they approached, it became clear that it was a huge field of ships, all derelict, with what appeared to be the shattered and ruined hulk of an ancient space station at the centre. Strange and massive emblems floated alongside the scattered bulks of uncounted vessels, shifting and rotating slowly in the darkness.

'Good to see you guys,' Yuri called. 'That was brutal.'

'You too ...' Raan replied.

'There's hundreds of traces,' Tsu whispered. 'How are we going to find this ship?'

'Bounty hunters won't take long to find us,' Raan said. 'If they get past our escorts ...'

Yuri's tones echoed across the comms. 'Old Arena trick, it's all about the heat sources. If it's got any kind of power, it'll be giving off a signature. Scan for low-level emissions.'

Tsu adjusted her scanner. Most of the ships were dead, their hulls reading nothing more than any other piece of debris floating in the void. A few gave off vague signals, but nothing definitive and nothing matching the outline of a Cobra.

The three ships carved a rolling trajectory through the graveyard, scanning and seeking their target. Time ticked away. They reached the far edge, turned and doubled back, still looking.

'This is taking too long …' Tsu said.

'Keep looking,' Raan instructed. 'It's here, it's got to be here.'

'What if it's already been destroyed?' Tsu said. 'They could have found it, they could have already removed the evidence …'

'Got something,' Yuri said. 'Low-level power emission, looks like a Cobra. It's dark, but … yes, confirmed it's a Cobra Mark III. Pretty old school by the paintwork.'

Yuri punched up the co-ordinates and the three ships converged.

A dark ship, a black paint job, hard to make out except where it eclipsed the stars. As they approached they could see its extremities were marked by bold white lines, giving the ship an almost skeletal, hand-drawn appearance, a small mesh of interlocking triangles outlining its form.

'I can see the hull plates!' Tsu said. '*Cor Meum Et Animam*. It's here, we found it! I'm pulling alongside …'

'We'll keep you covered,' Raan replied. 'Make it quick!'

***

The *Seven Veils* materialised in the Trianguli sector. The worlds of the core were close now. Tionisla was less than twelve jumps away. The pursuers had fallen behind; the combined actions of the shields, daggers, reapers and the allied coalition fleets causing disarray across the stars.

Untold battles raged in systems en route as supporters from all ranks attempted to guard or dominate strategic waypoints on the galaxy map, with hostile forces equally determined to frustrate those efforts or directly interdict and attack the fleeing protagonists, the bounties offered for them an enticing lure.

There was no let up.

Salomé found her hands trembling on the controls.

An hour now … we have been chased constantly throughout …

Her concentration was strained, sweat soaked her, despite the best efforts of her suit. Her head pounded with the exertion. She could feel the bruises on her hands where the controls had been wrenched on every interdiction. Her body was battered and sore all over.

No let up, no time to rest. I'm tired ... let this be over ...

The ship was damaged ... she felt its pain herself. Every jolt that broke a system hurt her too. She felt battered, exhaustion fell about her like a cloak of weariness.

She could hear it in the voices of her escorts too. The strain, the planning, the uncertainty. It was wearing them down. Something had to give ...

The ship lurched again ... the blueness of the frame shift drive disrupted.

No, please ...

She blinked, trying to force the weariness away. Adrenaline came to her rescue as she struggled with the interdiction. Once again she lost, unable to counter the skill of the attacking pilots.

Multiple contacts ...

'I have an Asp, an Anaconda and a Cutter!' Eisen called. His voice was strained, tense and alarmed.

'Choose your targets,' Eisen called. 'Salomé, you need to jump out the moment you can.'

The *Seven Veils* was still spiralling from the disruption. The onboard drives had to cool before she could trigger them.

Need time!

'Can't spool the drive,' she called. 'Too hot!'

'They're all over her!' Isaiah yelled.

The Asp was already firing. Salomé spun the *Seven Veils* aside. Her defenders were closing in. More fire punctuated the darkness. The shields flickered and flashed in response.

Then the big guns fired. Salomé gulped as she saw the weapons of the Anaconda and the Cutter attempt to converge on her ship.

'Got Commanders Demetrios, JT and Haloring!' Eisen yelled. 'Assume all hostile. We're outgunned. Salomé, you've got to get out of range, we can't handle this!'

Salomé looked at the temperature gauge. As she watched, the frame shift drive indicators flickered to green.

'Demetrios is clean, Demetrios is clean.' Isaiah called. 'It's Adle's Armada! Anaconda! They're friendly, don't fire ..."

'Charging,' she called, batting at the controls. 'Frame shift drive is ...'

Error messages flickered up on the display. Heart pounding, she read them with alarm.

Module Damage! FSD failed!

'Frame shift has failed!' she called, desperation clutching at her. She felt sick to the stomach, nausea swirled about her and bile rose in her throat. 'Come on ... engage!'

No, no, no ...

The onboard computers buzzed angrily as they tried to reroute systems to bypass the damage.

The ship jolted again. Salomé watched as the shields began to fail under the combined attack.

'The Asp is down!' Isaiah called. 'Can't touch that Cutter though!"'

'Salomé, jump! For Randomius' sake, jump!'

She tried again, rekeying the controls.

'Come on, come on ...'

Frame shift drive charging!

'It's working!' she yelled. 'Just give me a few more moments ...

Frame shift inhibited by factor of 27. Disruptive mass.

The attacking ship was big, too big. It was trying to hold her in place. She needed range. There was enough charge left in the damaged capacitors. She channelled it to the engines.

Boost!

She was flung back in her pilot's seat as the acceleration took her. The *Seven Veils* had that advantage at least, it was quick.

Then the drive engaged.

'Jumping now!'

***

'Got the airlock opened,' Tsu's voice was breathless and tinny across the narrowband comms. 'There's emergency power, but not much else. No atmo. I'm boarding the ship. No lights ... hang on ...'

'No contacts on the scanner,' Yuri confirmed. 'Good so far ...'

'Let's hope it stays that way,' Raan muttered.

'Keeping the comms open,' Tsu's voice crackled out, her breathing harsh in the receivers. 'No life support in here, I only have a few minutes on the Remlok. Just trying to get some light ... there.'

A crackling hum burst out before Tsu's voice could be heard again.

'The cargo bay ... oh god ... there is blood on the walls ... marks of weapons fire ... the panels are blasted ...'

'Any signs of life?' Raan asked.

'Nothing here ... the escape pods are intact and undisturbed. I'm making my way to the bridge ...'

'Still clear ...' Yuri said. 'Wings are reporting incoming jumps, though. They're decoying them. We're going to have company soon ...'

'Get them to notify us if we have incoming,' Raan said. 'We'll need time to get Tsu out ...'

'The door to the bridge has been forced,' Tsu said. 'More burn marks. Looks like it was barricaded. Someone forced their way in here. The bridge is intact, but there's no one here. Minimal power, but the console systems are still running. The pilot's seat ... there's bullet hole straight through the middle ...'

'Make it quick, Tsu,' Raan said. 'No time for a scenic tour!'

'I've got the access,' Tsu said. 'Let's hope Salomé's code works ... got something ... yes. The systems are powering up ... Some kind of transmitter just popped up on the hull.'

Raan looked at the darkened hull of the Cobra from the viewpoint of his own ship. Sure enough, a small dish had risen up and locked into place on the old ship's hull.

'I can see it, just coding the transmission frequency ...'

'Can you hear it?' Tsu asked. 'A message? What does it say? I'm blind in here! Tell me!

Raan flipped the narrowband comms over to the indicated signal.

AUTHENTICATION CONFIRMED. BEGINNING TRANSMISSION. TEORGE. TEORGE. TEORGE ...

'It's just repeating something over and over,' Raan said. 'Teorge ... what the hell does that mean?'

'It's a system, just next door,' Yuri confirmed. 'One jump, literally.'

'That's it?' Tsu asked, bewilderment in her voice.

'Company!' Yuri yelled. 'We have ships dropping in at the beacon! Get out, get out now!'

'I'm coming!' They could hear the sounds of her exertion over the comms. 'Get word to Salomé that we found it ...'

'Transmitting to Erimus now,' Yuri called out.

Marks were flickering into solid readings on the scanner as the *StarStormer* powered up and left the old wreck of the *Cor Meum Et Animam*. The three ships formed up and retreated from the graveyard, which continued to echo to the repeating transmission.

TEORGE, TEORGE, TEORGE ...

***

'She has been weakened,' came the report. 'Hull is still intact, but her ship has significant module damage. Her escort remains, but they are tiring, their strategy is played out. They can only run now. Course is clearly set for the Old Worlds region. Perhaps Lave or Diso.'

Besieger nodded.

'Sufficient. Place yourself in their path. I will do the rest.'

***

The wing jumped into the Anumclaw system, the star swollen before them, bright in the canopies. Three ships appeared, battered and damaged, but still intact. The pilots were in much the same condition.

'Six jumps out,' Isaiah breathed. 'Refuel as quick as we can …'

'Very low on fuel,' Salomé said. 'Need some time.'

'Loop around the star,' Zenith replied. 'We have you covered.'

'Eisen?' Isaiah called. 'Where are you?'

Static crackled back.

'We've lost him,' Zenith replied. 'Have no telemetry. Where …'

Salomé pulled the *Seven Veils* into a tight loop. Rising above the burning corona of the Anumclaw star were several points of light, glowing halos in formation, heading directly towards her. The scanners revealed nothing, but it was clear they were closing on her position.

Fuel scooping complete …

She jabbed the control for the frame shift drive once more.

Frame shift drive malfunction!

'Not again,' she said. The ship was falling apart around her. Systems status lights competed with each other to warn of impending doom. Overheating, failed capacitors, malfunctions, system surges … the ship was staggering from one calamity to the next. 'Come on, not much further …'

She tried again with the same result.

'I cannot get the FSD to charge!'

'Keep trying,' Zenith urged. 'I'm right behind you … wait … ships!'

Salomé knew it was coming. The lurching jolt told her all she needed to know. Through the twisting wrenching distortion of physics that was the frame shift drive, a spike of energy lashed out, a tether, connecting her ship with that of one of her pursuers.

The *Seven Veils* spun out of control in a blaze of coruscating energy.

'I'm being interdicted!'

She tried to wrestle the ship back on course, but it was limping, sluggish, barely able to respond to the control inputs. The HUD signalled confusing and overlapping messages, the escape vector wandered uncontrollably around the screen. The tether grew stronger as the integrity of the frame shift fell away.

With a crashing jolt the ship hammered back into normal space. The impact nearly knocked her out, her head slamming back against the pilot's seat, the inertia crushing the breath from her. It took several moments to register what had happened, more still to slow the gyrating vessel.

She blinked.

Before her was another Imperial Clipper.

'Zenith? Isaiah? Eisen?'

Weapons deployed from hardpoints. She saw the fire blister towards her. Instinctively she throttled up the engines, aiming directly at the other vessel. A collision course. A ram! It might do enough damage to allow her to get free.

The other ship veered out of the way, anticipating her move. A missile exploded out from its hardpoints, detonating against her shields. Alerts flashed up before her, not giving her a chance to read them.

She dimly heard the voice comms from the wing.

'I'm blue tunnelling ... can't get a lock ... can't get to you ...'

'Boost away, Salomé! Keep your shields at full ...'

'Tsu! She's made it. She got through! The others are safe. Make sure Salomé knows ...'

It is done then, they can't stop the truth ...

Then a voice drowned out all the others.

'You tried to kill Fleet Admiral Patreus, now it's time to pay the price. There is no mercy for murderers and terrorists.'

'I am no terrorist!' Salomé answered. 'You know nothing.'

The response was another volley of laser fire. The shields on the *Seven Veils* valiantly tried to repel it.

'The Empire decides your fate today.'

Salomé laughed. 'My fate was decided long ago and not by you, bounty hunter.'

'Know who killed you, Salomé. My name is Besieger. The justice of Patreus.'

The shields failed. The ship was moments from destruction. Another round of fire would be all it would take.

Salomé glanced briefly around the ship that had served her. Prism to Achenar, across the galaxy on endless quests. A good ship, a worthy vessel, but it was no fighter …

'Even you have been deceived,' she said softly. 'You have been played by a higher power. Claim your reward. I bear you no ill will.'

There was a brief pause in the barrage.

'I'm not the one you should have been chasing,' she continued. 'The truth is already being revealed. You, and those you serve, are too late.'

The other Clipper came about. Just seconds remained.

Salomé closed her eyes, placing her hands on her lap, leaving the deadened controls. The *Seven Veils* yawed out of control as its systems failed, the hull streaming debris and shattered hull plating. The engines flickered and died, cooling fins and hardpoints disintegrating as the ship broke apart.

'This time, it was my plan. Not his, not hers, not any of them. Mine and mine alone.'

The truth must be known … and all this pain will end … they will … remember.

Faces from the past flashed through her mind, decisions, regrets, joys and sorrows …

My parents, my sisters … Corine and Tala, Dalk, Hassan … Luko … I join you now …

Fire blossomed in the depths of space.

Martyr!

Epilogue

Deep space, Teorge system, Independent

The listening post hung in the darkness, its exterior pockmarked and tarnished after uncounted years orbiting the moon. There was nothing remarkable about its appearance. Teorge itself was a quiet system, far from the beating heart of galactic commerce, politics or government. It had a curious history, having hosted a complex and wide-reaching failed genetic experiment long ago in the past. Old-timers referred to it as the 'Clone World.'

The listening post had been inactive for years, forlornly awaiting a signal. Its passive systems had been tuned to listen for a particular code. Its ancient memory had no intelligence. Impatience and boredom were not things the technology within could suffer from. Each day passed without regret or frustration. Simply waiting.

But today was different.

A signal.

Verification algorithms decoded the message, analysing it for authenticity. Thus confirmed, the controlling memory carried out its instructions as it had been programmed to do all those years before.

Across the system, transponder points lit up. Passing ships immediately noticed the signals on their scanners. It wasn't long before one came investigating.

Commander Enshiv was the first. His ship dropped out of frame shift and made a cautious approach. The area was clear, the listening post sombre in the darkness. In the absence of any obvious threat, he moved his ship into narrowband range.

Automated scanning took over. The data appeared on his display.

Ragazza Log – 31/03/3275

'What the hell is all this?' he muttered, looking at the holofac display. It was an old woman's voice, her tones strident and agitated.

'If you just stumbled across this message, nothing of what I am going to relate will make any sense. My advice? Don't read on, kill this holofac now, don't go looking. You really don't want to be involved, trust me. Just fly on like nothing happened. People will kill you for knowing.

'If you found this because you were led here … congratulations, you must be reasonably smart.

'I don't know what you were expecting, but this probably isn't it. There's no payoff my friend, there's no money to be made. You haven't won. You may have just made things much worse for yourself. If there is any fame to be had it is what you make of it, maybe some chronicler will immortalise you in the future.

'I put this message in this system for a reason, the old lore will tell you why. I'm not the first and I'm not the last. I'm old now and it will soon be time for another to take my place. Maybe it's her who has led you here. If she's anything like me she'll be one feisty little lady, hope you had fun.

'By now you'll have been to the hind-end of space looking for, well … something. Guessing you found it. I make no apology for all your trouble, you decided to go out there, same as me. I don't know what tech you have in the future to make that voyage a little easier, but I spent years following this, trying to unravel it all and so did many others before me.

'You weren't alone, suffering that boredom and loneliness in the void. Don't expect any sympathy, no one told you to go. Decide for yourself if you think it was worth it.

'But I figure I owe you some kind of explanation. So here it is.

'They've known. They've known for decades, maybe centuries. There's something out there and it's heading this way. Everything you've seen: all the wars, all the investigations, all the abductions. It's their way of getting stuff done, getting things ready, keeping things quiet.

'You don't build a fleet of warships for no reason – too many questions get asked. So you manufacture a threat, you start a phoney war. You keep the populace amused with any diversion you can think of. You play powers against each other, you boom and bust the markets to tilt the economy. Anything to stop people looking at the real issues.

'Who are they? Don't go thinking this is the Feds or the Imps or even the Alliance, it's way beyond all that. Most of what you think you know isn't true. It's all a fabrication, woven by those who have appointed themselves the protectors of humanity. They've been keeping us all in the dark, hiding the truth, secretly prepping for a confrontation.

'If you're unlucky enough to stumble upon a part of it, they simply remove you. A shadowy revolution that decides what to reveal and when.

'But that's not all they've done. They had all manner of contingency plans drawn up over the years. Maybe they had a premonition of failure.

If you've got this far you'll have read the old lore, you know there was a conflict with an alien race. Yes, them. You know what they were capable of in the past. Who's to say what they could do now?

'Our so-called protectors thought the core worlds might be overrun. Maybe we might need somewhere else to go. That's what they were looking for out there in the void. Somewhere to flee to, somewhere to run and hide. An Exodus, the Dynasty plan.

'So they sent out ships, lots of ships, looking for Earth-like worlds in the far reaches of the galaxy. You know where, you've been there. When they had that data they planned to kill the crews and bury the missions. Some kind of suicide pact. No one was supposed to know. Some of those poor souls managed to survive for a few years it seems, marooned in the blackness, but none of them made it home. If you're here you've probably found what was left.

'But they didn't tell us plebs about this. No, not a word. They claimed it would cause riots, panic and confusion if the truth ever came out. Maybe they were right. So they lied, time and again.

'But you can't lie forever, truth is a dangerous thing.

'I figured someone should know the facts one day. So now you have it. What you do with it is your business. Could be they have let you find this message, maybe the time is right at last. Maybe there is nothing left to hide anymore. I don't know if I've played them, or they've played me.

'There's probably one last question burning in your mind. I know I'd be asking it. How do I know all this?

'That's simple. My memory has been shot to pieces, edited by them and by me over the years. But I finally put it back together, most of it anyway. Turns out I was one of them. I was part of it. I helped them do it. Somewhere along the line I had an attack of conscience.

'Guess they didn't take too kindly to that. Here's hoping I made a difference …

'Rebecca.'

***

Docking communications at Serebrov Terminal in the HR 6421 system continued as they ever had, hundreds of ships per hour were served by the station. Beyond the rugged backdrop of the moon lay the glory of the ringed gas giant that dominated the system.

Erimus had always found comfort in that view, but now he could only see shades of grey. The starlight seemed muted as if the universe itself were darker this day.

He had watched Salomé's wake live from the Prism system; the assembled commanders paying their last respects in speech and symbolism. He had turned away before the end.

How dare you die and leave us like this! How dare you leave me!

He cast his mind back over everything that had transpired since he'd joined the Children of Raxxla. The disenchantment with the established powers, the encounters with the mysterious; the subterfuge and the searching. The clues, the logs, the endless travels in the deepest void. All had led to the unmasking of a conspiracy beyond all the powers combined.

But without you …

A communiqué pulsed in his line of sight, a message from Tal Aldris.

'Regret to inform you that a vessel was accidentally destroyed by an unscheduled test of the station's defensive weapons during the memorial event. Malcontents had attempted to interrupt the ceremony, but were repelled. A ship belonging to a certain commander Besieger was inadvertently destroyed …'

The universe has its own karma …

Erimus would have smiled once, but not now, not today. Tal's report was the official version, and thus not the truth.

On the desk before him lay a letter, sealed with the emblem of the Children of Raxxla. He knew the contents, for it was he who had written them.

… we must find a new purpose … and there must be a new leader.

He stared at the letter for a long moment, before glancing around the conference room one last time. He'd summoned the consul, but the meeting wasn't for another hour. He'd be long gone by then.

To make an end is to make a beginning. So be it. Farewell, Salomé …

A woman laid her hand on his shoulder. He looked up into the eyes of a friend. Alessia Verdi had been there from the beginnings of the Children of Raxxla.

Grey eyes … funny … I never noticed that before.

'You did everything you could,' she said.

'Was it enough?' Erimus asked.

'Time will tell …'

Erimus nodded and then turned on his heel. Alessia watched him go, the conference room doors snapping closed behind him.

***

'A conspiracy revealed then,' Emperor Arissa said, 'if not unmasked. The threat is real too.'

'So it would seem,' Patreus replied. 'We know who we can trust at least, judging by their actions.'

'Yes,' Arissa said. 'The mouthpieces are known and identified. Lady Kahina's loss will be felt far and wide. Still, we must continue our preparations. Make the arrangements for the fleets.'

'It will be done, your Imperial Highness.'

Patreus strode purposefully out of Arissa's anteroom, not hesitating as he walked across the gently curving floor of the gravity-enabled sections of her Interdictor, the *Imperial Honour.*

A Courier took him back to his flagship, the *Imperial Freedom*, keeping station alongside.

Not until he reached his own quarters did he pause to take stock. He looked out at the distant stars; the Orion Nebula glowing bright with Barnard's Loop a subtle counterpoint.

A martyr then. Will the masses rise up in anger as we hoped? Only time will tell.

Carefully, deliberately, he pulled off his gloves finger by finger, before dropping them into the disposal chute. With a flare of laser light they were atomised. His knuckles clicked as he clenched his fists.

'Let that be an end to this sorry affair.'

***

Three ships. Deep space. Systems shut down save the life support. Only the faintest glow of starlight outlined the familiar hulls. Three pilots could just be seen in the cockpit of one of the ships, one keeping a wary eye on the scanner.

'She's set the galaxy on fire,' Tsu said. 'Everyone will ... remember. It's breaking on all the newsfeeds, everywhere ... she got what she wanted ... maybe that was her plan all along ...'

'Has she?' Raan shrugged. 'Give it a month, the masses will forget, the traders will go back to the money. Greed always triumphs. People don't care ...'

'They'll still be after us ...' Yuri said, sparing a glance out of the cockpit of Raan's ship.

Their conversation petered out, the silence broken only by the faint hum of the ship's systems.

Raan nodded. 'Guess this is it then. Not one for goodbyes. We'd better make a move.'

'Where are you going?' Yuri asked.

'With a two million credit bounty on my head,' Raan replied. 'I'm not telling anyone where I'm going.'

Yuri smiled.

'Had the same thought myself,' Tsu said. 'Stay out of sight. Not sure where ...'

'There's always Colonia if you fancy the long haul,' Yuri said.

'Doubt I'll be welcome back in the Alliance anytime soon,' she replied.

The conversation faltered again.

Raan held out his hand, the other two grasped it.

'We did good,' Raan said. 'Fly safe.'

'Fly dangerous,' Tsu and Yuri replied, their voices just above a whisper.

Minutes later the ships separated. Each pilot chose their own route, deciding their own fate, blazing their own trail. The flicker of a hyperspace transition briefly broke the monotony of the void, but then all was peaceful once more.

Amidst the glow of starlight, the emissions of nebulae, the twisted gravity of neutron stars and the bottomless pits of black holes, uncounted billions heard the story. Most discounted it, a fabrication, too unlikely to warrant serious consideration; a madcap conspiracy surrounding a crackpot messianic woman and her group of deluded followers.

Yet some heard it and resolved to take action. Some believed, some were just curious. Stories were spun, factions were organised. Across a thousand worlds, there were those who made their preparations and headed out into the void. Traders, bounty hunters, explorers and pirates.

Whatever was coming, the answers lay out there, beyond the worlds that humanity called home; over the edge, into the unknown. In the far reaches of space lay secrets that would freeze the heart and chill the soul, edging closer every day.

Eight sided shapes moved in the darkness, merciless, inexorable. They recognised no boundary or jurisdiction, edging closer every day. En route to humanity's small sector of the galaxy, a line was being relentlessly crossed.

They call it the Frontier.

About the Author

Drew Wagar is best known for fast paced science fiction adventure stories, including Elite: Reclamation and the Shadeward Saga. He also writes fantasy novels, including the upcoming Lords of Midnight. He lives in Kent, with his wife, two sons, a dog and a cat. Outside of writing he is an avid astronomer and likes to tinker with an old sports car which occasionally works. He can sometimes be found playing the piano and his favourite colour is dark green. You can find out more at his website drewwagar.com, on twitter - @drewwagar or facebook.com/drewwagarwriter.

Printed in Great Britain
by Amazon

23258459R00267